IMMORTAL FROM HELL

GENE DOUCETTE

PART I

THE OLD WORLD, AND THE NEW

I'm sort of fond of Paris.

This is a hard-won conclusion, because I don't care all that much for cities a lot of the time. I mean that kind of literally. I loved Constantinople for a couple of centuries but never liked it as Istanbul. I enjoyed London from approximately 1500 to 1600 and again for about fifty years in the 1800's, but not much since. And I've only ever liked parts of New York City.

Paris in the time of the Sun King was kind of awesome, got a lot less interesting after that— through the French Revolution and all the other revolutions—and then got really interesting again. I'm not sure why it never fell into disfavor with me. Maybe it's just that I wasn't there for *la Terreur* (although I lost a lot of friends, because while I was never royalty, nearly all the people I thought of as interesting were) so I had no opportunity to sour on the city.

It's also a great place to go if you need to hold a meeting with someone unsavory. I'm not sure why this is so, but it is. If you happen to be in the European theater, and you need to sit down with a person who specializes in the non-legal kind of merchandising opportunities that have existed since the word 'legal' was invented, your best bet is to hold that meeting in a Parisian café.

It makes no sense, because everybody knows this, and they still do it all the time. Possibly, there are too many cafés for the *gendarmes* to keep an eye on. Or maybe they're cool with it as long as nobody commits acts of violence right out in public. Or, they just don't care, which is probably the most likely explanation.

Anyway, as you may have guessed, I was sitting in a Parisian café while awaiting the arrival of someone unsavory. At least two other people in the café were doing the same thing, so far as I could tell.

I was alone at the table, but not alone in the café—Mirella was at a patio table near the door. She would signal when our man arrived, and also come to my rescue if someone went after me with a knife while I was sitting there. This wasn't a realistic possibility, but it was nice to know if the waiter went from *normal-French-rude* to *rare-French-psychopath*, she was ready.

I like to think I can handle myself just fine, but it's also pretty awesome having a girlfriend who can kill a man ten different ways in about two seconds. This is especially true if you derive endless fascination out of discovering hidden knives on your date, as I appear to.

We'd already been there two hours. The man we were meeting—astonishingly, his name was Jacques, which made this entire meeting so cliché it probably sounds like I'm making it up —was evidently based in a different time zone.

Or, he wasn't going to show.

Clandestine meetings need some kind of standardized rule, akin to the one American schools supposedly have, wherein after fifteen minutes, if the teacher doesn't show, everyone can leave. Something like, if it's been more than two hours, assume you're blown or the contact is dead. Maybe we could add some nicer options, like so-and-so just forgot, didn't mark it in his calendar, or turned up at the wrong café.

These were the things I was considering as we entered the third hour. The excellent coffee I was getting a steady supply of had already turned my stomach into an improperly functioning organ, and my kidneys were extremely displeased as well. The seats were also of the sort that were designed to be comfortable for only about thirty minutes. Anybody paying a bit of attention had to have figured out by then that Mirella and I were there together, since we were the only two tables that hadn't turned over all afternoon. The waiter already made a joke about combining the bills, twice.

Finally, Mirella gave the signal.

Neither of us had ever met Jacques; she was going on a crude physical description that fit roughly one in every ten people in the city, so I had no idea how she knew, but I trusted that she did. I shifted in the chair to get some blood back to my feet in case I had to move quickly.

Jacques was a white guy with unmanageably thick black hair that looked windswept on a day without any wind. He had a thin mustache, and coffee teeth, and lots of body hair. He was about five-foot-ten and looked like he could handle himself pretty well in a fight if it ever came to that. (Note that if someone had given me *that* much detail, I'd have picked him out just fine, but all we were told was five-ten, white guy, black hair.) He was one of those people who just radiated bad body odor that could be discerned even from a safe olfactory remove.

He signaled the waiter for attention, pulled out the chair opposite mine, and sat.

"You are Randall," he said, in French. "I am Jacques."

"You are late," I said, also in French. This was all I'd been speaking since our arrival in Paris, except when talking to Mirella, who wasn't good with the language. I'm fluent in all the European tongues—including the dead ones—because that's what happens when you live through the invention of verbal communication.

Randall was just the name I was currently traveling under. I wasn't fond of it, and planned to change it at the nearest opportunity. The problem was that when we left home, there were only a couple of aliases available for my use.

I have to adopt a fake identity to travel anywhere, because my real name—going back to the first one I ever used—looks like a computer glitch, and I was given it before there were borders.

I usually go by Adam, or I have for the past several years. No reason, I just like the name.

"I am late, yes," Jacques said.

The waiter came over with a cappuccino for Jacques, which was a pretty good indication my new friend was a regular in this establishment. Not because that's a drink reserved for regulars, but because all he did to get that cappuccino was wave to the waiter.

"I apologize," he added. "I have been watching from the building across the way for some time."

"Were you waiting to see if I could endure three hours in this chair?"

It hadn't been three straight hours. I got up a few times to use the bathroom.

"No."

He sipped his cappuccino and either paused to carefully formulate the next words, or because he was enjoying the drama. I was mostly annoyed that we hadn't decided to do this in a bar instead, because I would have much preferred spending the afternoon with a bottle of alcohol in my hand.

"This request," he said, "it is quite extraordinary. Not for what was asked but for who asked. If I may, who are you, sir? I know only that the name I am to use with you is Randall, and that you travel with the lethal woman on the patio. I also know she is not a woman, in the common vernacular."

"She's uncommon in many ways," I agreed.

Mirella is a goblin. He could have been referencing her uncommon beauty just as easily, but he wasn't.

It wasn't a big surprise that he recognized her for what she was, even though he was human, and I'm human, and everyone else in the shop was human so far as I could tell. Goblins don't appear non-human to the untrained eye, but Jacques took orders from elves so he would know what to look for. (Long story, but elves and goblins are basically the same species, it's just that neither of them want to admit to that.)

"Is knowing more about me required?" I asked. "Before the fulfillment of our request?"

"It is not."

He took a pack of cigarettes out and waved to the waiter again, who presented an ashtray. There were parts of Europe that hadn't gotten the memo yet about smoking in public places.

"You must understand, Randall, that the request I fulfill came to me as if on high, from God himself. And when your God tells you to do a thing, it is reasonable to ask—if only to oneself—why is this so important? Why are you so important?"

"We just wanted a particular bit of information," I said. "If someone asked you to sacrifice your firstborn on an altar, it didn't come from us."

He laughed.

"No, I'll allow, the request is not so extreme as that. Complicated, yes, but nobody is threatening the lives of my immediate family. That's an assumed consequence of non-compliance, but this is the case for all such demands-from-on-high, wouldn't you say? Irrespective of my great interest regarding whom you and the lovely lady outside might be, I do have what you asked for."

He pulled a scrap of paper from an inner pocket and held it up as if it were a communion wafer.

"This simple thing was exceedingly challenging to obtain. I had to burn a number of resources. I say this because I want for you—and for my god, assuming you are in the position of reporting my value upward—to understand what was involved. Corporate espionage can be lucrative, but it is also expensive."

"My benefactor will compensate you, I'm told."

"This is so. But human intelligence is difficult to put a price tag on."

"I'm sure you can arrive at a number. May I see it?"

He handed the paper across the table.

"I hope this satisfies your needs, and concludes our business."

He moved to stand.

"Hang on," I said, before looking at the paper. "I'm going to have some more traditional requirements shortly. Don't go anywhere."

There was an address written on the scrap, belonging to a commercial establishment in Chicago. That was the extent of the information we'd requested, so I shouldn't have been surprised by it. I was a little disappointed anyway that this was all he had. It was a necessary breadcrumb, but not a very large one.

My new friend Jacques remained in his seat. Only his eyebrow had gotten up.

"So?" he asked.

"I'm going to need some new travel papers, new ID's, and maybe some cash. I'll make a call; Dimitri will compensate you richly, I promise."

"Very well. But do both of us a favor and never again say his name aloud."

The version of Dimitri Romanov that existed in my head and the one that existed in Jacques' head were quite different, clearly. I thought of Dimitri as a pretty cool guy (well, elf) who also happened to be one of the most important mafia figures in the East. Jacques perhaps emphasized the second part more than the first.

"Right, sorry. He's a friend. I take it you never met him?"

Jacques looked uncomfortable about this line of questioning, which was probably my fault because I was kind of baiting him for kicks. I don't know why I do these things.

"Randall," he said flatly. "This is the name you're using."

"It doesn't have to be. Your man can create one for me, I'm not that particular."

"There was a rumor of a man who went by a different name, but who fit… well, not your description, as one was never paired with the rumor of his existence. But it fit the kind of access you appear to have, and the company you keep. Men do not simply appear out of the ether into our world with your connections. I'm wondering now if you are this man."

"Where did you happen to hear these rumors?"

"Oh, in places. On the lips of certain people. You know how it goes."

I sort of did and sort of didn't. Jacques was (obviously) a member of the European criminal underworld. If you go back far enough, you'll find at least five or six people who could have been identified with that same underworld and who also knew me either as Adam, or under another name. The thing was, those five or six people were surely no longer among the living. So what we were talking about now was a legend passed down among Jacques' people. Given the last time I lived in Europe was well over a century ago, it had to be one heck of an important legend.

There was a more obvious explanation that wouldn't occur to me until later.

"I'm sure it's a coincidence," I said. "I'm not from around here."

"American?"

"Sure, why not?"

I actually lived on an island until recently, and it was nowhere near the New World. The island was nice, until it wasn't. Identifying myself as a native of that island would do no good, since it was a secret island, but it was no more accurate to say I was a native of America. This was likewise true of everywhere else in the world other than equatorial Africa. That, I'm pretty sure, was where I was born.

"If you are an American, you surely don't need my help traveling to Chicago," Jacques said. He was playing, because we both knew he wasn't getting up from the table without promising to assist us. Just the fact that he couldn't say Dimitri's name aloud made that point pretty well.

"I'm not anything, not really," I said. "And the last version of me that could call himself a U.S. citizen died a few years ago. There are connections to my old life I can't restore without putting people at risk. And you don't need to know any of this to get what I need."

"You are correct. Here."

He took out a pen and jotted something down on a napkin, and then slid it over.

"Be at this address after eight tonight, and we will accommodate you."

I looked it over. "And the telephone number?"

"That's a message center. A woman named Sherri will answer. If you require anything else that you have not yet expressed to me, tell her and we will get it to you. Where are you staying?"

"I'd rather not say."

"Yes, all right. It's only that I may need to get a message to you."

"It would be better for everyone if you didn't need to do any such thing," I said. "If we see something we don't like… I'm sure we'll find a way to notify you of our dissatisfaction."

He stared at me for several seconds.

"Yes, I understand," he said. "Tonight, then."

~

"What did you think of him?" Mirella asked, later.

We waited another half an hour before leaving the café, to put some distance between us and Jacques. This was either so anyone following Jacques wouldn't also follow us, or to give whoever he paid to follow us around plenty of time to get ready. Either worked.

"He'll get the job done."

We were walking along Boulevard Saint-Germain. I'd set us up in a hotel not far from the piano-maker's shop where the guillotine was invented. I didn't do this out of any particular sense of nostalgia—probably—so much as that I happened to be pretty familiar with that part of town. Although, Marie Antoinette was a friend, so maybe there was more to it. Anyway, we were also right next to a McDonald's. You can make of that what you want.

"He had a man across the street," she said.

"I assumed as much. Is he tailing us?"

"No. I imagine he recognized this would be a discourtesy. I'm glad; I didn't want to have to kill anyone in Paris. I like this city, and we only just arrived. What about the information?"

"I have no way of verifying it. If I did, I wouldn't have needed him to get it for me in the first place."

"But your sense is that it's correct."

"The laundry tag on the blouse was in English, and the sizing was U.S. standard, so Chicago fits. Plus, it was one of the only places in the US where I'd previously spotted her. If Jacques was lying, he concocted a pretty convincing lie."

"Well," she said, taking my hand, "I will continue to distrust him, if that's all right."

"I'd expect nothing less."

"Good. Now take me someplace passably romantic."

～

*P*aris was just the second or third step on a journey of unknown length, and that was sort of exciting—who doesn't enjoy a quest?—or would be if the stakes weren't pretty high.

Here was problem number one: the only human being in the world older than I am had acquired some kind of disease.

A whole lot of impossible things are packed into that sentence, but let's start with *older than I am*. I'm roughly sixty-thousand, give or take a few thousand. (It can only ever be an estimate.) She claims to be a third older, which puts her at eighty-thousand. And look, that's kind of insane and hard to believe, but it helps to know that unlike me, she's spent part of her existence in a side dimension where time moves differently.

Yeah, I know, I'm not happy with *side dimension* either, but I think we can agree it's better than 'the veil', which is what she calls it. (Possibly worse: 'faery kingdom', which is what the man who first told me about it called it.)

The side dimension aspect makes this even more complicated, because it involves a trick she—we'll call her Eve for now—can do that I can't. That trick enables her to step off of this plane of reality and into a place where she can cover distances much faster. It comes with a time-jump, so it's not a great thing to do if you're late for work or something, because you might trade a week to go a thousand miles, and still end up late and possibly fired.

All of that means Eve can drop in and out of reality as we know it wherever she wants, which is important as regards the mystery Mirella and I are currently attempting to solve.

About six weeks ago, Eve stepped out of the veil and into a hotel room on a secret island in the South Pacific, said my name, and then passed out. We waited a month for her to wake up and explain herself, but once it was clear that simply waiting by the bedside wasn't getting us anywhere, I suggested we try to figure out where Eve was before she popped in. For an ordinary person, that's mostly just a matter of checking passport stamps, or ticket stubs, maybe leveraging a contact in an airport or getting close with someone in Interpol, or seeing what currencies are in her wallet.

For Eve, there was very nearly nothing to go on: no wallet to rummage through, no airline tickets, security checkpoints, nothing. She dropped in wearing a stolen set of clothes, and that was all.

The reason it was so important that we figure out where she'd been was the aforementioned disease, because there was a decent chance it was killing her.

We immortal folks don't get sick. We're not invincible, so you can certainly run one of us through with a sword if you get an opening, but we don't acquire illness in any form.

I say it like that's just a default state, like I pass through a world of disease just automatically immune, as if getting sick is just completely inconceivable…and, well, that's pretty much how I've always thought of it. One could sooner give a plague to a rock, was my thinking.

It isn't really that simple, but the germ theory of disease is only a couple hundred years old and I'm a ton older than that, so give me a little slack. How it really works is that I—and Eve, presumably—have absolute, state-of-the-art immune systems.

It may seem like there's no difference between "immune system that won't allow me to get sick" and "it would be easier to give a plague to a rock" because the outcome is identical. However, it looked like something in this world got through Eve's immune system, which means there *is* a difference.

That was bad, because whatever was making her sick was killing her and we couldn't do anything but hope she beat it. Far worse, if it could kill *her*, imagine what it would do to the rest of the population?

In short, there was something in the world that could possibly end all life on the planet, patient zero was comatose, and she had traveled in steps that were nearly impossible to retrace. We were nevertheless attempting to do exactly that.

Paris is romantic and quests are cool. But the threat of a global pandemic kind of sours the whole thing. The good news was, if all life on Earth were felled by a plague, it looked like this one could take me out too. It'd be pretty lonely otherwise.

That is, unless I was overreacting about the global pandemic thing.

It would definitely be an overreaction if Eve were the only one we found with it; she was actually the only *human* we found, but we'd seen it elsewhere. Technically, the real patient zero was either a now-deceased incubus, or a possibly-deceased mermaid. (Please don't make me explain that because it's a lot.) If all three of them could be traced back to the same source, I would tap the brakes on the *pandemic* notion. But they were probably the least likely threesome to ever turn up in the same place: an immortal woman who spent half her time in another plane of existence; a creature who lived at the bottom of the ocean; and an incubus from Eastern Europe. Throw in that we knew the disease could be acquired—we saw a demon perish from it almost as soon as he was exposed—and it seems like a fair word to use.

So, that was why we embarked on this quest. We were disease-hunters, off to save the world before it was too late.

Or something, A lot closer to the truth would probably be to say that I just couldn't sit around that hotel room any longer. Fortunately, Mirella is almost always in favor of a plan that involves travel, and the potential for violence.

~

After checking in at the hotel and deciding not to spend the afternoon indoors until it was time to meet with Jacques and his ID man—I actually wanted to stay in, but Mirella has this thing about not sitting around in the dark and drinking when there are other options—we went out and did something moderately romantic.

Or so I'm told. I am a profoundly unromantic person, but Paris is immune to my non-romantic wiles, and the Eiffel Tower is neat, so that was where we went.

"I remember when this was built," I said, as we took the elevator to the observation deck.

"Of course you do," she said, smiling.

"It was for the world's fair. It was the tallest free-standing structure on Earth for a while."

I didn't know Gustave Eiffel, but I think he probably built it on a dare. At least half of the 'world's tallest' whatevers were either the result of a dare, or a pissing contest between cities.

"Did you attend the fair?" she asked.

"No, I wasn't in France then, but I was just thinking how much I miss them. I did attend one in Chicago."

"What an interesting coincidence."

I'm not sure I believe in coincidences. This isn't to say I was or wasn't fated to go to Chicago. More like, I saw the address on the scrap of paper Jacques provided, thought back to my own time in Chicago, remembered the fair that I visited the city to see, recalled that the Eiffel Tower was built for a fair, and suggested we go see it. Which, since Mirella was looking for something romantic, made me come across as suggesting something inherently romantic.

Or, I'm just overthinking it.

"I think I've just been around long enough that every story I have sounds like that," I said. "Especially since history has a habit of repeating itself."

"You say so, until the oldest woman in the world ends up in a coma."

"Yes. That's new."

"But you remember when this was built."

"First time I've visited it in person, but it was a big deal at the time, so yeah."

I should mention that we weren't alone on the elevator, and we were speaking the same language—English—as everyone else, despite which the other occupants were doing a bang-up job of ignoring the guy who claimed he was alive in 1889. This sort of out-in-the-open conversation wasn't the kind of thing I used to do, sober, and I couldn't tell you for sure why I was okay with doing it now.

It might have been because I went through some trouble to kill myself a few years earlier, before disappearing to the afore-mentioned secret island. Once I did that, I started to look at the world-at-large the way I used to view new tribes in which I was inserting myself. Clean-slate thinking, in other words. It was probably foolish—a lot of the things I do end up being foolish in hindsight—but I was enjoying the freedom of being a nobody-in-particular again.

It could also have been a consequence of the lingering sense of my own mortality, (Eve was sick therefore I could get sick too, *et cetera*) which I frankly never bothered to confront because it hadn't come up all that often. Maybe as a mortal guy I'm loudly nostalgic.

Once at the top, I spent a good hour pointing out landmarks and providing Mirella with color commentary on whatever weird historical nugget I happened to recall. This is easy to do in Paris, because they haven't put up a ton of skyscrapers like so many other cities. (I'm told this is because of the catacombs—the ground can't support structures that heavy. This may not be true but it sounds good.) Thus, while it had been about three hundred years since my last visit, I still recognized a bunch of things. Entertainingly, two or three of the people who rode up with us lingered at the edge of our conversation, turning me into an unofficial tour guide. They probably thought that was exactly what I was: some kind of off-duty historical re-enactor.

This would be an excellent profession for me, by the way.

"You know what I'd like?" she said, as we held one another, while the sun began to set. "I would like to be able to do things like this with you without the world first sitting on the precipice of destruction."

"I only get out of bed for emergencies," I said. This was a joke, but only sort of.

"Yes, I know. And I know asking a man who has seen all there is to see, to approach the world as if he had not, is nigh impossible. But there are days when I'd like for you to try."

"Days like this?"

"Everything after the café. Yes."

"I can try. Hey, didn't we talk about going to outer space once? We could try that. I haven't been there."

"Let's work our way up to outer space. Paris is a good beginning."

"All right."

We kissed, and it was all kinds of romantic. A-plus stuff. If I could describe it better, I would, but as I've said, I'm really terrible at this.

I will add one thing: as much as we promised to do romantic, stop-and-smell-the-roses things wherever the days to come took us, this was pretty much the last time we got that opportunity.

$\mathcal{M}$y expectation of general seediness and bad-neighborhood vibes for the 8:00 P.M. meeting was not at all met by the trappings of the actual location.

The address Jacques provided belonged to a nice building with a doorman. My former papers man worked out of the basement of a pawn shop in New York City, in a section of town that looked like it needed to be hosed down with antibiotics, so I arrived carrying a certain expectation. I figured at minimum, Paris would provide us with a storeroom in a warehouse on a riverbank someplace where the odor of the river was particularly strong. But this wasn't even in a part of the city that hotels instructed tourists to avoid, which was downright disappointing.

The doorman directed us to the concierge, who held up a finger to cut off the greeting that was about to come out of my mouth. (I was going to go with, *hi, we're expected.*) He looked us over for a three-count before making a call on the house phone.

We must have matched a description. I'm thinking Mirella was described in great detail, while I was probably "...a guy." That's how I would do it.

"Penthouse," the concierge said, in English. "Take the middle one." This appeared to be in reference to the elevators, of which there were three.

He slid a key across.

"We're expected," I said, finally, even though we were past that part already.

"Yes, sir."

We had to insert the key in a slot next to the button for the penthouse, which was the only way to get the lift to go up there.

"Classy," Mirella said, once the doors closed and we were on our way up.

"Weird, isn't it?" I said. "I guess there's money to be made in counterfeit passports around here."

"It's… disconcerting. I'm not sure why."

"I feel the same way," I said. "Like we're in the wrong place, and someone screwed up the instructions."

"Yes."

What with the private key to activate the button, it was unsurprising that the elevator doors opened on the penthouse directly.

There was a man waiting for us. He was about what I was expecting, in thug terms: stocky, nice suit, shoulder holster for a sidearm, all that. No sunglasses, but it was nighttime. Basically, he should have been at the riverfront warehouse I'd been expecting, instead of inside a pricy penthouse.

He looked us over for a few seconds, and then gestured that we could continue into the loft.

"Not going to frisk us?" I asked.

"Well, don't know," he said, in an American brand of English. "You here to kill somebody?"

"We don't plan to, no."

"Cool, then I won't frisk you."

"Really?"

He shrugged.

"If you want me to frisk, I'll frisk, but most people don't get this far without being well-spoken-for. You guys look okay. But if you want, I can linger at the edge of the living room and stare at you menacingly. If it helps the mood."

"No, that's all right."

We left the entryway and stepped into the living room, which had a simply epic view of the city. The room itself was appointed with leather furniture, a grand piano, tables that were useless for anything other than a tray of hors d'oeuvres, and so on. Very clean, very antiseptic. There wasn't any art on the walls, books on the shelves, or family photos. It was homey, and welcoming, but it didn't feel as if anyone actually lived there. It felt like a movie set. But the view of the Paris skyline was great.

"Down the hall," the man said, pointing to the hallway at the other end of the room. "She's waiting for you."

"Thanks," I said. "Is Jacques here?"

"I don't know who that is, friend."

"Right." That was either a *no*, or a *don't mention anybody's name around here.* Probably the latter, since he hadn't introduced himself or asked our names.

There was an open door at the end of the hallway, out of which streamed the familiar glow of multiple computer screens. I was about to call back to the fellow at the elevator to make doubly sure it was okay to go down the hall, when someone poked a head out of the room.

"Ah, you are here, good. No, stay there, I will come to you."

The woman who emerged from the room was short and skinny, with army-cut brown hair, in sweatpants and a hoodie. She was holding a camera that looked heavier than she was, and moved with the kind of manic energy one usually only saw in coke addicts and tornadoes. Her accent—like the man at the door, she spoke English—was vaguely Germanic.

"Welcome, welcome to my home," she said, a burst of activity as soon as she made it to the living room. "Call me Ina! You, there, you sit, go, on the couch, it's very comfortable I'm proud of it. You, stand against the wall. No, not there, here, against the white background."

The first 'you' was to me and the second to Mirella. She likewise had no interest in getting our names, which was now sort of making sense, given we were getting new ones anyway.

"No, no don't smile" Ina said, attempting to direct my girlfriend. "Look displeased."

"I am actually displeased," Mirella said. "Can't you tell?"

"Then you are too pretty. Try anger. You have waited in line for days before this photo, you hate bureaucracy, give me that! Yes! More of that!"

I'm not an expert in fake passports or photography, but from where I was sitting every expression Mirella tried from the moment she was asked to pose looked like she was unhappy, so I didn't know what Ina was hoping for, but whatever. Goblins don't often smile for pictures anyway, because if their teeth show, it can be a problem: most of them have pointed teeth. I understand there's an entire clandestine dental industry catering to goblins and elves, which in addition to the usual teeth-cleaning and what-not, will cap teeth so they aren't pointy any more. It wasn't a procedure Mirella had gotten, though.

Ina took about twenty photos too many, then sent Mirella to the couch.

"You, man. Come here."

I stood up against the wall.

"You don't actually live here," I said.

"Hold still and look aggrieved. What do you mean?"

"You said welcome to your home, but this place doesn't look lived in."

She took three photos, and then lowered the camera.

"I didn't say I lived here," she said. "You are done. Go sit."

"You used up a whole roll of film on her," I said.

"I needed a bad photo, and she doesn't take bad photos so easily. You, very easy. Also, it is digital, there is no roll. I have better cameras that use film, but there is no darkroom in this penthouse, and you asked for a rush. Developing film takes too long."

"I'm not used to letting people I've just met take pictures of me," I said, because for some reason I felt like explaining why I was a good model for a bad photo.

Cameras, radios, and telephones are all 'new' technology from my perspective. (So are eyeglasses, indoor plumbing, the printing press, and so on. You get the point.) I'm not always good about embracing new technology, especially when it complicates my passage through a world in which I often prefer anonymity.

I will say that I'm glad we got past the part where we had to stand motionless for an hour to get a photo taken. I'd just rather not have the photo taken.

"Yes, fine. Now. Tell me where you are going?"

"Is that important?"

"Everything is important. Some borders are inhospitable to people from certain places. Are you visiting a sanctioned country? How many languages do you speak? Why are the passports you used to get into France no longer adequate? I am very expensive and I do very good work, but I traffic in a level of realism which requires a thorough perspective on my clients. If you are concerned, much of what you are paying for is my silence. So. Tell me what it is I don't know, so that we can get you to where you would like to be."

I looked at Mirella, who shrugged.

"We're going to the United States," I said. "I've been there before, and she was raised there, but we don't want there to be any connection between the last time we were in the States, and this time."

"This is not your ultimate destination."

"I don't know if it is or not."

"Multiple identities, then. I'll arrange three. Are you criminals?"

"I don't understand the question."

"Are you on any watch lists? Is Downing Street looking for you, or the CIA, or Mossad? Who are you hiding from?"

"That's complicated."

The reason I killed my 'self' and broke off all contact with the outside world was that a small number of incredibly wealthy people happened to know I was immortal, and had already exhibited an unseemly degree of motivation in attempting to exploit that fact. I wanted nothing to do with them. This was partly because their plans didn't include my surviving the experience, which was an admittedly selfish motivation.

The less selfish motivation: sharing total immunity and effective immortality with the richest .1 percent of the planet would be a disaster from just about every angle. If I knew exactly who these people were, I could maybe develop a strategy to avoid them. But I don't. And, based on everything I've come to understand about the world of high finance—holding companies, venture capital firms, offshore accounts, and all that—the people behind it might not even know they're behind it. They could just be rich people investing in an untested medical procedure.

That wasn't the only reason, though. We had to burn all connection between what we were doing now and the secret island from which we came, both to preserve its secrecy and to protect Eve, who was convalescing there. This was maybe just paranoid thinking on my part, but I thought it would be best if nobody knew where she was until we better understood how she'd gotten sick when that was supposed to be impossible.

"This is a yes?" Ina asked.

"We are not wanted by Downing Street," Mirella said. "Nor by Mossad, so far as we're aware. The CIA, possibly."

"Don't hold out, pretty woman," Ina said. "Any others? Interpol?"

"I don't think so."

Ina checked with me.

"The Inquisition," I said. "But they've probably stopped looking for me by now."

She grunted.

"Show me the ID's you've already used, please."

I tried to come up with a reason for her to need these, without asking, because it was becoming obvious that her answer wasn't going to change the end-result of us handing them over. Then I tried to come up with a reason why showing them to her would be bad, and came up with only one: if she didn't give them back, we'd be stuck in Paris.

That was a good reason to hang onto the passports, but at the same time I was standing in the living room of a master forger already, so other options were available if this became an issue.

I handed mine over, and Mirella did the same.

Ina examined both for several seconds, nodding slowly.

"Yes," she said. "I know this work. Very good. There's a bar behind that wall. Sit. Drink. Wait."

〜

*Y*ou may know this about me already, but the very best way to get on my good graces is to share your large stash of expensive alcohol.

The secret bar behind the wall was fully stocked with top shelf liquors, plus a couple of wines older than everyone who wasn't me, and Ina was now my best friend. I went straight for the bourbon, because decent bourbon is harder to find than you might think, and this was on the good end of decent.

"Careful," Mirella said, as she took the bottle out of my hand —I'd filled a glass, drained it, and was about to refill it—and poured a drink for herself. "We could use you clear-headed right now."

"Same to you."

She smiled. "I handle my liquor better. We both know

cirrhosis would have claimed you a millennium ago if you functioned like the rest of us."

"So, you're saying try not to get drunk."

"I am saying that, yes."

"But I do some of my best work drunk."

"This is only something you tell yourself. It isn't true."

"I think I'm supposed to be offended now," I said, somewhat close to being genuinely offended.

"You would be if I was wrong."

I don't let a lot of people get to know me as well as Mirella. Maybe one person every third generation. When it happens, I make it a habit to not ignore their wisdom as it pertains to my behavior. Usually, they're right. Sure, a lot of the time they have a crummy way of making their point—lovers habitually leave, for instance—but they're still usually right.

The point is, I took her concern seriously.

Mirella scooped up her glass and took it to the window to get a proper look at Paris at night.

"I've been in rooms such as this before. You're right, I don't believe this woman lives here. I don't think anyone does. I suspect it's loaned out for parties and the like. The bar makes that point strongly."

"You've been to parties in places like this?" I asked.

"I've guarded people who went to parties in places like this," she said, referencing her prior career as an expensive bodyguard. "I met you in a place like this."

"That was a hotel room."

"Similar view, different city, same size bar."

"Better alcohol here."

"Fair."

She downed the glass and went back to the bar.

I snuck a peek around the corner and down the hall to see if there was any way to discern exactly how long this was going to take. (You would think I'd be more patient, given boredom has been the defining mood of almost my entire existence.) There wasn't; I'd have to break whatever politeness protocol we were observing and walk into the room at the end of the hallway to get an idea.

Mirella watched me fidget.

"I feel it too," she said, quietly. "This was not a night I expected to feel safe and relaxed, and with a drink in my hand, and so I don't feel safe or relaxed. If it puts you at ease, I've checked the windows for sniper positions four times and identified two likely fire exits. I also believe I can shatter the overhead window if we need immediate roof access."

"That does make me feel better, thanks. And I can add that the man at the door is right-handed and has a Glock holstered on his left side. He favors his left leg. Knee problems, I'm thinking. He looks like he's carrying about twenty pounds more than he should be for his frame, and his peripheral vision sucks."

"Don't we make a pair," she said, smiling. Casing a room is kind of like foreplay for us.

"I think maybe we shouldn't be released on the world," I said. "Let's go find another island, or we'll never get to relax again."

"Certainly. Right after we save everyone once more. It's your turn to pick the island."

"Here we are!" Ina said, from halfway down the hall. "I will show you the first set, and then we will talk some more."

She bustled into the room with two passports in her hand. She tossed one to each of us.

"Sit!" she said, before taking a seat of her own in a lounge chair opposite the couch.

I flipped open the new passport immediately, to see what my new name was about to be.

Frederick Mayall. Didn't roll off the tongue, but okay.

"I have a large list of appropriate names from which to choose, with the paperwork already completed and ready to go," Ina said. "All of this documentation cost time and money to obtain and create, and so it only wastes my time if there is a name which I cannot use, about which I'm not notified."

"Sure," I said. I wasn't at all clear on the point she was trying to make.

"I will explain. You are better known by the world at large as an immortal man named Adam. Knowing this, it would have been unfortunate had I used one of the two 'Adam' documents I have available."

I looked blankly at Mirella, and she back at me.

"Neither of us gave you that name," I said.

"*Exactly*. And you ought to have. Now, let's discuss why Dimitri should have never let you leave the island."

INTERLUDE (1)

From the journal of Dr. Lew Cambridge

Day thirty-seven since the patient arrived.

The patient remains in an unresponsive state. I continue to have reservations regarding the customary terminology—e.g., a 'coma'—to describe this state. In the most important sense, that's exactly what it is, as she's alive, not conscious, and not merely asleep. According to the EKG, her brain remains active.

Coma, then.

Yet her body, which seems to be *essentially* that of a normal human female, periodically acts with a type of self-defensive agency which we are at a loss to explain, without using a word like "magic": sometimes, somehow, she disappears for a little while.

I've been examining all of the historical and medical documents, books on mythology and legend, and religious texts, and I can find no antecedent for these periodic disappearances.

(Actually, this isn't entirely true. There are numerous such examples in the religious texts, but I'm discounting those for the fact that while one might argue our patient vanished because she was assumed into heaven, after that assumption she returned. There is no history of that happening as a matter of routine. A few thousand years apart, yes, but not twice in an afternoon.)

There's no biological explanation for the disappearances, although in fairness I wouldn't know where to look for a biological explanation. And, although we have only a few examples to study, there doesn't appear to be a connection between the disappearances and external stimuli: in some instances, it's defensive, but in others it just happens.

When I approached Adam on the subject, in the hope that he would have an insight he could share—and could furthermore perform the same vanishing act, so it could be studied more concretely—he recommended I skip the biology textbooks and study the physics textbooks instead. Then he said something about a fairy kingdom, which I would be extraordinarily surprised to find covered in a physics textbook.

But I'm not a physicist, so I'll allow that I could be in error.

Adam is no longer available to answer questions, not without placing a call I'm told not to place short of an emergency. It's been seven days since his departure, and I've heard nothing since.

As his intention is to get to the root of our patient's evidently impossible sickness, I'm holding out hope that his efforts are more fruitful than mine. Understanding how she can dematerialize is a close second on the ledger of things about which I'm curious. Figuring out how someone who never gets sick got sick is a much more important question.

~

Day thirty-eight.

We tried to move the patient again today, and it was as fruitless as ever.

We'd like to do this for a few reasons.

First off, it would be much easier if she were in the hospital, because some of the equipment I'd like to use for diagnosis just can't be relocated, or if it can it won't fit through the hotel room door. We have a basic setup in the room, and that's all.

Second, I've been told by hotel management that they would prefer she not remain in the hotel room, as it's interfering with their cleanup. I'm taking this as the exaggeration it must be, because the entire island still looks more like a war zone than a vacation spot. We're as aware of this as anybody.

All of the surviving hospital staff, along with the new arrivals from the mainland, have been working non-stop to deal with the injuries sustained either from the tsunami or the siege that followed, and yet we have the better task. Yes, we are seeing patients die, still—sometimes tourists, sometimes neighbors—but our work is primarily with the living. The larger challenge is having to deal with all the debris, because there are bodies in the debris, and they're only getting riper in the heat. I don't envy anybody that task.

I think we're a long way from the hotel serving as a proper hotel again. Were it not for the fact that an incredible amount of money was buried in this island already, I'd say it shouldn't be expected to ever recover. Surely, an insurance executive somewhere is saying exactly that to the council members, or whoever is making decisions these days.

And so, the patient is hardly our biggest concern. On top of that, there doesn't appear to be anything to treat: she's sick, but with something we have no cure for. Even if we did, Adam mentioned in passing that—and I'm quoting—"drugs don't work on us."

(Is this still the case? If she was sick with something for which we had a cure, would the cure really not work?)

Without a treatment protocol, the hotel bed may as well be as good as the hospital bed… except for the part where we won't really know if this is genuinely the case until we've had a chance to study her, using all available technologies. And as I've said, some of those technologies aren't portable.

But she continues to not let us move her. Today, we shifted her onto a crash cart, made sure she was comfortable—as much as one can determine this sort of thing with an unconscious person —and rushed her from the room. She made it all the way to the ambulance before disappearing.

We found her lying in the parking lot where the ambulance had been parked. The hotel's satyr manager looked quite put out, but the only thing we could do was bring her back to the room again. It was either that or risk her vanishing while the ambulance was in motion. I know nothing of the nature of this trick of hers, but I suspect it would be bad for her health if she reappeared on the open road while unconscious, and still carrying the vehicle's momentum.

I'm thankful that to this point, she hasn't materialized in the middle of a solid object. This would, I expect, be fatal.

CHAPTER 3

$\mathcal{I}$ am beginning to hate the information age.

I'm really fond of my secrets, although I honestly don't have all that many right now. I've *had* thousands of really good ones, but secrets only last as long as there are people around who care about them. Eventually, I end up being the only guy who knows enough about the secret to know why it's a secret at all, basically, and then it no longer matters to anybody except the occasional historian.

For a really long time I could keep all of those secrets in a place where nobody could get at them: in my head, most obviously, but also written down in a ledger I kept on my person, or locked up in a place only I had access to.

There were also secret societies that were good for keeping information secret. Sometimes, they were secret societies that, by virtue of being secret, became good places to store information. Other times, there was a bunch of information in need of being kept secret, so a society was formed to keep it that way. Honestly, once things got going it was hard to tell which came first: the information, or the organization. They both looked the same after a generation or two.

Being associated with one of these groups meant a new place to store my own secrets, which did mean they tended to last longer.

But not *too* much longer. A lot of the secret societies are gone, a few are still here but not all that private—the Freemasons, for instance—and a handful still exist and nobody knows about them but the members. I can name five of these off the top of my head. I'm sure there are more.

Beyond those kinds of explicit secret-keeping endeavors, there are the things I *think* should be secret but somehow are not any longer. Like, where I ate breakfast, when I crossed a border, whether or not I wore a hat last week, and what kind of hat it was. They're not really secrets, but they are things I feel shouldn't be straightforwardly obtainable.

That's what I don't like about the world so much. It wasn't that long ago that I understood when I was entering into a high surveillance situation, and what to do with myself in that circumstance. No sudden movements when meeting a head-of-state and all that. Nowadays, there's no such thing as a low- or no-surveillance environment, not if I want to go anywhere and do anything. (Aside: I do not want to go anywhere or do anything, which was why we moved to an island, but that's another story.)

"You know about the island?" Mirella asked.

"I do," Ina said. "But not that you came from there, not until I saw your papers. Dimitri always uses the same man."

"That doesn't seem like enough to put us on the island," I said. "Other than when we confirmed it for you about ten seconds ago."

"No. But I knew of *you*, the man who doesn't age. It has been some time, hasn't it? Since you last poked your head out of the grasses and looked at the horizon?"

"I planned not to stick my head up at all, but events conspired."

"I see."

She stared at me for an uncomfortably long time. It was a little like how it felt to be stared at by an oracle or a prophet. Like my *now* wasn't the only thing being perceived. Fortunately, I had a drink in my hand, which leavens discomfort sometimes.

"Your disappearance was a death gesture, I take it," she said.

"Yes. I didn't plan to go anywhere until the people who knew me aged out. Death by other means."

"You didn't wait long enough."

"I already know that. As I said, events conspired."

"We severed the connection," Mirella said, "between his life before and now. This is why we're hiring you, and the man who did our papers before now. To keep the separation clean."

"It didn't work," Ina said. "Someone, it seems, knew you were not dead, and now associates of that somebody appear to be aware that you are currently in Paris."

"Associates," I repeated, as that seemed important. "Is there a bounty on me? Because I've been through this before."

"Not a bounty, immortal man. A hit. A longstanding one, as it turns out. The contract was initiated three years ago. I assume you were on the island three years ago? It's the only thing that would have protected you."

"Oh," I said, "yes. I was."

There was a great deal of vetting involved in even visiting the island. I always thought it was sort of paranoid, initiated by the council to prevent some of its more controversial residents from an assassination. It never occurred to me that I might also benefit from this protection.

The bounty I previously had to get out of was very different from whatever this was; the people behind that one wanted me alive. This was clearly someone else.

"What is the source of the hit?" Mirella asked.

"Unknown. It came via the usual channels." Ina took a longer look at Mirella. "You swam those waters for a time, I can tell. You're armed, and not with the usual sort of weapons."

"I'm not unfamiliar with murder-for-hire," Mirella said. "Is it reputable?"

"Five-star, and for quite a lot of money." To me, Ina said, "I don't know how much you were worth before your paper suicide, but I would wager you are now worth much more as an actual dead man than you were in that life."

"I seriously doubt that," I said. "But I get your point."

I was one of the richest people in the world, for a little while —probably the second or third time I've been able to make that claim in my lifetime. It depends on how one counts personal wealth, and probably also how one defines the 'world'. I think it's probably a more impressive claim now than it was a few thousand years ago, just because of the size of the population.

"Thank you for the warning," I said. "As soon as we have those other two passports, we'll be out of your way."

"That isn't the only reason I'm telling you this," she said. "I wanted it out in the open now, in case you thought whatever steps I took after this were in some way *up-selling*, as it were, to an imagined threat."

"I don't know how to take that. What do you mean, up-selling?"

"I understand," Mirella said. She stretched, and raised an arm until her hand was tickling the hasp of the sword sticking out of the scabbard on her back. She did this when she was expecting violence.

"When will they be arriving for us?" she asked.

I was just slow enough to need a couple of beats to fully comprehend what Mirella meant. I'm not prepared to blame the alcohol, because that would just prove she was right about recommending I stay sober. But it was probably the alcohol.

Anyway, what I had missed and my girlfriend hadn't, was that the part about there being a contract on my head wasn't an abstract conversational point. There was an immediate, practical application.

"We have time," Ina said. "I don't expect them to enter the building at all, as the wise thing would be to await your departure. Right here, you're cornered. The only way out is down the elevator and through the lobby. A smart play would be a sharpshooter across the street, but they may not be smart. We will see."

"Fire escape?" Mirella asked.

"Yes, there is one of course, but the door is alarmed. You'll just be notifying them of where to expect your exit. And the stairwell releases into the lobby, so as long as you're using public exits, a sharpshooter across the street is still in play."

"You have another way out," I said.

"I do. It's in the event someone decided they felt the same way about my life as someone does about yours, but it will suffice here."

"I'm going to go back to *up-sell*. What do you want in exchange for this safe passage?"

"A good word with your benefactor, on the occasion of your continued survival. Imagine how this could go: you exit my home and are assaulted. You survive, or you don't survive; in either case, I was here, you were here, now I look involved. It could be argued, that were I an active participant in the execution of the bounty, the financial benefits would make becoming an enemy of Dimitri Romanov tolerable."

"Does it?"

"No, immortal man. I have money. I value peace more highly. In this, I can only speak for myself. The man who referred you here follows his own conscience."

"Jacques was so afraid of Dimitri he couldn't even say his name," I said.

"A healthy terror for one in his position. But greed can convince a person to try and outrace the devil. I'm sure you're no stranger to the siren call of avarice."

"I grew out of it a long time ago. How do you know he *did* betray us?"

"I don't, but someone knows you're here. Assembling killers on short notice creates ripples, and I've been seeing those ripples all evening. It was only after we met that it became clear what the cause was."

"So, you can get us out of here," Mirella reiterated.

"Out of the building, and as far as the airport, if you need. My advice would be to take the earliest flight back to the South Pacific and disappear yourselves once more. The island remains off-limits to those in the know and secret to those not in the know. Dimitri can send someone else on this errand of yours."

"That isn't really an option," I said.

Not said, was exactly how unsafe the island had recently become, thanks to a tsunami and something like an attack by an invasive species. It was good to know this wasn't public knowledge, even if it seemed insane for it not to be, given how many had died as a consequence of those two events. But, most of the dead were non-human, and as weird as this seemed, they valued secrecy more highly than their own lives.

"Surely, you have turned your back to impending cataclysm before," Ina said. "I would say your survival depended on such an attitude. Unless the contract is mistaken, you have no special abilities."

"Well that's just hurtful."

For the record, she was right; I don't get old and I can't get sick (so far) but that's about it.

"It isn't Dimitri Romanov's problem to solve," Mirella said. "He's only providing tactical support for the expedition."

"Then perhaps you should consider another era in which to tilt at this windmill."

There was a DING from the end of the hallway, prompting Ina to jump to her feet.

"The second passports are done," she said, heading for the back room. "The airport, then? Assuming you haven't concluded

I'm inventing a threat to improve my standing with your sponsor."

"We believe you," I said. "Just get us out of the building, we'll figure out where we're going from there."

"Very good."

She got halfway down the hall when we all heard another DING. This one came from the front entryway.

"Oh dear," Ina said.

"Was that the elevator?" I asked.

"It was. Someone with a key engaged the penthouse level."

"I take it you weren't expecting any other guests?" Mirella asked.

"No. I apologize, it appears they are opting for a frontal assault after all, and we have less time than I thought."

It seemed like we were jumping to a lot of successive conclusions at the same time, but these weren't people I was intimately familiar with, so Ina's understanding of the situation was the one that made the most sense at the moment.

Still, Jacques didn't seem all that betrayal-ish when I sat with him, being far more concerned with getting out of our transaction okay. He was also reluctant to involve himself in the part where he got us in touch with Ina. If he'd been planning to betray us all along, he would have had a different way to do it, and then decided what was about to happen was a better plan. Or, it wasn't him, and someone else—presumably someone close to Jacques—was behind this.

Or nobody was coming and we weren't about to get attacked.

"They opt a closed-quarters attack over hidden sniper," Mirella noted, as she drew her sword. She keeps it aligned with her spine, and short enough to allow her to still bend at the waist without it being awkward. She owns a larger sword, but that's for special occasions. "Interesting decision."

"A stupid one," Ina said. She looked at me. "Are you armed?"

"She's my weapon."

"That's lovely, but unhelpful."

Ina put her hand on a spot on the hallway wall, and a panel slid open, revealing a nifty collection of guns.

"The goblin is a fine weapon, but maybe you can back her up with more than confidence in her abilities," she said.

"Those might help. It depends on what's coming up in the elevator. Any ideas?"

"I assumed they would be intelligent enough to wait until you exited. I don't know how much I trust my own answer to this question."

"Best guess."

"Human. I don't think Jacques has anything more interesting on his payroll."

I took a Glock from the cabinet, and confirmed that it came with a full clip.

"I wouldn't be too hard on yourself," I said. "The best way to keep Dimitri from finding out about a betrayal is to either pay off or eliminate everyone who could tell him, so this sort of makes sense."

It could have also been that whoever was doing this wasn't smart at all, but very, very stupid. This was the option that had me sort of worried, because if we were dealing with the exceptionally dumb, there was a good chance a demon was riding up the elevator.

We gathered in the entryway. The man at the door had his gun out and was watching the number above the elevator doors go up. I didn't remember how many floors the building had, so I couldn't tell when it was close, but given he was holding his breath I thought we were probably about there.

Ina positioned herself between us and the door, armed with what I would call a small cannon. I didn't know what kind of gun it was, but that was what it looked like. Mirella was next to me, sword out.

"Hey, I have a question," I said. "Do you have to be in the lift in order for it to reach the penthouse?"

Ina looked at me for a hard second.

"No. It's a direct trip when the key is engaged and the button depressed. One could turn the key, hit the button, and step out if so inclined. Why?"

This was what was bugging me. Anybody coming up the elevator had to know that there would be a ton of forewarning to the occupants of the penthouse that someone was coming, that nobody was expecting them, and that there would be a lot of bullets flying in their direction as soon as the doors opened. So either they were bulletproof—which meant standing there to defend ourselves in this manner was a waste of time—or something else was being sent up the elevator.

The door dinged again. The guard whose name we never got crouched down and prepared to shoot whatever came through the doors. I felt sort of bad about never getting his name, because he was about to die and I had no time to warn him properly of that fact.

All I did have time to do was grab Ina's collar and yank her backwards. My other hand (I dropped the gun) had a hold of Mirella.

Other than those two things, I had time to shout one word of warning, so it had to be a decent word. What I came up with was, "BOMB!"

I'm pretty sure the door opened at that point and the explosive device inside the elevator did what it was supposed to do. I can't be a hundred percent positive that's precisely what happened, because I didn't hear the doors slide apart, and after the explosion I couldn't hear much of anything at all, not right away. However, I can speak with great confidence that my guess was correct, and there was a bomb on the elevator, since once the detonation occurred it was pretty impossible to deny this.

When I pulled everyone back it was to get behind the nearest wall, which happened to be a retaining wall. Anything less than that and I wouldn't be around to tell you about it. There was, for instance, another wall consisting of not much more than plasterboard, separating the entryway from the kitchen, and that wall vanished in a puff of white dust. Ina's doorman had been in front of the wall, and he too vanished in a puff, albeit a much more gruesome one.

I think I must have lost consciousness for a minute or two, because the next thing I was aware of, after the blast knocked us all backwards—I landed on the couch—was Mirella shaking me and saying something I couldn't hear.

Ina, she was asking, *where is Ina?*

I staggered to my feet, decided that was a bad idea, and sat down again. The room was full of smoke and dust, and smelled like pulverized human. (One of the many unfortunate things about being immortal is that I've smelled this often enough to know exactly what I'm smelling.) There were cracks in most of the windows on the ceiling and wall, and a few of them were growing as I watched. Soon, we would be exposed to the night air. That wasn't necessarily a bad thing, except for the part where the glass had to fall somewhere and we were under a lot of it.

Mirella found Ina lying beneath part of a table on the other side of the room.

I didn't appreciate the urgency of the task in the moment; my head was too scrambled. I figured the fire department was undoubtedly on their way, and those guys were trained to do things like help tiny women with vaguely German accents out from under a pile of rubble. There was no rush to get it done ourselves. Then, I decided Mirella did this in order to interrogate our host on the subject of where the fire exit was, so that we could leave that way ourselves.

I was half right. That was obviously the question asked, but once Ina told Mirella where it was, Mirella ran in that direction alone.

I probably said something out loud about this, along the lines of *hey, don't forget me*, but I still couldn't hear so I don't know how audible I was. She kept going, sword in one hand and a dagger in the other, looking like she had been somewhere else when the bomb went off. Maybe goblins just didn't get concussions.

Then I understood.

You don't just send a bomb up and hope for the best, not when there's money in proving it killed who it was supposed to kill. You send a team up the stairwell to make sure, and to deal with anybody still breathing.

I watched my girlfriend disappear into the smoke, and then got to my feet and tried to find a weapon with which to provide some backup. Hand-to-hand was out of the question, as my equilibrium was shot: it felt like I was the bad kind of drunk.

What I found was Ina's cannon. It looked like something between a rocket launcher and a shotgun, but it had a trigger and a barrel, and was probably loaded and ready to fire. *What* it would fire was a good question, and one I really should have sought an answer to prior to using it, but: my girlfriend was facing off an unknown number of people alone, somewhere in the middle of the smoke and plaster dust. Time was at a premium.

My hearing was starting to return, so I followed what sounds I could pick up through the smoke until—all at once—I came on the scene.

I was too late, but in a good way; she didn't need my help after all. Mirella was standing over possibly three bodies, covered in blood and looking happier than I'd seen her in a really long time.

We don't talk about it, but she likes killing people a whole lot more than she probably should.

"Put that down before you shoot me with it," she said.

"Any more coming?" I asked.

"I don't know. But I would recommend we find Ina's third way out rather than attempting the stairs."

Just then, a loud CRASH took away my hearing again for a few seconds. We were standing at one end of a side corridor that had been behind a door, with the fire exit at the other end of the corridor. This was a part of the penthouse that was covered by a non-glass roof, which was good, because that was what had made the crashing noise: the ceiling had caved in.

Mirella ran back to the living room. I followed as quickly as I could.

As I said, being open to the night air was probably ultimately a good thing, as the Paris winds cleared out the smoke and dust almost immediately. The winds were also strong enough to tip someone with equilibrium issues off the side, though, so I stayed far from the edge and let Mirella dig out our host. Ina looked to have avoided damage from the falling glass thanks to the tabletop she was beneath.

Ina pointed, and Mirella got her to her feet. *Get me to my office,* Ina was saying. The three of us stumbled down the hall.

Her computer room was largely undamaged by the explosion. It also still had power, which was a little surprising.

"I have to destroy all of this," Ina said, reaching into one of the machines. She pulled out two passports. "My apologies, I will be unable to provide you with the third identification this evening."

"That's okay." I said. "How do we get out of here?"

Ina stepped past the computers to the wall on the far end, reached down and slid up a panel.

"It's for laundry service," she said. "Don't worry, there's an electrical lift; you won't be free-falling into the basement."

"Will they be surprised to find us instead of laundry down there?" I asked.

"It's a prearranged escape route; they will know what to do. Hand me that gun."

I did.

"I'm going to shoot the electronics as you descend, and then go down after you, so don't be alarmed by the report of the gun. I trust you will be gone by the time I reach the basement, and so: best of luck to you both."

"You too," I said. "Sorry about your place."

She laughed.

"This is one of many. You can never be too cautious, can you, immortal man?"

From the journal of Dr. Lew Cambridge

Day forty-three.

Adam's limited understanding of the patient's physiology led to our assumption that she's fully human, in the same way that he's fully human.

This may not be the case.

There are a tremendous number of qualifiers in this assertion. Both Adam and (ha-ha) Eve are human-but-immortal, which by default means they are *not* human in the same sense that the rest of mankind might be called human. Leaving aside, for the moment, genetic markers, a minimum expectation of a human being would be age and infirmity. Adam neither ages nor becomes sick. Eve does not age, and until whatever happened to her sometime in the past year transpired, she didn't become sick either.

This should mean they're something other than human.

Adam agreed to donate blood and hair samples before leaving the island. He was exceedingly reluctant to do this, citing the multiple occasions in which a medical professional attempted to use such samples for ill—something about a secret government project, on which he declined to elaborate. The argument that this testing might in some way aid me in curing Eve was what won the day. This was even after he made the point that he and the patient are from different "stock", as he put it.

I've run extensive tests on the samples he provided, and have found no evidence to contradict his self-identified humanity. I don't have the material or the time to do any DNA sequencing (I'm sure he'd be happy to know this) but I don't think it would lead to any different conclusions. At the same time, I can appreciate his trepidation, because my curiosity is positively afire: if I had a sequencer, I would definitely be using it.

We ran the same tests on the patient as the ones on Adam's samples. The patient yielded slightly different results, although I'm becoming convinced that what I'm looking at may be a cross-contamination, because the tests indicate she's both human, and goblin.

It was an odd result for many reasons, the primary being that there's no such thing as a human/goblin hybrid.

Species hybridization is not at all unheard-of, but the only confirmed instances are: incubus-human; satyr-human; and imp-human. My unusual field of study admittedly has more unknowns than knowns—for instance, next-to-nothing is known about the breeding habits of rakshasas, wraiths or the yeti. I have also never been able to get a straight answer from an iffrit. And of course, there is a lengthy list of creatures whose existences I can't confirm at all, never mind gaining a substantive understanding as to how they reproduce.

The point remains: to my understanding, goblins and humans cannot produce an offspring. There should ergo be no reason to expect to find traces of both species in one donor.

Upon receipt of that unusual result, I took a second blood sample and re-ran the test, taking extra caution to avoid any contamination. (I don't know how the first sample could have become contaminated, as neither myself nor my lab assistant are goblin-born. However, it's the most likely explanation, and so the best thing to do is attempt to control for that.)
The second test yielded the same result, but a different ratio: the percentage of the sample that could have been called goblin was only slightly larger than the error margin of the test itself.

This presents a tantalizing possibility.

To date, we have been unable to fully isolate and examine the disease within the patient. We had a similar problem isolating it in the residual samples we had left from the mermaid, but this was in large part due to the lack of information we have on mermaid biology as a whole. (This study is ongoing, on the remaining liquefied samples. The living mer-folk have all left the island, blessedly.) There are no other active carriers of the disease at this time.

It has been a cardinal frustration for myself and my team, that despite the patient's evident biological humanness—about which we know a great deal more than we did about the mermaid—we still can't definitively isolate a sample, even though she clearly suffers from the disease.

I'm left with the cynical conundrum: I'd like samples of the disease so as to develop a cure for it, so that the next being to be afflicted can be saved; and I would like another being to contract the disease so that I can get a clean sample.

Finally, there's this: if the presence of goblin within the patient is declining, I can't escape the notion that her body's strikingly effective immune system is busy eradicating it.

On many levels, this is preposterous, and seems even more preposterous now that I've committed the notion to paper. The test we performed wasn't designed to identify infections or contaminants in the patient; it was only to flag the genetic markers of the patient's species. If there were goblin within her—if, for instance, she was injected with the blood of one—it wouldn't present in this way at all.

Yet, I can't shake the idea that this is what we're seeing happening.

We have decided to wait a week and then take a new sample and re-test it, to see if the markers for goblin continue to decline.

CHAPTER 4

*I*na's people got us out of the building in the back of a van holding soiled linens, to an alley, four blocks away. We were on our own from there, which was really okay. Separating from Ina as much as possible as soon as possible was better for everyone concerned.

We headed back to the hotel on Boulevard Saint-Germain and camped out across the street for a half an hour, both to wait for my ears to stop ringing, and to see if anyone obviously problematic surfaced—the police, an armed goon or two, or something non-human would all qualify. Nobody like that did, so we went in.

"We need to be out of here before they realize we aren't in the bomb wreckage," Mirella said, almost as soon as we got back into the room.

I was already busy throwing my clothes into a suitcase, so I wasn't sure what she meant about hurrying; I sort of already was. But she had this weird habit of never unpacking when we stayed in hotels, so there was nothing for her to do but watch me emptying drawers. In hindsight, this was probably the exact kind of situation she was anticipating when deciding not to unpack.

"That'll take them a while," I said.

"They only need to find the bodies near the fire exit to know I lived."

"Fair, but they weren't trying to kill you."

"I'm only saying to hurry."

"I get it."

Trying to get the hell out of town while also trying to work out exactly what was happening was a little exhausting. I'm never comfortable with the kind of uncertainty a fluid situation like this engenders, because the way to survive is to be the one to not panic. This works in a lot of situations, actually: gunfights; fires in public places; stampedes. I didn't like that we were reacting to the situation without fully understanding how we got into it in the first place.

"I want to make a phone call before we go," I said.

"We can do that later."

"I'd rather do it now."

She glared.

"Come on," I said, "let's not overreact here."

"There's been a bounty on your head for three years, and the entire criminal element of Paris is evidently aware of this fact, so we need to leave Paris right now. How is this an overreaction?"

"I get all that, but running is also when we're most exposed, so let's do it right. Look: how many exits do we have?"

"Five to the public, plus a service exit to the delivery dock. Two more with alarms. This is provided we can get off the floor, which only has two stairwells and an elevator."

"There, see you've already scoped out the routes."

"We need to get to the airport before they know we're going to the airport, Adam."

"There are a lot of different ways to flee a city, and we don't have to go to the airport at all. We'll be fine."

She harrumphed.

"Fine," she said. "Call. I don't like waiting, and I don't like standing still."

From my pocket, I pulled out the phone that was only meant to be used to make this particular call, and dialed.

"Look at it this way," I said, as it rang, "if they catch up to us now, you'll get to kill more people. Don't tell me you aren't looking forward to that."

Mirella stuck her tongue out, by way of response.

The call connected.

"Hello, Adam."

The man on the other end of the line spoke with a terrifyingly deep voice. You'd think a voice like this would be soothing, but it was less Barry White and more, Angry Gregorian Chant. Also, he wasn't a man.

"Grundle," I said. "We're burned."

Grundle was a troll who lived in a cave, on the island we called home until our house was destroyed. He was the first intelligent troll I ever met, and also something of a genius when it came to all things relating to the Internet. Admittedly, the bar is pretty low when it comes to me and the Internet; I don't even understand how radios work. Basic competence with search engines looks advanced to me.

It's hard to make clear how unlikely it is to find a troll who can use a computer, to someone who's never met a troll. (Almost nobody has.) It's a little like finding a five-year old with a firm grasp of non-Euclidian geometry. Just trust me: it's weird. About the only thing about him that was standard for his species was the home in the cave.

Well, that and the prodigious body odor.

"Explain," he said. "Provided you're speaking non-literally, and not dialing from the burn ward."

"Someone sold us out."

I decided to leave Jacques out of this conversation for the

moment. Ina's logic was compelling, but I wasn't entirely convinced he was behind this.

"To whom? I'm not sure I understand. Who is out there prepared to buy you?"

"Sorry, I guess that doesn't make sense. It's been a long night. We just found out there's a price on my head. I don't understand how, but I have a feeling getting to the *who* will help with that, because as long as every thug in Europe means to put a bullet in my brain, we're going to have a lot of trouble getting around."

"I see. Is there a concern that Dimitri's local cohort will be unable to resist the temptation?"

"There is. Although, if it comes up, the counterfeiter named Ina is pretty definitely not involved. Maybe Di-Di can post a positive review for her or something."

"I take it you're cutting ties, then. Can I help?"

"Only if you have your own secret criminal empire. No, we'll make do; I have other options. But it would be great if you could figure out where the bounty is coming from."

"Yes, I'll see what I can find out."

I used to have a guy I could rely on to do this sort of thing. His name was Tchekhy, and he also did my passports, so as you can imagine, I kind of missed him at this moment. But, he was one of the people I couldn't contact now that I was 'dead'. It was annoying, because this was the kind of thing he'd be able to get an answer about before I even hung up the phone. Although there was an equally good chance he wouldn't take the call, because the line was insufficiently secure.

"Good, thanks. Actually, maybe we should keep the detail about the contract away from Dimitri until we have more. I don't know how much money this is for, but if it's enough he might be tempted himself."

Grundle laughed. His laugh was terrifying, even at a distance.

"He would never do that, Adam. He owes you his life."

I wanted to say, *yes, but he's a criminal,* but decided not to.

Grundle literally lived in a cave; he might not appreciate this side of Dimitri Romanov.

"I know. Keep it between us anyway. Tell him we're taking our own path, and we'll fill him in later."

"Adam," Mirella said, in a tone of voice that made me want to duck. She was at the window.

"I have to go, Grundle," I said. I nearly hung up, but there was one more thing.

"How is she?" I asked.

"Oh! She's awake."

I nearly dropped the phone.

"She's awake?" I repeated, almost too loudly. Mirella, on the other side of the room, stopped caring about what she saw out the window for a few seconds, because this was news.

"Why didn't you lead with that?" I asked.

"You jumped right in, I'm sorry. About the burnt thing. It was very confusing."

"Right, right, right, sorry, so she's awake, did she say what happened?"

"No. It was only a day or two ago. Lew said she has no memory of what happened. She didn't even know where she was, and she's too weak to get out of the bed."

"All right. Um. Please update us if that changes."

I didn't entirely know what to say, because the fact of Eve being unconscious was sort of why we were doing what we were doing. It knocked me for a loop.

"Of course," Grundle said, as if this was the most reasonable thing. The most reasonable thing would have been to call me two days ago, and that hadn't occurred to him. I would have given him some grief about that, but Mirella was glaring at me again, so I just hung up.

"So your terrifying dream girl is awake," Mirella said. "Good. Now let's get out of here."

For reasons I will never be fully clear on, Mirella sometimes acts jealous of Eve. Granted, Eve is beautiful and also immortal, but she also sort of hates me.

I decided to ignore the *dream girl* classification and skip ahead. It was an argument we'd probably have to get through eventually, but in a more leisurely setting. Assuming we found one.

"What are you seeing?" I asked instead, getting to the window.

"Oh, nothing," she said. "Not yet. I just wanted you off the phone."

"Really? I figured an army was outside."

"You would have been another half an hour with the troll otherwise, and then there *would* be an army. Can we go now?"

~

We were traveling pretty light, with one bag apiece. On a good day—meaning, a day in which Mirella didn't feel any compunction to arm herself—about a quarter of her bag was taken up by weapons. No guns, just a variety of knives. Roughly a third of my bag was occupied by cash.

It was actually sort of amusing. Depending on the problem, we would either open up my money belt or her knife collection to solve it. It was also ironic, given she's wealthier and I've definitely killed more people. I've had a longer time to work on my body count, though.

We exited through a loading dock that opened on an alley next to the hotel. From there, we reached the sidewalk, which was busy with tourists—I'm pretty sure on any given day, Paris is about 60% tourist in every direction—and blended into the crowd.

An hour later—reasonably assured nobody was in pursuit—we were at a table at a pricey restaurant with a view of the Seine. The seats were at the corner of a railing with a twenty foot drop on the other side. Unless they were gifted with the power of flight, an attacker would have to get through the entire restaurant first to reach us. I could tell it was an effective defensive position because it was the first time Mirella really relaxed since we'd walked into Ina's penthouse.

Me, I was just happy to have somebody bring me alcohol.

"So," Mirella said, after ten minutes of eyeballing everyone sharing the patio with us. "Who did you piss off this time?"

"Well that doesn't seem fair. What makes you think I brought this on myself?"

"I didn't mean it that way."

"You sort of did, but that's okay. It's not like I haven't racked up a decent number of enemies, it's just that none of them are still alive."

She laughed.

"I think perhaps you're mistaken about that."

"Yeah, maybe. This feels like something new, though. I mean, for starters, I don't exist anymore."

"That could be the part where you're mistaken."

You probably don't think about your own life like this—or if you do, not often—but you're leaving a footprint everywhere you go. What I mean is that you've got one life, and in that life there are family members, friends, enemies, coworkers, and so on. As benign as that existence may or may not be, if one day someone came up and said, *there's a bounty on your head,* you would at minimum have to evaluate your life to come up with the name of somebody who felt strongly enough about you to do this. That evaluation would take a while, because you've left a lot of footprints.

I've obviously left a lot of footprints too. More than anybody. But the difference is that my footprints are largely historical.

"The who, seems less important to me right now than the why," I said. "I think if we get the why down, we'll find the who."

"Something you did, then, rather than someone to whom you did something."

"Or, something I'm going to do."

Mirella tensed, but not because of what I'd just said. Movement across the room caught her eye. Whatever it was, it was a false alarm, because she relaxed again almost immediately.

"What do you mean," she asked. "Do you plan to do something in particular?"

"Other than find out what made Eve sick, no. But we could still be in the middle of a prophesy."

I hate to keep saying *long story*, but this is also a long story. I ran into a prophet on the island, and that prophet seemed to think I was important enough to save, to the extent that she effectively traded the lives of hundreds in order to ensure my continued existence. I'm still a little upset about this.

"Goodness, Adam, how long do these prophesies last?"

"Who knows? There are parts of the bible that haven't happened yet, right?"

She laughed.

"That isn't a prophesy."

"Depends on who you're talking to," I said. "I don't think I slept through the Second Coming, though."

I never met any of the folks who wrote the Christian Bible, nor the guy who inspired them to write it. I did meet two or three of the old testament scribes, and there were definitely prophets and prophesy involved there. (Generally, the person named as the prophet in the Bible was actually the scribe for the real prophet, which means the raw prophesy was being filtered through someone before anybody even heard it aloud.) My point is only that while I was joking, it wasn't a very good joke.

"We could still be in the grip of one is what I'm saying," I said.

"How would that impact the questions we have now?" she asked.

"Not sure. Another prophet? If someone wants to stop me from doing something I haven't done yet, how do they know I'm going to do it?"

She sighed, and paused, as the waitress brought over a new round of drinks.

"Perhaps we should take all of the magical hand-waving out of the conversation and stick with available facts," she said. "We don't have enough of them, but I will not come out of it with a headache."

"Prophets aren't magic."

"Call it what you want. Magic to me is the ability to do something for which there is no available science."

"A whole lot of things through history were mislabeled magic using the same reasoning."

"I know. You've told me, many times over. It doesn't invalidate my point. You just don't like the word *magic*. All right, so we don't know who's trying to kill you or why they're trying to kill you. We assume the bounty is generous enough to send all capable hands in your direction, as there's plenty of evidence of that. This means we can't trust Dimitri's people, as you've already concluded given the part of the phone conversation I heard with the troll. Where does that leave us?"

"We have money and two clean passports each. That'll get us pretty far."

"It doesn't give us the protection we were counting on, and the anonymity of clean passports is somewhat overrated. You know this. I'm wondering if the woman was right and we should go back to the island."

"That seems extreme."

"Someone tried to blow us up not three hours ago."

"Yes, I remember."

She downed her drink and signaled for another. This happens around me sometimes.

"Why continue?" she asked. "Eve is awake. By the time we return to the island, perhaps her mind will have recovered enough to provide us with more thorough information than where she shoplifted her clothing."

"Unless she never remembers."

Mirella nodded slowly.

"You're frightened," she said.

"Why do you say that?" I asked.

"I should have seen that sooner. I thought you were in this to save the life of this unattainable woman of yours, but that isn't it at all. You want to solve the mystery before *you* get sick."

"That is entirely too insightful. I hate you a little for even suggesting it."

"She's getting better, so now you don't have to worry. Let's go back. Dimitri can find out where this contract came from, Eve can tell us where she became ill, and the next time we leave it will be with a better plan than this one."

I didn't answer. It was hard to deny the reasoning. At the same time, we didn't need to be on the island to hear what Eve had to say. We could be in Chicago already.

Mirella could tell I wasn't changing my mind. Not only would I have jumped at the suggestion otherwise, I'd have suggested it first.

"Smaller steps, then," she said. "We can't stay in Paris, which is fortunate as we have no reason to stay in Paris."

"Aside from the romance of it all."

"Its charm has worn off. Airport? You said no earlier, but it's the fastest way to Chicago."

"No, not the airport. If there's one thing I'm an expert at, it's fleeing parts of Europe."

"You have a plan. Can you tell me what it is?"

"Only part of it," I said. "The rest is a secret."

She laughed.

"You're serious?"

"I might be. You'll think it's dumb. Just trust me."

"All right. As long as it's better than escaping France on foot. Or swimming."

She tensed up again, only this time she didn't calm down. Something had changed in the restaurant in the last few seconds.

"Do you imagine that this bounty is rich enough to entice a person to open fire in a crowded restaurant?" she asked.

"I don't like a single thing about that sentence. What do you see?"

"Go ahead and turn around, I don't think it matters if they see your face; they clearly know you're here."

I turned.

There were three men of note: one at a table on the left, one at a table on the right, and a third standing at the bar at the far end of the room. As Mirella said, the place was crowded, so the men weren't easy to spot if you didn't already know to look for them. This must have been why Mirella only decided they were a threat in the last few seconds.

"Can we make the jump over the railing?" I asked.

"I can. I don't think you can."

"Twist-an-ankle bad, or break-a-leg bad?"

"The second one."

"So, we'll call that a last resort. Who's the guy at the bar talking to?"

"You'll see."

A series of gestures passed between the man at the bar and the two at the tables, and then he stepped aside, and the fourth man revealed himself. It was Jacques.

"Oh, well that's all sorts of interesting," I said.

"I can probably kill him from here," my girlfriend declared. She's the best.

"No, better not."

Jacques raised his hands to show that he didn't have a gun. It didn't mean anything—surely the other three were packing—but it worked to secure his personal safety as he made passage from the bar to the table.

"How about now?" Mirella asked under her breath.

"Maybe."

"Can I sit?" Jacques asked. He was speaking in English now, undoubtedly for Mirella's benefit. That was smart.

"Sure," I said. "We'd both like to kill you, just so you know."

"I thank you for the warning."

He pulled a chair up to the table and sat.

"I want you to understand," he said, "that I had nothing to do with what happened earlier, and further that it is still my intention to help you reach safety, wherever it is you intend to next travel. Chicago, or elsewhere."

"Thanks. What do you think, honey?"

"I think that sounds like what someone who would like to get us alone and away from all of these people would say," Mirella said.

"I agree. Jacques, unless I'm confused about something, you're the only one who knew we'd be at Ina's, so that narrows down the suspect list an awful lot."

"I can only agree with this reasoning, Randall. I came to the same conclusion the second I heard of what took place in the penthouse. But as I told no one, and none in my organization knew enough of what our meeting entailed to connect you with the bounty, I was stymied by this information. I began to wonder if perhaps I had made the arrangements and then immediately suffered some kind of head injury. But I also knew that it hardly mattered if it was I or no, as nobody but me would pay the penalty for it. Truthfully, my only solution was to find the true source of the information, and if possible, bring them to you. And so I have."

"This seems…awfully convenient," Mirella said.

"Again, I agree. No sooner did I decide this course of action but I came upon the man, because as it turns out he was looking for me at the same time. It seemed hardly possible, to the extent that I fear we may have damaged him somewhat in the intervening minutes, as we attempted to tease out more information.

He continued to refuse disclosure of his source, but did allow that were we to come to this restaurant we would find you. And so, we did, and here you are."

"That's a pretty crazy story," I said.

"Most of what has happened since this afternoon qualifies under that descriptive. I've since learned you may be the oldest living being, and that is undeniably mad, would you not agree?"

"Sure, that's fair."

"According to this odd little man, everything I just told you should be enough to spare me from the wrath of your benefactor..." he looked at Mirella. "And from you."

"That depends," I said. "What's his name?"

"He gave me seven names, each more preposterous than the last. Here."

He took a phone from his pocket, called up an image, and slid it across the table.

"Maybe you can tell me which of his preposterous names I should use?"

I took a good look. The guy in the picture was tied to a chair and looked pretty roughed up, but I still recognized him.

"Yeah, okay, this is starting to make some sense," I said.

"I'm glad someone feels this way," Jacques said.

"His name's Thelonius D'Artagnan. Take us to him; we have a lot to talk about."

INTERLUDE (3)

From the journal of Dr. Lew Cambridge

Day forty-seven.

The patient is conscious.

I was at the top of the island when she awoke, dealing with a medical matter that was urgent only in the mind of the person who was afflicted, and about which I won't commit to in detail here. My frustration at having been away—it's been twenty-seven hours—is mitigated only marginally by the satisfaction in learning that she's conscious.

Per Janet's notes:

--at 10:42 A.M., Janet proceeded to change the patient's IV drip and perform a regular vitals check.

--at approximately 10:49 A.M., Janet became aware that the patient's eyes were open. At this point, Janet attempted to engage the patient in conversation. Patient appeared to be aware but unresponsive.

--at 11:02 A.M., Janet contacted the hospital and updated the team regarding the newest development. Efforts were begun to reach me telephonically. (Note: these efforts did not succeed. I returned unaware of the change in the patient's status until my arrival at the hospital this afternoon.)

--at approximately 11:32 A.M., the patient moved her head, and it 'became clear she could hear me', in Janet's words.

--11:35 A.M., or thereabouts. Despite Janet speaking only in English, the patient began attempting to communicate with Janet in an unknown tongue. This continued for forty minutes. (Note: approximately twenty minutes of it was recorded on Janet's phone. As I write this, I have not had an opportunity to listen.)

--at approximately 12:15 P.M., the patient began speaking in French, which Janet could identify but not speak. This was followed by German, 'something like Spanish', and an unknown fourth Latinate tongue.

--patient finally arrived at English at roughly 12:18 P.M. Her first words were as follows:

"Where am I?"
"I will kill you."
"Why am I so weak?"
"What has happened?"

Janet answered the first question, requested politely that the patient not kill her, and then explained that she was unsure how to answer the other two questions. It was impressed upon the patient at this time that what happened to her and why she was so weak were things she was best positioned to answer herself, given our current uncertainty.

The patient stated that she did not know, and that she would like to sleep.

All other communications from the patient have been requests for privacy. I will be interviewing her myself shortly.

CHAPTER 5

*I*t was just after Midnight by the time Jacques was able to put us in the same room as Thelonius D'Artagnan. The meeting took place in the office of a storeroom that looked a lot like the kind of place I had been expecting to end up in at the beginning of the evening, way back when we were planning to meet the passport counterfeiter. It wasn't *on* the river, but it was close.

Thelonius was sitting in a wooden chair in the middle of the room. It looked like he had been tied down for a portion of the evening, and also for that portion of the evening someone had been hitting him hard in places that bruise visibly. That he was no longer tied down or being struck by someone could have been because Jacques informed the necessary parties—Thelonius shared the room with five armed men—that we were coming, and to please stop trying to beat information out of him. It could also have been that he talked his way out of the beating.

Thelonius was a portly being of indeterminate age—anywhere between 40 and 140—with a round face and a thick beard. His hair was long and stringy, covering ears that were just a little too large and floppy to be associated with that of a human.

(Although you had to know this already to look.) Had the hair been whiter, he would have looked a lot like Santa Claus. Since it was graying, he gave off more of a Jerry Garcia vibe.

He was an imp. And actually, since we're here, so was Santa. But that's a story for another time.

When we walked in, he was in the middle of a tale. Because of course he was.

"…and then," he said, in perfect French, "to the surprise of all, the tiger sprang up!"

The five men ostensibly guarding Thelonius jumped back in surprise, as if the tiger were in the room with them.

"But, it was dead!" one of them said.

"That is what they thought! But no!"

"Excuse me," Jacques said loudly, "if we could bring story time to a conclusion?"

At least one of his guys looked ready to draw on Jacques for interrupting.

"But I'm nearly finished!" Thelonius said.

He did not in any way sound like a man who had been held against his will for the past few hours. He sounded like he was exactly where he wanted to be. This could either be because we were fulfilling a predicted sequence of events—so none of this came as a surprise to him—or because this was just what imps did.

It would be an understatement to describe imps as gifted storytellers. That would be like calling a fish a gifted swimmer. They lived and breathed stories in a way that made things which were self-evidently impossible sound not just feasible, but likely.

I don't think it's an understatement to say that a large portion of the world's myths and legends could be pinned on an imp. One of their kind is the reason a name I used to go by—Dionysos—was considered a god. I'm still kind of pissed about that.

"I'd wager you have another hour left," I said, in English, stepping into the room.

He saw me, and grinned.

"The eternal man arrives!" he said. "And yes! You have it correct. Another hour at most. That is what I meant when I said it was almost finished."

The fact that he wouldn't be telling the rest of the story was nearly enough to cause a mutiny among Jacques's men, something he didn't appear entirely aware of. This is another interesting thing about imps: they could probably start revolutions if they wanted. I've never met one who *did* want to, but it's reasonable to argue that a decent number of revolutions took place because of an imp anyway, whether or not it was intentional. Good storytelling can be a superpower.

"Leave us," Jacques said, to his men, in French.

This didn't go over well, but they left.

I pulled up another chair and sat opposite the imp. Mirella closed the door and took up her usual defensive position near it. If I didn't know her really well, I'd think she did this in every room she was in. It was *nearly* true.

"I don't even know where to begin," I admitted.

"The beginning is always the best place for a story," Thelonius said. "Start there!"

"That's the problem, I don't know where that is. Earlier tonight, we were getting passports and heading out of town, which we couldn't do until we got the information Jacques here supplied for us. That should be the beginning of the story. But it turns out there's been a price placed on my head, and that pre-dates our arrival in Paris, so that could be the beginning, except I don't know who's sponsoring the bounty, and I definitely don't know why, or how they know who I am and that I'm alive. That seems like a crappy place to start a story, don't you think?"

When engaging in conversation with an imp, it's always a good idea to treat everything this way: as a tale with a beginning, middle and end. It's how they ingest information.

"When I am faced with an unknown element in a story," he said, "I often speculate on it until the truth comes to me."

"You mean lying. That's what regular people call it. Making something up and passing it off as equivalent to the verifiable bits."

He shrugged.

"Who is to say?" he asked.

Mirella groaned, from the corner.

"No wonder you couldn't get a straight answer," she said, to Jacques.

This is the thing about imps: from their perspective, every story is true. It makes the tales they tell incredibly compelling, no matter how fanciful. If you hooked an imp up to a lie detector, you'd find that he is *never* lying, because he doesn't think he is. (This says more about lie detector tests than imps, actually.)

"I'm hoping you can fill some of this in for us, Thelonius. Somehow, you came to Paris knowing both about the contract and about the fact that I happened to be here, and you also knew who to provide that information to. In doing so, you nearly got both of us killed, and the last time you and I spoke, that was clearly not on your agenda."

"May I call you Adam?" he asked.

"Sure."

"Adam, I cannot talk freely in this company. As you're intimate with my kind, you surely appreciate how much it pains me to say this."

I glanced over at an impatient-looking Jacques.

"He means you," I said. "Can you let us have the room?"

"You aren't the only one this little person has put at risk on this day," he said.

"I understand, but if he's saying he can't answer questions with you here, he means it, because there are few things imps enjoy more than an audience."

"Did you say, imp?"

"I did. Not, 'little demon', if you're a Christian. I mean, obviously."

"So, he isn't human?"

"He's not, no. You must be used to this by now."

Jacques didn't look like someone who'd ever really get used to any of this.

"All right," he said, "I'll leave you. But I would like an explanation sometime before the sunrise."

He exited.

"All right," I said, to Thelonius. "Now can you talk?"

"Alas, no, I still cannot." He looked at Mirella. "Can you hear?"

She looked confused.

"I don't understand," she said. "Can I hear *you*? Of course."

"No, not me. There's a device in the room."

"A microphone?" I asked.

"It offers aperiodic feedback, and echoes when one's voice exceeds a certain pitch. I identified it earlier this evening and strove to fill up whatever recording device might be installed in here. I'm now of the opinion that we're being listened to from another room in this building, and possibly recorded there, as none bothered to flip a tape whilst hearing my earlier tale."

That Thelonius wasn't familiar with digital recorders indicated he was one of the older ones.

As I said, he could be between 40 and 140, and there would be essentially no way to tell from looking at him. I've never known what the average imp lifespan was, because I could never get one of them to give me a straight answer to the question. (They might not know, for the same reason.) Possibly as high as two centuries, though.

Mirella began circling the room. Aside from the chairs we were in, there were a bunch of crates in the corner and an old desk against a wall, but that was about all. There was a cheap drop ceiling missing several panels, and for illumination we had bare fluorescents.

It was a big enough space to make a completely thorough search impossible—again, because digital recorders were a thing that existed, and were small enough to live in any one of the crates—but we only needed to find the one that was bothering Thelonius.

Mirella eventually located it, in the ceiling. She cut its cord with a well-aimed knife.

"Much better," Thelonius said. "I confess to surprise that you couldn't detect it directly. The heightened senses of your kind are legendary."

It should be said that imps have exceptional hearing, thanks I guess to those big floppy ears of theirs. Being able to hear things nobody else is supposed to hear is undoubtedly a useful skill for inveterate storytellers.

"Legend doesn't improve my hearing any," Mirella grumbled. She went back the door to see if anyone was going to come running in, now that they couldn't eavesdrop electronically any longer. Nobody did.

"All right, now explain yourself," I said. "The last time we saw you was on the island."

"Indeed! And my goodness, what a tale that was! I cannot tell you how difficult it has been to not recount *that* story. Mermaids! Prophesy! But the island, as you are aware, is a forsworn secret to all who visit, even the ones who arrived surreptitiously, as I did."

I found it hard to believe there was anything an imp couldn't find an excuse to repeat in a story.

"Why don't you begin with after we rid the island of mermaids?"

Again, this is a long story, although probably not as long as Thelonius could have made of it. There was an invasion of mermaids and a tsunami, and we lived through all of that so we didn't really need for him to give it back to us in more fanciful language. However, the last time either of us saw the imp, it was in the hospital as the prophet he was following died.

Her death made Thelonius D'Artagnan a lot more important, because he was her scribe.

~

*P*rophets are really bad at sounding intelligible. Their brains aren't wired in a way that makes comprehensive sentences an expectation, which is why the good ones—by which I mean the ones who survive long enough for somebody to figure out what's coming from their mouths are predictions of the future—end up with an interpreter. That's really what a prophet's scribe is: an interpreter of what might sound to the rest of us like gibberish. We call them scribes because what they're supposed to do, after the necessary editing, condensing, and interpreting, is write down the stuff. That way, all of us can go back later and read what was written and go, "ohhh, that's what this was about." Because to be honest, these kinds of predictions are hardly ever actionable beforehand.

There are a lot of reasons it's a bad idea to hire an imp as a scribe. Number one, the predictions require a modicum of interpretation already, so while we're talking about a species that can spin all kinds of nonsense into a story, they'll also fabricate freely to make that story better. It isn't that an imp scribe would or wouldn't embellish a prediction so much as that they wouldn't themselves know where the embellishment began. Number two, it wouldn't occur to an imp to write any of it down. They are—and this is an extremely generous definition—oral historians.

This prophet happened to see a future in which I died, and took direct action to alter that future, at great cost to a lot of lives and a few fortunes. Then she passed away, and now the only location of whatever remaining prophesy she left behind was stuck in the mind of Thelonius D'Artagnan…because he couldn't be bothered to write any of it down.

I knew exactly how important he was, but didn't bother to

alert anybody to grab him and hang onto him, because I was occupied with other things. (Eve in a coma sort of took up all my free mental space for a while.) At the same time, i was under the impression nobody was leaving the island for a while, so I didn't concern myself with the possibility that he would vanish on us.

Then, he vanished on us.

~

"How did you get off the island?" I asked.

"On Lorelai's instruction, I was to seek the future elsewhere."

Lorelai was the name he gave to the prophet. Nobody knew her real name.

"She was dead by then."

"Yes, but we are still in the thrall, eternal man! Surely you have come to this understanding on your own."

"Whether or not I have, I think I've made it clear I don't care for prophesy, and plan to ignore it whenever I can."

"But that hardly matters! Did you ever hear the story of the frog and the castor oil? It seems that many years ago…"

"Please stop. I asked you how you got off the island and you began with *why*."

"The frog and the castor oil is a quite illustrious tale."

He looking incredibly put out, at not being able to convey the story of the frog and the castor oil.

"Thelonius, I promise that you have never in your life met a person less interested in hearing a long-winded story from an imp than I am."

I actually enjoy the company of imps during times of peace, which is to say when there's alcohol and no curfew, and there isn't anyone trying to kill me. They're incredibly annoying when you're in a hurry and require information, because imps have no off-switch.

"For the purposes of allegory…" Thelonius began.

"Good lord, Adam, can we just beat him up some more?" Mirella asked. Going by her expression, it wasn't a casual threat.

"Why?" I asked. "It didn't work when Jacques tried it."

"I meant, for fun."

"I left the island by boat," Thelonius said, possibly deciding on a direct response or two before Mirella acted on the torture idea.

"What boat was that?" I asked.

The first boat to take survivors off the island didn't do so until two days after the last time anyone saw Thelonius, and I'd seen the travel manifests already. It was the first thing I did after realizing he'd gone missing.

"On a merchant vessel, full of hard men and captained by a leathery woman as old as the sea itself. She took to anchor on the leeward side late one night, two days past the calming of the sea. We rowed by lantern from the jagged rocks that punctuated the shoreline to the breast of the old fishing scow. Never before have I…"

"All right, stop," I said. You have to know where to interrupt imps to get what you want. Like I said, this is a process. "Lorelai chartered a boat for you to leave by, after the threat was over, do I have that correct?"

"The old woman of the seas owed a favor, it was no charter. Or, more fairly, Lorelai dealt in a different manner of coin than most of us. An open channel to the fates was her currency."

This made a lot of sense. I had to think any merchant vessel given advance warning of a tsunami might be inclined to do a favor for whomever provided them with that warning.

"Who is *we*?" I asked.

"Is this a philosophical question?" Thelonius asked. His eyebrows twitched, which I guess was a display of excitement for the many hours of verbal sparring that would follow if my answer was yes.

"You said *we* rowed by lantern. Did someone leave the island with you?"

"Oh. Yes. Henri. Fortuitously, we did not depart during a full moon, or my lupine companion would surely have been a hefty challenge. He is far stronger than appearances indicate, and indeed rowed us there unaided."

There was a lot going on in that explanation. First off, Henri was a werewolf, which was why Thelonius brought up the full moon. But, as anyone who's spent more than thirty days with one knows, the entire full-moon-transformation thing isn't true.

Werewolves are the occasional genetic byproducts of a mating between a satyr and a human woman. (There are four options, with the most likely by far being a male satyr or a female human. Male werewolf is less likely. The fourth option—female werewolf —is so rare I've only ever heard of it happening once.) The imp undoubtedly knew this about werewolves, but since the idea of them transforming into monsters by the light of the full moon was a much better story, it wasn't a surprise that he leaned in that direction.

For the rest, I doubted Henri decided to do all the rowing by himself so much as Thelonius declared he would be unable to. Imps don't do manual labor except under threat of death. I said before that the Santa I met was an imp, and while there's nothing about the myth of Santa that corresponds to the reality of the man, the part where he doesn't build any of the toys himself is pretty on-the-nose.

"Is Henri still with you?" I asked.

"Alas, no. After we were reunited with the shore, he fell ill. A terrible malady the likes of which no man had ever suffered before!"

I shot a glance at Mirella, who looked about as concerned as I suddenly was.

"I hate to say this, Thelonius, but could you elaborate?"

"Certainly! We holed up in a ramshackle hovel at the edge of a town with no name on the Indonesian coast, close enough to the ocean we could smell the changing tides. It was balmy, and water was scarce, but the local delicacies…"

"Sorry, can you elaborate slightly less? What did Henri die of?"

He looked aghast.

"I didn't say he *died*!"

"Oh, he didn't? He got better?"

"No, he perished tragically, and most painfully. It's only that you gave away the ending. How did you know it? Has someone else recounted Henri's death?"

"No. No, sorry, I jumped ahead. Maybe you don't realize this, Thelonius, but we're sort of on the clock here."

"You *guessed?*"

"I'm very sorry. Tell me how he died anyway."

Mirella was trying to roll her eyes all the way out her head, but I sort of understood his mortification. There's nothing that can ruin a story faster than someone blurting out the ending beforehand.

"It was a wasting condition. The local practitioner—a wise herbalist of great renown—claimed to have never seen such a thing as this. After Henri died, the herbalist ordered the hut burned to the ground, and had I not chosen to depart when I did, I suspect he would have insisted I be included in that fire."

"Wasting how?" Mirella asked.

"His body became dissolute, and ran like a frozen treat in the midday sun. It took many days."

"He dissolved," I said.

"Yes, I suppose you could say this. Only, that word implies a suddenness that doesn't correspond. As I said, this took many days."

I'd already witnessed an incubus die in this fashion, and Mirella and I both watched a demon fall apart in the same manner, albeit much faster. The mermaid—whose apparent captivity on the island caused a lot of things to go very badly—also suffered from some form of this disease.

And there was Eve, who exhibited the same symptoms. If we added her to the list, Henri made the fifth species to come down with the disease. I was growing more comfortable with the word *pandemic*. Also, I'm in no way a medical doctor, but I was pretty positive this wasn't normal behavior for a disease.

"All right, so: Indonesia. And from there?"

"Why, Paris. Of course, as this is where you have found me."

"It seems more accurate to argue that you found us, than to say we found you. How did you know where we were going to be?"

"This portion of my tale was where I met the most…violent skepticism from the men by whom I was previously questioned, Adam. You see, I did not know that you and I were to encounter one another again, here, under these circumstances. I also did not know the consequences of my actions would put the two of you in danger. All I have is my faith in Lorelai's words: that my deeds, performed at a certain time and in a certain place in a certain manner, will bring about the preferred future."

"I can see why they had a problem with that," I said. "What were those deeds, exactly?"

"The passage I followed was: *bald anchor rues peace, mister fortunate rooftop German found.*"

I blinked a couple of times.

"That's…nonsense," I said.

"Of course it's not nonsense! Why, it's all right there!" He laughed heartily. Imps have pretty infectious laughs; it was honestly a challenge not to join him.

"I mean, it's obvious," he continued. "I went to the pub and told the man I met there that the one he was looking for was in the penthouse. I didn't know *you* were the one he was looking for, nor did I know the intent was to kill you. I only learned this later."

"Sorry," Mirella said, "what pub?"

"The one on *Rue de la Paix*, of course! With the ship on the sign."

"Where you saw a man?" she asked.

"The bald man!"

He looked at me and shrugged, as if he and I were in on this and Mirella was the one who couldn't grasp basic English. I was just as mystified as her.

"It's hard to argue with the accuracy of your interpretation," I said, "but we're clearly missing some of the nuances. So, you don't know who this bald man was, and it sounds like you also don't have any useful information about the contract he was trying to fulfill."

"Again, had I known I was putting the two of you in danger, I'd have never done it! But, such is the nature of prophesy, is it not? Truly, the greatest kind of story."

"Do you have any information on this man now?" Mirella asked. "A name? We could find him and work our way backwards to the source."

"Alas, no. It was as if he had been sitting in that pub just awaiting the news I provided. He thanked me, and left with a phone in his ear. I have no direct knowledge as to what happened next or to whom he spoke."

"And then another aspect of this prophesy you're working from led you to one of Jacques's men," I said. "What did you tell that man?"

"Only that I'm the foreigner he seeks. I've gathered that by that time, an active search was being undertaken. And now, look! We are reunited, and together can continue in your quest."

Mirella shot me a look.

"Give us a minute," I said.

She and I stepped out of the room. It was only separated from the rest of the warehouse by a thin wall with windows that looked like they belonged on the outside of a building. Jacques was out there, waiting.

"I know what you're going to say," she said. "You're going to say, better to have him with us than out there spilling his bits of prophetic doggerel on the wrong people. I agree with you, but that doesn't mean I intend to enjoy it. The last one we traveled with who was this annoying, was small enough to fit into a sack."

She probably meant Jerry, an iffrit who could indeed be shoved into a sack and carried around. He was doll-sized. There was also a chance she meant Clara, my ex-girlfriend, who was a normal girlfriend-size, but who Mirella probably could have crammed into a sack if she really had her heart set to the task.

"I'm glad we agree to the thing I didn't even suggest yet," I said. "I'd add that since we're evidently still working through the predictions of the dead prophet, her scribe might come in handy. I hate prophecy, but I'm not philosophically opposed to knowing the future."

Jacques, lingering at the edge of this discussion, but probably only caught some of it, as we were trying to whisper.

"What did you learn?" he asked.

"Only that he knows as much as he said he did," I said.

"But how?"

"It would take too long to explain. Right now, I need for you to arrange passage for the three of us out of the country."

He nodded.

"Of course. Are you certain you wish to include this… imp in your plans? I could dispose of him for you, it would be much more efficient I'm sure."

I put my hand on Mirella's shoulder, to stop her from jumping at the offer.

"No, he'll be useful."

"All right. Do you mean to fly? The airport will be…I wouldn't recommend it. I can do it, but it will take time and there will be risks."

"No, a boat."

"To America?"

I imagined he was trying to remember whether Chicago was on a coast.

"No, just as far as England. We need to get to Devonshire. Can you do that?"

He looked immensely relieved.

"This I can arrange."

He walked off, pulling a cell phone from his pocket.

"Devonshire?" Mirella asked.

"I told you, I have another solution. We can't use Dimitri's network any longer, and I'd rather not trust Jacques any more than we have to. We need a new way to get around."

"And that way around begins there."

"It does. I have an old contact. They just don't know it yet."

TRANSCRIPT (1)

TRANSCRIPTION OF INITIAL INTERVIEW WITH PATIENT 'EVE', CONDUCTED BY DR. LEW CAMBRIDGE, DAY FORTY-EIGHT

CAMBRIDGE: Hello, I'm Lew Cambridge. I'm going to call you Eve, is that all right?

EVE: Yes, it's all right. Did he tell you to call me that?

CAMBRIDGE: If we are speaking now of the man known as Adam, yes. Would you prefer it if I called you something different?

EVE: No, that will do.

CAMBRIDGE: Eve, do you know where you are?

EVE: I'm told I'm in a hotel room on an island.

CAMBRIDGE: That's so, yes. Do you recall how you got here?

EVE: No. (*In thought.*) I expect I passed through the veil to reach these shores.

CAMBRIDGE: The veil? Can you tell me what that is?

EVE: No. But that way is closed to me right now. Are you doing that?

CAMBRIDGE: I wouldn't know how to do such a thing. We understand you appeared in this room from empty space. Is this what you mean when you talk about the veil?

EVE: Yes.

CAMBRIDGE: We've had a time…keeping you here. No, let me restate that. We've had a time moving you from here. You keep disappearing when we try.

EVE: (*Smiles.*) I cannot explain that, because as you can tell, I'm unable to do any such thing now. Otherwise, I would have. I appear to be too weak to rise from this bed. Are you here to tell me why this is?

CAMBRIDGE: You were sick. You still are, but it appears you're improving.

EVE: That's impossible.

CAMBRIDGE: I've been told. I can't explain why or how, because there's very little I do understand about your biology. There are only two of you available for study.

EVE: He's not here. I can tell. He would never miss an opportunity to speak to me under these circumstances.

CAMBRIDGE: Circumstances?

EVE: As a captive of this bed.

CAMBRIDGE: I think I've explained that this isn't something we've done to you.

EVE: A poor word choice, I apologize. I only meant to underscore my current sense of helplessness. I'm not used to feeling this way, and in truth the last time I did, it was because of him. Can you say where he is?

CAMBRIDGE: Adam is trying to retrace your steps in the world in order to figure out how the impossible happened. Now that you're awake—

EVE: No.

CAMBRIDGE: No?

EVE: There are more than two. You said there are only two of us to study but that's not right. There's…there's a third.

CAMBRIDGE: A third immortal?

EVE: Yes.

(*Eve looks confused, falls silent before speaking again.*)

EVE: Oh, he's in danger.

CAMBRIDGE: The third immortal is in danger? Is that who you mean?

EVE: No, Urr. Adam. Adam is in danger.

(*Eve concentrates in silence.*)

EVE: I don't know why I came here, and I can't remember where I came here from. I'm so tired.

CAMBRIDGE: You came here to see Adam. You appeared before him.

EVE: That seems unlikely.

CAMBRIDGE: We took it to mean you needed his help. Or, to warn him about something.

EVE: Those are also unlikely. But perhaps. Perhaps. Only no, not here. He would have been safe had he stayed here. It's all… I can't think straight.

(*Eve is silent for a long while.*)

CAMBRIDGE: I'm told…I took a family history of Adam before he left. We were looking for anything that could help. He mentioned a woman with whom he fathered a child. Could one of those be this third immortal?

EVE: The woman, yes. Yes. Clara. She called me all-mother. I remember her. She is not like us. She is now, but she was not. I'm sorry. I'm very tired. I've never experienced sickness before; it's ghastly. She could be the third I'm thinking of.

CAMBRIDGE: Why do you think Adam is in danger?

EVE: I don't know. I can't remember. I need to sleep.

CAMBRIDGE: All right. I'm sorry, I have a lot of questions. We can talk again later, after you feel better. There is…I'm sorry, just one more question. When we were trying to figure out what's wrong with you, we found some evidence of goblin in your genetic signature. Do you understand?

EVE: I know what a goblin is, and I have heard of genetics.

CAMBRIDGE: Can you explain this? We're stumped.

EVE: No.

CAMBRIDGE: All right. I'll leave you.

(*Eve thinks.*)

EVE: Wait. I think I remember putting my hand through one.

CAMBRIDGE: You…put your hand *through*…?

EVE: Yes. I apologize. I can't remember why I did that.

CAMBRIDGE: Can you recall what happened to the goblin?

EVE: I'm sure he died. That is generally what happens.

CHAPTER 6

$\mathcal{I}$ have a decently long history with England. I lived there on four separate occasions, twice in and around London. This may be surprising given how often I've picked on that city for being unpleasant, but for the most part that's a *post facto* judgment on my part. That is to say, I didn't really appreciate how unpleasant it was until after I'd left. Also, that unpleasantness didn't keep me from going back again later.

Cities in general hold a lot of obvious advantages over rural areas. They're usually the center of whatever progress one happens to be enamored of, along with the kinds of progress one might find distasteful. Progress, either way. Cities have the latest in art—portable art, mostly, but also the architectural kind—and inventions. I saw my first flush toilet in a city, and the first timepiece that didn't rely upon the sun. They also tended to be the center of commerce. I could go to a city to buy things that were native to a wide range of territories it would take months to travel between on my own. And the latest in political, philosophical and religious thought didn't really receive any kind of attention until it surfaced in a city somewhere.

At the same time, if you wanted to catch up on the newest

plague, by literally catching the newest plague, a city was probably also the place for you. They were also insanely overcrowded, smelly, and just in general not the kind of place to be if you valued your privacy.

Unless you were rich. Then it wasn't so bad. You could buy some privacy, and some soap too, if you couldn't stand the smell. (Most of the really wealthy citizens made their own soap. It wasn't to keep themselves clean so much as so they could smell something nicer than the people around them.) You could also own multiple properties and the means to travel between them: keep an apartment in the city, say, and an estate in the country.

This was a popular rich-people thing to do in London, but was a practice I witnessed in some form or another as far back as the height of Athens. Earlier than that, if we're counting the pharaohs. (I don't, because they weren't a wealthy family within a merchant economy; they were incarnations of gods on Earth who effectively *were* the economy. At the same time, they did have their own summertime getaway temples, so maybe.)

My last time in London—and England in general—I was a modestly wealthy merchant. It wasn't the kind of wealth that resulted in a lordship or anything, but that was how I preferred it. Titles are meant to be hereditary, and I would never have offspring to pass it down to, so it was better for everyone that I didn't end up Lord Duke Viscount Earl something.

I was well-off enough to keep an apartment in London and a small cottage in the countryside, which was nice. I used the cottage for weekends with interested women when I could find interested women. (Or succubi. It worked much better for succubi, because they tended to not be interested in furthering their lot in life via marriage.)

I sold fabric. It's not flashy or exciting, I know, but I had long-standing contacts I could rely upon, some dating back to when the Silk Road was still a thing, so I did pretty well. And the city had a *lot* of tailors, dressmakers and haberdashers, who needed a regular supply of bolts of fine cloth.

It was a good business to be in. I was able to travel freely among all classes of citizen in London and take time off whenever I felt like doing so—I had surprisingly little overhead without a family to support, and by the end I'd been running this 'family' business for over fifty years, so I had a lot saved up.

It did end, though. Usually, my merchant ventures ended because they ceased being profitable, or because the civilization collapsed around them, or there was a war, or just that I got bored of pretending to be my own son to every new generation.

This was the only time I abandoned a business because of murder. A lot of murders, actually.

~

They were called the Whitechapel murders at the time, but you probably know them better as the Jack the Ripper murders. (I preferred the Leather Apron murders, personally.) Now I know you're probably thinking less of me right now, a little, because this is going to sound like what you'd expect from every immortal (humor me): claiming to be in all the interesting places at all the right times. But look, I wasn't at Woodstock, I really never met Jesus, I was out of town when Rome fell, and on a different continent when the French Revolution got interesting. But, I was there when Mount Vesuvius erupted, I knew Marie Antoinette, and I was in a few other significant places at particularly important times. And, I was in London during the Whitechapel murders.

I'm only being honest here.

The thing is, it wasn't really all that big a deal as it was happening, unless you were a journalist. If you talked to anyone else who was alive back then—and you can't, unless you know a jocular vampire who's lasted more than a century—they'd probably be about as amazed as I am that anybody is still talking about these killings at all.

Maybe it's the name: Jack the Ripper. It's a good name. Catchy. Whoever dreamed it up was on their game.

But it all lasted only about four months, and took place in what was frankly a pretty nasty part of London already, the kind of neighborhood where it just wasn't surprising to learn that people were ending up violently dead. It was overpopulated with poor Irish immigrants crammed together on a hot summer at a time when we were all wearing too much clothing in general, and certainly nothing breathable, where everyone drank too much all the time, and where law enforcement was largely indifferent. Violence was an inevitable consequence.

It's not impossible to imagine that if, today, five women were killed in the same section of a major city, the same way, over a period of only four months, it would be a big news story. But would it be so big that we'd still be talking about it more than a century later?

It's just hard to believe is what I'm saying.

It could be argued that there were more than five women who were killed—I saw as many as eleven attributed to the killer—but this seems specious, and besides it only further illustrates my point that Whitechapel at that time was kind of brutal.

I'm pretty sure the media is the best explanation for all of this. There was what might be called a subscription war going on at the time, and the newspapers were all trying to gain a monopoly on the interests of Londoners. That led to a lot of problems with the investigation itself, up to and including inventing the name Jack the Ripper in the first place. I mean, the media today is bad, but not "write up a fake letter from the killer to boost readership" bad. At least, I don't think so.

Anyway, so I was there, and it was big *news*, but almost everyone I knew, on reading about it, just shrugged, said something bigoted about the Irish, and moved on.

~

J'm not a very good bigot. As a species, we've pretty much always hated people we could identify as being 'not of our tribe' in some way, whether that was by skin color, language, nationality, immigration status, or just that they were *over there* and we were *over here*. It never took much. But considering I've never been a native-born member of any tribe—save for the first one, sixty-odd thousand years ago—I pretty much see everyone the same way.

Which is a long way of saying I was friendly with a fair number of people in the Whitechapel district, and I didn't think anything of it. Oh, and also, the number of those people who were prostitutes was larger than zero.

I used to give them my scraps. Cloth was usually sold in full bolts, but sometimes tailors bought lesser quantities of the pricier stuff—the silks, mainly—meaning that I'd have to cut the necessary measures off the bolt for them. By the time I got to the end of the roll, there'd sometimes be an unsellable scrap amount left over.

All they were good for were as patches on existing clothing, or maybe as a very thin scarf. So, I'd give them as gifts sometimes.

Or, you know, in a trade for services rendered.

My best friend at the time was a man named Herman. He had the same problem with my frequenting the local prostitutes as most people have when one says, *I spend a lot of time with prostitutes*, except he threw in a lot more bigotry.

"It's...well, it turns my stomach, if you want the God's truth," he said one day. We were at a pub in a much nicer part of town at the time. "I don't know how you can do it. I don't know *why,* moreover."

"You don't know why?" I said. "You're familiar with the mechanics of the act, I trust."

"That isn't what I mean. Honestly, Jack, I would be less appalled if you were putting it to a farm animal."

So, here's an uncomfortable detail. The name I was going by at the time was Jack, which was a really unfortunate coincidence.

"You're exaggerating," I said.

"Not in the slightest."

"Exaggeration is in your national character, sir. I daresay it's your distinguishing characteristic."

"Nonsense!"

Herman was an American, which was one of the reasons I'd decided to make him a friend, because he was one of the first ones I'd ever met. He said he was from New Hampshire—which I learned was in New England, leaving me to wonder if everything in the United States was established as a form of envy for all things Britain, going according to how they named their locations.

I was, of course, around for the American Revolution, but that only means that I happened to be alive when it was going on. I wasn't there, and I wasn't in England. I also wasn't in France. I actually can't remember where I was, but it wasn't in one of those three places.

Probably, I was drinking.

I recall hearing later that 'the colonies' had revolted and it was a big deal, but honestly I may not have even known which colony they were talking about. Europe had a fair number of them, and they revolted semi-regularly.

I did eventually work out that the American colonies were no longer a part of the British empire and had decided to become their own nation, and I remember thinking that was sort of cute and endearing, but that was probably the extent of my opinion on the whole thing for a decent amount of time.

Herman was a medical doctor studying overseas on what I gleaned was his family's fortune rather than an official exchange program of some kind. He told me his work involved studying patients at St. Mary's Bethlehem Hospital, and I had no reason to question that, because I didn't care for doctors all that much and so was trying not to listen about his work, as I didn't want those details to result in my disliking him.

(Side note: you've probably heard of St. Mary's before, only referred to as Bedlam, which was its nickname at the time. You would be correct to infer that bad things happened there, given a common-use noun came out of the place's nickname.)

The larger point was that when you worked in a place like St. Mary's, you tended more often than not to deal with the poor, and the poor more often than not (for this particular period in London's history) were Irish.

So, what I was getting from him was that he didn't think all that highly of his patients. I can't say this was something I found surprising. Again, I'm not a fan of doctors.

"Here," Herman said, pulling a newspaper from his valise and slapping it on the table. "Proof of their savagery, as if any were needed."

My memory of the period isn't stellar, but I think this conversation took place at the beginning of October. The papers were calling him Jack the Ripper by then, and there had been four bodies.

"That only proves someone's killing them. Unless you know the killer, and can vouch for this Irishness, I say it goes too far to argue that they do this to themselves. Any man could walk those streets at night and do those things."

"Any man?"

He smiled gently. Herman had a round face and an enormous mustache that obscured a portion of his mouth. It was the style at the time, but one I couldn't abide; every time I wore my facial hair that long it ended up in my beer. It was, anyway, a trustworthy kind of face. I imagined that made him a good doctor, regardless of what he thought of his patient's lineage.

"I'll amend," I said. "Any man could walk those streets at night. Only one could do those things to these women."

"Ah, I like this direction."

He held his mug up to get the attention of the keep, who refilled the draught. For the time, he was something of a lightweight, as this was only his second stein. I was on my fifth.

"I think, Jack, that I prefer your initial overestimation to your correction," he said. "Any man could, and quite a few are inclined. This fellow, your namesake… not only is he not unusual, he's not even particularly exceptional."

"The police would disagree."

"They are also not particularly exceptional. But look: this man—and surely, it's a man who does this—wants to cut up women, and so he does. Bully for him. Only he does it all wrong."

When Herman questioned whether or not we spoke of a man, my inclination wasn't to imagine instead that it was a woman; it was to think of other species that might do this sort of thing to a person.

I couldn't think of any. It wasn't that this kind of predation never turned up in other creatures—demons, for example, are notoriously bloodthirsty—just that the killer's particular methodology seemed uniquely human.

I took another look at the tabloid page, which included a gruesome description of the state of one of the victims. If I have the date right, this was shortly after the 'double incident' in which two women were killed on the same night, so we wouldn't have suffered from a lack of detail.

"As I'm not sure of his intent, I can't say whether he does what he does correctly or well," I said. "Perhaps this is going exactly as planned."

"I'm assuming his goal is to cut up women," Herman said, "and he's doing it poorly."

"His surgeries appear quite extensive, and the deaths are

entirely irreversible. If he means to kill and also to dissect… again, I fail to see how he does a poor job of this."

"Obviously, he does it poorly because we know he's doing it."

"I see. And if he were better—"

"If he were better at it, these women would have simply disappeared."

I looked down at the story again, and realized I was looking at the description of someone I knew.

"…all that difficult," Herman was saying. Something about how easy it was to dispose of a body; I wasn't paying attention.

"I know her," I said.

"What, really? One of the victims?"

"Kate, yes. Catherine. She was more of a Kate than a Catherine."

He snatched the paper from the table to re-read the section on the death of Catherine Eddowes.

"Oh, I see how you could have known her," he said. "Were you a regular?"

"I didn't know her like that. We shared an interest in a local establishment."

This was true but also not entirely accurate. I recalled negotiating a price with her once, but we either never arrived at an agreement or I forgot to counter-offer or something.

The establishment was the Ten Bells Pub, a much rowdier spot than the one I was sharing with Herman. I doubted it was the kind of place he'd have enjoyed, but it was one of my favorite spots in the city.

"Well then, it sounds as if you'd make a fine suspect," Herman said.

"Stop that."

"I mean it! You knew one of the victims, you spend plenty of time in the neighborhood, and best of all, your name is already Jack. I wager that's all the CID would need to hear."

I laughed, but he was actually right, and that was a problem.

Things have gotten a whole lot worse since 1888, but even back then my background wasn't the kind that stood up to extensive scrutiny. I was fortunate in that I dressed and acted like a gentleman, which pretty effectively insulated me from a lot of attention I might otherwise draw, but that was only true as long as the police continued to assume the killer was a low person. Already, news reports had begun to suggest that "Jack" was clean and well-dressed, and a member of the upper class.

Incidentally, this was how murder investigations used to go. The people who committed murder were, of course, uneducated drunk immigrants from the worst part of town—how could they not be!—so that was where the police started. It didn't matter if there was no proof that the crime was committed by a person matching this description: some people were just expected to be murderers.

I had cover, then, because I didn't look or act like *that kind of fellow*, and I was wealthy enough and had the right kind of manners to indicate a high-class upbringing.

But only for a while.

It was obvious even from a relatively safe remove that the frenzy surrounding the killings could easily end with someone getting railroaded for the murders, despite a lack of real evidence. (Or so I thought at the time. Obviously, nobody was ultimately charged for the crimes, which is both a testament to the honesty of the police force, for needing real proof, and a criticism of them, for never having found that proof.) For someone like me, getting out of that kind of situation would require friends in high places. I had a few, but I didn't think they were connected enough to help me out of that particular hypothetical jam. Nobody close to the crown, certainly. And it didn't matter how long I'd been alive up to that point; being hanged by the neck would be just as effective on me as on anybody.

All of that ran through my head as soon as Herman suggested

I'd make a good suspect. And I wasn't nearly sober enough to convince myself it was just paranoia.

"Oh! My goodness!" Herman exclaimed. "You should see your face! I'm sorry, Jackie, I was only having you on. There are a legion of men in this city who would make a more likely suspect, myself included!"

"It's all right," I said, "I'm only wondering if I should verify my whereabouts during the killings, just in case."

"Stop. I know you, now you're going to dwell on it all night. Forget I posed the notion. If you're really concerned, I'm sure I could dig up an adequate suspect from the depths of Bedlam to take your place. The police would no doubt be happy to put a lunatic down for it, and the right lunatic might like it as well."

"That would be splendid, right up until the real killer does another girl."

"Nonsense. They'll just say it was another killer altogether, and if there are a few more after that, I'll kick another lunatic to them. We could empty Bedlam and Whitechapel at the same time."

"You know Herman," I said, polishing off my ale, "I can't believe it took this long to realize exactly how unsettling your sense of humor is."

He laughed.

"It's thanks to my grim side that we're friends in the first place, Jack. You have one too, don't think I haven't noticed."

~

"Call the inspector, boys, I've got Jack right here."

A pair of large hands clamped down on my shoulders a great deal more tightly than was really justified, given the owner of those hands was only joking. But Rob was one of those people who became more aggressive the drunker he was, and he was hardly ever fully sober.

"You're a riot," I said, wriggling out from under those hands. They smelled like urine, which matched the rest of him. Rob was a tanner, and that's how they smelled.

"You leave him be, Rob," the bartender said. His name was Eric, and he was probably half Rob's size. But Eric always seemed like the biggest fellow in the pub, which was an important talent to have in this part of town.

I was at the Ten Bells Pub, roughly a week after that conversation with Herman, and thus about a week after I should have probably just left town. I'm obviously working with the benefit of hindsight here, but I've abandoned identities sooner for more petty reasons than sharing a name with a killer.

I think I probably didn't want to leave before learning who the killer was. This also undoubtedly sounds silly in hindsight, but remember that at the time, I had no reason to think this was ever going to be anything but a regional story.

I've always found it odd, how people treat serial killers as if they were a modern concept. The only thing new about them is the term 'serial killer'. If anything, humankind evolved to the point where we stopped having destabilizing local wars every generation, which was where people like this tended to be most at home.

I can recall a similar killing spree in Baghdad sometime around the ninth century. It, too, centered around one neighborhood, and was quite the talk of the city. I left—I was a traveling merchant then too—before learning if the killer was ever caught, and if so, who he turned out to be. By the time I returned again, thirty years had gone by, and when I asked if the killer had ever been caught, nobody knew what I was even talking about. The same thing happened in Bangladesh sometime in the 1200's, Tyre sometime before the birth of Christ, and Athens on two occasions during the Classical period. I can think of four Roman protectorates that suffered from the same malady, too, during the height of the Empire.

These are just the ones I know about. There were obviously more. And except for one of the Roman killers—in Gaul, if I'm remembering right—I couldn't tell you if they ever caught any of them.

"Ahh, he knows I'm riding him, yeah?" Rob said, clapping me on the back. He shoved up to the bar and took a seat that wasn't actually unoccupied at the time. The guy who was already there recognized a losing situation early, and got out of the way before Rob sat on him.

"Might be wisdom in changing your name 'til this blows over," Eric said.

"I thought of that," I said, "but decided it might draw more attention for my having changed it. "And none of you lot would use the new name."

"Change it to arsehole," Rob said, "we'll call you that all day."

"You're a prince among men," I said.

"Tell my woman that."

"I would, but I can't afford her."

Rob grabbed me by the collar and glared, like he was about to brain me with his teeth. It lasted about a second-and-a-half, before he burst out laughing.

"You're a fine fellow for a gentleman, Jackie. And that's a damned lie, she's right affordable."

He smacked me hard on the shoulder and then turned his full attention to the ale.

It's difficult to explain why I liked hanging out in East London. I couldn't put it to words in the moment, when it was Herman asking, and I still can't now. I mean, I can get close, I guess, but every explanation feels a little inadequate.

Victorian era London was pleasant for a few, and nasty and terrible for almost everyone else. The city's population was something over one million, but built on top of an infrastructure that was only intended to support a few hundred thousand, so for starters the whole place was basically one enormous toilet.

I'm not exaggerating; I mean this literally. Nobody knew what to do with their feces, other than to keep putting it where they always did: in the sewers the Romans built a millennium earlier, or in holes in the ground, or their basement if they had one.

The overcrowding was largely thanks to the Industrial Revolution, which was also doing a stellar job of polluting large portions of London. A lot of that manufacturing was done outside of the original city limits—East London being one of those places—so that was where the poorest lived, and in the worst conditions. Basically, nobody on this side of the Thames could breathe they air, drink the water, or get any rest in the substandard housing that slept as many as twenty to a room.

The solution to not being able to drink the water was to drink alcohol instead—this was, honestly, one of the reasons alcohol was invented—which meant an epidemic of public drunkenness was stirred into this overpopulated, underfed stew.

So, why did I like it there? Could be, I appreciate savagery more than is entirely healthy, I don't know. Maybe I would have felt differently if I was biologically capable of catching one of the many, many diseases that perpetually made the rounds in East London. I could get beaten up or shot or stabbed (although I'm quite capable of defending myself) but when it came to sickness, I may as well have been looking at a zoo through a glass observation window.

"What's the word on the Ripper, then?" I asked. The question was put to whoever was in earshot.

"You're seeing the same papers as we," Eric said.

"I am, but what's the word? There's what the pages say and there's what you lot say. I'll take you over the ink."

By this time, probably half the people in the pub had been questioned by a constable—even me, informally—and everyone there knew one or two of the victims.

"Coppers are looking wrong," said a man to my right. I recognized him, but didn't know his name. "They think it's one of ours, but it's one of yours."

Meaning, I think, not an East Londoner.

"I have heard that," I said. "That's not passed out of their consideration."

"Oh, they say it, but I don't believe it."

"Mary seen him," Rob said.

"Mary?"

"Pretty girl, from Limerick. You know her, she's been 'round. Boards near here."

An Irish girl named Mary, currently residing in or around Whitechapel or Spitalfields, was a woefully inadequate description. About one in ten local girls matched that description.

"She goes by Marie at times," Eric said. "Likes to pretend she's French or summat. There she is, back of the room."

"Oh, Marie?"

I turned to look, because I did know who this was. She had indeed been 'around'. I'd been around with her on one or two occasions myself. Eric caught her attention and waved her over.

"Hullo gents," she said, "hi Jackie, what's your fancy?"

She squeezed my arm and leaned in a little too close for a sober person, which she was not.

"I'm told you saw him," I said.

"What, the Apron?"

As I said, *Leather Apron* was another name for the killer. It possibly didn't catch on because there were more men walking around East London with leather aprons on, than were walking around with the name Jack. It wasn't a helpful description, I'm saying, although if it was an accurate description, it did narrow the identity of the killer to one of the locals.

"I'm told."

"Yah, no it weren't me, it were Mary Ann that seen him. I passed it on is all. Well-dressed fella, she says, came and went in a carriage. Saw 'im off Dutfield's the night he got Lizzie. Clear as you see me now, she says."

"How'd she describe him?" I asked.

"Just like you, luv," she smiled. I must have gone a little pale at this suggestion, because in the few seconds that followed, I was busy planning my escape route.

"Aww, look at 'im!" she said, laughing. "I'm kidding you, Jack, Mary knows your face all right. Man she saw weren't you."

"Coppers don't care," Rob said. "She told 'em, yeah?"

"Oh sure," Marie said, "Told 'em straight away, but they don't bother. Think they don't know who the Ripper is? Oh, they know."

"They'll let him kill us all," Eric said, shaking his head. Given the killer had exclusively targeted women, I didn't think he had much to worry about.

"Yeh," Marie agreed. "Nothing to be done. So, Jackie, what's hidin' in your pocket on this fine evening?"

~

*M*uch later, after a substantial portion of the day laborers had called it a night, I decided to trade a few of the coins in my pocket—I had no silks this time—for Marie's company.

(I feel like I have to defend myself for this, even though it was one of the most common transactions imaginable for a significant stretch of human history. I like to think of sex as recreational, but most of the time it was transactional, and that's just how it went.)

Marie claimed to have a private room not far from the pub, which was a refreshing change from the usual back-alley fumbling, and so I agreed to head with her in that direction. At minimum, I could say I got her home safely on a night when the Ripper was still at large.

We only made it halfway, before her friend Mary Ann spotted us and came running.

"Mary, I seen him," she said, breathlessly.

Marie—or Mary, I guess depending on who was talking to her —was by then quite loudly drunk. It wasn't a surprise her friend knew she was there, because Marie had been singing a shanty a few seconds earlier.

"What, I know, Mary Ann," she said, "you tol' me."

"No, again, I seen him again, just now, round the corner."

"Around what corner?" I asked. "Is he still there?"

Mary Ann jumped back, because I guess she hadn't seen me. This was sort of fair given it was the middle of the night and the 'fog' was thick. (*London fog* is the pretty title for what was actually factory smog.)

"Yes sir," she said. "Up 'round the corner, as I said. Swear, on my mum."

"Can you show me?"

She looked terrified, which was enough of an answer already.

"Jest as soon head that way," she said, pointing in the opposite direction, "if you mind, sir."

"Right. Mary Ann, is it?"

"Yes sir."

"Can you see about getting Marie to her bed for me? I think I'll have a look around that corner for myself."

Marie was leaning heavily on me, and muttering the same stanza of whatever song from her childhood was stuck in her head.

"That's a right lot of trouble, sir," Mary Ann said. I knew what she meant, so I pressed a coin into her palm and handed over Marie without waiting to see if Mary Ann upped her price. This wasn't the time for a negotiation.

Around the corner from where we stood was Whitechapel High Street, the largest thoroughfare through this part of town.

One of the efforts currently being undertaken to clean up the nastier sections of London was to forcibly evict the working-class poor from their tenements and shanties by building roads through their homes. Probably half of the major roadways outside of London proper were created in this way. It had the advantage of improving commerce by making travel easier, while at the same time moving the poor to…well, to somewhere else, anywhere else. It was a little narrow-minded, but that was one of the things that made London special.

Whitechapel High Street and Whitechapel Road (they connected, so I don't know why they had different names) wasn't that kind of road. Rather, it was the kind of road other areas used as a model for what they wanted to build themselves. It was established by the Romans as a way to get out of the city and to the docks. Probably. It was eminently practical, anyway, which was exactly the kind of thinking made the Romans equal parts efficient and dull.

It was well past one in the morning when I rounded that corner onto High. There were very few carriages about, in this part of town or any other part of it, really. So it was easy enough to spot what Lizzie described, and easier still to see the man she thought was the Ripper.

Seeing his face? That was difficult.

As I said, there was the fog to contend with. The street lamps, when they existed at all, did almost nothing but light up the fog and make it even harder to see. The carriage did have a lantern hanging by a crook next to the carriage man, and that was my best bet at seeing the gentleman's face. I just needed him to turn in the right direction at the right moment.

That didn't happen right off. They weren't leaving straight away—a conversation was taking place, and not between the driver and his passenger. It was between the passenger and someone I couldn't see inside the carriage.

If I wanted to force the issue, I could have just charged the carriage. That would have afforded me a clean look at the well-dressed man's face before he had a chance to disappear into the back of the carriage. But I suffered a modest lack of nerve—one didn't run up on an upper-class gentleman in the dark in the middle of the night, whether he was a murderer or no—and held back. Instead, I made my way down High Street as if I were a local, wandering home from the pub.

I got a clean look at the man in the carriage first. The two of them were in a heated discussion, but the details of that discussion weren't audible. Sound carried all right in the pea soup pollution, but the interior of the carriage was eating up their voices. The man inside leaned out in the midst of emphasizing a point, and showed himself to the world in the driver's lantern.

I didn't know him. He was thick, wide, and disheveled, was missing some teeth, had a dirty face, and was definitely a human. He looked a lot more like what I'd expect to find in the back of a butcher's shop, than in the back of a hackney.

He caught a look at me, muttered something to his compatriot in the nice clothes, and disappeared into the interior again. Then the gentleman turned…not all the way, just enough to side-eye me, which was why I didn't think he knew who he was looking at. I did, though.

It was Herman.

⁓

In the days that followed, I tried to put together how it was that I ended up becoming friends with Herman in the first place, because that suddenly seemed terribly important. For instance, if we had mutual friends, and those friends were connected enough to put me into trouble, what would be the consequences of accusing him of something?

And I mean *anything*. I was reasonably certain he wasn't the actual Ripper, although knowing what I know now I couldn't say where this certitude came from. But my impression of the

Whitechapel killer was that of a brute savage who'd gotten lucky in not having been caught, and he just didn't seem to be that kind of person.

(I liked to think I didn't seem like that kind of person either, and yet I've killed a ton of people in my lifetime—albeit mostly in wartime or for self-defense—so this was perhaps also an ill-conceived assertion.)

However, for someone who stridently insisted no true gentleman would show his face in Whitechapel for any reason not pertaining to their role as captain of industry or something—and then, certainly only during the daylight hours—there had to be an explanation for his presence there in the middle of the night. And I wanted to know what that explanation was.

After a good deal of consideration, I decided we were friends because he reminded me of someone else. Or, multiple someone elses, I guess.

When you get to know as many people as I've known, you become accustomed to a certain…type. I don't know how to put it better than that. Essentially, I can figure out pretty fast if someone I'm talking to is going to be a friend, a guy I sort of know, or a person I'm going to avoid because of how annoying they are. (This is for men. I have a similar sliding scale for women, only *lover* is one of the options.) Setting aside that we appeared to have nothing in common, in temperament or world-view, something about him felt familiar enough to be likable. Maybe we were only friends so that I could figure out what that something was. It was hard to say, because of course alcohol was a factor.

I also began interrogating how I'd arrived at that corner at that time of night in the first place. I was relying upon the word of a friend of a friend, who insisted this well-dressed man was none other than Jack the Ripper. Her evidence seemed to be that she saw him around the area where Elizabeth Stride was murdered, at around the right time to have done it. It wasn't exactly unlikely for there to have been several men matching that description in the right place at the right time, and further, that none of them necessarily would have been the killer.

She essentially identified a man who didn't look like he belonged where he was, and concluded that he must be the Ripper.

It wasn't actually that much of a leap, provided one felt confident that this Jack was preying upon people outside of his normal circle. As I think I've proven, I've known a fair number of murderers. One thing most of them had in common was an ability to separate themselves from their victims in some logical (to them) way. Whether they're killing people of a different ethnicity, or gender, or social standing, it was always easier to see themselves as a thing that was different from what they hunted.

Mary Ann had a good point, then: the fellow who didn't belong was in-profile for the man who would be capable of slicing up local girls. Unfortunately, as I've said, I fit that profile pretty neatly too. I liked to think otherwise, especially when exchanging pleasantries with the local roughnecks at the pub, but my clothes and business and money marked me as an Other. The only way that would change would be to give up all my money and start working in one of the factories. That seemed extreme.

Anyway, I had solid reasons to doubt her, not the least being that she'd pointed out a friend of mine. At the same time, he really didn't belong where I saw him. And I had no idea who was in the carriage with him that night.

I didn't end up seeking Herman out to get the answers I wanted, but mostly because I couldn't. We had no standing appointments, and I didn't know where he lived. We crossed paths two or three times a month, usually at the pub but sometimes out and about. I could recall accidental encounters with him in shop-heavy areas like Piccadilly Circus and Charing Cross but—and it only came to me in this moment that this was odd—if

I had to actively find him, I wouldn't know where to begin. We always just…ran into one another.

I supposed I could find him at Bedlam, but that was a large building with lots of men who called themselves doctors. One couldn't simply look up one of them in the directory at the entrance, because we didn't have directories then—too large a portion of the population was illiterate to make one useful—and goodness knew what the public entrance even looked like. Besides, I'm an immortal man with no traceable family history. I wanted nothing to do with an asylum. It wasn't a rational fear, but the idea remained, that I might get jumped and locked up until one of these 'doctors' figured out how to convince me I wasn't in fact immortal. I didn't even want to be in the same part of the city where such a place existed.

So that was out.

I decided to just wait until the next time I saw him, as that would surely be happening any day.

I'd also like to take a moment to note that this was yet another chance I passed on, to flee the country before things got dangerous.

~

*W*hen we did run into one another again, it was in the closest thing the city had to a place I called home.

I belonged to a gentlemen's club. Several, actually, but I only kept a room in one of them. (Two still exist, and I technically remain a member at both, although I doubt they'd accept my bona fides.) These clubs popped up all over the place in the late eighteen-hundreds, for some reason. I think at one point there were something like four hundred, and London's just not that huge. The better ones—and by better, I mean older, more prestigious, and harder to get into—had such high entry hurdles and long waiting lists that eventually the people who couldn't get in decided to form their own clubs. Then those clubs ended up gaining prestige and long waiting lists, and so new clubs were formed as a consequence of *that*, and on it went until the city ran out of gentlemen who were actively interested in getting away from their wives.

That wasn't really the full functional intent of the clubs, but sometimes it seemed that way. It was as if London had been struck by a powerful distaste for women, to a degree I hadn't seen since the height of Athens. Different reasons—I think—but similar approach. Members with families routinely deposited their wives and children in one part of town (or in their country estate) while they stayed in the club all week. In some clubs, this was advantageous for business reasons, especially if the other members of the club happened to be important, but "making important business contacts" was more often than not an excuse for the wife and not a truly solid explanation.

I had no wife to hide from. I was there because this was easily the most convenient way to exist in the city.

The club I stayed at was actually pretty basic. It had a large study with enough books to keep me content for quite a long time, a laundry service, a full kitchen, and a staff that could bring over a drink at any time of the day to any part of the building. There was also a billiards room, but other than the quarters—which were all little more than a bed and a dresser—there wasn't a lot more to it. Mostly, it was clean, it was exclusive, and it offered all the privacy I could ask for.

What it didn't offer, was women. I'm making that point for a couple of reasons. First, if you read *gentlemen's club* and thought *strip joint*, that's because strip clubs borrowed the term semi-ironically a long time ago. Second, there were clubs in the city that did cater to certain proclivities, and this wasn't one of those places.

Some of those proclivities were very much in line with what

was going on in Athens back in the day, but others were actual (hetero) sex clubs. These were *not* places to conduct business or stay overnight. In a couple of ways, they were even more exclusive, only because you didn't have to be a member to know the existence of (for instance) the St. James Club. It was right out in the open. But it was difficult to join a sex club about whose existence you were unaware.

Clubs were also useful for certain species. Vampires had at least two, one of which I was an honorary member of (vampires routinely mistake me for one of them), and there was at least one for elves. I heard tell of an underground club for goblins, but never confirmed that. And you would think that succubi and incubi would have something, but so far as I know they never did. They aren't really social creatures, at least among their own kind.

I was a legacy member of the club I called home. That meant I inherited my membership from my father, who was one of the first members, which is to say that I was one of the founding members and so far as the British Commonwealth was concerned, I was my own son.

It was *extremely* exclusive. According to the stories about the place, actual royalty had been turned away at the door on more than one occasion, for attempting to enter without an invitation from a member in good standing. It was also said that Scotland Yard's jurisdiction ended at the door. This wasn't true, but it made for as good a story as the one about royalty being barred, so it was oft-repeated.

I felt safer there than I had in all but a few places on the planet during my lifetime. It was therefore the last place I expected to run into Herman.

"It seems I've discovered your other favorite hideaway," he said. The statement was delivered from behind, as I sat in a large leather chair with a high back, near a fireplace that was full-on hunting-lodge-chic. It even had a rug in front of the hearth made from the pelt of a dead tiger. The whole set-up made me feel particularly comfortable, as someone who used to hunt large cats and wear their hides. This one was a lot cleaner than the kind I used to wear.

It was also all a ridiculous fire hazard. The fireplace was open, and we were surrounded by wood. In hindsight, I'm surprised we didn't all die there.

I jumped when he spoke, and turned awkwardly to see if it was possible that the voice I was hearing was actually who I thought I was hearing. Thus, my greeting was somewhat flat.

"Herman. Hello."

"Hello to you, Jack!" he said, shaking my hand, which was only accidentally outstretched. He took the seat beside mine, with a table between us for the drinks the staff had been bringing all afternoon. "Or is it Lord Jack in here?"

It was actually Lord Davis in this club. A byproduct of my legacy appointment was being stuck with the surname I used when the club opened. They didn't know me as Jack in the place, nor did they know anything about my mercantile business. The people in this club weren't supposed to be so uncouth as to have to work for a living.

"Jack is fine," I said. "If you don't mind my asking, Herman, what the devil are you doing in here?"

"I heard great things about the meat pie," he said. "I thought I'd try for myself."

"You're being cagey."

"So I am. I'm a guest, of course! One of your fellow club-men owed a large favor. As my entry for a few hours into this place eradicated his debt entirely, I expected greater things, I'll be honest. This is quite sedate."

"It's a proper place," I said. "I dined last evening with three members of the house of commons, and a crown prince."

"Yes, that's lovely. But I was anticipating something more debauched."

"You'll be needing a different sort of club for that."

"I guess I will. Or, I can do as you, and risk my life and health in the rougher end of town."

"Yes. Perhaps you should do that."

We were interrupted by one of the house-men, with a refill for me and a drink for Herman. In the pub, we drank ale. Here, a decent bourbon or a gin and tonic. Brandy, if it was a holiday. London was largely without wine, which meant that was what I craved the most when I was there.

Herman asked the man for a cigar, and so we both had one of those as well, silent for a time as we drank and smoked.

"I have to say, I don't think you're glad to see me," Herman said.

"It isn't that," I said, although he was correct. "It's disconcerting. I know a great many people, from a number of avenues. Each occupy a narrow spot in my world. Seeing one of those people in a place where I should not expect to see them, I find arresting."

He laughed, loudly enough to draw the temporary attention of some of the other men sharing the vast study. That kind of boisterousness was sufficient to get one shown the door.

"You *did* see me!" he said, slapping his knee. "I knew it!"

When I didn't respond to this, he leaned forward into a whisper.

"In Whitechapel. Your hunting grounds. You saw me."

"I did see you. And you me. I think we've established why my appearance on those streets is not unexpected. Why were you there? I'm sure an innocent explanation exists, but I admit I haven't been able to settle on one on my own."

"Innocent?" he laughed again. Quieter, this time, and with less evident mirth. "Benign, yes. I find things like innocence and guilt to be all but meaningless when self-reported. I will await your adjudication on the point to determine my degree of innocence."

"All right, what is your benign explanation?"

"I was conducting an experiment."

"Did it involve the man in the carriage?"

"It did."

"I was under the impression a medical professional such as yourself only conducted experiments in the hospital. A ditch on the side of High Street past Midnight seem less than ideal conditions."

"That depends on the experiment, Jack. Do you know what I do?"

"You've described yourself as a surgeon."

"I am. And do you know what that means? It means I cut people up."

On the whole, he was doing a terrible job of convincing me he wasn't Jack the Ripper. I wondered if he was even trying. Granted, I hadn't accused him of anything like that, but he must have known this was one of my concerns.

"You…"

"Professionally. I do it to figure out what's wrong with them, and then I put them back together again, if I can. Sometimes, I remove something to see if that was the cause of their malady. Other times, it's to see what happens once it's removed. Is it essential? We know there are some things we simply can't live without, of course. The heart, or the lungs, as examples. Do you know why I'm at St. Mary's?"

"Because that's where the sick people are?"

"That's true, but not the sort of sick you may be thinking of. Here's the dirty secret: a poor, institutionalized madman with no family, no prospect for release, no expectation for a future of any kind that exists outside the basement walls of Bedlam, is still a man. His mind may be malformed, but his body works like any other man's body. Women likewise, of course. More commonly so, I'd add, for they suffer from hysteria at a much higher rate."

"I'm not sure I understand what you're telling me, Herman. Are you saying you perform surgeries on madmen, just to see what's going to happen? How can they let you do that?"

He laughed.

"Oh, my friend, we *all* do that. Medical science can only learn so much from corpses."

I think of this conversation whenever someone asks me to explain why I dislike doctors so much.

"So you were performing a surgery on this man in a coach on the side of the road."

"No, no, don't be absurd. Unlike my colleagues, I was trying to actually help him. You see, my companion that evening was a man who was locked away for being criminally insane. By all rights, he should be at Newgate waiting to hang for someone's blood, only he was tossed into Bedlam before provided that opportunity. I don't fully know the circumstances—a head injury is my wager—but something happened to him upon reaching adulthood which fully converted him into a murderer. But in theory alone; not in practice.

"His history makes him a valuable subject. Since he hasn't killed anyone that we know of, and yet is so undeniably marked by Cain, it's our hope—more so my fellow doctors than myself— that we might find wherever in the body this mark is located, so that we might eradicate it."

"If I'm following," I said, "you mean to cut off body parts until he doesn't want to kill anyone anymore. Is that right?"

"You are always so quick to the point. Yes, that's exactly right. Only that isn't what I want to do. These efforts are all irreversible, you see. What's removed can't well be reattached. Yes, it's of value to know what humors to drain to alleviate a man's bloodlust, but whatever cures obtained would no doubt end up applied successfully to the next patient, not this one. I'm looking for a more compassionate alternative. I mean to cure what's gone amiss in his head, not his gut."

"Surgery on his head?"

"No, something much simpler. A wartime solution, if you will."

"I'm not following."

"How many of us come back from war with an abiding desire to kill more people?"

I could think of hundreds who did. Probably half of European history could be summed up by the maxim, *give young men more people to kill, before they decide to kill us*. That was almost the entire point of the Crusades.

I didn't say that, because it wasn't the direction he meant for me to go.

"You mean, war trains soldiers to develop an aversion to killing," I said.

"Over time, the passion for it is worked through, and they can retire to civil, non-violent lives. Yes."

Then I understood.

"No," I said. "Tell me this isn't what you've been doing."

He put up his hand, as if to signal me to halt before charging.

"I've given you the wrong impression. I haven't done anything. It was an idea."

"You meant to bring him to Whitechapel to… to what? To work the murder from his system?"

"He's an unrealized killer. I supposed that were I to give him an outlet for his unquenched need, it might cure him. That's all."

"That isn't all. What about the life he takes?"

"Oh well… look at who we're talking about. Beyond this Ripper…did you know someone is killing women and dropping their headless torsos in the Thames? Just the torsos, Jack. They're *all* animals, and if it weren't for the knack your namesake has for capturing the imagination of the dailies, nobody would care. It isn't as though getting captured for the act was likely. The Yard would pin it on the Ripper, and they're having no luck landing him as it is."

I'm probably not the best person to go with in a debate on applied conditional morality, because my record isn't all that tremendous. Basically, I've done a bunch of things that seemed like a good idea at the time, but look pretty monstrous in retrospect. I know that about myself, and I'm mostly at peace about it. So, I don't know what it means that I could see no angle of Herman's "experiment" that was anything other than morally reprehensible.

"I appreciate how little you think of the people in the East End, Herman, but they're still people, as you have yourself pointed out. They live and breathe and feel pain and have aspirations and souls. Encouraging a man to butcher one of them just to see what happens is without justification, regardless of what you learn from it. You must see that."

"Hardly any encouragement is necessary."

"You understand my point."

"Yes, of course. But I'm disappointed I can't make you see this from my perspective. I imagined us more alike than that. I didn't proceed, though, if you must know. Once I recognized you, and you me, I corralled my patient and returned him to his cell. No harm done."

"It was my arrival that stopped you? Why was that?"

"I knew you'd step in. Most men—most gentlemen—would frankly walk past. Do you think Lord Pish-Tosh-Farthing over there would step in to save the life of a whore? But you would. It's both your most fascinating and confounding quality."

"Kudos, I suppose, for knowing me as well as you appear to."

"Yes. Well. Sleep easily with the knowledge that you have, in fact, stopped me. If I can't convince you of the value of this work, I can scarcely proceed."

He put his empty glass down on the table and got to his feet. I think I was probably supposed to urge him to stay or something, but I couldn't wait for him to leave.

"Besides," he said, "were I to continue, I suspect you're also the sort of man who would alert the necessary authorities, irrespective of our friendship. Would you agree?"

"I would, yes."

"As I thought. It was a great pleasure running into you here, Jack. Pity membership is so challenging, I think I'd really like to come back sometime."

He clapped his hand on my shoulder and stepped around the chair.

"One thing," I said, "before you go."

"What's that?"

"The girl recognized you."

"I don't understand."

"The reason I was in a position to see you that night was that the girl recognized you, from another occasion in which you visited Whitechapel. But you've told me it was your first effort, and I thwarted it."

He smiled, but at the same time didn't smile at all.

"How interesting! Well that's remarkable. That a case of mistaken identity would nonetheless put you in exactly the position to witness my departure. I of course spotted you before you reached High Street. You must have worked that out already. Otherwise, why would I have been in the midst of leaving?"

"Yes, of course."

"Of course. But, I promise, it was my first time. You know, that's the interesting thing about being dressed properly in a place like that: to an extent, we all look alike to them, don't we? Good day, Jack."

"Good day, Herman. Be good."

He smiled, and walked off.

❧

I was in Whitechapel on the night of the final murder.

It happened about ten days after that last encounter with Herman, which was nearly long enough to have put it behind me and forgotten about it. I was certainly no longer including him on the list of my close associates—I didn't anticipate enjoying long conversations with him over a pint in the future, which is really the extent of my measure of friendship for most—but that was about all. What I mean is that I didn't in any way anticipate how things would end up playing out.

The last victim was Mary Jane Kelly, but I knew her as Marie Jeannette, because she liked to pretend she was Parisian. Nobody believed her, and in fact one of the accoutrements she used to cement this assertion was a silk scarf that was just an old discard scrap I'd given her. Still, I called her Marie, because she wanted to be called that, and I am not one to ignore one's chosen name, given how often I changed my own.

That Marie happened to be the last victim is something I blame myself personally for, because I remain almost positive she was targeted based on my associations with her. Aside from having been out with me the night I'd spotted Herman on High Street, on the night of her death I'd been seen speaking to her by at least half a dozen people at the Ten Bells.

We'd made plans to connect with one another later. Those plans weren't met because she failed to show, but I had no witnesses to her not showing, and plenty to the promise of a later engagement.

In other words, a whole bunch of people could list me as one of the last people to see her alive.

As it happens, I was also one of the first people to know she was dead. But I'm getting ahead of myself.

My final conversation with Marie took place fairly early in the evening, at Ten Bells. She was still moderately sober at the time, so there was every reason to think that after she'd had more she would either forget about our plans or sleep through them on accident. It wouldn't be the first time.

The plans were to meet at the corner of a specific street at or around the midnight tolling, and to go from there to the room she said she had. I didn't know where this room was; she'd mentioned it on several occasions, but I'd never been.

When she didn't show, I sounded no kind of alarm, because again, this was how things went with her sometimes. Instead, I went to another pub—I forget which—and continued to drink.

I could have kept with that all night, and on a number of occasions, I did. But I had a standing arrangement with a coachman associated with the club, which was for him to appear on nights such as this at a certain corner of High Street at or around three in the morning, and to wait there for a half an hour. He was to leave after that, whether or not I turned up for a ride. I paid him in either case.

It meant that right around two in the morning I had to decide what I was in the mood for: a continuation of whatever carousing I happened to be enjoying, or a quiet ride to a private bed.

I'd like to say I decided on the latter most times, but it's more accurate to say I probably *should* have every time, but did not. I am a poor judge of my own mood when I've had a decent amount of drink, and I appreciate any situation in which the people with whom I'm drinking can keep up. This used to happen all the time, and hardly ever does now.

On this night, I decided to call it an evening, left the pub, and made an earnest effort to orient myself toward High Street. It was a large road, as I've said, and since it cut right through the middle of the borough, it wasn't that hard to find, provided one began walking in the correct direction initially.

This was harder than it sounds, and why I gave myself a full hour; many an early morning was spent wandering in the fog, looking for a singular wide road.

I found my way pretty easily that night, though, arriving at the wrong end of the road, but with plenty of time to walk down it and meet up with the coach before he departed. What I came across instead was another coach, and Herman standing next to its wheel.

My first instinct was to run away, right then. I could already foresee a future in which I never crossed paths with him again, and I was really happy with that future.

But then he made it clear that he'd seen me, and I had to stay at least long enough to find out what was going on.

"There you are," he said. "I thought you'd never leave that horrid little rat-trap."

The cabin door was closed, and his driver was absent. We were either alone, or whoever was with him was in the carriage.

"What are you doing here, Herman?"

"Waiting for you, Jackie." He noted my review of his coach. "The driver's off having a piss somewhere. It's just us."

"Who's inside?"

"And him. We'll talk about him soon. He's not up for company just now."

"All right. Why were you waiting for me?"

The hairs on the back of my neck were standing at attention, which tended to be a good indication that I was in some immediate danger. I couldn't see a way in which Herman represented an actual physical threat to my person—he wasn't a man of slight build, but I am a very good fighter—but there were other ways to define danger.

"I was dissatisfied with our last conversation," he said.

"Were you. And this seemed the best time to pick it back up? Come by the club tomorrow, I'll invite you in and we can work through whatever you'd like."

"I'm afraid we're facing some urgency, Jack. You see, it came to me that you might get it in your head to relate portions of our chat to a local constabulary, and I couldn't have that."

"Well, you didn't do anything, Herman. You told me so yourself, and I believe you. Why would I tell anyone anything?"

He laughed.

"Oh, come on. Another week, maybe two, and you'd be talking to *someone* about it, whether you planned to or not. Get a little drink in you, and who knows what will come out. Especially if another body is dropped. Let's be adults."

He was right; I hadn't believed him at all. At the same time, I was having difficulty coming to grips with the notion that my erstwhile friend was actively ferrying around a lunatic and setting him loose on local prostitutes, just to see if it would make him less of a lunatic. Even if I decided it was definitely true that he was doing this, I could think of a dozen different ways my bringing it to the attention of the police would backfire on me personally, with one of those ways being that they would then know I exist.

Despite all of that, another week before I started talking sounded pretty accurate.

"Are you saying it *was* you?" I asked. "All this time?"

"Not me personally, Jack."

"Right. Who's in the carriage, Herman?"

He ignored the question.

"Here's what I will allow. Without confessing to any prior abetting of sins, I'll have you know that I didn't appreciate the notion that you had the power to do me harm. And so, I took the necessary steps to wrest that power from you."

He took a pouch from his pocket.

"Here."

He tossed it to me, which was necessary because I was keeping a distance between us that was greater than the reach of his walking stick, it being the only visible weapon.

I opened the pouch. There was a scrap of silk inside.

"I think that's yours," he said. "I did you the courtesy of removing it from the scene. That's the extent of my charity."

I recognized it as the pattern on the scrap Marie liked to wear.

It was wet with something dark. The light from the lamps combined with the fog to make the crimson difficult to make out, but I knew blood when I touched it.

"You've killed her," I said. It probably should have been a question, but it wasn't.

"No, not me. He did. I just directed him to the right person. She was recently seen in your company, I believe? She told me as much; I found her not far from here, awaiting your arrival, and so drunk she didn't much care that it was I that came instead of you, especially once I told her you and I were friends. That's all it takes to get invited into a young woman's home in these parts."

"Where is she?"

"As I said: her home. Or her flat, or… I'm not aware of precisely what the rental agreement consists of, Jackie. It was private, which was exactly what had been missing in my prior experiments. I'd hoped that given an opportunity to fully explore his itch of madness, he would finally be freed. But even after an hour of cutting, he's no less a gibbering lunatic than before."

"I'm sure you're disappointed," I said. My heart was racing.

"Oh, I am! Mind, I didn't expect to publish my results in either case, but it pains me to realize all of this work was for naught. No, that isn't so: I learned that my thesis was untrue, and that's valuable."

"Can you tell me where her flat is? I should…"

I didn't know what I should do, but something. I was still catching up.

"Jack, I promise, she is very much beyond earthly help. He made an extraordinary mess. He still has her heart, if you don't believe me; I can show it to you, unless the idiot's eaten it or something. You can't save her, and if you're the first person on the scene—"

"I'll be the most likely suspect."

"Yes. Although you already are."

He was right, and I was being a fool. He'd already set me up to be the most probable suspect, which effectively nullified any accusation I might make against him. Add to that all of the things he couldn't have known, such as that my family history was essentially a fabrication and I was called by two different names in different parts of the city. Despite being an American, his background had better provenance than mine.

"What are you going to do with him?" I asked.

"Oh, he's done. Regardless of what you decide to do with my gift, I've marked him down as a failed experiment. I'm going to drop him off in the river before he has a chance to get any more blood on the inside of the carriage. Nobody will miss him."

"The killings end here, then."

"They do."

"Good. Now what the hell kind of gift are you talking about? This scarf?"

"No, no, no. The gift is a solid head start. Get out of town. She's not lying out in some alley; it will be hours before anyone but you and I know she's passed. And in honesty, if I were you I'd get out of Europe entirely; he really did make an awful mess, and the papers are going to turn this into quite a big deal. I suggest considering a trip to the New World."

~

*A*nd that was what I ended up doing. I abandoned my business and whatever portion of my English accounts I couldn't turn into currency immediately—most of my funds were in a Swiss account anyway—and fled the Isles stowed aboard a cargo ship bound for Germany. Six days later was aboard the S.S. Lahn, a steamship bound for New York from Breton.

So far as I know, Herman did exactly as he said, and dumped the actual killer in the Thames somewhere. I never wondered how this might be accomplished, as surely the man was quite large and violent, but maybe Herman just convinced the guy to take a swim with a brick tied around his neck or something. Either way, whether the man drowned, or was shoved back into whatever corner of Bedlam he came from, the killings did stop.

Later—much, much later—Scotland Yard's investigative files became publicly available, as a consequence of the fervor over the Ripper case, which has inexplicably never died out entirely. The name I was using isn't on the list. This could mean I overreacted when I fled town, but I'm pretty okay with the decision.

I still beat myself up about this entire episode. I was right there, I knew two of the victims and the guy who was responsible for the Ripper murders, and I was either too drunk or too clueless to recognize it early enough to make a difference. On my worst days, I blame myself entirely for all of it. On my best, I point out that maybe the murders *did* stop because I called Herman on it and besides, how could I have possibly anticipated all of that?

The truth is, I dwell on that period mainly because I was outwitted, outmaneuvered, and forced into self-exile from a place I kind of liked. I am almost never out-anythinged, because being the cleverest person around is how I've lived this long. I think I hate the reminder—and every time there's a new Jack the Ripper theory (which is often), I'm reminded—that someone out there got the best of me.

I'd like to say I never saw Herman again, because he's definitely on the list of people I wish I'd never met, much less encountered repeatedly. But I did see him again, and it didn't go a whole lot better the second time around.

We'll get to that.

INTERLUDE (4)

From the journal of Dr. Lew Cambridge

Day fifty since the patient's arrival.

The patient has provided additional insights into the meaning of her assertion that she "put her hand through" a goblin.

To gain even a modest understanding, I first required an explication of the process by which she arrived on this island.

She called the medium through which she traveled, "the veil", which I believe is a non-scientific term. Adam recommended I consider a study of physics books for a better grasp, but neglected to offer exactly which physics books, encompassing what topics. Eve was equally unable to color in the details. But since her appreciation of what it is she does, and how, is on the distant side of mysticism, I'm not surprised.

As she described it, she can "travel up" and away from this dimension. If she goes far enough "up", she reaches a level where she can no longer see what's transpiring in this world, but if she remains close to—and again, this is deeply non-scientific—the edge of the veil, she can witness events, and walk through solid objects that exist in this world. Time, she claims, moves at a more rapid pace the further she travels "up".

(Note: "up" is an arbitrary direction Eve uses, denoting little more than the fact that from her perspective, she grows larger, the deeper her travel in the veil.)

(I appreciate how ridiculous this sounds.)

In short, when just on the other side of this veil, she can observe the events of our world, happening at a slightly accelerated pace.

This is a particularly interesting assertion, because I'm told—both Eve and Adam volunteered this detail—that she spent a portion of our history "deep" on the "other side" of this veil. Thus, while she claims to be older than Adam by twenty- to thirty-thousand years, she may not have *lived* longer than he has.

With the capability of moving unseen and passing through solid objects, she can also defend herself by reappearing when a part of her is *within* someone or something, which is what she meant when she said she put her hand through a goblin: in an act of self-defense (this is assumed, not confirmed) and while on the other side of the veil, Eve positioned her hand in the chest cavity of a foe, and then exited the veil.

My theory is that when she did so, her body chemistry became commingled with that of the goblin's, and that goblin happened to already be sick with our mystery pathogen.

To say this theory is medically suspect is to give it too much credit, but it matches the available facts. It further argues that Eve herself was not the one who was sick at all. The part of her that was goblin was what was sick, and once her body replaced the goblin cells with her cells, the sickness went with it.

This would get me laughed out of any medical school in the world if I were to offer it as a legitimate theory. But, so would most of my other work.

CHAPTER 7

"What's on your mind?" Mirella asked, as we watched the sunrise.

As is usually the case when one is smuggled out of a country, we were taking a less than ideal method of commercial travel. Jacques managed to get us on board a cargo ship across the channel. It departed from Le Havre and was docking in Brighton, which wasn't where we wanted to go, although it was closer to it than Paris had been. But the ship met the minimum requirement of leaving at a time of night which corresponded neatly with the immediacy in which we preferred to leave France. To hook up with a vessel heading directly to Devon, we would have needed to wait another twenty-four hours, and that didn't sound reasonable.

The difference between a dock in Brighton and one in Torquay (The nearest available dock in Devon) might have been more substantial a couple of centuries ago, when the on-land options consisted only of walking or riding by horse, but now they were just about a day apart by car.

"I was thinking about the last time I was in England," I said.

"Is it a good story?" Thelonius asked, from a chair behind us.

He was bundled up in a wool blanket someone from the crew lent to him. There was a chill, but I wasn't feeling it as much as he was, clearly. I hadn't spent part of my day being tortured for information, either, so I wasn't really in a position to judge.

"You know, I think I've probably said this to every other imp I've met, but not everything is a story."

"Why that is simply untrue."

"Either way. It *is* a story, Thelonius, but not one I'm going to tell right now. I don't like the ending."

"Then change it!"

Mirella groaned, and walked halfway down the railing so as to position herself out of earshot. Imps can be exhausting, and we were both already pretty exhausted.

"You know what the problem is?" I said. "I know what you're saying, because I've spend plenty of time with your kind in the past. If I told you that a few minutes ago, I left the deck to go to the head, then came back again, and that's all that happened, you'd probably want to know if there was a dragon involved."

"You exaggerate to sell your point, and I find that fantastic!"

"I'm sure you do. The thing is, there wasn't a dragon. I didn't meet anyone along the way, I wasn't nearly crushed by loose cargo below-deck, and I didn't have to wait for anyone to get out of the john before I went in. Nobody forgot to flush. I washed my hands. There's nothing else to say. And…let me stop you, because I can see it dancing along your eyebrow, the next thing you're going to say. It's okay that nothing happened. I could try to turn that little non-event of a thing into a story that sounds far more interesting than it actually was, but I have no reason to do that."

"No reason! But this is life!"

"Sure. And life is mostly boring. Some of us happen to like that about life."

He wanted to interrupt again. The only way to shut up an imp is to talk longer than them, so I kept going.

"Look, I don't know how old you are," I said. "I have a feeling

I'd have trouble accepting whatever answer you gave, because I wager you're not sure yourself. But it's not as old as I am. I've been alive for sixty millennia, at least, and I'm telling you, if I tried to turn every dull moment into a story of its own, I wouldn't have made it half that long. What I don't think any imp has ever understood is that *something* happening is important to the rest of us in part because it's not *nothing*. If something is always happening, it devalues what *actually* happens, do you understand? I'm far more interested in the things that actually happened than the things that didn't. Whether I like the ending or not."

Thelonius, to his credit, didn't respond right away, but appeared to take everything in and give it a good think.

"Can I tell you a story, Adam?"

I think I probably sighed audibly.

"A short story, I promise," he added. "Pertinent to the moment."

We were coming in to port, but it looked like we had some time. Docking ships always take about four times longer to tie up than it feels like they should.

"All right. Go ahead."

"Very good. Once upon a time…"

"Oh, please no."

"You said you'd let me tell the story."

"Sorry."

"Once upon a time, there was a great king. His lands, though modest, were rich with natural goods. The state's taxes were also modest, his subjects were well-fed and content, and his queen and children were healthy and well-loved. But, he was bored. Terribly, terribly bored. And in his boredom, he cast his eye on his neighboring kingdom, a kingdom where his younger brother was ruler by marriage.

"He started to wonder if this other kingdom was in fact larger than his own. And so he called the royal mapmaker to his chambers and put the question to him. After a lengthy consultation, the king and the mapmaker concluded that yes, his younger brother's kingdom was indeed larger.

"The king then decided that this was a great effrontery, and considered if he should do something about it."

"He could get the mapmaker to draw a better map," I said.

"Yes, he could! Indeed, one could argue that this is precisely what the mapmakers responsible for our current world maps have done. But that is not what this mapmaker did, and for an important reason: he saw that no answer other than the one he gave would mollify the king. And so, he gave the answer the king wanted to hear, rather than the truth, which was that the kingdoms were almost perfectly equal in size."

"The moral of this story appears to favor my point."

"Only because I haven't finished! The king took the map to his high counselor, and asked him what would happen if he, the king, were to lay claim on enough territory to ensure that his kingdom was larger than their neighbor. His counselor responded that such an action would surely constitute an act of war, to which his king replied, 'splendid!' And then he asked his counselor to plan for war.

"In this, the king's high counselor was no doubt exaggerating as well, as the kingdom was on good terms with its neighbor. Assuming the land was taken peacefully, it would at worst trigger furious acts of diplomacy. In his attempt to tell the king what he thought the king needed to hear—instead of the truth—he inadvertently told the king precisely what he wanted to hear. And now the kingdom was planning for a war."

"Telling the better story instead of the truth got him into trouble," I said. "Again, you're making my point for me."

"No, that is not the point. The point is, regardless of what is true, a good story-teller should know what his audience *wants* to be true, before he even begins to speak. But this isn't the end of the story either.

"There was more advice to be heard, but none could do much to temper the king's ardor for a war. The queen tried to reason with his sense of brotherly fealty, in ignorance of the fact that he happened to greatly dislike his brother. His generals tried to point out that the army's troops were ill-prepared for a war, which only made him more resolute. His tax collectors pointed out that the income from the new lands wouldn't offset the increase in taxes that would be necessary to feed a standing army, which only encouraged the king to consider taking even more land.

"Finally, the court jester came to an audience with the king."

"An imp, no doubt," I said.

"Of course. All the best were! The jester said that he understood the king was making plans for war. When the king affirmed this, the jester said that he would be happy, in the king's absence, to fulfill all of the other royal duties.

"The king laughed, thinking of how little he actually had to do from day-to-day when *not* planning to go to war, and told the jester that this would be fine, if indeed the jester could think of anything that wouldn't have been just as well left undone.

"The jester then proceeded to describe a single day in the life of his liege. Every step, every greeting, every nod and tick and gesture, every signature and announcement, and meeting, and so on. And he did so in such a way that the king was enthralled. More, he realized that no man could possibly be bored with such a life as this, so full as it was.

"And so, he declined the jester's offer. Soon after, he announced that a war was surely an unreasonable thing to do, given how occupied he was with his regular duties. Then he had the royal mapmaker killed, and everyone was happy again."

I laughed.

"You need to work on that ending," I said.

"Parables are the hardest," he said. "They have no punchline."

"I take your point to be that sometimes the ordinary has to be dressed up into something extraordinary, or we all go to war."

"Something like that."

"I appreciate you giving me the short version of that story. I have a feeling the longer one would have taken us to mid-afternoon."

~

We finished docking a few minutes later. Getting off the boat was a modest challenge because we weren't supposed to be on the boat at all, and smuggling passengers into any sovereign nation comes with complications, even when we're talking about two European countries during peacetime. We disembarked while inside a box, basically, and didn't get released from that box until we were on the other side of customs.

From there we met a driver in Jacques' employ, who had a large SUV, and who could take us to Exeter, which worked fine, because that was the part of Devonshire I was interested in.

I would describe the drive down, but I slept through most of it.

"Adam," Mirella said, sometime later. "Wake up; we're here. Did you have anywhere in particular you wanted to maroon us?"

"Here?"

"We've just entered the town limits."

"Right. Right."

I sat up, and spent several seconds trying to remember why I wanted to go to Exeter in the first place.

"A church," I said. "Have him drop us off at a church."

"Any particular one?"

"One in the middle somewhere."

"In the middle. Right."

She shook her head, then relayed the information to the driver, after interrupting the imp in the passenger seat who was either talking to keep the driver awake or to keep himself awake, or some combination of both.

The driver was one of those people whose nationality remained entirely ambiguous until he spoke. I hadn't heard him speak yet, but for all I knew, he didn't understand a word Thelonius was saying.

Mirella leaned back again.

"All right," she said. "Is that all? A church."

"Yeah, any one will do. Oh, and I need something to write on."

Fifteen minutes later, and I was ready for some food and a cup of coffee, and a bathroom, so I sort of wished I'd asked for a church that was near a café, assuming they had street cafés in Exeter. It was my first time there, so I couldn't be sure.

"Here you go," the driver said. Caribbean island accent. I wasn't good enough at those to pin down which island.

He pulled over in front of a church. We got out, stretched for several days, and then I took the pad of paper and pen the driver handed over.

"I just need one page and then you can have it back. Hang on."

Using the hood, I drew a quick design that could best be described as a triskelion, if drawn by a child. Art was never one of my skills.

I handed back the pad and the pen, keeping the drawing, and sent the driver on his way.

Mirella stood at the curb as the SUV drove off, our bags at her feet.

"So," she said. "You appreciate we have only the cash in your suitcase, and the only parties offering us assistance to America have taken us as far as Southern England."

"I know."

"Which is not a part of America."

"I know this too."

"You also know that walking to Chicago from here is neither timely nor feasible?"

"I do. But I have this!"

I held up the drawing.

"Yes, it's a lovely doodle, Adam. What are we doing here?"

I looked up.

"Going to church. Except not this one. Wrong kind."

"Is there a particular denomination you're looking for?" Thelonius asked.

"Not really. I'll know it when I see it. See any steeples?"

"There's one over there," Mirella said.

"Great, let's go."

There was a diner halfway between the first church and the second, so I got my food and coffee and bathroom, and Mirella got to be loudly grouchy for a while, which was what she wanted.

"I would just like it if you told me what we're doing here, rather than waiting for me to guess," she said, over a plate of eggs.

"I don't expect you to guess," I said. "I just…okay, I'm not supposed to tell you. It's a secret."

"You are as annoying as he is," she said, pointing to Thelonius. He was busily devouring a steak with his hands, for some reason.

"I am perfectly willing to await the grand reveal, Adam," he said, "in the event my input is of use here."

"I'm sure you are," she said, before turning back to me. "The problem is that once you've committed to one of your plans, there's no room for anyone else to say, hang on, that's a stupid plan. It was all right back when I was your bodyguard and you were my client, because you were paying for everything and were welcome to do as you pleased. That's no longer the case. Now, what kind of secret is it? Is there a single living person who would care if you told us what this secret was, or are you honoring yet another oath to dead people?"

"It's a little of both. Put it this way: if I'm only honoring an oath to dead people, we really are marooned here, so let's hope I'm not."

"I see. And when we get to whichever church in this place meets your criteria, do you anticipate blindfolding us, or some other nonsense?"

"You usually like blindfolds."

"I will kill you with the knife the imp isn't using," she said, although she was smiling. "What are we looking for? On these churches."

"A symbol. And there won't be any blindfolds. You'll both just have to swear the same oath of secrecy."

Then we were both staring at Thelonius,

"I can keep a secret!" he said. "And if you must know, steak tastes better this way. Would you like to know why?"

"Absolutely not," Mirella said.

We reached the church a few minutes later, and walked around until we came across a side entrance. Above the entrance was a window with a carved-wood circular design.

"There it is," I said.

"The bunnies?" Mirella asked.

"Hares. I don't actually know the difference, but I've always seen them described as hares."

"I'm underwhelmed," she said.

"Why, I've seen this before!" Thelonius said. "This is splendid!"

The image was of three hares running in a circle. It was perfectly normal in that regard, except that their ears didn't make sense. Each appeared to have two ears, but there was a total of only three. The ears formed a triangle in the middle of the image.

"Why is it splendid, imp?" Mirella asked.

"Because I know of four different stories involving the hares. They are all completely different, largely contradict one another, and are each absolutely true. I would love to learn a fifth!"

"As long as you keep it to yourself," I said. "Come on."

We went inside. It was one of those great old wood churches, with dark browns everywhere offset by light through stained glass and pews too narrow for people on a modern diet. We entered through the side, meaning we came in on one of the cross arms, where the layout of the church approximated a cross from a bird's eye perspective. It was modest compared to most, but that was fair given we were within walking distance of another five that probably looked just like it.

I thought the place was empty, until a priest popped up from the room behind the altar.

"Hello," he said, in a weighty local accent. "Can I help? Confession times are afternoon."

"I hope you can," I said. I held up the piece of paper with the spiral doodle. "*Zurgaan gurvan ni neg yum.*"

There was a long pause, as the priest considered what I'd said.

"I'm sorry, is that supposed to mean something?" he asked.

"Evidently not. Is there a…more senior pastor on hand?"

"Father Bates, you mean? I'm afraid he's taken ill. It's just me for the mo'. Can I…? Not sure what you're asking of me."

"Never mind."

~

"That went well," Mirella said. "I think you had him until you started talking in gibberish."

"It wasn't gibberish. And we'll just have to keep looking."

"What did it mean?" Thelonius asked.

"It's a saying. Come on, I thought I saw another steeple down the road."

The third church had the three-hares symbol, but its doors weren't open. The fourth was both not open and had no symbol. By the time we reached the fifth—open, and appropriately adorned—it was late afternoon.

I don't actually know what priests do, and what churches are for, outside of holy days, because I'm not really a guy that goes to church as a matter of habit. This has a lot to do with being older than all the religions—and to be honest, each of them was a little silly and cultish at the start—but also, I find I'm less compelled to look to deities for things when I have no expectation of dying one day.

My point is, walking into these churches, I didn't know whether to expect to come across a lot of people, no people, or a small gathering. I also didn't know when or if to anticipate a ceremony of some sort. Do they hold mass every night? Do weddings happen during the week? How about baptisms? Or exorcisms, if that's still a thing?

It was an instructive little mini quest, I'm saying. Or, I took it that way, even if Mirella didn't.

"Paris was prettier," she said, under her breath, as we walked the aisle of the fifth church. It was the biggest one we'd been to yet, and it was the most architecturally impressive. It wasn't the Hagia Sofia or anything, but it was okay.

"People were trying to kill us in Paris, dear," I said.

"Yes, and wasn't that fun?"

"I think Thelonius has a parable about boredom to tell you."

I waved down a passing priest who looked as old as the church itself, which I thought was a good indication that I was talking to the right guy. But when I showed him the symbol and spoke the phrase, he looked as perplexed as the last one.

"I'm sorry, are you selling something?" he asked. This was directed at Mirella, in case she could explain me.

"No, it's all right, thanks for your time," I said, patting him on the shoulder.

"Whatever this is," Mirella whispered, "it isn't working."

"We'll find the right person."

"During my lifespan? Or yours?"

Thelonius, meanwhile, was trying to get our attention from

the back of the church. We headed over to him.

"I would like you to meet Oscar," he said, barely containing his excitement at having met Oscar. "Do you know, he's eighty-two years old this week?"

Oscar was a bent old man who was using a push-broom to keep himself aright.

"Is that so?" I said. I couldn't possibly match Thelonius's enthusiasm, and didn't try.

"Yes sir, eighty-two this week," Oscar said. "And I been cleaning this holy place sixty-eight of them years. Started when I was wee. Time off during the war, but mostly straight ahead. Oh, the things I could tell, yes sir."

"I told Oscar here that we're looking for someone just like him, for a special project!"

"Special…? Okay. Oscar, can you see this?"

I held the doodle up under his nose.

"Course I can. Eyesight's always been perfect, they say. Why this is…hm."

He looked like he might actually recognize it, which was a reaction we hadn't gotten from anyone else.

"*Zurgaan gurvan ni neg yum,*" I said.

He went very pale.

"*Zam neegdene,*" he muttered, entirely on autopilot.

It was the right response.

"Can you help us?" I asked.

Oscar looked ready to drop dead, which would be terrible; we'd have to go find another church and do this all over again.

"I never… they taught me, but I never expected anybody to come. I mean, at first, it was made out to be a big… but nobody ever…"

"Can you help us?" I repeated.

"Yes." He snapped out of whatever reverie he was caught in. "Yes, of course. Yes, follow me. I'll bring you down."

He took us around the pews and into a side door, which led to the church's green room, I guess, where the priests warmed up before going out to hold their ceremony. (I'm sorry, like I said, I know a lot about the history of religion because I lived through it, but I know almost nothing about church services themselves. Is there still a goat sacrifice? I'm really asking.) From there we went to another door, and then to a staircase that looked as old as I am, and a lot less stable.

At the bottom of the stairs, Oscar fiddled with a set of keys, while we acquainted ourselves with the smell of mildew and the steady drip-drip sounding out in the dark. There was a sense that we were standing at the edge of a large room. Probably a boiler room. Or, an old Inquisition dungeon, but that was less likely to be the case in Britain.

Oscar unlocked the door and held his hand on the knob.

"I call it a storage closet," he said. "I'm the only one who ever goes in."

"What's it really?" Mirella asked. The only light we had was what came down the stairs behind us, but I could tell she was fixing me with a glance at the question. She really hated it when I didn't give her all the information I had as soon as it became relevant. The problem was, we had different ideas of when something became relevant.

"A storage closet," Oscar said.

He opened the door, threw on a light inside, and beckoned us through.

Calling it a closet was unfair, because it was easily large enough for the four of us to stand in. However, it did look like a yard sale for discount religious artifacts, so the 'storage' portion seemed accurate.

"At last," Mirella said, "we're saved."

"You're not impressed?" I asked.

"We could perhaps corner the marketplace on used thuribles," Thelonius said.

"You are both a great disappointment to me," I said.

Oscar, meanwhile, had begun moving things away from the back wall of the room.

"Do you need help?" I asked. He really looked like he was about to fall over, permanently, now that he was no longer being held upright by a push broom.

"No, no, this duty's mine. My own fault, I put this junk here, didn't I? Never figured to host someone on the Path."

Mirella looked as if she'd just figured something out. She stepped into the center of the room and spun in a circle.

"Unless I've become turned around, this room is smaller than it should be," she said.

"That's better," I said.

Oscar crouched down at the corner, and began extracting a brick. The wall was a patchwork of what had to be the original stones—varied in size and shape—and the more modern red brick variety. It was the latter type that he pulled out of the wall. It slid out cleanly and loudly. He placed it on the floor and then went back for the next.

"Oh my goodness, Oscar, don't be ridiculous," Thelonius said.

"It won't take long, I promise," the old man insisted.

Thelonius jumped in to help anyway.

I was wondering if Oscar meant to take down the entire wall. It soon became clear he only had to open a small passage, though, which was a few minutes of brisk work and that was all.

Notwithstanding the dirt and dust, no masonry had been done on that part of the wall; the bricks were loosely stacked so that it appeared otherwise. Basically, an extremely low-tech secret door that could be foiled by anyone who bothered to lean on that part of the wall, whether they meant to find it or not.

"Are you going to tell me what's back there, or make me wait?" Mirella asked.

"I don't know exactly, because I've never been to this location before. I have a rough idea, but they're all a little different. Probably not a cask of amontillado, if you had any hopes."

She laughed.

"I had no such hopes, but you raise a point, intended or not. We don't know what we will be eating or where we will be sleeping tonight."

"One thing at a time."

Once Oscar cleared up a wide enough space for a man to step through—albeit a very short man, or one in a deep crouch—he disappeared through the opening. A moment later, he reappeared, his hair thick with dust and cobwebs. He had a torch in his hand.

"Can I trouble someone for a match? I'm afraid this side was never wired for electricity."

Thelonius had a book of matches. Soon—after working through a number of non-trivial concerns regarding ventilation and the potential lack thereof—we were all on the other side of the wall and staring at a space that hadn't been stared at in decades, by torchlight.

More than anything, it resembled one of those family burial temples they have all over the place, where there's a bunch of small squares in a wall, with each square containing—either in fact or only in spirit—the remains of a member of the family. The squares in this wall had no names on them, however, just symbols. They didn't have cremated remains behind them either, or if they did it was because somebody fundamentally misunderstood the function of the Path.

Opposite the wall of squares was a wooden table and a couple of chairs, a leather-bound ledger, and an old rotary dial telephone.

Curious, I picked up the receiver. Dial-tone. It still worked. They may not have run a line for power, but a phone they were good for.

"Have you ever done this before, Oscar?" I asked.

"Only once, sir," he said. "In my training, when I was a lad. Will you be wanting the wayfarer's standard or...?"

Instead of finishing his sentence, he nodded at the squares. He was somewhere between nervous and excited. My fellow travelers had landed firmly on confused and tired.

Oscar was asking whether I was a simple traveler on the Path or if I was a legate. That was what we called the owners of those boxes. It was an outdated phrase that made a ton more sense when the Path was first established, but there are a lot of old titles humans stick to long after they no longer make sense.

By way of answer, I sat at the table.

"Do you have something to write on?" I asked.

"Yes, under the ledger."

The ledger book was heavy, more from the binding and the thick paper than because it was particularly voluminous. It was intended as a record of transactions that passed through this station, and by what Oscar was saying, there hadn't been a transaction in something like sixty years. I resisted the urge to open it and see what was on record there. Instead, I pulled out the pad of paper. Next to it was a thoroughly useless fountain pen.

I waved it around.

"Don't suppose you have a ballpoint pen on you? I never much cared for these."

I write with both hands, but that's largely because when I first learned to write, it was with ink that didn't dry immediately. That wasn't a big deal for languages that were read vertically, and it didn't much matter when recording numbers, or using a chisel in stone. I also distinctly recalled a type of ink that dried and/or was absorbed refreshingly quickly when used on certain types of papyrus. But for a decent portion of the time, writing was done left-to-right, with ink that needed time to dry, using a quill or a fountain pen. Doing this with the left hand—which felt more natural to me—meant smearing every word immediately.

Anyway, I prefer ballpoint pens almost without exception. (An exception: if I need to use the pen to defend myself, fountain pens are better.)

Oscar had one, and handed it over. I spent a few minutes writing down the key, which was a series of characters in three different alphabets, a couple of random symbols—a triskelion was in there—and a hieroglyph belonging to the god Anubis. It looked like what happens when a bored archeologist doodles while on the phone.

"Here you go," I said, handing the pad and pen to Oscar.

"Which box?" he asked.

"You're going to need a ladder."

His eyes drifted upward.

"Oh. How far?"

"Top center. I wrote it for you."

The symbol on the top center square matched the first one I'd written down. It was a character in a language that didn't exist any longer, and the symbol corresponded to my name in that language. For good measure, the three-hares symbol was above it.

Oscar laughed.

"But that's the founder stone," he said. "That isn't…it doesn't open, it's just there for…you're serious."

"That's me: the keeper of the Path. Nice to meet you. And it better open. I put entirely too much time and effort into this for it not to."

⁓

The three-hares motif was already around for a while when I decided to make some good use of it, primarily because I thought it was neat. The first time I saw it was at the China end of the Silk Road, so I'm pretty sure it came out of China from somewhere, as much as something this widely-used can be held to a single origin story.

I moved merchandise along the Silk Road for a good long while, and became enamored of the way the Buddhist monks set up shop at certain way-stations along the route. These were safe spaces for travelers to bed down for the evening, where they could expect to wake up alive the following morning, which was something considerably less guaranteed on most other parts of the road.

One time, for reasons I can no longer recall, I was at one of the monasteries with a supply of heavy goods—bulk spices—when I had reason to very quickly travel in an unanticipated direction. The ideal way to do this was to find someone to guard my expensive and heavy spice jars while I went on this errand, until I came back. The short version of the story is that I asked the monks to hang onto the spices in exchange for a portion. They agreed, I took off and did the thing, got back and retrieved my spice, paid them for their service, and everybody was happy.

I should mention one other thing about this time-period, because it's slightly relevant. We didn't have banks. What we had to do, if we wanted to move money—gold, typically—from one region of the world to another was use a Hawala. I'd pay money to one guy in one part of the world, and tell him it's for my account in another part of the world. He'd keep the money I gave him, and send a letter to his partner in the other part of the world telling the partner to credit my account the same sum I gave to him, minus the fees for the handling of this transaction. Really simple, and not all that different from how electronic funds are moved now, I'm told.

So here was my big idea: a private society made up of fellow travelers who were looking for additional security for their liquid funds. Originally, this was just for the folks like myself, who traveled the Silk Road, but the network grew to cover most of Europe, got as far as Britain, and eventually set up in the US in at least two cities I'm aware of.

At first, that was the extent of it: a sort-of Hawala for a select group, with a location—you can think of it as a bank with branches if that helps—every hundred miles or so. The bonus feature was that each location also had a vault (safe deposit boxes, if you will) where things could be stored.

It was the second part that was an evolution into something slightly more useful to a general traveler—merchant or no—and especially to someone who happens to be immortal. It basically solved a large number of problems I was having with my stuff.

I've owned a lot of stuff. I've lost most of it, sold some of it, and broken some of it, but I've managed to keep a select few things I like and consider important. This has been incredibly difficult, because private ownership of things is not something that mixes well with immortality.

What I needed was a few places to store a private cache of things, with a caretaker to keep them from falling into a volcano or whatever, and with enough secrecy around it so that it wouldn't get discovered by someone operating under the assumption that the owner was long dead.

So that was the first function of the secret society I invented. The second was what gave it the name, *the Path*. (Technically, it never had a real name. I would have probably called it something cooler, if anyone asked.) If you've done any traveling, you've probably figured out that it's a lot easier getting around some-place new if you're being helped by a local. Take that sentiment, and factor in that being a stranger in a land with unusual customs could well get you killed, and you can see how I devel-oped this idea.

Once it was up and running—it took a while—I had a network I could rely upon to help keep me alive during a particu-larly tumultuous part of history. If I traveled to a new city, and needed immediate assistance, the Path would provide a place to stay and, if I needed it, funds from my account, whose balance was kept in a shared ledger across the network. If I knew where I was traveling next, and that I would need help, word could be sent down the path, ahead of time.

It worked really well, in part because we all kept it a secret, and in part because we kept it very exclusive. My initial investors —and it was an investment, as this kind of thing isn't cheap— were all hand-picked. Almost all of the users of the Path after that were legacies. That was what all the squares in the wall represented: legates.

The other users of the Path were people who had been given the means to use it by a legate. We called them delegates, or wanderers. The delegate's use of the path was meant to be only a one-time thing, although it occasionally became a means of recruitment and fund-raising. Help out a well-to-do delegate, offer them a proper membership, refresh the society's coffers a little. Kind of like how professional sports leagues expand, only less expensive and a lot more private.

Another reason it worked really well is that none of us used the Path all that often. For a fair number of legacies, they may not even be fully aware what the dues they're expected to pay are for.

~

Given my arrival was the first time Oscar had even had to open up this room, it sounded like for this part of Europe, the Path was effectively no longer in use. This wasn't a huge surprise; Devon wasn't precisely a large travel destination. If I could be certain a way-station still existed in London itself, I would have gone there instead. But one of the things the churches in Devonshire were known for was the peculiar three-hare decoration that seemed to be everywhere. I don't know why this is—I think it's possible the decoration was borrowed by another tradition for a different reason. Your guess is as good as mine on that. But I figured if I wandered around long enough I'd find one that was dedicated to the Path.

"That's quite a story!" Thelonius said.

I'd given him and Mirella the basics while waiting for a deeply shaken Oscar to find a ladder that could reach the top shelf.

"You have to keep it to yourself," I said. "Can I trust you to do that?"

"I will find a way to recount it by couching the details in such invention that none could find the true Path, I swear to you,"

"Well, that's almost a yes."

"I find this difficult to fathom," Mirella said. "A thousand-year old travel agency?"

"Kind of."

"It's difficult to believe something like this could remain a secret."

"None of us tried to profit off of it, by design. I think that helped. It's strictly a co-op. Or, it used to be. Like I said, I haven't had to rely on it for a really long time."

I wanted to add, but didn't, that Mirella was probably under-estimating the number of secret societies currently in existence, about which the general public is largely unaware. It sounds sinister when I put it like that, but the reason they continue to exist without being detected is the same as the reason I gave for the Path remaining secret: nobody tried to profit. More exactly, these clubs aren't seeking any kind of world domination or what-ever. More than half of them are trade organizations, which means they are just incredibly boring unless you happen to be highly enthusiastic about that particular craft.

Anyway, it's not a big deal. It's what happens when communi-ties grow to a certain size: people try and organize small tribal groups of like-minded people. As long as they aren't lynching anyone, they're mostly harmless.

Oscar returned, shoving one end of a ladder through the hole. Thelonius helped get it in the rest of the way, and then the frail old man was climbing to the one box nobody expected to access.

The decoration on the front of the box hid indents that were meant to be used as a drawer handle, which was how he managed to get the front opened. The stone face flipped downward on a rusty hinge. Behind it was a metal box, and a second handle.

Oscar pulled that handle, and got the box out. All three of us made some effort to help him with the box at that point, because it really looked like we were going to be dealing with a broken bone and a ton of questions from whatever paramedic arrived to deal with that bone, but he made it down okay.

"It's the rules," he said, panting from the exertion. "I have to do it myself."

I cleared off space on the table for the box. He put it down, opened the top, and extracted a rolled-up bit of leather from inside. Then he re-closed the box.

He untied the strap around the leather parchment and rolled it open, then spent several seconds comparing what I'd written on the paper to what was burned into the leather.

"Well, sir," he said. "It's impossible, but you appear to be who you claim. You are a legacy, I gather. I was told the founder had no offspring, but clearly we were misled."

"No, that's right. I'm him."

He laughed.

"But this is…hundreds of years of tradition, my prior told me. Hundreds, and you're just a lad."

"Well thanks, I'm older than I look."

He shook his head, and stepped back so that I could examine the contents of the box.

Inside, there was a pouch containing gold coins. It wasn't a fortune in gold, and it was frankly a lot more trouble than it was worth to even try and turn it into traveling money. This was the downside of relying upon a system this old. True that gold retained value even after all these years, but I couldn't pay for a room with it, or book passage on a boat or an airplane.

This was just the seed money from the foundation of this way-station. If it was heavily trafficked, I might have expected to find regular donations to the box as well, in more fungible currency.

Unfortunately, there wasn't anything else in the box. That

wasn't necessarily a shock since, again, I'd never been to this location, so I never stored any personal items here.

I sort of regretted not having thought of this a little sooner. It would have taken up a lot more time than we had, but I'd left an incredibly rare sword of Damascus steel in a way-station somewhere in Austria. It would have been just as unhelpful for the present situation as the gold coins, but I sure did miss that sword.

But, the main reason for opening up the box was to establish my identity, not to fund our quest. That said, if we needed more usable currency, a portion of the ledger should have been dedicated to the Hawala aspect of the Path—it would have had a record of my account. There was really no telling how that balance converted to modern money (unlike banks, Hawalas don't compound interest) but it was bound to be worth more than the coins.

I put the sack of gold back into the box, put the leather scroll in on top of it, and closed the lid.

"We're going to need travel assistance," I said. "I assume that process has become much easier in the telephonic age?"

"I imagine it's… why, I don't even know how it could've been managed otherwise," Oscar said. "But yeah, of course. I'll make the call. No trouble, it's all coming back to me now."

The difference between now and back before there were telephones (and cars, and airplanes) was that none of us were in as much of a hurry to get someplace. If I turned up at a way-station needing full travel arrangements, it could be taken care of, but it would require a month or two of planning before I went anywhere. Most times I just stopped in long enough to ask the location of the next way-station and maybe drop off a few things, and then made my way to the next city, but I wasn't nearly as allergic to foreign cultures as some of the other legates.

Oscar sat at the table and opened the ledger. After a few minutes or poring over different pages of numbers and letters, he found the phone number he was looking for, and dialed it.

"Hello, luv, my first time on this line," he said. "I have a traveler…right…Yes, I'm excited too."

He put his hand on the receiver.

"She's excited," he said. "Her first time."

He got back on the call.

"Yes. Yes, dear, I can't do long distance from…oh, right the number. Hang on."

He flipped through the ledger again. What he was looking for now was the code corresponding to my account, which should provide them with an idea of precisely how much service they would be offering. A delegate off the street would probably only be smuggled over the nearest border. This was sometimes incredibly dangerous, so it was still a decent service. My rank, I suspected, could get me anywhere in the world, provided the people I was dealing with still had the infrastructure to handle that kind of request.

He found the code and read it off. There was a long pause as he waited for the woman on the other end to find a match.

"Yes," Oscar said. "Yes, no I'm not joking, he…he passed the *test*, luv…well yes, I agree, and it's a good thing we're already in a church, ennit?…well I can't ask him that."

"Ask him what?" Mirella asked.

"All right, hang on."

He put his hand on the receiver again.

"She wants to know if you're Satan," he said. "You're not Satan, right?"

"I'm probably not," I said.

"He says he's probably not," Oscar said on the phone. "No, I think he's having us on…no, not about that, about being…right. Look, dear, can we get this rolling, I don't want to keep them all day….yes. Yes, call it in."

Oscar turned to us.

"Sorry, I should have asked," he said. "Where are you going?"

"Chicago," I said.

"Oh, all right. Dunno if we have one of our…one of these little ports in the States or not. Guess it don't matter, we can get you there either way, I guess. You know, you can fetch tickets online these days, it's really very easy."

"Yes, I've heard that," I said. "And there are a couple of stations in the U.S. that I know of."

"Oh. Very good."

Whoever he was talking to came back on the line. He spent a few minutes muttering and taking notes, relaying that we needed to go to Chicago, and that we appeared to be unwilling to buy airline tickets online, and that I continue to probably not be Satan. Then he hung up.

"All right. What I understand, she made a call to another one of our people, and they're making some more calls, and eventually we'll be reaching up high enough to get this sorted. If I'm guessing, you won't be headed to Heathrow tonight. There's a lovely little inn up the road, if you're looking."

～

After helping Oscar hide the hole in the wall behind a rack of priest robes and an old confessional, we headed down the street, to an inn that was indeed lovely and little, and whose sole apparent employee, Bridget, was happy to have us.

"Is this the most expedient way to do this?" Mirella asked, once we'd gotten to our room. We could afford two rooms, so Thelonius was down the hall.

"Do what? Get to America?"

"Yes. I know your concern is valid, but relying on a technology that last made sense for an overland merchant route? Perhaps we can use one of our aliases now and just book our own flight. They're likely still looking for us on the continent."

"I think this will happen faster than you realize."

"And then, we don't even know what we're going to find once

we get there. This is a small needle, and America is a very large haystack."

I stopped to look closely at her. She was sitting on the bed, and displaying an emotion I was frankly not familiar with in her.

"Are you…worried?" I asked. She'd been a lot more sarcastic and irritated than usual for the past day, but I attributed that to the thing about keeping things from her. Maybe it was more complicated.

"Of course I am," she said.

"About me? I don't even feel sick. And like you said, we can always just go back to the island again, if things get bad. But we're fine. You've got my back, and I have yours. And Chicago is where I think we're supposed to be."

"I no longer feel heading to the island is necessarily the best approach. I'd just like to get to Chicago by plane instead of rowboat. And I'm not worried about you."

She hesitated. I didn't say anything, because it looked like there was something else on her mind.

"I need to show you something," she said.

"Okay."

"But I want you to understand that this doesn't change anything. I feel fine."

Now I was the one worried.

She took off the light jacket she'd been wearing since the boat, and rolled up her sleeve.

"Touch my arm," she said. "Right there."

She directed my fingers to a small spot on her left arm. I did. It was tacky.

"So you need a shower," I said.

"In that one spot?"

"That doesn't mean—"

"I think it does. Whatever killed the incubus, and Thelonius's werewolf friend, and the others…I think I have it too."

TRANSCRIPT (2)

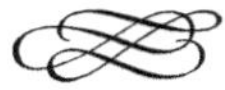

TRANSCRIPTION OF SECOND INTERVIEW WITH PATIENT 'EVE', CONDUCTED BY DR. LEW CAMBRIDGE, DAY FIFTY-THREE

CAMBRIDGE: I'd like to play a recording for you. I think it could help with your memory.

EVE: All right.

(Dr. Cambridge plays a fifteen second snippet of Eve, speaking in another language.)

CAMBRIDGE: Do you recall saying any of that?

EVE: Is that me?

CAMBRIDGE: It is. Don't you recognize yourself?

(Eve laughs)

EVE: It's the first time I have ever been recorded, that I am aware of. The voice sounds strange to my ears.

CAMBRIDGE: Do the words sound strange?

EVE: No, those are familiar.

CAMBRIDGE: What language was that?

EVE: That was what's now called Elamite. It's the same language as what is written on this wall above my head.

CAMBRIDGE: What were you saying?

EVE: It's part of a ceremony. Who wrote this? On the wall. I assumed it was Adam, because to my understanding nobody else could have, but I now question this assumption.

CAMBRIDGE: It was written by someone else. I don't think she knew what it meant either. Adam identified the tongue, but said that he couldn't read it, because he never learned the written form of the language.

EVE: I understand. He was a farmer then. We didn't teach farmers to read. Who was this someone else, that wrote Elamite but couldn't understand Elamite?

CAMBRIDGE: She was a prophet. Remarkable person. She was my patient, until she died.

EVE: I see. I think these words were how I came here. That must have been why she wrote it. In my state…

(*Eve concentrates, in silence for several seconds.*)

EVE: Yes. I was looking for Urr. I recall this.

CAMBRIDGE: And Urr is…

EVE: Adam. His older name is Urr. I was trying to find him. I don't know why, now, but I remember wanting to do this.

CAMBRIDGE: You said before that it was because he was in danger.

EVE: I was in the veil, looking for him, and evidently feverish… and these words drew me to this place. Where he was.

CAMBRIDGE: The prophet wanted to help you find your way.

EVE: Yes, I understand this now. But why?

CAMBRIDGE: If you've met a prophet, you already know getting a straight answer on any kind of question is almost impossible. If it helps, Adam asked the same question. She was her customarily opaque self.

EVE: Yes. They're very annoying. It's why we usually kill prophets.

(*Cambridge coughs for several seconds.*)

CAMBRIDGE: Can you…um…tell me about this place? Elam, yes? Where Elamite came from?

EVE: It was called Haltamti then. I don't know where the name Elam came from, but history has a habit of retitling places at whim. There was a city there, called Susiana. The largest city in the world.

CAMBRIDGE: For the time.

EVE: I suppose. It was a matriarchal culture. It was founded before I ever happened upon the city, but when I arrived it was an easy enough matter to assume the role of their god-priestess. I find this is often the easiest way to interact with cultures. Or it was, back when there were gods.

CAMBRIDGE: And the ritual was for you? On the wall.

EVE: It was for their god-priestess, and so for my stay in Susiana it was for me. The ritual written on the wall was chanted aloud by the acolytes, sometimes for several days. The functional intent was to coax me from the temple, to hold a day of blessings. For the crops, and…

(*Eve falls silent for several seconds.*)

EVE: Yes. The crops and fertility and so forth. Things ended poorly in Susiana. I don't fully engage with many societies any longer. Hardly ever, now. The inevitable descent is difficult to witness.

CAMBRIDGE: It ended poorly in what way?

EVE: The usual way. As I said. Every society in the world of men eventually falls prey to war, rape, murder. This is what Urr built.

CAMBRIDGE: You blame him?

EVE: Because he is to blame.

CAMBRIDGE: His actions brought down the city of Susiana?

EVE: No. No, you misunderstand. His crime was more…originative. But there was a priest…

(*Eve trails off, lost in thought.*)

CAMBRIDGE: You were saying? A priest?

EVE: Where is Adam going? Do you know? Has this been shared?

CAMBRIDGE: I'm told he's trying to book passage to America. I don't know which part.

EVE: Is it Chicago?

CAMBRIDGE: I don't know, as I said, but why did you suggest Chicago?

EVE: I'm not certain why. It came to mind first. But if that's where he's going, he cannot. Anywhere else, but not Chicago.

CHAPTER 8

It took a couple of days to get out of England.

After settling in and verifying that Mirella wasn't on the actual verge of death, we spent the better part of a day in the nearest pub. This was ostensibly done in order to map out our journey from the island to England, in order to identify the moment in which she might have become infected. The pub seemed like the best place to have that conversation.

It was an impossible exercise, of course. We knew nothing about this disease, and outside of what we'd picked up from movies and televised medical dramas, we barely knew anything about disease in general, never mind how it might be transmitted. (That last part was mostly me. When you've spent most of your life being told that an illness in the village means the gods are angry, getting up-to-speed on germ theory takes some doing.) Our conclusion—after much alcohol—was that there was no way to pinpoint the exact moment of acquisition, especially given the last non-human we came into contact with was Thelonius, and he wasn't sick.

A brief sidebar took place as we considered if perhaps he was a Typhoid Mary of some sort. It seemed like a promising pursuit insofar as the last non-human *he* was in contact with died of the thing. I was especially fond of this theory because I personally remembered Typhoid Mary, having been in the States (but having left New York City) around the same time she was in the news.

But once we broached this idea—that Thelonius was carrying it—we didn't know what to do, other than to find another non-human and see if he could infect them too by his presence.

After enough ale and British pub food, which I actually like a lot, we dropped the matter entirely, and decided it would be more fun to keep drinking and pretend Mirella wasn't dying.

Then Thelonius told a lot of really long stories, built up an audience, and created an inexplicable economic spike the pub's bookkeeper would never understand. We ended up getting all of our meals and drinks comped by the tender, which is probably the best thing about drinking with an imp.

Somewhere in the downtime between his long-winded bits of fancy, I got the idea to ask Thelonius if any of the prophesies he was carrying about in his head had something to say about Mirella's life or death.

He didn't answer right away, which I took to be a bad sign.

"No, I don't think so," he said, with reticence. An imp being reticent was an even bigger bad sign. "I'll re-evaluate, and let you know."

I was pretty sure he was lying, and also pretty sure I wasn't going to get a better answer. I made a note to revisit the question later, the next time I was out of earshot of Mirella, who had already indicated that her solution to this problem was to pretend there was no problem. and would be expecting both of us to follow suit.

The next morning, back at the inn again and cursing the same ale and pub food I'd been celebrating just a few hours earlier, I found that a note had been slid under our door. It instructed us to be outside the inn at four P.M., where a car would be waiting.

~

*A*nd so it was. The car—driven by an extremely truculent fellow who only knew yessir and no-sir—picked us up promptly at four and took us to Heathrow...or rather, to a private hangar *near* Heathrow.

"This would explain why no-one has provided us with airline tickets," Mirella said, as the car pulled up to a rolling staircase.

It was a private jet.

"Nice," I said. "I used to own one of those."

Thelonius looked inquisitive.

"Did you crash it?" he asked. "Donate it to an orphanage? Parachute into the Andes as it was being shot at from the ground?"

"No, but those all sound much better than what actually happened," I said. "It was sold along with the rest of my estate when I died."

"Aha! You died!"

"Only on paper, and I'm not going to tell you that story either."

We were met at the door by the captain and crew, who notified us that they were all very, very happy to have us aboard, and also that takeoff wasn't until Midnight, and would we like to make ourselves comfortable and have a drink?

Things got a little weird once we made it into the cabin.

"As you said, you used to own one of these," Mirella said, looking around and sniffing. "I would swear this is that very plane."

"I have the same feeling," I said.

There were a couple of minor changes, but they weren't profound enough to argue that it was a different plane. Chief among them was that someone had affixed much more thoroughly effective shades on the windows to prevent even the slightest chance of sunlight getting through. I could sympathize.

More than once, I'd woken up on the couch/bed with sunlight hitting my face through a crack in one of the windows. (It was uniquely the case on an airplane that there could be no place to put the bed where it wouldn't be sun-facing part of the time.) But for the rest, the chairs and desk were the same, as was the aforementioned couch/bed.

"Your Path would appear to be exceptionally well-funded," Mirella said. "I was expecting a slow trawler to the States, and that was optimally."

"I kind of was too. But, I mean, I am the founder and all. This is how it's supposed to work."

"But you didn't expect it to."

"Not really, no."

A day earlier, waiting for Oscar to give us our travel instructions, I was thinking I should have left some of my money to the Path before I pretend-died. I imagine getting that done would have been more difficult than it was worth, and I was under something of a time constraint, but it would have still been a decent idea.

Now, it looked as if that sentiment was unnecessary. The Path's coffers appeared to be full.

The bar was also full, which I would have been much happier about were I not still feeling the effects of the prior night's ale.

There was also a bottle of French champagne on ice. I was pretty sure the champagne was a message of some kind, but I couldn't figure out what that message could possibly be.

The hostess—the flight had a hostess, which was super—opened the bottle without prompting, and passed a plastic cup to each of us.

"I was told to open this right away," she said. "Are we celebrating something?"

"It would appear," Mirella said. "Who told you to open it?"

The hostess laughed, as if this was a silly question.

"My dear, *life* is a celebration!" Thelonius said, raising his glass. Then he dove into a story that sounded like it was going to last all the way to the States.

It was going to be a long flight.

~

My first direct experience with the United States was New York City, at the tail end of 1888. I didn't choose the city—it was the only option. I arrived as a deck hand on a cargo ship, and at that time most cargo ships made port in New York Harbor.

Honestly, on arrival I wasn't terribly impressed with New York, or with the country surrounding it, and I remained underwhelmed for the first few years that followed, right up until I left the city.

In a lot of ways, if you see one city, you've seen them all. It's true that New York has since evolved into something larger and louder and somewhat more interesting, but in 1888 it wasn't that big a deal. It had all the same smells and the same division of labor, the same diseases and the same ethnic biases. There were admittedly fewer titled nobles, but that wasn't obvious from the bottom rung.

All cities started out as marketplaces that just got out of hand. The ones that lasted had certain geographical advantages over other areas, like having multiple paths for goods and decent weather most of the year. They also had to be easy to defend and difficult to attack, although that requirement was barely the case by the time we were calling New York City a city.

So I could understand how New York became important, and why my cargo ship headed to it, in the same way I understood Carthage, Tbilisi, Constantinople, Athens, Cairo, London, and so on. What I didn't get was why New York won this stateside economic lottery and not one of the other emerging cities on the continent. It seemed like Boston had a better claim, unless it was too cold, or the harbor too small. If not Boston, maybe someplace in Virginia.

I'd expected New York to feel like someplace new, and it didn't. It felt a lot like London, which I'd just left after residing there for (off-and-on) close to a century. Sure, the population in the States was more diverse, and the class distinctions weren't nearly as well-established, and it felt a bit roomier, but it was just as filthy, the working poor were just as poor, and the taverns were just as violent.

In that sense, then, I felt right at home.

I didn't come in through normal immigration channels—Castle Island in those days; Ellis Island wasn't a thing yet—which is another way to say I was there illegally. I had paid the captain of the cargo ship to get me there, and then I spent my time on-board learning how to pass as a crew member once. Then, once we docked, I just hopped off the boat one night and walked away.

Getting in was that straightforward. Nothing that came after was, though, because I was carrying a currency that belonged to the wrong country, twice over. I didn't have German Gold Marks —as would be expected of someone fresh off a vessel from Breton—and I didn't have U.S. Dollars. I had British Pounds Sterling.

If this had been anything other than a midnight escape—if I'd had proper time to plan things—I would have managed to exchange what I had with what I needed. I also would have probably used proper channels, taken a decent ship with nice sleeping quarters, and most importantly, I would have taken a lot more cash and a proper international visa.

This was the second half of my problem. A distressing amount of my London wealth was a combination of non-liquid goods, and credit. I had other money sitting in a bank account in Switzerland, but of course I didn't flee to Switzerland. I could get the money *out* of Switzerland if I had to, but first I would need to do a lot of things, like establish a new name and address in a country where the person whose name and address I was using was legally residing. Then I'd have to get a bank account and have that bank send a letter to the Swiss bank. To even get that to work, I'd need to communicate with the Swiss by providing documentary proof that I was the person whose name was on my account there. This wasn't a problem when I went there in person, because I had a passbook, but it was a big problem remotely, because I had no documents the Swiss bank would recognize under the name on that account. To get those documents, I'd need to hire a forger who would take Pounds Sterling. Because again, that was the only cash I had.

I thought about all of this on the long trip across the ocean, and decided that absent a way to to pull all of that off, I was probably looking at the long game: I'd have to start from the bottom of whatever kind of society I found myself in, and work my way up. Maybe after twenty or thirty years I'd be well enough established to tap some of the Swiss funds, if I still needed them at that point.

Of course, the correct solution would have been to have gone to Switzerland instead. I can't remember why I didn't do that; I had the passbook, and I thought the funds on deposit were probably considerable. And I liked Switzerland just fine. I think I maybe just wanted a new experience, and had had my head filled with Herman's descriptions of the New World. Sure, he was kind of a terrible person, but I had no reason to think he was lying.

So to recap: I ended up in New York knowing nobody, with no proof of citizenship I could use, and money that was difficult to exchange. That probably sounds like a desperate situation except that I'd faced similar circumstances hundreds of times in the past. Here, at least, I spoke the language already. It could have been worse.

The thing is, there are always jobs nobody else wants to do. If you're willing to do an obscene amount of work for very nearly nothing—and risk getting literally nothing, since there wasn't exactly an H.R. rep to complain to if the foreman decided not to pay you that week—then there are ways to get by.

So that was what I did for my first couple of years in America: I cleaned things in which fecal matter was an expectation; I built things that were likely not to last; and I carried things that should have been carried by more than one person.

If it looks like I'm skipping through this part, it's because I can't remember precisely all the things I did do, possibly due to the fact that I spent a decent amount of what I earned on alcohol. Everyone else did, too. I do recall being glad I couldn't get sick, because aside from drinking, trading communicable disease was everybody's favorite pastime.

I was working and living in an area of town called Five Points, a neighborhood that I think doesn't exist any longer, and thank goodness for that. More than any other part of the city, it reminded me of the London slums. I felt at home there, but not entirely for the right reasons. If you had qualms about killing another man in order to prevent him from killing you, it wasn't the best place to live, basically.

And again, had I not been going between work, drink, food, sleep, and work again, I would probably have a colorful story or two about this time, but I can't really remember much of it. Did I kill anyone in self-defense? Sure. Did I sleep with a lot of women? Absolutely. But only an imp could turn those years into a proper story, and it would take a lot of talent.

What I do remember is how I got out of this cycle.

One afternoon, a job took me east of Five Points and into a small neighborhood that was an entirely different kind of dangerous: Chinatown. The Tongs ruled the streets there, in the same way the Irish ruled Five Points. The difference was that I could pass for Irish.

The job required I move something heavy to the far end of Chinatown. I don't remember what. Wood, or paving stones maybe. I used a cart and an ass, neither of which were mine.

This took a decently long time. I know everyone who has visited New York, or who lives there now, has a complaint about the traffic, but you really have no idea how bad it used to be—narrow dirt roads with no real transit laws to prevent someone from just stopping in the middle if they felt like it, combined with a seriously ridiculous variety of conveyances. It all conspired to make it faster to travel very nearly everywhere on foot if you could.

At least, that was the case in the part of the city I was in. On my one or two trips to midtown, I noted everything was a lot cleaner, the buildings were taller, and the roads wider and easier to get around on, so maybe the congestion was specific to the poorer neighborhoods. (I remember being modestly impressed by the first skyscraper I ever saw, but only modestly impressed, because I was comparing it to the pyramids of king Khufu.)

I ended up stuck behind a cart that was selling dead chickens. The driver stopped right in the middle of the street, because people kept running up to buy chickens from him. It was kind of like how ice cream trucks operate now, only it was blocking traffic and nobody was eating what they bought as soon it was in-hand.

As I waited—I didn't have a horn to lean on and it wouldn't have helped if I did—I got a good look around, and that was when I spotted it: the three-hares symbol. It was above a door between two shops, painted in gold on a black background.

I was stunned, because it never even occurred to me the Path might have made it to the New World…assuming it even had. It was, as I've said, a common enough symbol, so it was within reason that somebody in Chinatown was using it to symbolize an entirely different thing. Selling dead rabbits, perhaps.

Without thinking much about the consequences of leaving the cart and the ass in the middle of the street, I hopped down, walked over to the door, and went inside.

It led to a staircase, at the top of which was a second door, with a different symbol but the same motif: three dragons chasing one another in a circle, red-and-gold on white. This had no symbolic relevance to the Path that I knew of, but it was cute.

The second door was locked. I rapped on it, and waited. After a decent delay, an elderly Chinese woman opened the door. She looked me up and down, came to a couple of obvious conclusions —I looked like an Irish dockworker, and smelled like one too— and shouted something I couldn't understand. It was delivered angrily, with a couple of gestures that were universal, so the meaning was clear enough.

I've said before that I'm not fluent in "Chinese". The reason I say this isn't because I never tried, or that I don't have a limited set of phrases I can lean on (as I do in most languages) as an entry-point to fluency. I say it because there isn't a single language called Chinese. There's hundreds.

This is sort of true everywhere, but the difference was that I was around for all the early European dialects, but only a couple of the Chinese ones.

I'm pretty good in Mandarin, and that's just about it.

The woman didn't yell at me in Mandarin, or in English, and so we were nearly out of luck from a communications perspective. However, I did have a phrase that belonged to neither tongue.

"*Zurgaan gurvan ni neg yum,*" I said.

It means, approximately, *six and three are one*, in a Mongolian dialect.

She blinked for an eternity or two, as I held my breath.

I had no reason at all to think this was actually the Path. As I said, the symbol is used for other things—the trip to Devonshire certainly proved this—so she could have been a purveyor of rabbit carcasses, or just about anything else. She could have also been confused, not because I'd spoken the phrase of the Path, but because she had yelled at me in the same Mongolian dialect. If that was the case, her confusion was entirely warranted.

"*Zam neegdene,*" she replied, quietly. (If I'm remembering right, this means *a way opens.*) The confusion in her expression hadn't gone anywhere, but at least she wasn't yelling at me any longer.

"Do you speak English?" I asked.

"No English," she said. Then she looked to the side of the doorway and nodded at someone I couldn't see.

"In," she said, stepping aside.

Inside the room, to the side of the door, was a large Chinese fellow with one eye and a machete. I wondered if he'd lost the eye before or after he decided to carry a blade around. I was guessing after, because, again, he was quite large, and assuming he knew what to do with the machete, I expected getting close enough to blind him would be a real challenge. I did note that the blade was in his right hand and the eye he'd lost was his right eye, which could be a tactical advantage if it came to that.

"Do *you* speak English?" I asked him. The man lowered his blade, and nodded.

"Yes, *Gwailou,*" he said, using a derogatory term I'd heard before. It meant something like ghost-man, in reference to my skin color. It was sort of unfair, because I had a decent tan, but whatever.

"Good, you can translate."

He grunted.

There was a small bamboo tree in a planter at the door that had no excuse for being alive given the lack of sunlight in the corner. The man stabbed the machete into the dirt of the planter and left it there. Not a good way to store a machete, unless you were hoping it rusted, but it wasn't my machete.

I followed the old woman past the entryway, to a large table, on the other side of which was a long wall of cubbyholes. Each space held a jar, and each jar had a Chinese character on it.

"You're an herbalist," I said. I had a sudden craving for green tea.

She was more or less ignoring me.

"Sit," the one-eyed man said, pointing to a stool at the table. "I am Lo. Her name is unneeded. Who are you?"

I did a mental review of the list of names I could have provided, from the one associated with the Path, to the name on the last legal document I had—as an Englishman named Jack—to the Irish name I was currently using.

"No name," the woman said. "Traveler."

She took a jar down from the second shelf, opened it, and pulled out two dollars, intending to hand it over.

That doesn't sound like a lot of money these days, so I wish I could say it was a fortune in the 1890's. But it was only about fifty bucks. So, still not a lot of money.

"Ah, of course," I said.

She said something in whatever dialect they were using, to Lo.

"She asks if you need temporary lodging," he said.

"No."

"Then take the traveler's pension, and be on your way."

"You misunderstand," I said.

"You are not owed more than this," he said. "A roof, and assistance. These are the only tolls a traveler such as yourself should expect."

"You take me for a delegate. But I'm more than just a traveler, and am owed more than the traveler's pension."

He translated, and then they proceeded to have a heated argument for a good thirty seconds. I kept waiting for someone to give me something to write on, but that didn't appear to be happening.

"What's going on?" I asked, during a pause. The old woman had shoved the money back into the jar and put it back on the wall, and was now facing away from both of us.

"She told me to kill you," he said.

"That's certainly not good news. I'm glad you disagreed."

"It isn't that. I'd rather not do it indoors. It took months to clean up, the last time."

"The…last time?"

"The smell was terrible as well. Very off-putting for an herbal shop. She will ignore us until I do this."

"You're being serious."

"Oh, yes. She is very stubborn. There's an alley out back. I don't imagine I can convince you to go out there with me?"

"To murder me?"

"I can't let you leave, if you know this much of the Path already. Self-evidently, you are not a legate."

"How would you know this if you don't allow me to provide proof?"

He laughed.

"Because you reek of a dockworker, which is surely what you are, and no more. Everyone knows the legacies are all Chinese, which you are not. That you do *not* know this betrays you as much as anything. It is this ignorance for which I must now kill you."

"All of them were Chinese? No, that was never true; I don't know who told you that. Look, can I just get a pen and paper for a proper test? You should both know how this is supposed to go. I mean, unless the Path has changed a *lot* since I founded it."

He raised an eyebrow.

"Your claim is not only to a legacy, but as a founder, am I hearing this correctly?"

"I didn't say, *a* founder, I said *the* founder. I don't want two dollars and a bed for a night, because I'm no mere traveler. I want the full services of the Path owed to me."

The woman, still refusing to turn, had stopped what she was pretending to do—organize herbs or something—to ask a question over her shoulder.

"All right," Lo said to her. He looked at me. "What is your name, then?"

"I thought you didn't want it?"

"Now we do."

"Depends on the audience. For you guys, the name you're probably looking for is Li Yuan, or Li Tieguai."

Both of those names belonged to an immortal being who was ugly and elderly-looking and walked with an iron crutch. (Tieguai means 'iron crutch'.) I'm still kind of insulted that I've been conflated with him, but it's not the kind of thing I have any control over. It was very specifically a Chinese legend, which was why I thought they'd recognize it. Also, the top, center cubby didn't have a jar, just a box with *Li Tieguai* in Chinese characters. I can't read Chinese worth a damn, but I know what the name they call me looks like.

Lo didn't laugh this time.

"She was right, I should have killed you right away," he said.

"You're welcome to try."

He got up to fetch his machete from the bad-place-to-store-a-machete, when the woman stopped him.

My name came up three or four times during their heated conversation, which was a little entertaining if only because now it seemed their positions had switched. Where before, she thought he should maybe kill me, now he was thinking he'd better and she disagreed.

"She is a superstitious woman," he said, after this had gone on for long enough to be a little awkward. "She believes these ridiculous old things. Li Yuan appears as a beggar in the bedtime stories her grandmother recounted, and now a beggar appears before us. I don't know what game you're at."

"You think it's a con. I mean, that's what I'd think, if I were you."

"Yes. But I don't know what you hope to gain. That box is symbolic; it has nothing in it."

"If she believes the legends, and she mans this station, then that box is not empty, and it's not about the box. You owe me more than its contents. But you have no reason to take my word for any of this. We established the tests for a reason. Are you going to get me a pen and paper now, or would you prefer it if I took away your machete first?"

Lo had something of an internal argument that went on a few seconds, and then he stood, grumbling, and extracted a piece of scrap paper and a fountain pen from underneath the table.

I took a few minutes carefully writing out the necessary symbols—again, I don't much care for fountain pens—and slid it over. Then Lo took down the box, while I appreciated the part where he was surprised to not find it empty.

He compared what I wrote with what was on the parchment inside.

"It's a parlor trick," he said. "It has to be."

"The Chinese legacy to the Path descends from a founder named Xuangang. A second legate named Hsu might have established another blood line, but that he died before this could come to be. These were the only true Chinese founders. I, as you see, belong to all nationalities, unless you prefer the inverse, which is more accurate. I'm Iron Crutch Li, and also Dionysos, and a few others if you'd really like to dive into it."

He harrumphed, but then the old woman was yelling at him again, and so he translated everything I'd just said.

"It's nonsense," he insisted again, after the translation.

"You don't have to believe a word of it," I said. "It doesn't matter. The Path wasn't intended to prove the impossible to the unwilling. I met the criteria. Whether you believe me or not, you —or her, because she seems to be the one in charge—owe the owner of this box its contents along with whatever aid I ask for, within your power. And I've just proven ownership of the box."

The old woman didn't wait for the translation. She pushed the box to the edge of the table in front of me and waved over it, as if to say, *here you go.*

"What you want?" she asked.

I wasn't going to count the money, but there was a decent amount of it, all balled up and slipped into the box at different times. Down at the bottom, there was what looked like pre-Civil-War coins. I wondered if they were still in use.

The bills looked to be about $200, which *was* a lot of money, more than I really needed at the moment. I took a handful, tossed a couple of balled up bills across the table for the house's other jars—being a legate meant always paying forward—and closed the box again.

"Thank her for keeping to the tradition. This is more than enough money for my current circumstance."

Lo translated.

"What you need?" the woman repeated. She had a way of shouting almost everything, so it difficult at first to tell she was offering hospitality, and not demanding that I finish and go away.

"I could use a good forger," I said. "Also, I'd like to get the hell out of New York, because I've learned to hate this place. Are there other stations in this country? Maybe I'll go there."

Lo and the woman talked amongst themselves for a good thirty seconds.

"We know of only one other house such as this," Lo said. "Her discussion of the subject is full of obvious exaggeration, so I can't say for sure if there are actually more, or if she just has faith that it must be so."

"What is she saying?"

"She claims the Path stretches to all corners of the world. I don't know why she speaks this way. She knows the world has no corners. She imagines if you are a legate on the path, you can walk anywhere and find evidence of the Path ahead of you. But practically speaking, we have only ever been contacted by one house in America. If there are more, I suspect they will know. It also meets your needs, as it is not located in New York."

"Chicago," the old woman said.

"Yes," Lo said. "I understand it's a terrible place, but truly, I'm sure the same is said of this city. And, they are having a fair shortly."

And that was how the second city I ever visited in the United States ended up being Chicago. Lo was right about the fair, as I arrived in time to experience the Chicago World's Fair, which was one of the highlights of the 19th century, so far as I was concerned. It was interesting enough that I decided to stay in the country for the next hundred-plus years.

With the benefit of hindsight, it was also the moment when everything began to go wrong.

INTERLUDE (5)

From the journal of Dr. Lew Cambridge

Day fifty-five.

The patient is feeling well enough to walk around the hotel room. We've asked her to consider relocating to the hospital— conveying the needs of hotel management as gently as possible— but she didn't seem at all interested in the idea.

It's likely the words on the wall are giving her solace in some way. That would correspond to her unconscious reaction to our attempts to move her previously.

While declining to leave, she has offered to satisfy my curiosity regarding this veil. Her strength has been restored sufficiently that she was able to take "quick trips", as she described it. And so, while I observed, she walked from one end of the room to the other, without traversing the distance between.

It was precisely as had been described by others witnessing the feat. She literally vanished, with the tiniest of audible 'pop' sounds, and then reappeared. (The 'pop' is, I believe, the air rushing to fill up the space she vacated. There was no such sound when she reappeared.) I asked her to walk across again, only without leaving. It took seven steps. Then I asked her to do it through the veil, and after, I asked how many steps it took.

She said six.

The difference in elapsed time between the control and test attempts was negligible enough to be accountable to slight variations in her pace, but the self-reported difference in the number of steps required was not at all trivial.

She was unable to fulfill my next request, which was to provide a more direct experience: taking me to the other side of this veil. This was something I'd been told was possible—by Adam—but while confirming that it was indeed within her power to do, she wasn't strong enough yet. She was already drained, clearly, from the effort of going across the room alone.

In other good news/bad news, my non-serious plea for another test subject has been answered, twice. Gordana the succubus has checked herself into the hospital with the disease, as has an iffrit named Carlos.

I would love to tell them there's hope for a cure, but the truth is, the fact that they are ill only makes it slightly more hopeful that the next one to acquire the disease will have a cure waiting. I'll do all I can for them, of course, but the prognosis is not positive.

I've asked permission from the council to reach out to the mainland for medical expertise. Ordinarily, this wouldn't be an issue, as there are a number of off-island physicians I could touch base with, no permission needed. (The reason this is so, is obvious: they already know about the island because they've vacationed here.) However, my request would go to an outside lab, where the island's secrecy can't be guaranteed. We'll see if the council continues to value privacy over life.

~

Day fifty-seven.

Eve is gone.

I wasn't in the room when it happened. According to Janet, she arrived to check on Eve, and found her pacing the floor. When Janet asked what was the matter, Eve said that she remembered. (Or that she "figured it out." Janet's recollection is foggy on the precise wording.)

Janet asked what it was Eve had figured out, and/or remembered. Eve stared at Janet, and said—and on this Janet claims her recall is precise: "he'll do it, just for fun."

Then, Eve stepped into her veil.

She hasn't been seen since.

We have no idea who the "he" was that she spoke of, or what it is that he would do just for fun. I'd like to think, had I been there, I would have gotten more information from Eve, but perhaps not. Hopefully, she'll turn up again soon, and explain herself.

CHAPTER 9

Chicago was where I fell in love with America.

Actually, that's not entirely right. Chicago was where I *understood* America for the first time. More accurately still, it was where I understood what America was trying to be.

To get to where I was, you have to come at this from the other end of history. Large societies had an approach to things that was refreshingly straightforward, while at the same time hugely unfair to the majority of the people who made the mistake of being born into families with no connections. What I'm talking about is basically a bastard form of feudalism. The modern versions in Europe and Asia were built on a structure established by the Romans and colored somewhat by early Greek and late Turkish and Muslim caliphate philosophies. Throw in the tribal god-king idea, and you're just about there.

Here's how it worked. Fundamentally—and this is going to sound dumb the more basic I make it, but here goes—entire societies were built on the idea that a certain subset of people was just *better* than another subset of people. All the way back to Athens, you had people who were citizens, and people who were laborers or slaves. Citizens got to own all the land and had all of the money, and because they had a labor class beneath them, they also had all the time in the world to better educate themselves. That freedom meant they were the only ones who could read and write, so that was where the poets and the sculptors and the mathematicians all came from. Meanwhile, other people were building their houses for them, hunting for the food they ate, making their wine and—a lot of the time—fighting in the wars the ruling class started.

That's honestly how it worked. Everyone just agreed that so-and-so born to such-and-such a house was *better* than the so-and-so born three blocks away. Whether that first person was *of royal blood* (which, again, is just a holdover from every culture that considered its king an actual god), or happened to have fairer skin, or whatever, they were just supposed to be inherently better.

It wasn't even a wealth thing, a lot of the time. The poorest nobleman was still generally considered a person of higher character—more noble, if you will—than the richest merchant of modest upbringing.

But there weren't any noblemen in America. It was the first country I'd been in where they flat-out discarded the concept and put the merchants in charge of everything.

Well, all right, it didn't actually end up working like that, which was why when I landed in New York City, initially I couldn't see the difference between where I was and where I had been. America was still founded on the back of a laborer class—worse, really, because the country was built by slaves as much as by anybody. The early colonists also had a big leg up on most of the other British colonies, because the first thing they did was clean out almost the entire native population, which left a ton of space, some of it already cultivated for farming. And, every wave of immigration to the country renewed the notion that the newly arrived *they* was inferior to the existing *we*. Some things are just hardwired in human minds, and that impulse appears to be one of them.

But they *aspired* to be more egalitarian than just about any of their government contemporaries. The cynic in me would argue here that all the founders did was establish royalty-by-other-means. The optimist sees a nation where that royalty can be acquired through one's actions in life, rather than one's accident of birth.

I thought that was great. It took the Chicago fair—plus a shower or two, some sleep, a little sobriety, and affordable room-and-board—before I saw it that way, but once I did, I was hooked.

❧

The first thing I did, on reaching the city of Chicago (I took a train,) was touch base with the local Path way-station. They'd been sent word of my arrival, but I still had to go through a second lengthy vetting process under an implied threat of violence, because modern man isn't good at embracing the idea of immortality. Like in New York, they were Chinese, and were just as confused to discover that I was not. (This was actually a larger hurdle to get over than the part where I happened to be a founding member of a 1000-year old secret society.)

I had arrived with what was left of my last paycheck, plus the money given to me by the New York satellite. It was a decent sum, although I say that with the important caveat that I was measuring the value of my money according to how many bottles of liquor I could acquire with it, which is a fairly limited metric. I also had just-forged paperwork that provided me with my new American name: Stanley. This was possibly of greater value than the cash.

What I needed from the Chicago office was whatever additional cash was owed from the founder box, and a place to stay. I also asked about—and was provided with—a way to exchange the British pounds sterling I'd absconded from England with, as I was under the impression these funds would translate into a decent pile of US dollars. Like, a hundred bottles at least.

I considered requesting a letter of introduction, so that I might obtain gainful employment in a profession that didn't require the lifting of heavy things and the fighting of Irishmen to the death behind bars. But by the time all of the pounds were converted and added to the dollars I arrived with, plus the dollars in my Chicago box, it turned out I was really quite well-to-do. Not wealthy enough to require no employment for the foreseeable future, but well enough to not have to concern myself with a job for a good year or so.

So began what ended up being one of my favorite summers. I appreciate that this sounds like a tremendous exaggeration in the context of my lifespan, but…well, all right, it is kind of hyperbolic, especially given how the summer ended. I liked it, though, enough that I stayed in Chicago for the next fifty-odd years, and in America for the next hundred plus.

All of that was because of the Chicago World's Fair.

That wasn't its actual name. Its actual name was World's Fair: Colombian Exposition. Also acceptable was Chicago Colombian Exposition and World Colombian Exposition. Every version with the word "Colombian" in it was a mouthful, basically, and probably half the people attending didn't know the reason that word was even involved, which was why we mostly called it the World's Fair and left it at that.

There *was* a reason, though: it was the four hundredth anniversary of Columbus discovering the New World, for a very specific subset of European humans. I always thought this was sort of funny, because Columbus was most certainly not the first person to notice the continent, even if one excludes the people already living there. His claim as the person who discovered America was about as solid as Amerigo Vespucci's claim that the place should be named after him because he was the one to draw the map. Basically, the country's purported discovery and naming can both be traced to someone exaggerating on their résumés, which is just about perfect for this country.

It's possible my reaction to the fair (and the United States, by extension) could be because I was a whole lot more tired of everything Europe than I appreciated up to that moment. It's also possible that the best way to enjoy anyplace, New World or not, was to have enough funds to not have to worry about where one is eating, drinking and sleeping from day to day.

I want to explain how breathtaking the fair really was, but it's hard to impart that, because everyone stopped having World Fairs, so for the most part the modern person doesn't even know what I'm talking about.

Try and imagine the Olympics, but for technology, during a carnival.

That's not really right, but it's close.

Let me try again: a technology convention, but it's every kind of technology you can think of, and it's taking place at the world's best amusement park, and the park is in the middle of a city.

Better.

At the fair, I saw electrical light for the first time. I saw my first camera—although those had already been invented, I was just late to it—and posed for my first photo. (This ended up being a tremendous mistake.) I had my first bite of sweetened chocolate, rode the first Ferris Wheel, saw my first Wild West show and my first hula dance, and saw the sedentary culture of the future in the form of a walkway that did the walking for you. (It even had chairs.) I also decided I disliked a number of things for the first time, such as breakfast cereal and American football.

The fair took place in Jackson Park, a decent-sized stretch of greenery on the shore of Lake Michigan, and a pretty good distance from what anyone would consider to be the proper downtown portion of the city.

(Chicago is huge. It was one of the first major cities I came upon that didn't take defensibility into consideration. The best you could say is, if Huns showed up to lay siege, they wouldn't know where to start, because the city limits aren't in any sense obvious. Los Angeles is just as bad.)

What they did was, they built a bunch of temporary buildings, just for the fair, right in the middle of Jackson Park. So, to the list of things I'd never seen before I got there, we can add 'temporary buildings', because this is just a lunatic concept to me. I mean, I guess you could say I saw a lot of temporary buildings in my time, but they were either A: meant to be permanent, but someone made a drastic construction mistake, or B: a tent.

These kind of were tents, I guess. Big rectangular ones. The facades were made of plaster and designed to look like stone, but beyond that I have no idea what went into putting them together and making sure they stayed that way for the whole summer.

A lot of the buildings mimicked a style I'd been looking at for a thousand years already, in several parts of Europe. Lots of columns and what-not, and all of it painted bright white. Hosting a big fair to say, *hey, America is totally different from Europe* and then borrowing all of your architectural plans from Europe didn't make a ton of sense to me, but I'm not an architect, so I don't know. Maybe there are only so many ways to make a temporary building.

Other countries had their own areas at the fair, which was probably pretty fantastic for all of the local American citizens who'd never been overseas themselves, but for me it was *amazing*. It was like a This Is Your Life: Greatest Hits special. All the best things about these countries and none of the violence, disease, and war, essentially, along with a glimpse at a few countries I hadn't been to yet, like Mexico and the Philippines.

I spent a stupid amount of time at the German pavilion

because they had beer there, and up to that point my experience with American beer hadn't been all that positive. I remember on one occasion having partaken of too much and then stumbling on the Norway exhibit at twilight. The Norway exhibit included an authentic built-from-scratch Viking ship. I can't begin to tell you how confusing that was. Were it not for the fact that the electrical lighting on the grounds was impossible to miss—and thus served as an ever-present reminder of what era I was in—I probably would have started speaking Old Norse just out of habit.

The World's Fair gave me everything I needed to understand America.

There was the good version: a little artificial and with a tendency toward grandiosity, but trying very hard to be authentic about something.

And there was the less-good version: a grand White City in which black people went almost entirely unrepresented, and the murder of Native Americans was re-enacted twice a day at the edge of the fairgrounds.

Then there was the bad version, which I didn't really come to grip with until the last few weeks of the Fair. That was when I saw my old friend Herman.

~

As I think I've mentioned before, I have a real problem with faces.

I'm guessing this is a problem unique to me. I've met so very many people in this life that almost everyone looks sort of familiar. People with more of the usual lifespan probably don't have this big of a problem, I'm guessing.

(The exception—and I apologize if this makes me sound like a pig but it's still true—is women I find particularly attractive. They all manage to look distinctive.)

So, when I saw Herman, I wasn't sure at first if I was looking at who I thought I was looking at.

I was on the Midway at the time. This was the part of the fair-grounds dedicated to the traditional amusement park kind of stuff, which were admittedly a lot more limited in those days. Among other things, it was where the Ferris Wheel stood. (This was the first one ever built, and it was gargantuan and terrifying. It fit something like thirty people per car and felt like it was going to fall over every time the wind blew. I loved it.) I don't remember why it was called the Midway, but I do recall that after that section of the park was claimed by an athletic field, the team that played on the field was nicknamed *the Monsters of the Midway*. They might still be called that—not sure if the field still is—even though I'm the only one alive for whom that appellation makes any sense.

Anyway. I was walking along the Midway when I spotted a man accompanying two women. He had on a suit and a hat, and wore a big bushy mustache.

None of that was unique. We all wore suits and hats even though it was the middle of summer because that was what men did at this stage in history, even when some of us remembered with great fondness how comfortable a *chiton* was in the heat. A lot of us also wore big bushy mustaches. But it was the combina-tion of these things, along with the roundness of his face and, perhaps, just his general stature, that left me nearly convinced that this was Herman.

We were walking toward one another, but they were coming along slowly, so I had plenty of time to step off the path, collect myself, and do the math. This is something I usually have to do after stumbling upon a familiar face in an unfamiliar place, because the odds are usually in favor of the person I think I see being long dead from old age. But I had last laid eyes on Herman in London in 1888—it had only been five years. Also, he was an American, and I was standing in America. I didn't recall him discussing Chicago, but all the same the odds that this was him remained *incredibly unlikely* rather than *literally impossible.*

After that was settled, I had to decide what I was going to do about this. He was the reason I'd fled London in the first place, and was possibly also indirectly responsible for a number of murdered women, a couple of whom were friends. I couldn't involve the police because nobody would believe me, so the only remaining options were to flee town and start over again, or hope he didn't notice me and pretend I didn't notice him either, and go about my day.

There was a third option, which was to kill him where he stood, but, annoyingly, it was no longer commonplace to walk about with a murder weapon all the time. (I miss swords.) I could have done it with my hands, but it would have taken a lot more effort. Plus, the lighting on the fairgrounds made murder really challenging to pull off without drawing a crowd.

I was in favor of pretending this never happened, which would have meant turning around and walking away from the man I thought was Herman, so that later I could convince myself I'd been mistaken all along.

I tried it, for about ten steps, before deciding it wasn't going to work. I simply had to know for sure. So, I turned back around.

Within ten feet, I was positive I had the right man. He and the women he was with were laughing at a joke he'd just told, and all I could do was stand in the middle of the path and stare as they approached.

It soon became obvious that I was staring.

"Hello, sir," he said, as the three of them stopped in front of me. "Can I help?"

"Herman," I said.

He blinked a couple of times, but it wasn't in recognition.

"I'm sorry, you must have me mistaken. Excuse us?"

One of the girls laughed again, and called him Henry. Then

they stepped around me and continued down the path, while I tried to process what had just happened.

I could have sworn it was him. Was I really that wrong, or was he pretending he didn't know who I was because of the women?

It was substantially more likely that I had the wrong guy. The timbre of his voice did seem a little off, and his mannerisms slightly different… but I couldn't shake the idea that I had the right guy.

Without being entirely cognizant that I was doing so, I began following them.

It ended up being the kind of long walk that should have made it impossible for the people I was following to not notice that I was doing so, except that they were too caught up talking about the fair and acting out some sort of three-way flirt to look over their shoulders.

They left the park by way of 63rd St. and just kept on going. It was a good three miles, the sort of distance people were okay with back before the invention of sidewalks that did the walking for you.

Their destination was a three-story corner building, with a shop on the ground floor. The other two floors looked residential. I couldn't tell much more than that without entering, which I wasn't going to do. They would definitely know I was following them if I tried that.

By then it was getting late, and I was standing in Englewood, which wasn't particularly near the flat I was renting in Chinatown. I hailed a cab, and tried to put Herman/Henry out of my mind.

~

*I*n this, I failed completely, because the next morning I was back out in front of the building. It looked like I was going to end my summer obsessing over this.

It was late morning by the time they emerged, this time hailing a cab at the corner. That should have been the end of it (since I was without a cab of my own) except the traffic on 63rd was scarcely faster than traveling on foot, so I didn't have any trouble keeping up. Even if this wasn't the case, it looked as if they meant to return to the fair, so I knew which direction to go and where to hunt for them.

At the fair, once I figured out that they preferred the attractions on the Midway to the rest of the exhibition, following them around without being detected became almost mundane. Espionage of this variety is something I've gotten a lot of training on, and am modestly good at; once I had their patterns down, keeping track without risking exposure wasn't tough.

That was assuming the people I tailed had no counter-espionage experience. The fact that they stuck to predicable patterns should have been an indication that no, they did not, but this turned out to be an overly generous assumption on my part.

I didn't really know why I was bothering, but once I decided to start following them around, I couldn't seem to stop. There was no endgame. Maybe I was holding onto the hope that Henry would eventually break down and admit to being the very same Herman who tried to pin the Ripper murders on me, but even if that were to happen I didn't know what to do after.

It was something I couldn't admit at the time, but I think I probably missed him, in some weird way. He did convince me to go to America (I mean, before I was forced to flee to the States as a consequence of his actions) and aside from the difficulties that were New York City, I'd found the place to be exactly as exciting as he'd said. So I sort of owed him for that—in a good way—and I was a little sad I couldn't talk to the man I thought he was about this country, because of the man he turned out to be.

I followed them for four days before their pattern changed. First, on the morning of day five, nobody came out of the building at all. This was a Sunday, but the fair was open on Sunday so unless there was a religious element to their threesome, the day of the week didn't offer much of an explanation. The following day, they didn't emerge all at once. At around the same time the three typically showed up on the street, Henry came out alone. Whether the women were lagging, decided not to attend the fair, or there was some other explanation, I couldn't say, because I decided I would follow him. Probably, they would exit later, and meet up with him.

Following only him was slightly more of a challenge, since he had nobody by his side to serve as a distraction. However—after stopping in the store on the ground level (it was a drug store)—he went to the fair, as before, and on foot. I was able to put more distance between us as a consequence.

The next change in pattern was that he went to the White City proper, instead of the amusements promenade. The White City was the part of the World's Fair dedicated to the country-specific pavilions, and the technology displays. The part of the fair *I* preferred, essentially, but which he and the women didn't evidently care to see.

For half a day, we went through different country pavilions, as Henry showed at least nominal interest in the dioramas. He looked more like someone trying to pretend he was interested than someone who actually was, which was when I thought for the first time that he knew he was being followed. Perhaps we had reached the point where he'd confess to being Herman.

I lost him in Cairo.

The Streets of Cairo was one of the most popular spots in the fair. I personally found it a little hokey, and a good indication of the fake foreignness that was always popular with 'civilized' people. They served mocha drinks, and had fake mummies, and exotic dancers the likes of which I never actually saw in Egypt in any of the three or four times I was there. It was no different than the artificial authenticity that made up the whole White City, but somehow in Cairo it bothered me more.

Anyway, because it was so popular, it was harder to tail Henry through it. Obviously, because I lost track of him.

Wandering around, trying not to look too much like a guy who was just tailing another guy, I ended up in a fake mausoleum with a fake sarcophagus.

"He does know you're following him," a man whispered in my ear. He was standing directly behind me, which was something I might have noticed had the place not been so crowded. "He's no simpleton. Not like the last one."

I turned, and there was Herman.

As soon as I was face-to-face with the man, I realized that Henry was indeed a different fellow. But the differences were subtle enough that mistaking one for the other was something anybody could have done.

"Hello, Jack," he said. "Happy to see you made it out of London all right. You look healthy!"

"*Are* you happy to see me?" I asked. My heart rate tripled, as my fight-or-flight instinct pushed the needle firmly to the *fight* side of the dial. I started assessing the surroundings, to see if I could get away with killing him right there. Since there was just one exit, the only chance I had was if the sarcophagus was real enough to be opened, and was also empty. Otherwise, I'd have to get him out into the open somewhere.

I wondered how he felt about taking a boat onto Lake Michigan with me.

"Of course I am!" he said. "What kind of friend would I be otherwise? Come on, let's go find a proper meal, we have so much to talk about."

"No, I don't think so. I'm considering wringing your neck."

"Well! I'm sure a number of people feel that way, in a place like this. Such a funereal atmosphere. But, I mean it, I intend no harm, and I feel as if we simply must catch up. You've spooked my associate quite enough, wouldn't you say? It'll be a public place, but if you want to wring my neck later, I understand entirely."

When I still didn't move—honestly, I was counting witnesses —he laughed and clapped me on the shoulder.

"I'll tell you what, Jackie, there's a German restaurant on Adams Street, can't miss it. I'll be at a table in the back, tonight, holding a seat for you. Why don't you get yourself together, gather whatever implements of violence you'd like to have on hand, and we can get a pint and talk this whole thing out like civilized men."

I found him exactly where he said he would be, five hours later: at a table at the back of the restaurant.

It was really more of a pub than a restaurant, but the distinction was pretty muddled back then, before people concerned themselves so much with things like legal drinking age, which wasn't invented until around the time child labor laws were invented. (I'm guessing.) I could probably make a compelling argument that the reason I spent so very much time in bars and pubs over the centuries was because that was the only place to get a meal when you didn't have a proper home to go to. It wouldn't be accurate, but I could make the claim.

"There you are!" Herman greeted once I stepped into view. The pub had too much tobacco smoke, too many people, and not enough lights. At the table in the back, I probably could have murdered him and left, and nobody would have been wise to it for a good hour or two. Oddly, I thought this choice of venues was a deliberate gesture of hospitality on his part.

I took a seat in front of a pint of ale.

"I ordered it an hour ago," he said, "to give it time to reach room temperature. Half of the places in this county chill their beer, which is a special sort of madness, I think."

"You talk of it as if you weren't born here," I said. I tried the beer. The German pavilion's draught was better, but this was okay.

"And you talk as if you were," he said. "I notice your accent has undergone some sort of transformation. If I didn't know better, I'd say you were born to an Irish wench fresh off the boat in New York. You're quite the chameleon, my friend."

"Let's dispense with the *friend* talk, Herman. You tried to pin the Whitechapel murders on me, and that's frankly not the thing I expect from friends."

"Only because you had me in a corner! We both know you were preparing to attach *my* name to them."

"Yes, but you were actually responsible. Do you see the distinction?"

"A minor difference," he huffed, taking a sip of his own beer.

"Is Herman even your name?"

"Oh excellent, good question. Herman is not my real name. It belongs to the man you've been following."

"He says his name is Henry."

"It is *now*. He changed it."

"When I called him Herman he acted as if he'd never heard the name before."

"Well, he's a decent actor. A terrible person, but…let me put it this way: Henry's something of a professional confidence man. Which is really interesting because he's also an actual medical doctor, and one almost never sees those two things together. Certainly, a man might exaggerate his credentials, for example, by lying about going to medical school. But he actually did go, albeit as Herman Mudgett, and not Henry Holmes. Not that this in any way stops him from calling himself Dr. Holmes. Honestly, I wonder why anyone bothers to actually attend medical school, when one merely needs put 'doctor' in front of their name and hang a shingle."

"All right, let me see how much of this I've figured out," I said.

"You knew this Henry person, realized you bore something of a resemblance to him, and then… what? Pretended to be a doctor yourself?"

"I wanted to travel overseas, and Henry, as I said, is more of a confidence man than a doctor, but that doesn't mean he's necessarily an exceptional confidence man. There was a decent amount of legal issues attached to the name Herman Mudgett, and so I proposed two solutions. First, he should change his name. Second, to prevent anyone from connecting the old name to the new, I could take on the old name and escape the colonies with it for long enough to allow him to establish the new persona. That's how I ended up traveling London under his name, ducking his creditors."

"And pretending to be a doctor. I'm assuming you're not really one."

He waved his hand in the air, a dismissive gesture.

"It hardly matters, as I said. I think you and I had more than one conversation about the shabby condition of the medical sciences. But if you needed to understand why my focus was more on the infirmity of the mind than the infirmity of the body, now you do. I could pass more easily that way. Although I did participate in a number of surgeries, and frankly nobody noticed. Appalling. As for Herman's family background and finances, all of that was true. While I traveled Europe with his name, those finances came very much in handy."

"I see. And then I show up out of nowhere and call him by his old name."

"He was left to assume that you were either there to collect money for one of his old debts, or you were someone who knew *me* as him. He reached out to me in the hopes that it was the latter and not the former, as would anyone who'd gone through so much trouble to distance himself from his old name."

I nodded, and drank some more. It was a ridiculous story, but I believed it anyway.

"Does he know you're a lunatic?" I asked.

"Well, that's just unnecessarily combative. I thought we were past that."

"We're not getting past that, no."

He laughed.

"I'm no lunatic, Jack. I'm in perfect retention of my faculties. And I'm rather insulted! I've met actual lunatics, as you know better than most anybody. What I am is a student of the human condition, that's all! Sometimes, given my chosen field of study—murderers—this requires that I make good company of unsavory types. If anything, my lack of inhibition in doing so marks me as a true man of science."

"That's a convenient rationalization," I said.

He ignored the point.

"So, to your question: Henry thinks I'm no less a lunatic than he himself is," he said, "which is fair, only because I would argue he is not a lunatic either. Let's say he's quite the engaging subject for my continued studies."

"Ohh, you've adopted another one to do your killing for you, I understand. I can't wait until your studies are complete and you look to publish the results. I don't think I've heard of anyone being hanged before for a medical thesis."

"No, no, no. No. They aren't doing my killing. I'm not interested in killing anyone at all! What I am is a student of killers. It's true that I can't study them if they don't actually murder somebody, but they're the ones choosing the victims and performing the act. You can put me to task for not stopping them—"

"I will. And you aren't just observing them, you're putting them in a position to commit the act."

"I did in London, yes. Not my greatest showing; I think we're in agreement on that point. All right, you have me there. But I promise, Henry is not at all like that other fellow."

He gasped.

"You know, I've actually forgotten his name?" he said. "How

curious. Here I am, the only man alive who can put a name to the Ripper of London, and I don't even recall it. At any rate. On the matter of Dr. Holmes. The implication of *lunacy* is a lack of self-control, a sort of raving…well, the sort of fellow I dug up from the dungeon of Bedlam. *That* was a lunatic. Henry is entirely in control. That's why he's so fascinating. He has an extremely flexible morality."

I thought back to the number of times I went a little insane, which I could count on happening every few centuries. It manifested as my no longer being able to discern the present from my old memories, and probably was the inevitable consequence of having a brain that wasn't supposed to be around recording things for this long. *Loss of control* was absolutely a hallmark. So maybe I was closer to the term *lunatic* than anyone else we were talking about.

"What does it mean to you, to have a flexible morality?" I asked.

"Well. I guess from someone else's perspective, it means he has no morality whatsoever, but that's not the case. He just values different things than the average person. Although he does appear to dislike women quite strongly, but that's surprisingly common, actually. Even in men who purport to feel the exact opposite. No, Henry's moral sense doesn't extend beyond what's good for Henry."

"That's not that unusual."

"Yes, but no, what you're talking about is self-interest. We all have self-interest. To further *his* interests, my friend will do anything. He'll kill. And think nothing of it."

I took a sip of beer and tried to reconcile the man I spent five days following around with the one being described. Henry struck me as a gadabout, when he was with the women he supposedly hated. *Potential killer,* didn't spring to mind easily. Maybe that was how he got away with it.

"And he's done it already," I said, for clarification. "Murdered someone."

"More than once. Very economically, too. He owns that building, did you know that?"

"I didn't go digging up any property records."

"He flim-flammed the funding to get it built. He's better at getting financiers to back him than he is at just about anything else, I'd wager. He has the means to make bodies disappear, in that building. I won't say how; it would put you off your food. But it's rather elegant. He's even made a profit off the remains, at least once. Sold the skeleton to a medical school. I heard at that Wild West show that the plains Indians found a use for every part of the buffalo. Henry's nearly as industrious."

"Except these are people," I said. "Not buffalo."

"Yes, I appreciate the distinction."

His expression implied this was, at worst, an inconvenient detail.

"And this is the sort of fellow you have no compunction about befriending," I said. "More than that; you're helping him. Not like you helped the London Ripper, but abetting anyway."

"I told you, my interest is clinical, that's all. Why do you think I became your friend?"

"I'm not sure I understand."

"Come on now. You move effortlessly from country to country, from the lowest rung on the social ladder to the tea room in an exclusive Gentleman's Club. You've done it here and I bet my hat you did the same in England, given how at ease you were in the East End. You know who accomplishes that kind of social climbing in a single lifetime? Nobody, that's who, and you've pulled the trick twice. How many people did you kill to get those fine threads, Jack? Is that even the name you're using now?"

It was actually an impressive bit of deduction, even if it was incorrect. It took multiple lifetimes to accomplish that in England, and I had the help of a secret society in the U.S. He was also wrong in thinking I'd killed people to get where I was at this moment, but not wrong in that I had taken lives in the past. I took them in self-defense, but I was capable of it. Granted, my definition of self-defense was probably not one a court of law would agree with. For instance, I considered killing Herman a self-defense exercise, even though he wasn't currently posing a direct threat to my health and well-being.

"You're wrong," I said. "My finery is attributable to the funds I brought from London, and the shop was my father's."

He smiled.

"That's a lie. You're a killer. I knew it when we first met. You're here to kill me tonight. I know that's not bravado. You have it in you."

I didn't come to the restaurant with a weapon, but I didn't have to. When they cleared off the table, they'd discover a steak knife missing.

"I feel as if we're approaching the end of our conversation, Herman. I've given you a chance to explain yourself, and you have. It hasn't changed my feelings regarding your continuing to breathe."

"Thank you for your honesty. But before we reduce ourselves to that level, I'd like to make a proposal."

"I decline."

"You should listen to it first."

"Fine. Go on."

"The proposal is this: you'll never see me again; Henry Holmes will vacate his property within a few months, and never return; nothing that happened there will be connected to any of us, you included."

"You've decided to stop pinning murder sprees on me? Is that what I'm getting out of this arrangement?"

"I know you've had to restart once already. I have to think that if you killed me tonight and then—and I'm just guessing but I've no doubt it's crossed your mind—went calling on Henry with the same murderous intent, you would have to flee once more. Only this is a much larger country and you are very much in the middle of it."

"I've heard good things about Canada."

"I've been. It's cold."

"Herman, you're asking that I leave you alone so you two can button up whatever else you've got going on here that you haven't told me about yet, and what I get in exchange is the freedom to pretend we never came across one another, plus the weight on my conscience of however many deaths happen at your hands between now and whenever someone puts a stop to it. Are the women still alive?"

"The women?"

"I saw Henry with two women, and then I didn't. What did he do with them?"

"Oh, they're fine. No, no, he likes them quite a lot. Told me so."

"Now who's lying?"

He smiled.

"In truth, I can't speak to their health in either direction. If you'd like to make their survival a condition of our agreement, I can arrange it."

"I don't think you can. And I don't feel like making any kind of deal with you. But I did enjoy the meal."

I got up and walked away before he could try and entice me with a variant of the *ignore all the killing* scheme. I heard a loud sigh, but no other protestation.

～

So, there I was, standing in a pass-through next to the restaurant, wondering about murdering a man.

Adams was a decently busy street, much more definitively 'downtown' than anything associated with the fair, but it was also late at night in a world with no electric street lamps outside of the White City itself. If you wanted to kill a man and then walk away, I'm saying, it was still possible to do it, even in the middle of a large metropolis.

I already knew this, from my New York experience, although I wasn't what anyone would call in the middle of that city then.

If you're wondering, I'm entirely capable of straight-up killing a guy, both in terms of execution and general intestinal fortitude. In that regard, Herman was right. True, it isn't often I'm put into a position quite like this, where I'm *creating* the act of violence rather than *defending* myself from it, but these were unique circumstances.

If Herman was without an accomplice, I could see letting him walk away in the expectation that our paths would never cross again during his lifetime. I might have to relocate again, but that was well within my capabilities. But there was Henry to consider. It was made very clear that Henry needed to be stopped, and unlike in London, it was within my power to do that. I'd have to go through Herman first, though.

I was ruminating on the subject of precisely how good my ex-friend might be in hand-to-hand combat, and what would be involved in dragging him from the street to the back of the building, when a large man came up from behind.

I heard him coming, and figured he was a restaurant staffer, leaving by way of the kitchen exit in the rear. I stepped aside so as to give him plenty of room to pass. But that wasn't what he was interested in.

"Hey," he said. "You can't be here."

"Here, in the alley?"

"That's what I said."

I looked around for a sign or a gate or something.

"It's a public alley."

"Nah."

"I'm… *nah?* That's what you're arguing? Look…"

I didn't get to finish what was going to be a positively devastating bit of sarcasm, because he decided to escalate the situation drastically. With one big, meatball of a hand, he grabbed my shirt collar, picked me up, and threw me a few feet further down the alley. I landed awkwardly on a metal trash can, and lost the steak knife I'd been keeping in my sleeve.

I was back on my feet before he had a chance to press his advantage.

"If you wanted me out of the alley," I said, taking a defensive stance, "you threw me the wrong way."

"Funny."

"I know, I have a great sense of humor. Ask anyone."

He swung at my head. I ducked, and jabbed two fingers in a spot below his ribcage. This took all the air out of his lungs, which he needed, both for his monosyllabic communications and to breathe.

"Leave it, friend," I said. "I don't want to hurt you."

He grunted, still on one knee. Then he was up again, only with a switchblade in one hand.

"C'mon, don't be…look, so it's your alley, fine. I'll head out right now."

"Man said you'd be tough," he growled. "He wasn't lyin'."

"Wait, did someone put you up to this?" I asked.

He ignored the question, and came at me with the blade.

Large men should carry large knives. Or swords. It's a truism I just made up, but I think it holds, especially if they're using the knife as the vanguard of their attack. For instance, if you happen to be a nimble enough large person, you can grab someone with one hand and stab them with your small knife with the other. That's a perfectly valid method of assault. But if you're leading with the switchblade—as he was—you're going to be off-balance most of the way. Because the thing about being very large is that you tend to put a lot of confidence in your strength. The idea, then, is that even if the blade in your hand is tiny, if you thrust it forward with tremendous strength, it will do more damage.

And, I mean, that's *true*, but not really sensible if the person you're going after is capable of independent movement. Also, if the thing is sharp enough, you don't need a lot of force.

He was using it wrong, is my point. Yes, you can slip a switchblade into a pocket and walk around with nobody being the wiser. That's the whole point of them. But you have to know how to use it or it's not doing you any good.

His initial stab was wild to the right, and easy to evade. He tried to paw at me with his left arm—the knife was in his right—but that was also clumsy, and simple enough to duck under. I did, and kicked his legs out from under him. He went face-first into the trash can that cushioned my fall a few seconds earlier.

"Look," I said, "this isn't going to end well. Did he pay you already? You should probably just take the money and get out of here."

I'd have had just as much success getting through if Herman hired a dancing bear instead of this oaf. He scampered to his feet and tried again.

"You're squirmy," he grunted.

"I'm going to have to really hurt you if you don't stop."

He roared, and performed what was actually an effective attack for a person his size. He wrapped me up in both arms and ran us backwards into the wall.

High grades all around: he used his size and the narrowness of the combat area to counter my quickness. I would have applauded if I thought it was going to be received well.

"Last chance," I said.

He laughed, pressed me up against the wall with one hand, and tried to stab me with the knife.

Again: high marks. But he should have taken the offer.

The blade never landed true—obviously—because my hands were still free. I caught the wrist with a left-hand sweep and grabbed the arm that was holding me against the wall with my right hand. This provided enough leverage for a kick in his groin with a decent amount of force. Then I was no longer being pressed up against the wall. I drove the palm of my right hand up into his chin, pinched his right wrist in just the right spot, and a second later he was on one knee and I was holding his knife.

"Just go, friend" I said. "Run off, please."

He didn't. He got up and charged yet again. I ducked under the attack, and jabbed him three times with the switchblade, in and around the heart.

See, that's how you're supposed to use a small knife: quick, deep, targeted jabs. If you know where the arteries are, and you're fast enough, it's nearly impossible to defend against.

The big guy grabbed his chest, more surprised than in any real pain.

"I'm sorry," I said. "I gave you at least four chances to walk."

His heart was busy exploding in his chest, so as much as it would have been cool to get a *hey, no problem, my mistake* from him, he mostly just fell over and died.

"I see you've proven my point," Herman said. He was standing at the back end of the alley, where the exit from the kitchen was located.

"If you've been there all this time, you know I didn't have a choice."

"Oh, but you did. Once you took the knife from him, you had an opening. Clearly, you're faster than he was. Why didn't you simply run? The street's right there."

"Because…"

I didn't know how the rest of that sentence went. He was right; I could have run.

Herman laughed at my perplexity.

"So, you hired this guy to kill me," I said. "And you were sure of this outcome. Now we're both standing in an alley, I've already killed one man, and I'm holding a knife. Are you sure this is how you wanted this to go?"

"Yes, I absolutely counted on it."

"You think you've got a better chance than he did?"

"I definitely do, yes."

He raised his arm to reveal a handgun.

We'd really just entered the era in which handguns became accurate enough weapons to be considered reliable in a circumstance such as this. Ten or fifteen years earlier, I'd have taken the knife over the gun.

We were also about ten paces away from one another. If I wanted to live, all I had to do was turn around and run, like he said I should have done once I'd disarmed his hired man. Regardless of what kind of rigged trick shots went on in Wild Bill's Wild West Show down the street, a kill shot with a handgun on a guy running in the wrong direction, in the dark, at more than ten paces, was pretty tough.

"This is just to keep you from coming any closer," he said. "Laura, why don't you step over here?"

A frightened-looking woman—I thought she might have been our serving-girl—emerged of the shadows next to Herman.

"Tell us what you saw."

"I saw…I saw that man kill Benny," she said.

"Very good. And who is that man?"

"His name's Stanley."

Then she recited my address in Chinatown.

"Thank you so much," he said. "Now run back inside."

She did.

"What is this?" I asked.

"Well, I felt terrible, about how we ended things in London. It was wrong of me to try and pin murders on you which you didn't commit. To make amends, I've decided to run you up on a murder you *did* commit, in front of a witness."

"I see. And how much money is Laura getting to pretend you weren't here as well, confessing to have set up the whole thing?"

"That's not important. Look, Jack—or, excuse me, Stanley now—the offer still stands. I'm just trying to broker an arrangement where we're all getting what we want. You leave us alone. You'll never see me again, and Henry will leave Chicago for good. I know you like it here. So stay."

"And Laura?"

"Laura will hold her tongue as long as you mind your business."

"Suppose I'm not okay with that."

"I guess you could kill her. But I don't think you have it in you."

"I could take my chances. It's her word to mine."

"Yes. And who *are* you? Stanley isn't your real name. Neither is Jack. Nor was the name you were using in…New York, wasn't it? You know, I spotted you long before you spotted Henry. I've been following you around for half the summer."

"Impossible. I'd have noticed."

He laughed.

"I didn't look like *this*. Nor was I born looking exactly like Herman Mudgett of New Hampshire. This is why, no matter how many times you work out the angles, you're not going to come out ahead. You may be able to stop Henry, but when I say you'll never see me again I mean it. Even if you *see* me again, you won't know it. In the meantime, Laura will go to the police and you will be forced to flee and start over yet again."

He lowered his gun.

"Take the deal," he said.

"What about him?" I asked, in reference to the large corpse lying nearby.

"Killed by street ruffians in a random attack. No witnesses. Probably won't find him until morning. Do we have a deal?"

I took the deal.

I hated myself for it, for a pretty decent stretch of time, but fortunately self-loathing is one of those things I'm comfortable with.

As promised, I never saw Herman again.

I did see *Henry* again, but not in person. He ended up being decently famous for all the wrong reasons, once someone figured out that people associated with Dr. H.H. Holmes of Chicago had a tendency to disappear. He was caught and convicted, and gained the kind of notoriety that put his picture in all the papers.

They executed him, which was probably for the best.

I have no idea how many people died between the time I could have put a stop to what he was doing, and the time he was arrested, but nobody else does either, because there's no exact headcount on the number of people he killed. (He claimed something like 200, but I don't think anyone believed that.)

Anyway. There's a list of the famous people I've known over the course of my stupidly long life, and depending on how one defines fame, it's a pretty big list. On it, are two of the most famous serial killers in history. They're the only ones that bug me, because I was close enough to stop them, and I didn't.

And people wonder why I drink.

CHAPTER 10

One of the most important rules of the Path was that none of its members were supposed to derive undue financial benefit from its maintenance and use. Or rather, no direct benefit. One wasn't supposed to establish tariffs at the way-stations, or use the Path to smuggle stuff. It functioned as a sort-of Hawala and a sort-of safe deposit box. (I actually prefer to think of them as train station lockers, but you get the point.) It was also a good thing to fall back on in an emergency. Smuggle drugs out of the country: no. Smuggle a legate whose life was in danger out of the country: yes.

I was thinking about this as the plane landed in Chicago. I'd hoped the Path would be a decent way to get into the United States without having to worry that the people arranging the trip might sell us out for a cut of the bounty. I didn't expect to travel quite like this, though, and to that end, I was growing concerned that perhaps someone figured out how to turn my little backdoor to the world into something profitable.

My concern didn't abate when we touched down in a private field, where a limousine was waiting.

Mirella noted my interest in the limo.

"I have never seen you so displeased to have a driver at your disposal," she said. "Were you hoping for a hatchback?"

"I was hoping for something a little less conspicuous, yeah."

"This way is faster."

"You're not the one with a bounty on your head. I prefer the anonymity of crowds. How are you feeling?"

"Don't worry about me," she said, with just the right amount of gruff in her voice to ensure that I would continue to worry very much. "Let's solve our mystery."

The driver was an Asian fellow named Han. He met us at the trunk of the car, bowed deeply, then loaded our suitcases in the trunk. I was about to suggest a destination for us—my instinct was to head directly downtown—when he shoved a hotel room key into my hand.

"The Path provides," he said.

"That's great, but we were really looking to keep a low profile," I said.

I didn't mean that a low profile meant not staying in a hotel; it meant not staying in a *good* one. Given my self-identification as founder had so far gotten us a private jet and a chauffeured limousine, I was a little concerned that the lodgings on the other end of this key was of the five-star variety. I like high-end hotels just fine, but not if staying in one will get me killed.

"This concern was anticipated," he said. "It is a very unpleasant hotel."

"Lovely," Mirella muttered.

"That sounds wonderful," Thelonius said. "The ramshackle establishments always have better stories. Hello, Han, my name is Thelonius! Would it be all right if I rode up front?"

≈

he hotel was, as promised, unpleasant—a scary-looking eight story beast on the South Side of Chicago. It took up half a block, and was conveniently close to both a subway station and a walk-in clinic. I needed the former, not the latter, but I suspected most of the clientele leaned the other way. The lobby make me want to go get a tetanus shot, and I don't even need those.

The lobby also had a bar, which was great news.

"I will leave you now," Han said. He was standing in front of our luggage in the aforementioned lobby. His limo was double-parked outside, and probably about to get stripped for parts.

"Okay, thanks," I said.

"The Chicago way-station is always available for your use, if you require."

He handed over a cell phone. It was a flip-phone, the kind of thing that looked state-of-the-art a decade or so ago. (Although all phones look state-of-the-art to me; I don't even understand how land-lines work.)

"What's this for?" I asked.

"If you need assistance, call the number in the preset. There is only one."

"What manner of assistance?" Mirella asked.

"That was unspecified," he said. "My understanding is that there are no limits to the nature or urgency of the assistance we will be providing."

"Who instructed you, exactly?" I asked.

"That was also unspecified, sir."

"Another legate?"

"As I said—"

"Right, that's okay," I said, slipping the phone in my pocket. "Thanks again."

I could hear my old tech guru, Tcheckhy, lecturing me about how easy it was to track someone through their cell phone. It was definitely true that with the phone they could follow our movements during the day, and since they booked the hotel they also knew where we were staying, down to the room number. The smart play would have been to toss the phone in the trash and find a different hotel. I wasn't going to do that, but it's what I was supposed to do.

"You aren't keeping that?" Mirella asked as Han exited the lobby, unquestionably thinking along the same lines.

"If anyone other than a representative of the Path had handed it to me, then no, I wouldn't."

"Trust the Path, then."

"Trust the Path."

She shook her head, but didn't try to talk me in another direction.

The key went to one room with a double bed and something that approximated a couch for a third person. It was a little gratifying to see that whoever was making the plans on the other end of the Path didn't know enough about us to register for two rooms. It certainly wasn't due to a lack of availability at the hotel, which appeared to have hourly rates, and highly flexible vacancies.

An hour later, Mirella and I were down in the lobby bar, to discuss how to proceed next, and to give Thelonius the room for a proper shower.

"So," Mirella said, over a neat bourbon that may have been distilled in a bathtub somewhere in the basement, based on the taste. "Now we are in Chicago. What's the next part of your plan?"

"We need to get downtown," I said. "The train across the street can get us there. We'll head to the Loop."

"Yes. And then what?"

"Well I don't know."

Eve arrived at the island with only the clothing on her back as evidence of her travels. For most people, that wouldn't be worth anything, but most people don't shoplift to dress themselves, as she clearly did.

There was a plastic clip on her blouse. It was one of those things that would destroy the product (the blouse)—somehow—if anyone tried to remove it without the proper unlocking mechanism. Given what I knew about her, it was probably well within her abilities to get the clip off by other means, and it also probably never occurred to her. She probably thought it just came with the blouse.

As we learned, it was possible to track this device back to the store in which it was employed, provided one gained access to the right database. This was what Jacques had to look up for us, apparently at great expense.

So now, we knew the following: at some time in the past year, Eve was in Chicago for long enough to steal clothing from a department store on Wabash.

The problem was, we didn't know what good that was going to do us. Getting to Chicago was the first thing. After that…

"We shouldn't go to the store," Mirella said. "You know that, yes? The price is still on your head, and even if we've decided to trust Jacques, he may not be the only one aware of our destination."

"I don't know what else to do. The store is the only lead we have."

I was hoping just by walking into the place, I'd be struck by some sort of *eureka* moment, and then we would know what to do next. It wouldn't be the first time it had worked out that way. I don't think I ever had this little to work with before, though.

Plus, Mirella was right: even if I had that highly unlikely moment of realization, it wouldn't do me any good if a sniper took my head off as soon as I walked back outside.

"Suppose we just wandered about?" Mirella said. "She was in Chicago, and now we are. It will make sense eventually."

"Wander about," I said, laughing. "Have you ever been to Chicago?"

"No. But you have."

"Not since the war," I said.

I think I probably lived in Chicago longer than in any other city in the U.S. I nearly died there twice: once in a speakeasy fire, and once in a… well, in another bar, in an aborted mob hit. I should have maybe learned the lesson to not spend so much time in the bars there. Instead, I decided not to spend so much time in Chicago as a whole.

"Which war?" she asked.

"Um. Which one had the Germans on the other side?"

"Both world wars."

"Right. That doesn't narrow it down much."

"It reduces the possibilities to two."

"Nazi Germans," I clarified.

"World War two, then. Perhaps a lot has changed since."

"Oh, I'm sure it has. But I don't think there's a chance it's gotten *less* complicated. Wandering around here could take a really long time."

She shrugged.

"We'll start downtown, but stay away from the department store. Being large and busy should largely work to our advantage. You'll be harder to shoot."

~

Over the course of the next week, we spent the daylight hours riding the L, hopping off at one location or another, and wandering around. It turned out to be the case that my prior experience with Chicago was largely unhelpful, which became obvious almost as soon as the skyline came into view.

A hundred years earlier, Chicago and New York City were almost constantly trying to outdo one another in a competition to see who could build the tallest skyscraper. (I just assume this stopped happening, but maybe not.) That little competition apparently deposited a tremendous number of large buildings in downtown Chicago. Possibly more than in New York City, but Chicago always had a lot more room to work with.

I'm not saying nothing was familiar, but what was familiar was usually surrounded by enough unfamiliar things that I couldn't be entirely sure why it was familiar. Blessedly, the street map was still about the same, so I was usually able to orient myself pretty well.

There were no *eureka* moments to be had, though, not in that first week. The highlight was that after spending the day looking for something helpful, we spent the evenings sampling mixed drinks in the local bars.

Day eight was when Mirella suggested we modify our approach.

"At the very least," she said, "we should consider changing hotels and adjusting our schedule if we're to continue with this. We're creating a vulnerability, by doing essentially the same thing each time."

"We aren't doing the same thing," I said. "We're getting off at different stops each day."

This conversation was taking place on the train, on a part of the elevated line called the Loop. It took us right past Wabash, and that department store, which was somewhat ironically one of the few stops we hadn't gotten off at yet. We'd gotten to the Loop by way of an inbound train that we picked up outside of the hotel. We did this every morning.

"You know what I mean, Adam. This is basic craft."

"I know, I know. So we'll switch hotels."

What she wasn't saying was that this was turning into a dead end. The problem was that we didn't have any other ends to try, aside from going back to the island and waiting for Eve to recover her memory or Mirella to dissolve, whichever came first.

"Maybe if we knew why she came to Chicago," Mirella said.

"Maybe. But I think I know the answer already. She came here because she'd seen me here. I know that sounds a little egotistical, but the last thing I said to her was to try and reconnect with the world. I might have even suggested she get a job somewhere. If she was going to do that, a city in which she'd seen me do that exact thing would make some sense."

"Well then, if you suggested this, and she came here, someone in this city might know her, and what she did while she was here."

Somehow, this hadn't occurred to me. I couldn't imagine Eve making friends with people, even though that was my exact recommendation.

"That doesn't get us any closer to where we want to be," I said.

"It might. It's a...where is the imp?"

I turned to check. He'd been occupying a seat at the other end of the car, engaging strangers in conversation and generally being the guy I would have imagined people found creepy, but they somehow never did. Except now he wasn't doing that, because the seat was free.

"There," Mirella said, pointing out the window.

Thelonius was on the train platform, heading for the nearest staircase with a single-mindedness that didn't fit him at all.

"Well," I said. "Isn't that odd."

This part of the L was, as I said, called the Loop, and it was called that because it looped. However, the train we were on didn't just keep going around; it did one circuit and then went back up the track it came down, stopped at the end, and came back down again. Fortunately, there were four other trains using the Loop, and at least one of them went counter-clockwise around, all of which is to say that Mirella and I were able to get off at the next stop, hop a train heading back, and get to the exit Thelonius decided on his own initiative to take, in a lot less time than it could have.

"Maybe he saw someone he could harass into telling him a new story," Mirella groused, as we ran down the steps to the street.

"Let's find him and ask."

What we discovered on the street level was another reminder that there are too many people in the world: it was something like three in the afternoon, on a weekday, and the whole area was full of people. This appeared to be true at every stop, but it was still ridiculous.

"Don't they all have jobs?" I asked.

"Perhaps their job involves walking from one building to the next."

We were across from an outdoor shopping plaza nestled between a number of decent-sized buildings. A hundred years ago, any one of them would have competed for tallest-in-the-world. Now, they were one of many.

"Over there," Mirella said, pointing to a particularly congested area. I couldn't see him, but her eyes were better than mine so I took her word for it.

We ran across and meandered though the crowd until Thelonius came into view. He was standing beside a bench and spinning around slowly, while looking skyward, acting just strangely enough to ensure people gave him a wide berth.

"Thelonius," I said. "What are you doing?"

"Oh. Hello."

He continued his slow spin.

"Are you looking for something?"

"Yes."

"What is it?"

"Why, I don't know." He stopped spinning to address us more directly. "If I knew, I wouldn't be looking, would I?"

Mirella laughed, shrugged, and took a seat on the bench.

"Perhaps he's looking for snipers," she said. "He's brought us to the ideal locale for it."

"The whole city is ideal for snipers," I said. To Thelonius, I said, "why did you come here?"

"I think I'm supposed to be here."

"Um, okay."

As far as I could tell, this part of downtown looked like every other part. I didn't see the appeal.

"How come?" I asked, hoping the answer wasn't going to be a five-hour story. He had a lot of those.

"Well," he said, "there is this curious passage in the prophesies. I've never been able to tease out an understanding. Not until now. *The foul hog tide steers fish to market, where the wind has answers.*"

"You're right, that is curious. It sounds like nonsense."

"It *all* sounds like nonsense at first, Adam. That's what makes them interesting! The possibilities are nearly without end. But this one, I've never been able to make anything out of. Today, I think I understand. And I think before now I wasn't supposed to, which means I'm in the right place at the right time."

"But what does it *mean*, imp?" Mirella asked, impatiently.

"Look up, my dear. At the sign you can see from the elevated track."

We looked.

At the edge of the open courtyard was a billboard advertising a weekly farmer's market. The artwork attached to the words included: a trussed pig, a cow, a chicken and a fish.

"A tied hog, a steer, a fowl, and a fish," I said.

"My mistake was hearing 'fish' and 'tide' and imagining it related to tidal forces. We were on an island, after all. I suspect that same misapprehension allowed for my recall to attach an 's' at the end of 'steer'."

"*The wind has answers,*" I said, finishing the passage. "The windy city."

Incidentally, I lived in Chicago when it got the name *the windy city*, and I'm still surprised the city embraced that nickname. It was originally meant as an insult.

"Yes! And so, I leapt from the train to follow the prophesy."

"You could have told us beforehand."

"Oh, I knew you'd catch up."

Thelonius went back to spinning in a slow circle, looking somewhat skyward. I had no idea why he thought this was what he was supposed to be doing once arriving at the prophesied location, but it was no better or worse than any other thing he could have been doing, I guess.

I looked at Mirella, who shrugged.

"We'll look around," she said.

We left Thelonius to his bench, split up, and walked a wide circle around the courtyard. There was no farmer's market today—it was not, evidently, Wednesday, which was when it was supposed to be happening—so all we had to examine was the various individuals moving from one end of the plaza to the other, at a variety of speeds.

Nobody seemed particularly noteworthy. I did catch the fact that at least three types of non-humans were represented in the Chicago business class—I spotted two elves, a goblin, and an incubus—but that was only a little interesting.

After completing one clockwise circuit to offset Mirella's counter-clockwise circuit, we met up again at the bench. Thelonius had stopped spinning, apparently transfixed by something on the top of a nearby building. It sounded as if he was breathing heavy.

"Is he okay?" I asked Mirella.

"You are the expert in imps, not me."

"Is he having an asthma attack? Thelonius, hey, are you okay?"

He held up a finger to indicate he heard me, and continued with the weird breathing thing.

"Oh," Mirella said. "He's talking to a pixie."

"What?"

"There's a pixie above his head. She's moving too fast for you to see."

"Then she's moving too fast for him to see, too," I rightly pointed out. Imps weren't known for exceptional eyesight. "How does he know?"

"He probably hears her. I can't, but his ears are better."

"And he's talking to her?"

"*The wind has the answers,*" she said.

Thelonius held up his hand, and waited. Presently, the pixie landed on his finger, as a parakeet might.

"Adam, Mirella, let me introduce you to Dee."

Pixies are tiny women with gossamer wings. Picture Tinkerbell—who was clearly modeled after one—only with no clothes.

"Hello, Dee," I said.

"Hi," she squeaked.

"I'm not sure what just happened, Thelonius. Did you just tame a pixie by breathing heavily?"

He laughed.

"Adam, in all your time, you truly never learned to speak their language?"

"I…"

"And she is not *tamed*! She is in *love*! It's quite a story! His name is Rick, and he works in one of these buildings. She's waiting for him now."

"Is Rick human?"

"I believe so, yes!"

If this Rick person managed to tame a pixie, I definitely wanted to have a conversation with him. It wasn't the sort of thing ordinary people did.

"What is her story?" Mirella asked. "Try and give us a short version."

"I will give you the highlights. It seems she was introduced to Rick by a woman, whom she also liked, but not as much as she likes Rick. Rick liked the woman more than he likes Dee, and so Dee is glad she went away."

"This other woman…what did she call herself?" I asked.

"Dee never knew her name. But she had alabaster skin and long red hair."

~

*D*ee explained that she spent every weekday waiting for Rick to finish work, because he didn't like it when she went into the office with him. She couldn't tell time, but knew he showed up around when the plaza went from busy to extremely busy, so we took that to mean five P.M. or thereabouts. That gave us an hour to try and tease out a better understanding of how a human ended up with a tame pixie. (Or, how a pixie fell in love with a tame human, take your pick.)

It was hard to piece together. Since the time I met my first pixie, my assumption was that they were somewhere between unintelligent and naïve, but it turns out this was because I was trying to talk to them using whatever human language I happened to be conversant in at that time, rather than in their native language. I would have probably taken some time to learn it, had I known such a native tongue existed, but no pixie ever bothered to clue me in about this.

I didn't know how Thelonius picked it up, but assumed it was a professional requirement of some sort. Given the amount of information pixies could theoretically be privy to, being able to converse meaningfully with one had to be worth the time. It made me glad neither species took up espionage as a calling.

We relocated from the center of the plaza to a walkway between buildings. I'd have called it an alley, but that implied something that wasn't commonly in use, and this was. Still, it was slightly more out-of-the-way than the bench, which satisfied at least one of us.

"We shouldn't remain here," Mirella said, even after we moved. "We're too exposed."

She said a version of this almost every day, so our tour of Chicago, while exhaustive, had been conducted at a rapid walking pace the entire time. She didn't want us standing still.

"It won't be much longer," I said. "Besides, do you think someone's going to fire a gun in the middle of the day in the middle of the city?"

"It doesn't have to be a gun. And yes."

This, too, was a conversation we'd had a version of multiple times.

Through Thelonius, we got bits of information from Dee.

She'd previously had a pixie companion, named Cee (because, of course) who became ill. The red-haired woman called Dee one night, and Dee led her and Rick to find and help Cee, but Cee died anyway.

When I asked Dee how Cee died, she said that the red-haired woman did it, but only because she had to, because Cee was suffering.

"What was she suffering from?" I asked.

Thelonius whistled back and forth with Dee for a few seconds, then looked rather grave.

"Cee was melting," he said.

"Well, we're definitely in the right place. Ask her—"

"Hang on."

She wheezed something and then flew off.

"Rick is here," Thelonius said.

Dee disappeared into the crowd in the plaza.

"I've lost her," I said.

"I have her," Mirella said. "Near the bench. Do you see that tall black man?"

There were a few tall black men among the masses, but only one near the bench. He was standing still, while everyone else was in motion, which also helped with the identification.

He looked alarmed.

"Did you tell her to introduce us?" I asked Thelonius.

"Yes!"

"And that we're friendly?"

"Certainly!"

"I don't think that's translating well."

"He's running," Mirella confirmed.

Rick took one look at the three of us, turned, and ran in the exact opposite direction.

"He's athletic," Mirella added. She wasn't wrong. The man was in a suit and tie, and shoes that were definitely not meant for sprinting, and yet he was sprinting quite well. "Am I allowed to damage him?"

"Try not to," I said.

"All right," she sighed. "Keep him headed in that direction and I'll circle around. Look out for snipers."

She took off to the left, while Thelonius and I ran straight ahead. Well, I ran; he sort of just tumbled. Native athleticism is not what one keeps an imp around for.

It was a little easier getting through the crowd than I expected, because people were getting out of the way, on seeing us running directly at them. It helped that once I reached the bench I was heading down a path Rick had already cleared. This also made it easier to nearly catch up.

The far side of the plaza was defined by the street we'd originally crossed when exiting the L. Traffic on it was considerably worse than before, which actually made it easier to cross on foot; none of the cars were moving.

Rick got to the other side, went under the tracks, then crossed the street on the other side of the tracks, and entered what looked like a residential neighborhood.

When I lived in Chicago, high-end residential addresses that were also downtown were decently rare, in that while they definitely existed, they weren't exactly all over the place. I didn't recall what this section looked like a hundred years earlier, in other words, but if it was residential back then, those residences were probably slums.

I made it across both streets and to the neighborhood side in time to see Rick disappear halfway down the street. It looked like he'd ducked into a proper alley. It would have been a better decision had I not seen him do it, because in theory I could have just run right past. I did see him do it, though, and so I turned in behind him.

It turned out I was underestimating exactly how on top of things this guy was. If anything, he'd lagged a little in order to make sure I saw him cut down the alley, which he hadn't picked at random.

Halfway down, he stepped behind a Dumpster. I was about to shout something like *we mean you no harm, I just want to ask you some questions*, when he popped back up again, holding a shotgun.

"Hey man," he said. "How about if you fuck off?"

I stopped, and raised my hands.

"That's a good choice," I said. "Wide spread, you could clear the whole alley with one shot. Very smart."

"Yes, thank you, I know. Wanna see me do it? Get outta here."

I have had a lot of guns pointed at me in my time. More arrows than guns, but still, a lot of guns. I wish I could say it's easy to tell how likely it is that you're going to end up getting shot, by recognizing one or two specific characteristics, but since so far nobody's actually shot me, I couldn't say for sure. I do tend to find the ones who are legitimately freaking out while also pointing the gun to be more alarming. The barrel could shake all over the place, which improved the odds that if they did fire, they'd miss, but they always seemed the most likely to fire. The ones who presented as calm and cool—as Rick did—came off as the least likely to shoot, but most likely to kill me if they did.

They were also the type that seemed easiest to reason with.

"Is this how Chicago is nowadays?" I asked. "Shotguns just lying around in alleys?"

"Let's say I figured somebody would come for me one day."

"All right. So it's your gun. I guess that means you already know it's loaded and not likely to blow up in your face."

"I notice you're not fucking off," he said.

"No, but I will soon."

"It's okay, we can wait for the other two to get here, save me the trouble of reloading."

"I really think you have the wrong idea."

"Sure. I'm gonna believe someone that just chased me through town now that he's got a loaded gun in his face? What is it I have the wrong idea about?"

"A couple of things," I said. "We really are friendly. I think your pixie probably missed part of the explanation. Also, we're only waiting for one of us to get here."

Mirella's sword touched the side of Rick's neck. He froze, and also didn't pull the trigger, which I appreciated.

"You should put down the gun," she said.

"How long have you been behind me? I didn't even hear you."

"The gun."

"Dee, how come you didn't say anything?" he said, to the air above his head.

Mirella stepped around him partway, so that she was in his line of sight. Her free hand was a closed fist.

"She tried for my eyes, an attack I anticipated. She's fine, but if you don't put down that shotgun, as I've asked you very nicely to do, I will squeeze."

"All right, all right."

He lowered the gun to the ground, slowly. I appreciated this too; it's not the kind of thing you're supposed to drop from a height.

Then Thelonius arrived.

"Goodness!" he gasped. "Did I miss anything?"

"Look," Rick said, "I'm just trying to scare you off, okay? I don't know who sent you or what you're supposed to do to me, but as long as you're a threat, your lives are in danger."

"How very altruistic," Mirella said. "Explain." She'd neither lowered her sword nor released Dee.

"She won't let you hurt me."

"The pixie?"

"No, not her."

"He means Eve," I said.

He looked at me, and nodded slowly. He looked haunted by a memory; I recognized the expression well enough.

"Last goblin to hold a sword up to my neck ended up with her arm bursting out of his chest. I'm not kidding."

"I believe you. But she isn't here."

"Sure. If you know what she can do, you know there's no way either of us can be sure she's not here, or not going to be here in a minute or two."

I was starting to get the impression Rick had spent a lot of his free time worrying that Eve might do exactly that. I'd assumed he was a friend and perhaps lover—he was certainly attractive enough. (I didn't know what her type was, but 'attractive, young, muscular' was probably about right.) But if they were friends and/or lovers at one time, that time was probably over, as clearly, he was afraid of her.

What was sort of interesting was that he wasn't afraid of what she might do to him; he was afraid of what she might do to us.

Whatever he'd gone through, it must have been pretty interesting.

"I'm very sure she isn't here right now," I said. "Because the last time I saw her she was in a coma, and I don't think that's changed."

"A coma?"

"She's sick. That's why we've come to Chicago. We're trying to understand why."

He laughed.

"Now I know you're playing with me," he said. "She can't get sick."

"I know, but she is. How well did you know her?"

"Well enough."

"Maybe she mentioned me, then. My name is Adam."

"You mean, bringer of all terrible things in this world Adam? Person she hates more than anyone Adam? And you want me to believe you just left her, she's sick, and you're just trying to help? Come on."

I laughed.

"Yeah, I agree, that sounds like a stretch. Mirella, lower the sword and let the pixie go. I think it's probably sending the wrong message."

"He had a gun trained on you."

"Sure, but he didn't pull the trigger."

She lowered the sword, with great reluctance, then held her fist up to her mouth.

"I like my eyes, little one," she said, before releasing Dee. "Don't try that again."

The alley was filled with a frantic buzzing for a few seconds, as Dee dive-bombed the air around us, before settling on Rick's shoulder.

"You okay?" he muttered. I admit to being slightly relieved that Rick didn't speak pixie language too. It was awkward enough already.

"Okay," she said. "Go home now?"

"Nearly."

"You weren't expecting *us* with that gun, were you?" I asked.

"I was expecting someone. Not you specifically. I figured somebody would turn up one day, after what I know."

"That's interesting. We're here because of what you know too. Only, we didn't plan to get violent about it. Who's the someone you were expecting?"

"I dunno. They, them, somebody." He looked at Mirella. "You're a goblin, right?"

"Yes," she said.

"I hate that I know that. I hate that I can't look around and see just people anymore." He nodded down the alley. "You, big guy. Human?"

"I am an imp, sir," Thelonius said.

"Yeah? Super. Didn't know about you. That's some crazy ears." Rick turned back to me.

"How is she sick?" he asked. "Is her skin all sticky?"

"Yes," I said. "You've seen it before, right? Dee's companion."

"Yeah, her. But, I mean, look around. Everybody's got it."

He turned to Mirella to add: "Talk to your people about it, it's no secret. And if Eve's sick…damn. Maybe we're all going down."

"So, it's an epidemic," I said.

"Nah. Not really. Sure, if you want to call it that, but that's not the word I'd use. It's a genocide is what it is."

Well, that was considerably different from an epidemic. I suddenly felt cold.

"At whose hand?" I asked.

"They. Them. Somebody," he said.

"I need more than that if I'm going to stop it."

He laughed.

"It's already happening, man. I think you're too late. I'll tell you what: look up a company called Holitix. They used to have a facility on the edge of town. Burned down last year. I don't think it'll help any, but that's all I've got, so if you feel like torturing me or something to get more information, anything else I have to say will be made up to get you to stop torturing me."

"It's a start," I said.

"Great. Can I go now?"

"Yes, but we may need to get in touch with you again."

"I would very much rather you didn't. But look, if Eve pulls through…tell her I was thinking of her. She still scares the hell out of me, but I was thinking of her anyway."

"You want me to tell her all that?"

"Yeah."

He started heading down the alley.

"Do you want your gun back?" I asked.

"Nah, you keep it. I'll just remember to run down a different alley next time. I got 'em hidden all over."

~

*W*e didn't keep the shotgun. I was in favor of holding onto it—because I didn't want to find myself in a situation in the future where I had to say, *boy, I wish I had a shotgun right about now*—but we decided trying to get it across town was going to end up being more trouble than it was worth.

After discarding the idea of just sliding the gun back in the sleeve Rick stored it in (in a crack in the wall) we dismantled it and scattered the pieces in the Dumpster. Someone could dive in and reassemble it if they knew to do so, but they'd have to swim through a lot of rotten kung-pao first.

"Holitix," Mirella repeated, as we headed back to the L.

"Yes," I said. "That's what the man said. I've never heard of them."

"I think I may have."

"I think I have as well," Thelonius said. "I believe they are quite large."

"It should be simple enough to look them up online," I said. "Do we have anything with the Internet on it?"

I appreciate that this sounds like a naïve question, but the truth was we weren't traveling with a computer, and the two phones I had—the flip phone provided by Han, and the one I used to contact Grundle on the island—were both of the dumb variety. Unless someone else had a smart phone or some other kind of device, we were going to have to find another solution.

"I don't," Thelonius said.

"I don't either," Mirella said. "A library, if we can find one."

"Or an Internet café?" I said. "Are those still a thing?"

Mirella grabbed me by the arm with a sort of urgency that indicated bad news was coming.

"They've found us," she muttered.

Looking around was pointless, but I tried looking around anyway. We had just reached the street we'd need to cross to get under the tracks for the L. There were a hundred people and dozens of cars in view; I had no idea what was setting off her alarms.

"Where?" I asked.

"Be ready."

There was a whistling sound. It was manifestly different from the one the pixie made a few minutes earlier. I knew what this one was, but it was probably the first time I'd heard it while standing on a street corner in a modern city.

It was the sound of arrows in flight.

Mirella took out the arrow that would have otherwise landed in my head, with her sword, at the same time pulling us to the ground. We landed hard on the pavement behind a parked car that was sporting a recently-added arrow that was embedded in its hood. It was impossible to tell if that arrow was fired at the same time as the one that nearly hit me, or not, because everything was happening at once.

"Are you hit?" she asked.

"What? Where are they?"

"There's only one, above. Are you hit?"

"Above? The tracks?"

"Adam."

"No, I'm not hit. Are you?"

"I'm not. Where's the imp?"

"I'm all right," Thelonius shouted, from behind another parked car. I rolled over to get a better look at him, while trying to keep all of my body parts behind the car.

Thelonius was examining an arrow that was stuck in his shoulder, with a sort of dispassionate indifference that strongly indicated he was in shock.

"I'm sure it missed all the important parts," he said. "You two run ahead; I'll catch up."

PART II

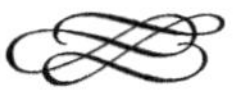

THE ROAD TO HELL

CHAPTER 11

*I*t's not every day a man is hit by an arrow at rush hour in the middle of an American city. Or, I imagine, *any* city these days.

That being the case, Thelonius made the evening news.

They didn't identify him by name, thankfully. I think if they had, a lot more people would know about it, because Thelonius D'Artagnan is one of those names that ends up being popular on the Internet. But no, they had him down as *local man*, which was untrue twice over. He was neither a man, nor—so far as I knew—a native Chicagoan. (Not that I knew where he was from.)

We learned of our imp's newfound fame from the television in the seedy hotel room at the seedy hotel. This was a couple of hours after leaving the scene ourselves.

According to Mirella, the assassin had been on the elevated track. After his initial volley, he (or she) disappeared, which was wise, because there were police only a couple of blocks away, and their response time was excellent. We barely escaped the scene ourselves before they dropped a cordon on the whole area.

"Goblin, I assume," I said, as the news went from *weird assault with medieval weaponry* to the weather.

"Yes," Mirella confirmed. She was in the bathroom, checking for wounds, or so she said. I think she was actually looking for sticky spots. In the days since she'd revealed that she was stricken with the disease, I'd had very few opportunities to glimpse her in anything other than a fully concealing outfit, so I was pretty sure it was getting worse and she just didn't want to talk about it. Not that there was anything I could do.

"Bad shot, for one of you. I'm surprised he missed."

"If you think so, you misunderstand what happened. He fired only twice, but let loose three arrows in the first volley, and one in the second, which struck the car we were behind. If you and I had been standing where we were supposed to be for the initial round, he'd have hit all of us."

"But he only hit Thelonius because…"

"I could only save one of you, yes. If he lives, I'll have to apologize."

"I wonder why all three, if the contract is only on my head."

"I was wondering the same."

She emerged from the bathroom in a towel, shaking her head before I even got a word out.

"I feel fine," she said.

"Wasn't going to ask."

She nodded at the TV.

"Should we retrieve him from the hospital?" she asked. "He knows more than he should."

"Do you think someone looking for us will grab him and torture him until he tells them how to find us?"

"It's not an impossible notion."

"It's not, but it isn't like Jacques had any luck getting information from him in Paris."

"Jacques is human. We have no guarantee the next inquisitor will be."

"Then maybe we should."

"Except they would expect us to."

"Then maybe we shouldn't," I said. "I'm not sure what the right answer is. I'm not even sure what we're supposed to be doing next. Do you have any ideas?"

I'm not saying my lack of creativity and increased aggravation had nothing to do with the fact that our cheap hotel room didn't come with a stocked mini fridge, but it was a factor. A good stiff drink was needed.

"Holitix," Mirella said. "That's what Rick said. That's our next step."

"Yeah, but I've never heard of them."

She sighed, and pulled a cellphone from one of our pieces of luggage, throwing it on the bed.

"I don't like you when you're this grouchy. Call Grundle; I'm taking a shower."

"*Talk to your people*," I said.

"What?"

"That was one of the other things Rick said, along with *genocide*. He looked at you and said to talk to your people. Is that a thing? Do goblins have some sort of party line?"

"No. I don't think that's what he meant by my people. Goblins, yes, partly. But he meant all of us."

"Us."

"Non-humans. We have…Adam, you know how many of us there are, don't you? Across the species, we number in the millions, surely."

"Nobody's managed to conduct a census, but sure."

"I ask because when I told you about the island, you had no idea how extensive the underground network of other-species really was."

"Sure, but it was a secret island."

"We have our own doctors, too. And dentists, and morticians, and insurance salesmen, and, you get my point."

"Doctors."

"As I said."

"Like Doc Cambridge?"

She hissed, because she didn't care for him.

"Yes, I suppose. Although his medical prowess ventures into superstition, where a general practitioner might remain fixed on known medical solutions to known medical problems."

"I think we should talk to one."

"Adam, I'm fine."

"No, no. I mean, yes, for Baal's sake, see a doctor already, but no, that's not what I mean. Just go over what we know: there's a disease nobody ever saw before; Eve has it; the last person we can connect to her seems to know what we're talking about and uses the word *genocide*, mentions a company I've never heard of and tells you to go ask a doctor for details. So maybe we'd better ask one of your special practitioners if they've seen it before, and what they're doing about it. Do these secret underground medical networks have symposiums or something? Or peer reviewed journals?"

"I don't know, I'm not a doctor."

"All right, well how do we find one?"

"They're by referral only. We would have to find a goblin and gain his…"

She trailed off, staring at the television. The news story related to sports, so I didn't think that was what had her so transfixed.

"What" I asked.

"We already know where to go to find a doctor."

"Thelonius? Will they call one for him?"

"It's a process, but yes. Every hospital has one or two specialists. He'll have had one assigned by now."

"So we have to go the hospital."

"Yes."

"Where they'll expect us to show up."

"Yes."

"Cool," I said. "It's a plan. Take your shower. I'm going to head to the bar, and make that phone call."

~

I was on my third glass of extremely bottom-shelf bourbon by the time I called up Grundle. I'd like to say I needed to be in the proper headspace to hear that Eve still couldn't remember anything, but it was more likely the case that alcohol was, at that moment, more important than an update.

So I was surprised to hear that I'd missed a few things.

"Say that again," I said, a little too loudly. I was at a table in the back of a space that doubled as a bar and the hotel lobby. I was the only patron, so my volume probably didn't matter too terribly much.

"She disappeared," Grundle said. "Eight days ago. I tried calling, but the line wouldn't open."

"Eight days? I was on a plane eight days ago, I think. You should have tried again."

"Yes, I apologize. I expected a call at some point, and here you are. I didn't think it would have mattered, you knowing. You can't question her if she's not here any longer."

"Grundle…" I held back a few curse words, even though he was right about all of that. I was basically back in the same place I was for a few millennia: knowing she existed, but not knowing how to find her. "Did she say anything? Before she disappeared?"

"I'll ask Lew. But it is good news yes? She recovered from the disease."

"Yes, fine, it's good news."

I was incredibly aggravated, actually, because at least a part of me felt as if I was doing all of this to rescue her specifically. Considering my girlfriend was now dealing with the same disease, this was a sort of awful thing to realize about myself, but there it was.

"As for the other thing," Grundle said, "I'm afraid I have nothing for you."

"The contract?"

"Yes. I don't think I'll be able to get what you need without going through Dimitri. Are you sure you want to keep this from him?"

"All right, bring him in. Only…try not to make too much noise."

I hung up, and wondered if I'd just made a big mistake. I could probably trust Dimitri, but every person he spoke to had to be equally trustworthy, and I didn't know enough about his organization to feel comfortable about that.

"You look no happier," Mirella said, as she approached the table. She looked geared up and ready to go. "Is it the alcohol?"

"It's crap, but that's not why. Eve's all better, and she left the island."

"Where did she go?"

"Where does she ever go?"

Mirella laughed.

"Of course."

She took a sip from my glass, and grimaced.

"Come on," she said. "We have to figure out which hospital our imp is in."

This was no small matter, because Chicago apparently has a lot of hospitals. Mirella's suggestion was to use the bow and arrow she apparently had in her suitcase—I didn't know she owned any such thing, but there's an outside chance every goblin is given one when they turn sixteen or something—and shoot someone downtown, then see where the ambulance took them.

I'm not saying I didn't consider it. But, summoning up memories from when I spent fifty-odd years in this city, I decided Cook County Hospital was probably the best place to start.

Then we had to get a cab there. The guy at the hotel's front desk looked deeply perplexed when we asked him to call us a cab, as if this was something nobody did, ever.

"Why don't you just Uber it?" he asked.

Then I was deeply confused.

I appreciate that technology changes at a certain pace, and sometimes that pace is a lot faster than what I may be accustomed to, and also that the pace has increased over the past couple of decades. But when that technological change involves borrowing words from other languages, it just gives me fits. "Uber" is a German word, and it isn't even a verb, and since I speak both English and German fluently (along with most of their antecedent languages) what I heard was *why don't you just above it?*

I looked to Mirella, in case I either misheard or was in the midst of having a stroke, but she looked equally confused.

Then I wondered if maybe the word "uber" had been adopted recently into English, because that happened all the time, except that really, that's how this language got the word "over", so there was no need to adopt it a second time.

The man at the desk waved a cell phone around, as if this explained matters better. It didn't.

"Um, no, just a cab, thanks," I said.

He grunted, and performed an excavation of the cluttered desktop until he came across a piece of paper with phone numbers on it.

"Uber would be way faster, but all right," he muttered.

~

J don't really do hospitals. The last one I was in was on the island, but I couldn't say how long it had been before that. I basically thought of hospitals the same way I thought of doctors and medicine in general, which is to say I had a poor opinion of the entire industry.

Part of it is just that I don't get sick, and when I'm wounded a medical practitioner is nearly useless; the only painkiller that works on me is hard alcohol, and for some reason people with medical degrees aren't cool with that. Another part is that I was around at the advent of medicine—which was routinely grisly and horrifying, especially before anesthesia was invented—and therefore the invention of hospitals.

I know hospitals are viewed somewhat positively these days (as are doctors and medicine) but that's because one expects to come home alive following a visit to a modern hospital. This was certainly not always the case. (Bedlam is a great example, but it was by no means the most extreme.) Hospitals were only occasionally the kind of place one visited in order to recover from whatever ailed you. More often, they served as a secure place to hide all the sick, poor people until they died. A public good to be sure, but less so for the hospitalized than for the people who otherwise stood to pick up the disease from the hospitalized.

They also made for a decent place to study disease, which was another common good that didn't necessarily roll downhill to the actual sufferers of the condition.

Cook County Hospital used to be one of those places, back when it was built, but when we pulled up in the cab it became clear rather quickly that it was no longer precisely that kind of place. Probably. I'm basing that on how it looked. In my day, the hospital was located in a big, scary-looking brick building (until it moved, to a newer scary-looking brick building); now it was in something that looked new and welcoming, and a little like an airport terminal. It declared, architecturally, *don't be afraid* and *come back again soon!* The old edifices were more along the lines of, *abandon all hope, ye who enter.*

We entered—without abandoning hope first—through the emergency room lobby, to the E.R. nurse's station.

That turned out to be the wrong place to go to find someone who had been admitted earlier with an emergency. It was where one went if one was personally experiencing an emergency at that very moment, which we sort of were, only not the kind that the hospital might recognize.

The emergency desk sent us to the admissions desk.

"Name?" the woman at admissions asked.

"Our name?" I asked.

"The patient's name," she said, less-than-patiently.

"Right. Thelonius D'Artagnan."

She stared at me for an extra couple of beats, because that sounded like a made-up name.

"Really," I added, in case this helped.

Her eyes went back down to the computer screen and her fingers tapped away.

"Ah," she said. "Him. Are you family?"

"Are we…"

"Because everyone wants to talk to him, and it's only family allowed."

"Who else wants to talk to him?"

"Reporters. They don't have a name, to them it's just the guy with the arrow in his shoulder. So, are you family?"

"Yes," Mirella said. "He's our father."

The woman behind the desk looked at the two of us with something that registered as skepticism.

"Different mothers," I said.

"Your names?"

"Adam, and Mirella."

She spent so long at her computer that I managed to formulate three distinct plans to find Thelonius without the willing assistance of the hospital. All three included at least one act of violence, so it was a good thing that when she spoke, it was to provide us with useful information.

"He listed you," she said.

"Really?" I asked.

"Yes, is that…? You look surprised."

"We didn't know he was conscious," Mirella said.

"They try to get next-of-kin as soon as they can. Plan for the worst, hope for the best."

She read off the room number and provided us with directions to get there. The directions were stupidly complicated, and involved following colored stripes painted on the floor. This was not improving my perspective on hospitals.

We followed the appropriate stripe to the elevator. On the way up, I took note of the knife in Mirella's hand.

"Trouble?" I asked.

"Not yet. But we should expect a trap, and the place to expect it is at the room, wouldn't you agree?"

"You think they had less trouble figuring out which room he was in than we did? Sis?"

"I'm less inclined to trust bureaucracy to rescue us than you appear to be."

"Well that, and they probably followed the wrong floor stripe."

The doors opened on a corridor that wasn't full of hitmen, which is always a nice surprise. Instead we faced another nurse's desk. From there, we received additional instruction on how to find his room, which included a different-colored stripe, and a buzzer to get through a locked door. I half-expected to come across a minotaur before we found Thelonius.

(Note: I'm kidding; minotaurs aren't real.)

This path took us across half the building, it seemed, to another gathering of nurses. Blessedly, that station was the last test we had to pass before getting to Thelonius's room, which was just on the other side of the desk. The attending nurse walked us to him.

"You can only stay for a short time," she said, on the way there. "Visiting hours end at 8."

"We would like to speak to his doctor," Mirella said, which I was glad about, because until she asked it didn't occur to me that the doctor wouldn't be standing in the room with Thelonius.

"I can have the attending swing by," the nurse said.

"Not the attending doctor. Our…father would have been seen by a specialist. We'd like to speak to that person."

The nurse crinkled her nose, which came off as a mildly repressed expression of displeasure.

"I'll see if he's available," she said.

We went in. Thelonius was awake and alone in a room with two beds. He looked to be in good spirits, but that was his default mode.

"There you are, my friends!" he said, a touch too loudly. The room smelled, oddly, of peppermint.

I closed the door. I didn't know if I was supposed to—all the other doors on this part of the floor appeared to be open—but he sounded like a loud drunk, and a drunk imp could say anything.

"Son and daughter, according to the hospital," I said, "not just friends."

He laughed, a little too long.

His shoulder was in a heavy bandage, and he had an arm lashed to the bed to prevent the IV needle from getting yanked. He was also attached to a monitor registering his heart rate. I knew nothing about what a normal heart rate was, but his seemed slow. Perhaps imp heart rates were just slower.

Mirella sniffed the bandage and checked the IV.

"Mint," she said. "How interesting."

"Yes! It's wonderful!" Thelonius said. "Peppermint! I *love* peppermint!"

There was a light knock on the door, and then a satyr in a doctor's white coat let himself in.

I've always found satyrs to be impossible to mistake for anything else. Every time I come across one mingling among humans and passing himself off as one, I wonder how I could be the only one to notice.

Satyrs are almost all over six-foot-three and really hairy, which can pass as human okay, but they also have ankles that are higher up their legs than human ankles. They tend to walk stiffly upright and wear baggy pants around mixed company, so nobody can see the bend. The gait causes a lot of lifelong back problems.

I took this one to be younger than most, but I was basing that on his beard. Most adult satyrs had big heavy beards they only trimmed reluctantly, while the doctor only had stubble. On the other hand, a big heavy beard was perhaps unprofessionally non-sanitary.

"Hello?" he said. "I'm doctor Ignacius. I understand you were expressing…"

He stopped when he saw the two of us.

"You are not the son and daughter I was told to expect," he said.

"What gave it away?" I asked.

"You could perhaps be. You appear human, and it's possible this man could sire a human child. But not the goblin."

"She could be adopted," I said.

He ignored the suggestion.

"Why are you here? And why does the goblin have a knife in her hand?"

"Mirella, put it away," I said.

Mirella held onto it for a beat and then slid it into whatever sleeve in which it lived.

I've seen very few interactions between goblin and satyr, but I didn't recall any historical animosity between the species. They were different kinds of warriors, certainly. I'd take a satyr over a goblin if the battle were to take place in a forest; otherwise, a goblin would probably be a better bet.

"Thank you," he said, to Mirella.

Under his clipboard, he had what I thought at first was a pen, but which turned out to be a wooden shiv of some sort. The satyros of the Athenian wood used to prohibit the use of metal for any tool, including weaponry. This little knife of his marked him as someone clinging to at least a portion of his people's traditions. It was probably only symbolic, given the metal stethoscope around his neck and the metal clip on the wooden board he was holding. I'm sure as a medical doctor, he had to learn to live with metal needles and scalpels and what-not as well.

Once Mirella had sheathed her knife, he did the same, albeit less dramatically. He had a leather sleeve for it on his belt.

"You must be the other two," he said.

"Other two what?" I asked.

"Eyewitnesses said three people were fired upon. You were the other two."

"Yes, we were there. I was the target. But we aren't here to talk about that."

He raised a bushy eyebrow. Satyrs have real non-verbal cue problems; an eyebrow raise is practically a scream. I had to wonder what his bedside manner was like.

"*You* were," he said. "Why is that? Are you important?"

"That really depends on who you ask. We wanted to talk to you about a different medical problem. In addition to checking on our friend."

"Why does Thelonius smell like peppermint?" Mirella asked.

"Is that the question?"

"No, I just want to know."

"Mint is an opiate for imps. Actual opiates are quite ineffectual."

"That explains a lot about Santa Claus," I said.

"Pardon?"

"Never mind. It's a good thing you were here when he was brought in."

The doctor laughed.

"Someone was shot with an arrow in the middle of downtown Chicago. The local news might not know what to make of such a thing, but I certainly did."

"Do most hospitals have someone like you on staff?"

"Usually, yes. Doubly the case here. This is a teaching hospital, with a long tradition of non-human research. These are surely not the questions you needed answering."

"They're here because these are my friends!" Thelonius declared—again, too loudly. Thankfully, the doctor had left the door closed behind him.

"How is he doing?" I asked.

"The prognosis is good, but I don't recommend moving him for a few days, if you mean to check him out early. His stitches need attending."

"I feel glorious!"

"Yes, Thelonius, thank you," I said. "Doctor, if I describe some symptoms to you, could you tell me if it was something you'd seen before?"

"In whom? An imp?"

"In anyone, human or otherwise."

"Well, I don't know. Let's find out."

I gave him as detailed a description as I could of the melting disease (for want of a better term,) and watched as his expression went from generic-helpful-doctor to inscrutable-satyr. Honestly, there was hardly a difference, but I'm well-versed in satyr facial expressions, such as they are. I took the change to mean he was familiar with the condition.

"Do you know someone who has this?" he asked.

Then he looked at Mirella. I was about to say, no, not her, other people, when she rolled up her sleeve to show the patch. It had grown since I last looked at it.

"Yes, put that away," he said. "You should be in quarantine."

"Quarantine where?" she asked. "Here?"

"I don't know. Somewhere."

He'd taken two steps backwards. Now, again, I don't know a lot about doctors and don't deal with them all that often, but backpedaling from a sick person was sort of the opposite of what I was expecting.

"You've seen it before," I said. "But you don't know anything about it. You don't even know how it's transmitted, do you?"

"Nobody knows," he said. "We're all trying to work that out."

"All who?"

He took a hard look at me.

"What are you?" he asked.

"Just an interested human party. It's not impossible for one of my kind to know about your kind."

"No. No, just rare. Outside of the occasional human medical doctor, you might be the first I've met."

If he was an adherent of a certain Dionysian mystery cult, I could have given him a better answer, but that wasn't the sort of thing one just threw around anywhere. The cult was nearly as big a secret as my immortality. Plus, the fewer people in this local other-species community who knew an immortal was kicking around town at the same time there was a bounty on the head of an immortal man, the better.

Besides, if I was the only human he'd met who knew about satyrs, he probably wasn't a member of the mysteries.

"When I say *all*," he said, returning to my question, "I mean, the medical community. Our medical community. We don't know what this is yet, but we believe it's approaching epidemic proportions."

"But that's good. It's being worked on. You can find an antidote or whatever."

He was already shaking his head.

"No. Yes, of course, eventually, but no, we're a good distance away from working that part out. We barely understand it, and it adheres to no historical standard."

"I don't understand."

"The cross-species aspect. It's not at all impossible for disease to jump species, but for a number of reasons it shouldn't have the same effect in all cases."

I considered mentioning Lenny, the demon, who dissolved within minutes of being exposed, but that information probably wouldn't be helpful, since you can also kill a demon with a head cold.

"How lethal is it?" I asked. "Like, how many have beaten it? In your experience."

"I've not heard of anyone surviving it." He said this to Mirella. "And as I said, it manifests the same. Aside from humans, who appear immune. All it would take was for one non-human species to show a resistance, and we would be much further along in establishing the parameters of a cure."

"I know a human who had it," I said.

"Really! Well that's…who is it, is he still alive?"

"Yes. Last I heard she'd recovered."

His eyebrows screamed.

"Can you tell me how to get in touch with her?" he asked. "Was there a hospital at which she was treated? If I could speak to her or her doctor…"

"It's not possible," I said.

"Even if it's a good distance, there are people I can call."

"No, I mean, I don't know how to find her, and you can't call the hospital."

His face fell.

"Maybe I can take your number," I said. "And have someone reach out to you."

I thought there was a decent chance Lew Cambridge would be willing to place such a call, even if he couldn't tell Dr. Ignacius where he was calling from.

"Thank you, that would be helpful."

"Who would you call?" Mirella asked. "If it were possible for you to send someone to look in on our friend, who would you call?"

"The research efforts are being spearheaded by a pharmaceutical conglomerate. They're the only company with enough capital to really attack the problem."

"You guys have your own pharmaceutical company?" I asked.

"It's a division of a larger corporation, but yes. If there's any chance of a medical cure, it will be coming from them."

"What's the name of the company?"

"Holitix. Have you heard of them?"

"Yes," I said, sharing a meaningful glance with Mirella. "But in a different context."

"Their products are so common, you might have seen them and not realized," he said. "That IV bag is one of theirs."

Mirella flipped over the bag so we could both get a look at the symbol on the back.

I'd seen it before, but it took a minute to figure out where: it was the three-bottles-on-a-table symbol I'd seen on the outside of the medical cooler on the island.

"This is Holitix?" Mirella asked, meaning the symbol.

"As I said. If you've been to one of our doctors in your life, you likely came in contact with one of their products at one time or another."

"How might *we* get in touch with the company?" Mirella asked.

"Or visit them?" I added.

He laughed.

"It's a shame, you know their only stateside facility used to be just outside of town. But everything above-ground was lost in a fire, and I guess they chose not to rebuild."

There was a lot to unpack in there.

"A pharmaceutical conglomerate with only one facility in the United States?" I asked.

"Oh, no, they have several, but only a few are devoted to *our* kind of research. As many of us as there are, compared to the human population as a whole, we're at most a side project. I doubt the shareholders have an inkling, for instance. That's why you can't just reach out to anybody at the company; it has to be a particular someone."

"Can you give us the number of that particular someone?" Mirella asked.

"It isn't a confidential number, so I suppose. If you tell them you have a human victim, I'm sure they'll be interested, even if you no longer know her whereabouts."

"Why did you say everything *above-ground?*" I asked.

"There were sub-levels. That was where the research specific to our interests was conducted. I visited myself once, for a symposium, and got a tour. I understand the fire took out the ground level floors and at least three of the basement levels, but there were seven sub-levels, total. I could be wrong, but given they cordoned off the building after the fire and haven't done anything with it yet, I always got the sense the bottom levels were at least partly intact."

"Just a sense?"

"Well, no, more than that. It's the way things work. If there are substances in the basement that are hazardous, moving them constitutes a risk that will have to be addressed. If they are also things not intended to be seen by humans, it complicates matters inordinately. I assume it's sealed and guarded until such a time as a non-human team of excavators with the appropriate biohazard equipment becomes available, so that they can empty out the labs safely."

"From hell," Thelonius muttered.

"Shh," Mirella said. To the doctor, she asked, "what sort of hazards do you imagine are down there?"

"Hang on," I said. "Thelonius, what were you saying?"

He seemed not at all lucid, which made what he said that much more interesting. He fixed on a spot on the wall somewhere above my head.

"From hell came the fires that burned the White City."

"He's babbling," Mirella said.

"I'm not so sure. Thelonius, is this your first time in Chicago?"

It was conceivable that he was in Chicago for the World's Fair too. It was a little outside of what I thought was an imp's life expectancy, but not impossibly so. Given the fair was called the White City, and given most of the buildings were later destroyed in a fire, what he'd just said strongly indicated an earlier visit.

"The infernal cane," he said, which wasn't any kind of answer.

"I apologize," Dr. Ignacius said. "The peppermint can cause this sort of thing. It's why I insisted on keeping him in a private room."

"I understand," Mirella said, leaning closer. "You're right, he's not babbling; he's repeating a prophesy. What about the infernal cane, imp."

"The infernal cane has found a new home!"

She looked at me.

"Anything?" she asked.

"He lost me after *White City*," I admitted.

"I'm sorry, a prophesy?" Ignacius said.

"Long story."

"What about the new home?" Mirella asked Thelonius.

"The new…oh! Hello, Mirella! What did you want to know? Would you like to hear a story?"

"And he's back," I said.

"An imp prophet?" Dr. Ignacius was kind of hung up on this. "I've never heard of such a thing."

"He's not a prophet. He just spent time with one. Hey, since he can't leave right now, what would it take to get him moved to another room and under a different name?"

We waited around until Ignacius was able to secure a different room and a new name for Thelonius. (He was now David Smith, and as difficult as this is to admit, he looked a lot more like a Thelonius D'Artagnan than a David Smith.) the doctor also handed over the phone number he had for Holitix.

"It's a local exchange," he said, "but I think someone overseas answers. I last called them a few weeks ago, and the man who answered spoke with a heavy Indian accent."

I thanked him, and said we'd be back to retrieve our imp once he was healthy. Mirella recommended the doctor not tell anyone about us, and also to watch himself. She didn't come right out and say that the people who had shot at us might also be interested in shooting at him, but it seemed as though that point was made in the margins between their words.

He took the suggestion in stride, which is what you do when you're six and a half feet tall with a twenty-foot vertical leap, I guess. Or maybe that's just how everyone in Chicago handles the threat of imminent death.

For his part, he told Mirella to keep the area on her arm clean, and to expect headaches, blurred vision, and increased weariness. He didn't bother to hand her any pills to help cope with those symptoms, but if he had and they'd come from Holitix, I doubt she would have taken them.

Mercifully, we were able to get a cab in front of the hospital without anybody using any misplaced German, and forty minutes later we were at the hotel.

"What do you think?" Mirella asked, after we'd made it safely past the downstairs bar and back to the room.

It wasn't a great room, as far as rooms go. We could hear most of what was going on in every other room on the floor, which was problematic only because from the sounds of it, there was an active prostitution ring in operation around us. It wasn't terribly clean, (the room, not the prostitution ring…well, maybe that too) the bed smelled of mildew, and the hot water in the bathroom appeared to only work during hours that were prime numbers.

However, the hotel remained perhaps the last place I would look for me, if I were looking for me, which made the other problems less of a problem. And, I'd seen worse. I probably had to go back to Victorian England for an example, but I'd still seen worse.

"I think I don't like anything about Holitix right now," I said, "but I can't put my finger on why."

"Yes, I agree. That seemed the most significant information the doctor had, whether he realized it or not."

I'd been running through the whole thing in my head during our largely silent cab ride. Mirella had evidently been doing the same.

"Here's what I don't like," I said. "If their drugs are used throughout this community, on the one hand, and on the other hand every variety of species is coming down with this disease… it sounds like a pretty clean one-to-one connection, doesn't it? I mean, we're dealing with a pretty limited information set, but even so."

It was a dangerous road to go down, because I could think of a lot of historical examples where that kind of deduction led to the wrong place, and it was often a bad place. In the plague years, for instance, a couple of towns in Europe killed all their Jews because the townspeople thought their local Jewish neighbors had poisoned the water supply. They reached that conclusion after it had been noted that Jews weren't dying at the same rate as everyone else. The real reason was that the Jews bathed more often, but nobody knew enough about the spread of disease to figure that out. And there was the old myth about how miasma—swamp gas—caused malaria. It wasn't true, but sure enough every time the local swamp was drained, cases of malaria went down.

Of course it did; there was less still water for mosquitos to lay eggs in once the swamp was emptied.

"I could imagine a scenario where their product was contaminated," Mirella said, "and they were controlling the research into the problem as a means to cover up the truth."

"That does sound like something a giant pharmaceutical would do. Especially one that catered to such a specific clientele. But nobody's getting the same pills, right? Thelonius got peppermint for his pain, but you wouldn't give that to a goblin, right?"

"No."

"And it's spreading naturally. You have it, and I've never seen you take medication. It didn't even look like you were familiar with the symbol."

"I am. And I've heard of the company, but I didn't much think about it."

"Did you ingest anything of theirs recently?" I asked.

"No."

"Then you caught it some other way. Eve is another exception."

"She's an exception in every regard," Mirella said. "Maybe *she* is the source."

"That's actually not a bad theory. If she's sick, she could have been exposed to a purer form of whatever it is. She can also travel to more or less anywhere."

"Even undersea?"

Mirella was referring to the second-most peculiar aspect of this disease: we'd seen it in a mermaid.

"No," I said. "Probably not."

She grunted and headed for the bathroom.

"There's no point in speculating if the answer is a phone call away," she said. "Dial the number. Maybe Holitix has a benign explanation. I'm going to go wash up."

"All right."

We were ignoring the part where she washed up before

leaving for the hospital. Maybe Ignacius's advice was on her mind.

I took out the cellphone I'd been using to call the island (I had two now, counting the one the driver for the Path gave me) and dialed the number for Holitix. I wasn't expecting much—in my experience, customer service representatives aren't in the habit of incriminating their employers—but I didn't see any harm in trying. At minimum, the answers could be interesting for what wasn't being said.

The number connected right away, and after going through the mandatory *press one for English* menu, I was put straight through to a person. No waiting, which I guess isn't a surprise when one is calling a secret division.

"Hello, yes, this is Arjun, thank you for calling Holitix, how can I help?"

He did indeed sound Indian, but the kind of Indian-by-way-of-Oxford I used to hear in Britain.

"Hi I was…actually, I'm not sure how to proceed."

"Yes sir. How can I help?"

"I was calling about a peculiar medical condition that I think your company is working on. I might have important information. Is there somebody I can speak to about that?"

"To whom am I speaking?" he asked.

"Call me Stanley," I said, deciding to reuse the first name I took in Chicago. Nostalgia, or something. Not sure why I didn't give him *Adam* instead; I just had a sense that this wasn't a good idea.

"And what is the condition to which you are referring, Stanley?"

"Well, it's kind of a thing where people…certain kinds of people…melt? I don't think it has a name."

"And you are calling from Chicago?"

I was worried at first that Arjun was tracing the call, but then I remembered I called a local number to get him; he undoubtedly knew what I'd dialed. Probably, doctors in Boston or New York or Los Angeles called different local numbers.

"Yes," I said.

"Are you or is someone with you in a state of emergency right now?"

"No."

"If this is an emergency, you should seek local attention immediately. I can recommend an appropriate hospital."

"I understand. It's not an emergency."

"And you wish to speak to someone—"

"Look, Arjun, I know this is a strange call, but I've seen at least one human—an actual human, not someone pretending to be a human—afflicted with this disease. I'm trying to get answers. I think there's probably someone there who wants what I know, and I want to know what they know. I appreciate that Holitix is a pretty large company, but from what I understand, the division I'm talking to right now isn't *as* big. I'm sure you can get me to someone, and if not, you can get me to a supervisor who can get me to someone."

By the way, I always thought telephones were a bad idea.

"Please hold," Arjun said, and then he went away.

The hold music was louder than Arjun by a decent quantity of decibels. It was also the same set of notes on a five second loop. If you wanted to get a confession out of somebody without leaving clear evidence of torture, this was what you'd play.

"How is it going?" Mirella asked. She came out of the bathroom in the same clothes as before.

"I'm on hold," I said. "It apparently wasn't a direct line to their finest virologists."

"Of course not."

Five maddening minutes later, during which I wondered if I would lose the signal if I took the cellphone down to the bar in the elevator, Arjun returned.

"Thank you for holding, Stanley," he said. "I have a few more questions."

"Sure, go ahead."

"Can you tell us how you obtained this private number?"

"I'm sorry, I'd rather not."

I probably could have, but for some reason the way he asked made me think it wasn't something I should be handing over. The use of the word *private*, certainly implied Dr. Ignacius had crossed some kind of line.

"That is all right. And you are a human, is that correct?"

"Yes. How did you know? I didn't tell you this."

He ignored the question.

"Are you alone right now?" he asked.

"Am I alone?" I looked over at Mirella, who shook her head. "Yeah, I am, but I don't see how that's relevant."

"Are you certain? Please, bear with me. I ask because we have an active concern that you may be sharing a room with someone who is afflicted, and as you have said yourself, even humans could become ill. Are you alone, Stanley?"

"I told you, I'm…why are you asking this?"

"As I said, for your well-being."

"Right, except you already told me if this was an emergency I should go to a hospital, and I already told you it isn't, so why do you want to know if there's anyone else here?"

"As I said—"

"Yeah. I think I'd like to speak to a supervisor."

"Yes, I understand. Please hold."

"This is weird," I said to Mirella, as the five-note hold music came back. "Is this weird? This feels weird."

"What are they saying?" she asked.

She was busy looking out the window, which was a long-standing habit of hers. It was probably why her dream house, on the island, had no outer walls; she could stare in any direction without getting up.

The hotel room window had a crappy view. It was of the front of the building and the street, so there were certainly worse views available, but since the street and the hotel were crappy, thus was the view.

"He's just asking a lot of strange questions," I said.

"Maybe they're only strange to you. When was the last time you had to deal with a customer service person on the phone?"

"I guess."

Arjun returned again after only a minute.

"Thank you once more for waiting, Stanley. I will transfer you to my supervisor in a moment."

"All right, thanks."

"Adam," Mirella said.

"I only have another question," Arjun said.

I sighed.

"All right."

"Adam," Mirella repeated. I didn't really catch the urgency in her voice when I should have.

"We have you at this address, is it correct?" Arjun said. Then he read off the address of the hotel.

"Wait, how did you get that?" I asked.

"Can you tell us what the room number is?"

"Hang up the phone!" Mirella barked.

"It's only so we may assist you better," Arjun said, before I disconnected the call.

"What is it?" I asked, not yet processing what just happened on the call. "Did you see something, or did you just want me off the phone again?"

Mirella closed the curtain and drew her sword.

"No, I saw something," she said. "They're here for us. We have to go."

CHAPTER 12

I'm not a huge fan of coincidence, as an explanation of concurrent events. It's a difficult line to straddle, because it's incredibly easy to draw conclusions based on one thing happening before the other, in the *this therefore caused that* vein. Where one tends to go astray is in the impossibility of *this* causing *that,* which is basically my problem with astrology as a whole. (I'm saying this as someone who used to be employed as an astrologer by kings.) Lean too far the other way, though, and you find yourself excusing two things that should absolutely be considered related.

For example: we've been trying to figure out which well-financed individual decided to put out a contract hit on me, while at the same time also trying to track down the source of the disease that was evidently gearing up to kill everyone. These appeared to be entirely separate things, with the first thing only showing up as an unfortunate hindrance in our efforts to resolve the second thing.

But now the two problems were dovetailing in a way that led to two possible conclusions: either it was a coincidence I happened to be speaking to a guy from Holitix at the same time our location was sussed out by whoever Mirella had seen out of the window; or the guy I was talking to tipped off the hit squad as to our location. Given I'd been on and off of hold for something like a half an hour, and Arjen the customer service rep had, in that time, traced the phone I was using well enough to read the address back to me, I was definitely on board with the latter explanation.

Holitix certainly had deep enough pockets to pay a ransom for my head. I had no clue why they would ever want to do that, but one thing at a time.

"You're sure?" I asked Mirella, while jumping off the bed to retrieve the suitcases from beneath it. She was wearing an army of knives and had a sword in her hand, but there was more equipment in the luggage, and I needed to arm myself with something.

"I'm very sure, yes. I saw seven, but there may be more. Two goblins, an elf, three humans, and a werewolf."

I found another sword, and tried it out.

Her swords always felt too light to me, but it was sharper than my fist and it had a better reach, so it would have to do until I disarmed someone and traded up.

This was the moment when I wished I hadn't gotten rid of Rick's shotgun.

"How do you feel?" I asked.

"I'm fine," she said. "Not that it matters. We're in a fight either way."

"Maybe we can get out the back before they close off the stairs. Or the roof. I think we can make a jump to the next building. We have time; they don't know what room we're in."

"They'll find out quickly. One of them arrived in a police car, and this doesn't seem like the kind of establishment that would take any legal risks to protect our right to privacy."

"No it doesn't. So, what do you want to do?"

"Kill all of them and flee the city? That went well last time."

"I was really hoping to flee the city without killing anyone first. That creates a lot of noise, and I like this country."

"I'm afraid we're past being able to make that choice for ourselves, Adam."

She got to the door, opened it, and peeked down the hall.

"It's clear," she said. "Are you ready?"

"I'm ready. Are we going up or down?"

"That will depend on which direction they're coming from."

"Kind of like how we hunted mammoths."

This was odd enough to earn a perplexed look over her shoulder.

"Except we're the mammoths," I added.

"I don't like this analogy. The mammoths didn't do so well."

She peeked out the door again.

"Run right," she said, then stepped out of the room.

We took off down the hall, away from the bank of elevators. The elevators were positioned at the left end of the hall, rather than in the middle, like they would be in a rationally designed building. The direction we were heading terminated at one of the two stairwells. (The other stairwell was next to the elevators.)

We didn't quite make it to the stairs when we heard the elevator ding. A guy jumped out, looked down the hall, spotted us, and reached the appropriate conclusion.

"Stop!" he shouted.

I turned to catch a glimpse: it was the police officer. He was human, and he already had his gun out.

By the time he was ready to bring the gun to bear and take a shot at us, we were already on the other side of the steel fire door which led to the stairway landing.

Through the square peekaboo window, I saw another door open in the hall, in response to his shout and the sound of our running.

"Get back in your room!" the cop (I was assuming he was a real cop) ordered, as he sprinted our way.

"That's only one of them," I said. "Wonder where the rest are."

Mirella was looking down. There was a straight drop to the ground floor—we were on the fourth—down the middle of the stairwell.

"Two more on their way up, she whispered. "Keep the officer occupied until I get back."

I didn't get a chance to ask her what she meant by that—I mean, I had a good idea, but this was a cop, and killing cops was extra bad—because she had already jumped by then.

I heard her land a couple of flights down, not because she made a lot of noise when she landed, but because there was a great deal of violence involved in her arrival. What I could pick up made it sound as if things were going great for our side, but it was tough to pay close attention, as I was soon fully occupied by the policeman.

He was a big guy. Older, but fit. Once he opened the door, I knew exactly what kind of battle I was in for, because it was obvious immediately that he didn't know what to do with himself if he didn't have a gun in his hand. (That I was in for a battle at all was equally self-evident. He wasn't there to take me into custody.)

The problem—for him—was that he lost the gun right away. He came through the doorway without checking his blinds first, assuming we'd gone either up or down. This wasn't bad thinking, not really. Most people, on discovering an armed man yelling at them tend to continue running until they're out of room, and the introduction of a badge to the dynamic probably doesn't change that. He wasn't prepared for an ambush, basically. And even if had been, he still entered the stairwell with the gun ahead of the rest of him, which is almost always a bad idea, because the gun doesn't have any eyes of its own.

Using the flat of the blade, I slapped his wrist and knocked the handgun to the floor.

He shouted something about being a policeman, and how I

was under arrest, and also a few curse words and something generically derogatory about my parentage, and then he swung at my head with his free hand.

I would love to tell you I knew some way to knock him out quickly, so maybe he'd wake up in an hour none the worse for having been concussed, but this wasn't a movie. Absolutely, I could have discarded the sword and beaten him up with my typically non-lethal fists until he was no longer awake enough to shoot me, but that kind of thing takes time. (Also, I don't know where movies get the idea that you can knock someone out, and then when they wake up later it was like they'd been napping, and they're otherwise pretty much okay. That kind of thing can take weeks to recover from. I know this from experience.)

I didn't have any time to fight him until he was unconscious, is my point, so when he took his shot with his left hand, I stepped aside, grabbed the hand and pulled so he was off balance, and slid the sword up beneath his ribcage.

I held it there until the life went out of his eyes, which was maybe ten seconds. Then I took the sword out and left him to sag against the wall in the pool of his own blood.

"Mirella, how are you doing down there?" I asked, while fetching the gun.

She didn't answer, so I started down to see if I could help. She met me on the landing between.

"I'm all right," she said. She was covered in arterial spray. "Human and goblin. You?"

"Just the cop. Human. Where are we going?"

"Up. More are coming. Let's hope you're right about being able to jump to the next roof."

The dead policeman on the fourth-floor landing didn't even give her pause. It made *me* hesitate, and I was the one who did it. The first thing I could think of was, now I had to steer clear of Chicago for a few years, like I did in Boston, which was the last city in which I ended up killing a human. It was a lawman then, too, although I don't think the police ever connected me to that one. They wanted me there for something I *didn't* do.

The hotel was eight stories and we had no idea—assuming we *made* it to the eighth floor—if we would find the stairs continuing upward to a roof exit. The building felt like the right kind of old to have a rooftop egress, but there were two stairwells; that exit could have easily been located at the top of the stairs next to the elevator instead.

Mirella was of the same mind. She stopped us at the seventh-floor landing in order to peer around the railing and get a look. I could hear people racing up the stairs beneath us. It sounded like two, but I'm much better at that kind of guess when I'm hunting in a jungle.

"No," she said. "No exit. We go here." She pointed at the seventh-floor door.

"We can go up to eight and across."

"Here," she repeated. "They'll expect us on eight."

Through the door, we found a hallway more or less identical to the one we'd just left. The lighting was a little different, and there was an ice machine, but that was all. A cache of weapons would have been nice.

It was all clear until about a third of the way down, when I heard the door open behind us, as the people on the stairwell caught up. I turned to check: two of them. If Mirella's count was accurate, we were only missing another two.

Unfortunately, a dead straight hotel corridor was a terrible place to be, if your concern was being struck by rapidly moving projectiles. We only had one direction to go, presenting a target that would have been easy to hit even if we were dealing with humans.

The first person through the door behind us wasn't human; he was a goblin, and the first thing he did on breaching the door was fling a knife at my back. I was aware enough to step aside, but a second knife had already been thrown in anticipation of the space I was about to occupy.

This one almost got me. My reflexes aren't nearly good enough to bat a knife out of the air—I didn't try—but I could get out of the way. Kind of. I twisted around, got my legs tangled up, and landed awkwardly on the floor. This was sort of a good news/bad news situation, because I continued to not be stabbed, but flat on my back is about the worst position to be in if I wished to evade additional projectiles.

But I still had Mirella. She spun around and threw a knife, which the goblin dodged easily. The werewolf behind him did not. He fell backwards with her blade stuck in his throat. I had to assume he was the actual target.

This bought enough time so I could regain my feet, and we were running again, but only for about five steps.

"Drop!" she ordered.

We both fell to the floor, as two arrows whizzed above us.

The goblin had a bow-and-arrow. I wondered if this was the guy who'd hit Thelonius, but again, it's possible they're all just given one at birth.

Mirella rolled over and threw another knife. The goblin was crouching in anticipation, and would surely have been able to dodge it had it come anywhere near his person...but it didn't It didn't come close. He didn't have to duck or anything.

Mirella had missed. By a lot.

All three of us stayed where we were for a second or two, as we contemplated the likelihood of such a thing.

The goblin snapped out of it first, notching another arrow.

"All right, I can do this too," I said.

I may not be very good at throwing knives, or batting them down, which was why I didn't have a knife in my free hand and the sword was only going to be useful if the goblin came a whole lot closer. But I'm an excellent shot with a handgun, and I had one of those.

I fired twice. Both rounds hit him in the chest. He looked shocked that a gun had been introduced to his bow-and-arrow fight, and annoyed in general. (Goblins and elves both consider firearms *gauche*.) Neither of these expressions helped him to continue breathing.

"Let's keep moving," I said.

"Adam…"

"Later. Just keep moving."

But then the door to the stairwell on the other side was opening, and the last human and the elf were there, blocking the way through.

"Okay, back this way," I said, but an eighth and ninth pursuer had turned up behind us already. They both looked human, which was great because I prefer fighting humans, except that one of them had an M16, which trumped the handgun. He didn't appear to have any misgivings about using it, even if it meant hitting the guys on the other side of us.

"Looks like you miscounted," I said.

Mirella threw knives in both directions, not hitting anything but keeping everybody back. I decided since my handgun wasn't going to be as effective against four as it was against one, I may as well use it as a hotel key substitute instead. I pointed it at the nearest door.

The doors in your better hotels have enough metal built in, so that even if you shoot and kick the hell out of them, they'll take a long time to get open. (I've kicked in a few doors in my time.) This was another reason to be glad we were currently in a substandard hotel. I fired twice around the knob, and then kicked three times. It flew open—wood splinters scattering everywhere—and in we went.

Nobody was in the room, thank goodness. We didn't need any hostages, and/or collateral damage to complicated this. Possibly —given all the violence going on in the hallway hadn't warranted a single curious patron—the entire floor was unoccupied. I couldn't imagine there was enough demand to fill the place on a weekday.

I shoved the half-shattered door closed behind us, as well as possible, took the mattress off the bed, and leaned it up against the door.

"Adam," Mirella said. "I can't see."

She was waggling her fingers in front of her eyes and squinting.

"At all?"

"I'm not entirely blind, but everything's fuzzy. And my hands are unsteady."

"We already know the name of a doctor, so let's get out of here and see about that," I said.

"Right, yes. After we get out."

She looked at the mattress, and blinked a couple of times, in case what she was seeing was actually a byproduct of her blurry vision.

"That won't hold," she said.

"It's just so they can't see in. Keep them guessing a few more seconds."

"How will that matter?"

"We won't be here by the time they shoot their way through."

I opened the window.

"C'mon," I said. "This side of the building has a fire escape."

She climbed out and tried looking around.

"Hang on."

She closed her eyes and slowed her breathing. Her hands steadied.

"We have to go up," she said.

"Why?"

"Because one of them in the hall was on the phone. They already know we're on the fire escape. Reinforcements are around the corner. They'll make it to the alley before we do."

"All right. You first."

We headed up. I hoped that if there was anyone already waiting for us up there, she'd hear them before whatever this disease had done to her eyes started to impact her ears as well.

I kept waiting for the wail of police sirens. I'd fired a gun in a building with paper-thin walls, and there were five corpses on various floors. Surely this was atypical for Chicago these days. But so far, nothing.

Once to the top—which was pleasantly unoccupied—we ran to the edge of the nearest building.

It was too far. From the ground, it looked like an easy jump, but now that I was standing there, it was clear this was no option. Only about six feet separated the buildings, but the other one was ten feet taller. Healthy, Mirella could make it, but I couldn't.

"What is it?" Mirella asked. Her eyes were still closed.

"I should have scouted this before now," I said. "Why didn't we scout this?"

It was much too late for this observation, but until we were running for our lives through the hotel, it never occurred to me that neither of us had taken the time to review the structure for possible escape options. Her getting sick had thrown both of us off our game, and made us sloppy. Now we were facing the consequences.

"It's too far?" she asked.

"Yeah, it is. We can either jump to the ground from here, or hope a helicopter touches down sometime in the next thirty seconds. Other than that, we're fighting our way to the street."

"Then we'll fight," she said, matter-of-factly.

She could barely stand, and hardly see, but Mirella wasn't going to check out before taking as many of them with her as she could. I sort of loved that about her.

I was about to check the gun to see what kind of bullet count I was down to when I remembered the second phone in my pocket.

I pulled it out and just stared at it for a second. The driver said it was for an emergency, and, well, this absolutely qualified. Sure, we were cornered on a rooftop and probably only had a few minutes left to live, and—I'm just assuming—the Path didn't have access to a SWAT team and a teleportation device, but I had nothing to lose. Maybe I could give them my last will and testament over the phone or something.

I hit the preset number. A woman answered.

"Hello."

"Hi," I said. "You guys gave me this phone, and—"

"Is there an emergency?"

"Yes, we're on the roof of the hotel and we're kind of cornered. The address—"

"I know where you are, Lord Venice."

Then the line went dead.

"Who was that?" Mirella asked.

"She called me Lord Venice," I said, which didn't mean anything to Mirella at all. I was still processing it myself.

The door at the other end of the roof opened up, and the four guys from the seventh-floor hallway poured out. The one I took particular note of was the one with the M16. He was probably our biggest immediate problem.

"She can call you whatever she wants," Mirella said. "If she can't help us it doesn't matter. You have to be my eyes; tell me where they are."

A fifth and sixth attacker came up the fire escape. About thirty seconds earlier, I'd have made a remark about how this is why it's a bad thing to be the mammoth in the hunt, because you eventually end up at a cliff with no choice but to run off that cliff.

I didn't say that, though, because we weren't going to be jumping off this cliff.

The fellow with the M16 stepped ahead of the pack.

"Hi there," I said. "Don't suppose we can talk about surrender."

"Sorry man," he said. He sounded like a Chicagoan by way of

Malibu Beach. "Contract's for a straight kill. We just need your face so we can send proof. I mean, if that makes you feel better."

"That you won't shoot me in the face?"

"Tell me where he is, Adam," Mirella muttered. "I'll throw—"

"I have it covered," I said to her.

"Yeah," the gunman said. "Oh, and we'd all appreciate it if you didn't take a header off that roof there. Then it'd be *really* hard to prove we got you, and you know, man's gotta get paid."

"I get you, but, I didn't mean our surrender, I meant yours."

He was checking his gun in the casual sort of way someone who's intimately familiar with a tool might. Like he'd raised it from childhood.

"Come again?"

The three guys behind him sort of laughed amongst themselves. The two at the ladder mostly just looked confused. Maybe they didn't speak English.

"Yeah, when I asked if we could talk about surrender, I was talking about yours. I thought it would be polite to give you a chance before you all died horribly."

"What is that?" Mirella asked. Her head was tilted up, toward the roof we couldn't make the jump to.

"Do you hear her?" I asked.

The guy with the gun shook his head at me.

"Pretty sure you're not gonna talk your way outta this, friend," Mr. M16 said. "Real sorry."

"Someone's running this way," Mirella said. "Quickly. Who is this?"

"An old friend."

The man with the gun didn't get a chance to do anything with it before a visually alarming blur leapt from the edge of the other building, over our heads, and directly on top of him.

Hopefully, he died on impact, because otherwise he was going to have a really messed up recovery.

It was hard to follow precisely what happened after that, to two of the three who'd been standing behind him. It was something like blunt-force decapitation, but it happened so fast, if someone were to claim a particularly violent god had struck them down with the power of the divine, from the heavens, everyone who witnessed it might have to consider taking the claim seriously.

The fourth guy, the elf, squared up to defend himself with a longsword. To face him, the visually imprecise blur that had torn through three people in two seconds slowed for long enough to reconcile into the shape of a young woman with auburn hair. She was wearing a blue track suit and running shoes, and had the hair back in a ponytail. If you added in a pair of earphones and took away all the blood, she'd look like your typical upper-middle-class jogger.

The elf made a game attempt to defend himself, but she had his throat out before he even finished his downswing.

The two humans at the fire escape ladder had enough sense to turn around and head back down as fast as they could, which wasn't remotely fast enough. One of them managed to disappear over the side, but she caught the wrist of the second, pulled him back up with one arm, and then threw him halfway across the roof. He skidded to a stop in the kind of awkward position that strongly indicated he wouldn't be getting back up again.

To deal with the last one, my friend in the tracksuit disappeared over the side for a few seconds. We heard a startled gasp, a not-at-all masculine shriek, then a long silence, and a squishy thud.

"What's happening?" Mirella asked. It had been only about six seconds between the part where we were about to die and the part where we were sharing the roof with a lot of body parts. Mirella still had the sword out, and was squinting to try and understand the inexplicable.

"I told you, an old friend."

"What do you mean? Who is this person? Not Eve."

"No, not Eve."

The woman in the tracksuit jumped back up onto the roof.

"Hello again, Lord Venice," she greeted.

Mirella crouched into a battle stance. She could barely see, but she could smell just fine.

"Vampire," she muttered.

"*Bonjour, Eloise*," I said. "Mirella, it's okay. We go way back."

"*How have you been?*" I asked Eloise, in French.

"Please, I am trying to remain in English now, while I am in this country."

"All right. I didn't even know you were in America." Last I checked on her, she was in Europe.

"Yes. It is the surprise."

Eloise looked around at the carnage.

"You should have called sooner. I barely arrived in time."

"If I'd known who I was calling, I probably would have. The Path isn't supposed to come with its own private, one person army."

"It does not. This is exclusive to founders service." She cocked her head. "We should be leaving."

"Sirens," Mirella said.

"Yes," Eloise said. "Five or six blocks out. They'll set up a blockade."

"Then we should be on the other side of it before that happens," I said. "I'd rather not kill any more cops today."

CHAPTER 13

*E*loise had to help us off the first roof. The next three were pretty easy jumps I could clear alone. I insisted—against my girlfriend's vehement objections—that Eloise help Mirella get across. Mirella looked ready to stab me, but in her current state I was pretty sure she'd miss.

Once we reached the corner where Eloise had a car parked, we hit upon a new problem: getting down to it. She'd evidently scaled the side of the brick building on which we stood, before traveling across the rooftops to come to our rescue. This wasn't an option for us, and neither was her leaping down while carrying us in her arms. It was a ten-story building; I was reasonably positive she couldn't cushion the impact so completely we'd come out of it undamaged.

We ended up forcing open the rooftop door and meandering downward.

This was an apartment building, which was less than ideal. If it were a hotel, nobody would blink at people they'd never seen before wandering the halls. If it was an office building, the place would be mostly empty. But we were going past people's living quarters, so we were bound to stick out. Also, we were covered in blood, and the night was full of police sirens. It would have been easy enough for anybody paying attention, to associate the bloody strangers with the law enforcement event taking place down the street.

The stairwell got us straight down to the lobby, with three chance encounters on the way down. None of the three people made eye contact with us or looked in any way alarmed by our presence, so there was a chance we weren't going to get noticed just thanks to the way people behaved in a city around strangers.

Then we got to the lobby. There was a rec room off to the side, containing four elderly women who were in the middle of a card game when we went by, and that was a different matter entirely, because they definitely noticed us.

I don't know if this is true in every culture, but I've learned that older people have no problem with staring, and don't bother themselves with whether or not it's rude to out-and-out ask someone if they're where they're supposed to be. I think it may be that they just have nothing better to do, so they might as well become witnesses to things, in case someone ever needs an official statement. Plus, who's going to get violent with an old person?

Even if none of the three residents in the stairwell elected to contact the police about our presence, I was pretty sure the old ladies in the card game would do exactly that just as soon as we'd exited the lobby.

Eloise asked the silent question, as one of the septuagenarians reached for her cell phone. I shook my head: no, let's not murder grandma tonight.

The car was right around the corner anyway.

"Get us back," Eloise said, just as soon as we were in. "Quickly."

The driver she was speaking to was Han, the same guy who'd ferried us from the plane to the city.

He got the car moving (no limo this time, this was an SUV

with tinted glass,) trying for a happy medium between very fast, and slow enough to not arouse attention. I just hoped none of the card players from the rec room got a look at the license plates.

"How are you doing?" I asked Mirella.

"I'm fantastic," she muttered.

The car was large enough for all three of us to sit comfortably, with Mirella in the middle, against me.

Eloise sniffed, and leaned away from Mirella.

"She is sick," Eloise said neutrally.

"She may be dying," I said. "It's kind of why we're here."

"Is this why? It's something I have been wondering, in these days. Explain, please, why there is a roving assassination squad wanting your head. I do not know this city well, but I don't think of this as normal."

"It probably isn't. There's a contract on me. I don't know why, or who's paying for it. Or, I didn't before tonight. I might now. Where are we going?"

"To the airstrip. And now that it's clear your life is at risk in this city, I think we must depart. Do you have a safe place to escape to? If not, I can provide."

"I do, but I'm not done here yet."

She crinkled her nose, which was a thing she did when expressing perplexity. I always found it adorable.

From a purely mathematical standpoint, Eloise was my lover for longer than any other person in my life. That was mostly because she could live as long as she wanted, and also because neither of us had anything else going on for a century or so. (It was the Dark Ages and all that.) To say we had a history was an understatement. Seeing that little nose crinkle took me way back.

"This is not the behavior of the Lord Venice I know," she said.

"Well, it sort of is. We killed a dragon together, remember?"

"Of course. Is there a dragon in Chicago? We can slay it together."

"No. Something harder to kill than that."

"What does this mean?

"No, hang on, you first," I said. "What are you even doing here?"

~

*E*loise and I met in France during the plague years, when she was a new vampire and I was the only guy in the village who knew what a vampire was. We ended up spending a century together while touring Europe, the Mediterranean, and northern Africa.

I'm a little hazy on how we ended up separating. It was a long time ago, so of course there's the vicissitudes of memory to content with, but I probably went on a drinking bender for a while and she just decided not to keep up. It's happened before.

I didn't bother to try to track her down, because I knew from prior experience that vampires don't typically make it past their third century. This isn't because of something physiological; they just run out of things to do, and eventually depression kicks in. And when depression is coupled with immortality, in a being who can commit suicide just by watching the sunrise, it doesn't end well.

By the mid-seventeen-hundreds, I assumed Eloise was dead. This is something I go through with everyone, which is why I also understand a vampire's depression better than most. (It's a good thing I'm not sun-sensitive, because I have had my moments.) She wasn't dead, though. Evidently, having spent a century with an immortal, she learned a few tricks about keeping active, and dodged the three-hundred-year curse.

Or something. I can't even begin to guess what it was I imparted, because I don't have any survival tricks that don't involve a pub, and alcohol doesn't do much for vampires.

I didn't learn that she was still alive until around the beginning of the twenty-first century. We were both being held captive on an old army base in a desert in the western United States at the time. Our escape involved her murdering about fifty people, which was bad for those fifty people but great for me, since I wasn't one of them.

We left one another's company in the desert. After that, knowing she was still among the living, I used a small part of my fortune to keep tabs on her. There was a five-year gap in there—falling between when we parted and when I was able to pick up her trail again in northern France. I didn't know how she got there, but I knew where she was, and that was good enough. I figured if I ever needed her help I could reach out.

I didn't, though. I thought about it a bunch of times, but inevitably decided it would be best if I left her alone. I figured it was indirectly my fault that she'd ended up half-starved in a box in the desert, so, all the better to let her live her life rather than risk dragging her into another one of my messes. And then I burned my old life down, and lost track of her again.

The two things I was missing: sometime between when we separated after a century together and the start of the twenty-first century, Eloise managed to amass a small fortune; and after we split up the second time, in the desert—in that missing five years—she used the Path to find her way back to that fortune.

She was familiar with the Path already, because I introduced her to it. It was one of the ways we used to travel across Europe.

When she came back to her senses in the desert, she couldn't speak any English and barely knew where she was or who she was. I could have helped her with some of that, but she didn't want my help. Instead, she struck off on her own. Her wanderings eventually landed her in Chicago, where she spotted the familiar three-hares symbol.

The Chicago way-station helped her get on her feet, and gain access to her money, and even got her some English lessons. She repaid them by literally paying them: the reason it seemed as if the Path was flush with cash was that it was. She put her own money in it.

Then came the day I turned up in England, looking for a ride to America. Not only did she send her own plane, she sent herself. She was sleeping in the cargo hold—in a coffin, which was sort of funny, because vampires hardly ever do this unless it's a personal fetish—when we flew across the Atlantic.

As to why Eloise didn't announce herself sooner, her explanation essentially amounted to not realizing I didn't already know she'd made the trip with us. She thought I would have figured it out from the champagne. Obviously, she overestimated my powers of observation.

That I didn't use the phone immediately to contact her was proof—in her mind—that I didn't want her around.

~

After Eloise explained all of that, it was my turn. It took the rest of the drive back to the airport to fill her in, starting with an explanation of what appeared to be killing Mirella, then to the corporate dragon named Holitix, ending with the league of assassins (or whatever) that evidently wanted me dead.

"They are connected, you're thinking?" Eloise asked. The question was in reference to Holitix and the hit squad.

"I think they have to be," I said.

"This makes little sense, if I am to follow the time correctly. You hear this name Holitix for the first time now, but the contract is from before now, and before you've left this island."

Mirella grumbled loudly but incoherently. She'd already lodged a semi-audible complaint at my mentioning the island, so I assumed this was an extension of that.

"This is the part I'm having the most trouble with too," I said, squeezing Mirella tighter. "They had to see me as a threat somehow, long before I knew anything about this. Then they had to decide it would be better if I was dead, at a time when, so far as the rest of the world knew, I already *was* dead."

Eloise laughed.

"I did not think a moment that you were dead. Who is behind the contract had the same doubts."

"That's fine, but that only gets us so far. I'm not nearly this important. If a conglomerate decides to murder its clientele, I can't imagine any scenario where I would be in a position to stop them."

"I certainly consider you important," she said. "Else I would not have gone through all of this to rescue you. And I remain in doubt regarding the conglomerate. I can neither imagine you stopping them from this than I can imagine them doing this."

The car rolled to a stop. I took another look out of the window to confirm that we'd arrived.

"That really is my old plane, isn't it?" I asked.

"It is. I bought it at auction. Your estate didn't know what to be done with a Gulfstream, and having one enabled me to see more of the world, without a kidnapping."

"I didn't know you had that kind of money."

"I do. It took some time to remember. Come, let us aboard. Sunrise is coming."

~

We got Mirella aboard and onto the bed, then peeled her clothes off.

It was bad. I didn't know if the disease had accelerated drastically over the previous eight hours, or if she'd been hiding it from me. It hadn't been at all long ago, that she rolled up her sleeve to show the patch to Dr. Ignacius, so I was leaning toward an acceleration, possibly connected to her adrenaline. I would have asked her, but he wasn't all that lucid so there was no point.

We got her some water, and made her as comfortable as possible, and then left her alone to finish our conversation regarding what was going to be happening next.

After securing the blinds to stave off the creeping sunrise, Eloise sat at the desk that used to be my desk.

"It is quite the problem, Lord Venice," she said. "You have a disease you can't explain, a company whose connection to it is either angelic or demonic, and a contract on your life that makes no rational sense. The contract, you connect to Holitix. The disease, you connect to Holitix."

"And you're dubious."

"I think yes. You are so sure about this?"

"Like I said, that team showed up while I was on the phone with Holitix, and the guy on the other end of the line asked what room we were in. That seems pretty explicit."

"Yes, I understand. And I recall well your disdain for coincidence. We will approach this from another angle. This company dominates an entire community, yes? For the purpose of the discussion, let's say I made my fortune by catering specifically to the vampire community, in the form of exotic human and non-human blood."

I smiled.

"Like, rare dragon blood?"

"This is just for example. I am not saying that is at all the case, I am using a hypothetical."

"Of course."

I immediately concluded that this was exactly how she'd made her money.

"This would mean I have exclusive access to a secret group of individuals. The fact that they happen to be a secret means I have no meaningful competition, which also means I can charge as much as I like, commanding enormous margins."

"A blood monopoly."

"If monopoly means what I think, then yes. But one day, I

decide to spike the blood. I add something that makes my clients sick, until they die. Why would I do such a thing?"

"To make money on the cure?"

"This is a consideration, but why? I already have this monopoly. Killing my clients achieves no goal aside for something to cover up."

"Maybe you just don't like your clients."

"Then I am in the wrong business. It makes no sense, do you see?"

"Maybe the why doesn't matter," I said. "Maybe just the fact that they appear to be doing it is enough right now."

"I think that if you go to Holitix for an explanation, you will be going down a drain."

"A dead end, you mean."

"Yes, that."

"All except for what happened to Eve," I said.

"The redhead."

"Yes."

Eloise's experience with Eve consisted of the two occasions during our century together in which I insisted I saw Eve from afar, and the time in the desert. Eve was another prisoner, but she escaped before Eloise did; I didn't know if their paths crossed.

"She thought it was Holitix?" Eloise asked.

"I don't know if she did or not. But we got to Chicago by retracing her steps, which was how we met Rick, and he was the first person to give us the name of the company. I still don't know how she contracted the disease, but the disease is here, and she was here, and the company used to be here."

"All right, this is stronger information."

"He also said it was a genocide."

"I see," she said, nodding slowly. "I think perhaps this man knows more than he provided. Would you like for me to ask him for you? I have persuasions you may lack."

"No, that's all right."

I thought she was underestimating how intimidating Mirella could be when she wanted, but Eloise did have a decent point. One of my remaining options was finding him again and questioning him more thoroughly.

"Then you say you are not done here, but you are. There is nothing else but assassins."

"No, I have another reason to stick around. Finding Rick again is the second option. The first is more straightforward. I can visit Holitix directly."

"You've already said they no longer do work here."

"That's true, their lab burned down. But the doctor we spoke to was of the opinion that not all the sub-levels were destroyed. I think there might be something down there worth checking out. If I'm wrong, I'll find Rick."

"You mean we, Lord Venice. This is your new dragon, and we will fight it together. Especially as you're now lacking support."

"Well that's not at all true. Thelonius should be checking out any day now."

She was about to argue the point that an imp could not in any way provide adequate backup, when she realized I was joking. She never quite got the hang of my sense of humor, which I always found amusing. I think I was probably the only one.

"You can't go forward alone," Eloise said, gravely. She never had much of a sense of humor herself, incidentally, so I had to have enough for both of us.

"I appreciate it, but I can handle myself okay," I said. "There's something I want you to do instead."

I took a pen and paper from her side of the desk and wrote down a set of GPS coordinates.

"Do you remember the secret island I told you about?"

"I do."

"This is the location. I want you to take Mirella there."

"She needs a doctor, not a trip to the beach."

"You're taking her to one. His name is Lew Cambridge, and

right now he's the only medical person I trust. Tell him I told you to do this, and also to not trust anything from Holitix. I'd call and tell him that last part myself, but I don't know the number, and my phone is in the hotel room."

She was shaking her head before I even finished.

"No, I don't like this plan. Better we all go to the island, and you return to Chicago later. We have a plane. This will be not difficult."

"It's just a burned-out old lab."

"Then we will go together and look at the burned-out old lab, and then we will fly to the island."

"Please. You're one of the few people alive I can trust, and right now I'm more worried about her than I am about me. I only need a few days, and by then you'll be back. I'll try to hold off on needing a last-minute rescue until then."

She stared at me for a period of time that was probably less than it felt. The thing about vampires is that since they don't breathe, they're missing a core piece of non-verbal communication. It's a little unnerving.

"Do you remember why we separated?" she asked.

"Honestly, I don't. I figured I went on a bender and lost track of a decade or two, and you didn't bother to go find me."

"No. It was a circumstance much like this. You are more predisposed to recklessness than I think you realize, Lord Venice."

"So you're not going to do it?"

"I will do it. But you should remember that luck is your god, and one day your god will turn his back on you."

∾

*S*he left the main cabin with a cell phone, to reach out to the local way-station and arrange for my needs. Those needs didn't extend beyond my needing a driver and a place to crash for a day or two, so leaving the cabin wasn't really necessary, but while she was doing that I had to explain the plan to Mirella. That seemed like something needing privacy.

Mirella looked pale, and terribly weak, which was something I'd never have used to describe her before. Her eyes blinked open.

"You are sending me away," she said.

"You heard."

She nodded.

"I tried to vocalize a protest," she said, "but the very fact that I wasn't able to, suggests perhaps you're right. I'm only a liability at this juncture."

"You'll beat this."

She smiled, and sat up.

"Whether I do or not, I don't believe my chances improve on the island. Better to keep me here and take the vampire with you. She's right, you need someone by your side."

"It's like you've both forgotten how old I am," I said. "I've made it most of my life without any kind of tactical support."

"Yes. In the days when the best defense against a foe was a larger rock, you did indeed survive. This is a different world, Adam."

"I'll be fine. You don't get to worry about me."

"No. Guns."

"What?"

"Get yourself some guns."

This was the first time I'd ever had firearms recommended to me by a goblin, so I took it seriously.

"I'll take one of your swords," I said.

"Yes, do that. And some guns. This is not about your combat skill. She's wrong, you know; it's more than luck. You've survived this long by controlling the circumstances under which your life might be at risk, and by running from the fire when it became necessary. You are not right now in control, and you're running in the wrong direction, and this is why she is worried, as am I."

"All right, fine. I'll load up."

"Promise."

"I promise."

They did sort of have a point, between the two of them. As Eloise said, luck has been a major component, probably more so than I spend a lot of time thinking about. For example, I've never died in an earthquake, despite that being the kind of thing one can neither defend against nor predict. And, they're very difficult to run away from, and I can't fly.

But to Mirella's point, I also excel at being the cleverest person in the room, and being sufficiently observant to recognize a threat before it becomes a threat, and then either removing myself from the situation or preemptively improving my odds. I did this by surrounding myself with people more lethal than I am.

Mirella and Eloise were both significantly more lethal, and here I was, putting them on a plane and sending them away.

It wasn't just out of character; it was a really bad idea in general.

I was gonna do it anyway.

Mirella nodded slowly, either accepting that I would do as promised and obtain some guns, or deciding there was nothing more she could say to convince me she was correct.

She reached out and took my hand. Her grip was hot and moist. I could feel her trembling.

"Listen," she said. "If this is the last time—"

"Don't say that."

She sighed, took a steadying breath, and tried again.

"If this is our last time together, I want you to know that I would rather to have died in your company, than like this."

"We'll see each other again," I said. "I'll find a cure, you'll get better, and then there will be plenty of chances to die fighting by my side."

"That would be nice."

We hugged, and kissed, and then I waited until she drifted off to sleep again, which wasn't long.

Eloise was standing at the edge of the cabin, meanwhile, looking concerned. Privacy on a plane this size wasn't really possible, but she managed to give it to us by slipping into the bathroom. A human might have accomplished the same thing by moving to the cockpit, or stepping outside, but the sun was up.

"What is it?" I asked quietly.

"The local news," she said, shoving a tablet in my hands.

There was a time when, if you missed the live broadcast of the news, you had to wait for the next time a story came up in another broadcast, or until the next day when it hit the newspapers. Nowadays, news stories were broken into three minute recordings and put online, so people could watch it on a loop all day long if they wanted to.

There were occasions when I thought this new approach to information distribution was much better. This wasn't one of those times. If anything, this moment made me long for when someone had to run twenty-six miles to deliver war updates.

I hit play.

"We have breaking news on the hotel homicides—a story we've been following all morning. As reported, at least five people were killed overnight in what police are calling a misunderstanding turned violent.

"Chicago police now say they are looking for this *man, in connection with last night's incident. We are told his name is Adam. No last name was provided. He is considered armed, and extremely dangerous.*

"If you see someone matching his description, police ask that you call the hotline on the bottom of the screen, and do not attempt to approach or apprehend him. Again: he is considered armed and extremely dangerous. If you see him, do not approach. Call the police immediately, at the number below."

The man in the photo was me.

"They called you Adam," Eloise said. "Is that not the name you've been using?"

"It is. Must have gotten the information from the hospital. The security camera footage too. But this is too fast. This is way too fast. Is this a local feed? How many people are seeing this?"

"Is it local? Yes, I think so, but it's all about the Internet. It is everywhere."

"Great. That's perfect."

"This settles it," she said. "You are not safe here. Come with us. If you still believe this Holitix is the one…there are other locations, yes?"

"Yes, but no. I just need a couple of days. This is where the trail goes cold, and if I don't figure out where it picks up again, I'm never going to slay this dragon. Otherwise…"

I nodded toward Mirella.

"Otherwise, I think people die," I said. "Besides, I don't think you understand what this means. If that news story is on the Internet, it isn't just a part of Illinois that now knows I'm alive. It's the whole world. And I don't want to get dramatic here, but I faked my death for a reason. The entire world is now theoretically unsafe. I can survive for a couple of days in Chicago."

She sighed grandly.

"I hope you are right," she said. "As you have run out of people available to come to your rescue."

CHAPTER 14

I have a complicated relationship with guns.

My first introduction to them came in the form of a cannon—large, barely-portable siege devices, either affixed to a ship or dragged across land. I considered them horribly impractical, and largely ignored the early adopters, whose insistence that it would change warfare meant nothing to someone such as myself, an active evader of warfare.

Those early proponents were right, and if I cared more about war I'd probably have agreed with them. As horribly loud and heavy and ill-tempered as cannons were, they performed one particular important function: they could enable an attack from a range outside of an opponent's capacity to counter. Basically, if you were the first country in the neighborhood to develop technology capable of flinging metal balls a half a mile with some kind of accuracy, you could park your army or navy at that half-mile point and just keep on tossing those metal balls until the opponent surrendered, or you ran out of metal balls.

Then one day some genius looked at cannon technology, and decided despite the incredible risk each person near a cannon took every time it was fired (a misfire can be devastating, and used to be entirely too commonplace) that it would be great if a portable, hand-held version of the thing existed.

I'm sufficiently risk-averse that I wanted nothing to do with these new portable cannons, and so I stayed away from them, effectively missing out on the vanguard of the firearms revolution that started as soon as gun manufacturers realized customers valued not having their fingers blown off above everything else. I also, not at all coincidentally, still have all my fingers.

So basically, I came in late, which was okay because in the interim I almost never had a need to shoot somebody. Likewise, it was almost never the case that someone wanted to shoot me.

Once I learned how to use them, though, I discovered that I'm a really good shot. It would be nice to say that I'm just a quick learner when it comes to new technologies, like I have a gift for this sort of thing, but there's ample evidence that this is untrue. (I will, for example, never be good at driving a car.) I suspect that I'm talented with guns because guns are used to kill people, and I'm good at killing people.

It wasn't something I talked about or advertised. I think it's likely Mirella didn't even know I was decent with a gun until she saw me use the police officer's handgun during the fight in the hotel. It's also likely that this was why she made the suggestion that I arm myself extensively.

Unfortunately, I left the policeman's handgun on the hotel roof. It was probably not adequate firepower anyway. If I was going to substitute an armed goblin and a six-hundred-year old vampire, I needed more than the six remaining rounds in that gun.

This was another one of the things that made the Path so useful. I told Eloise what I was looking for, she made a couple of phone calls, and two hours later I was holding a meeting with a local gun merchant.

I say "gun merchant" like this is a perfectly legitimate profession, and maybe it is in some parts of town, but those parts of town probably require that I have a license or something, and there was certainly no time for that. Plus—I'm guessing—most legal versions of gun sales aren't conducted out of the trunk of a car.

The man who owned the trunk and the stuff inside of it didn't seem to have a problem making house calls. He also didn't seem to be in any way concerned about conducting this transaction on the tarmac of a private airfield, with a guy who everyone in the news said was armed and extremely dangerous. Perhaps he decided that since the fact that I was supposedly armed was clearly untrue—or he wouldn't be there selling me guns—maybe the rest of it was also untrue. Or, he didn't watch the news, which was slightly more likely.

After spending a solid forty-five minutes going over everything in his immediate inventory, I only ended up taking two guns. I'm sure this was a huge disappointment to the man, who after the first fifteen minutes probably thought I was outfitting an army. I had a lot of questions and never really faced an opportunity like this to have so many of them answered, and there were about two decades of weapons technology to get caught up on.

I didn't expect to need either gun. Everything I'd been told about the facility I was about to break into, indicated this was an abandoned location that was at best lightly guarded to keep out stray trespassers. Given more time, I'd have had better information, because I would have scouted the spot prior to planning an incursion, but time wasn't something I had a lot of. (Ironically, for an immortal man.) I had no reason to expect a large occupying force, though, is my point. On the other hand, my margin of error when it came to being wrong about large occupying forces took off on a direct flight to the South Pacific a half an hour before the gun merchant showed up.

Besides, I had no plan to fall back on in the event I didn't uncover anything useful at the lab, but if such a plan were to exist, I could see it involving the continued need for firearms.

He had things other than guns and ammunition for sale. I picked up a bag (to carry the guns and ammo in,) along with a slightly used flak jacket, and a Bowie knife. I passed on the hand grenades—which I could hardly believe he even offered—and the sub-machine guns. The latter was too much gun for what I was doing, and every time I thought about a hand grenade I thought about it going off in my hand, which is not a happy association.

I paid him with some of Eloise's money. (She was quite generous.) Then he wished me happy hunting and drove away.

It's hard to believe how easy it is to buy a gun in this country.

~

The only other things I needed, to break into the abandoned facility, were a lock-pick set, and one of Mirella's swords. Close combat was just easier with a sword, especially when facing someone else with a sword, and since we'd seen our share of goblins and elves already, it just made sense to anticipate seeing more of them.

I already had the sword, but the lock-pick set took us a while to get our hands on. The gun merchant didn't carry one, Mirella didn't own one, and Eloise hadn't had to worry about opening doors since 1450.

Han and I drove all over downtown Chicago looking for one, with no luck. He ultimately ended up having to call in a favor to a local locksmith. What kind of favor a locksmith could possibly owe to a chauffeur remained unanswered.

I got to know Han a little as we drove around town, which just seemed like the polite thing to do, given I was implicating him in a large number of crimes just by being in the back of his car. Working for the Path wasn't truly his job, which makes a lot of sense given that's not really something with a full-time demand, and it's also more of a volunteer/family responsibility than a paying position. He was a chauffeur-for-hire, usually.

His family had been in charge of the Chicago way-station of the Path since it was founded in the city, which meant I knew his great-grandparents from when I first visited Chicago. I thought about mentioning that, but decided it would be easiest if I didn't. He acted as though my title as founder was hereditary, and that was fine. On the other hand, he clearly knew Eloise was a vampire, so maybe he would be cool about it.

Save for the occasional bathroom break, I stayed behind the tinted glass in the back of the car for the entire afternoon. The bathroom breaks were terrifying, by the way. They were in public places—side-of-the-road gas stations—and they were really quick, but I hated being out in the open for even that much time.

Eloise was right: staying in Chicago after my name and face were plastered all over the local news was unwise, and the longer I was there the more I was regretting not having stayed on the plane. Even if the story had already gone global, and the international interests who might find my continued existence interesting had already seen it, I was significantly more likely to be recognized in the Chicago area.

The last time I had to worry about something like this, in Boston, it was enough to just change my appearance a little: I shaved my head and put on nicer clothes, essentially. But that was to duck a police sketch in a newspaper. This time it was a video image, and it was on the Internet. Everyone with a smart phone could very well be carrying around an interactive 'wanted' poster of my face in their pocket.

Worse, because the Internet has the kind of reach a local newspaper never would, that image was technically available to anyone in the world. The very fact that people in other countries might know enough to look for me kicked off a part of my psyche that was evidently taking a nap when Eloise offered a way out. That part of my psyche was slightly paranoid, and certain there was no place left on the planet in which to wait this out.

Unless the island was still safe. But if I went there, it would definitely mean Mirella dies, and maybe everyone else who had this disease too.

~

By sunset, I'd learned enough about Han to make an imp proud. Likewise, he probably learned a lot more about me than he expected to, because while we drove around the city, I kept commenting on what used to be where. If he bore any illusions about this being my first time in Chicago, I'd undoubtedly disabused him of them.

It was fully dark by the time we reached the edge of the old Holitix facility, which was by design. The fewer eyes on us the better.

Han provided me with a tablet with Internet access so I could do some research on the Holitix facility, which didn't turn out to be all that fruitful. I suspected this was because a pharmaceutical research company on the outskirts of Chicago is only as interesting as it cares to be, and it didn't care to be that interesting. I got a decent overhead view of the area from a map, and a few short news reports about the fire, but that was it. The website for Holitix didn't mention the facility at all.

When it existed, the building stood at the center of a ten-acre compound—private land in a wooded area at the end of a private road. The setup reminded me of British country estates, where there would be a gate or decorative archway first, to mark the edge of the property, and then a mansion another half mile down the road that was usually not even visible from the gate.

There was a gate here. No archway, but they did have a big silvery sign with the word HOLITIX on it in big type beneath the company logo. Under that was the smaller "corporate headquarters" legend. It was set into brick and stone, and looked very welcoming. In contrast, the gate was a heavy steel barrier that barred further travel down the road, with a sign on it reading "Private Property: Do Not Enter".

Han pulled over at the locked gate.

"I can wait here for you, if you would like," he said.

"No, better not."

"It's only woods, and a burnt-out building. Are you sure? It would be easier to pull over down the road than to return in a few hours."

One of the things we'd discussed was the high likelihood that I wasn't going to find anything, this was a waste of time, and I would surely be reaching out to him again in the next few days for safe passage out of the city.

"I'd rather keep the trail leading from the airport to here as cold as possible," I said. "Give me a way to reach you, and if I need a pickup, I'll call. But not until tomorrow at the earliest."

"You're sure?"

"Han, we're the only apex predators for miles in any direction. I can survive overnight in the woods."

He shrugged, and handed over a new burner cell phone. Then he added a business card in case I lost the cell phone. The card wasn't to reach him; it was to reach the Path way-station, which was useful given I hadn't made direct contact with anyone other than him, locally. All it had on it was a phone number.

Then I was on my own. I waited until his taillights disappeared, before hopping the gate and heading into the trees.

⌁

One of the things not in my inventory was a flashlight. This was not an oversight; I'm more accustomed to moving through woods in the dark than not, and I've found that holding a light source when trying not to be seen is almost always a bad idea. It was also a full moon, so I was doing fine.

Plus, I wasn't really traveling through heavy underbrush here. There was a perfectly good road leading right to what was left of the building, and it was unlit. It looked like there used to be illumination along the route, but the lights must have been connected to the building's power grid, rather than to the local municipality.

I stuck to the edge of the road in the event someone came along. It was all private land, and I was assuming it wasn't heavily guarded on account of there being no reason to guard an old laboratory that had been leveled by fire a year ago, but that didn't mean just walking down the middle of the road was anything other than a dumb idea.

I arrived at the scene suddenly. It seemed for a long time as if the road was just going to wind through the woods indefinitely, until I turned a corner and there it was. From a landscaping standpoint, it was pretty well hidden.

The building—if you could call it that—looked exactly as advertised. Parts of two of the walls were still standing, and the center column for the elevator shaft looked mostly intact, but that was about all. The rest was rubble and loose ash.

I walked around the edge of the wreckage a couple of times, to get a decent idea of what I was dealing with. It was easy enough to figure out exactly where the structure used to be, because at least two or three sub-levels had been destroyed in the fire along with everything that had stood above-ground. There was, in other words, a pretty steep drop that would have been easy to miss were it not for the yellow Do Not Enter ribbon along all the parts that didn't have a wall in the way.

On the first pass, I could only conclude that this trip was indeed a mistake, because the place certainly looked abandoned. The second time around was when I spotted the ladder.

It was easy enough to miss. The safety ribbon skirted the

entire edge of the hole, all except for an opening for a door that was in one of the free-standing walls. The ladder was on the other side of the doorway.

I took the ladder down. At the bottom was a well-trod path through the ashes: more than one person had made their way along there, and not just once.

I followed it to its end, which at first looked to be the elevator shaft in the center, but that wasn't right. The door to the elevator was there, but the makeshift pathway went past it and around the side, to where there was a more standard door.

It led to a stairwell. That was obvious from the markings around the door, which indicated exactly that, graphically, with a symbol for a staircase on the wall next to something that looked like it used to hold an EXIT sign. The stairs appeared to exist within the brick column that also held the elevator.

There was no lock on the door to pick, but I also couldn't get it open. Next to the doorknob was a black panel with a blinking red light. It required a keycard.

The first thing I thought of was, this was why finding a lockpick set was so difficult: nobody used pickable locks anymore. The second was: this facility still had power.

The part about there still being power was great news, because it meant I was actually onto something. Unfortunately, that didn't help me get inside.

I looked around to see if anything in the rubble could be of use—like an extra keycard or a crowbar or something. If necessary, I thought one of the guns could do the trick, but that would be a real risk. For starters, it was a metal door, and dying from a self-inflicted wound on a ricochet was not near the top of my list for acceptable ways to go. Also, it would make a godawful lot of noise, which I was trying to avoid.

I found another solution, of sorts, a few yards from the doorway: a big stone block that looked about perfect if one wanted to have a seat, which was evidently how it was being used, insofar as on the other side of the block there was a pile of cigarette butts.

Not only did the remaining underground levels of this supposedly abandoned facility have power, someone down there had a nicotine habit.

So, I took up a position on the other side of the elevator shaft, and I waited, and hoped the smoker was on duty, and hadn't quit the habit yet.

It was a solid four hours of standing, roughly, according to the moon's passage. (I didn't have a watch, and I wasn't going to open up the cell phone in the dark to check the time, for the same reason I wasn't using a flashlight.) I spent the time wishing I had a drink, and a chair, which was what I wished for most of the time anyway.

Finally, the door opened.

I could have just as easily positioned myself on the blind side of the door, and then, when it opened, snuck in behind whoever emerged, but I decided this was a bad plan because I didn't know if only one person would come out, or if I was going to need a keycard to get anywhere else once inside. Ambush was a much better plan.

The guy who exited looked like such a prototypical security guard, I had to wonder if someone was having me on. He was portly, short, and had on a loose-fitting security guard outfit, with a cap. His belt—holding up his pants beneath an ample gut —had a handgun, a walkie-talkie, and a keycard on a cord.

He grumbled as he walked, which made it incredibly easy to come up behind him despite making a little noise along the way. By the time he noticed I was there, I had the tip of a sword pointed at his chin.

"Jesus Christ!" he exclaimed, dropping his lighter.

"Sorry," I said. "Do you want to find that? I don't want to interrupt your smoke."

"Who the hell are you?" he asked.

"A guy who wants to get into the lab beneath us. I assume that card on your belt will do the job?"

"Buddy, is that a *sword?*"

"Yeah."

"Okay. For real?"

"Yes, it's a real sword," I said. "You act like you've never seen one."

"The fuck, of course I haven't, we don't get ninjas in Chicago no more."

"Do you want the smoke or not?"

"Yeah, yeah. Jesus."

He had the unlit cigarette dangling from his lips. The lighter on the ground was a lost cause, though; he didn't even bother. He pulled out a book of matches instead.

"Is this some kinda joke, man?" he asked, taking his puffs.

"No joke. You think I'd come all the way out here for a prank?"

"I dunno, maybe. One of the other guys could…you wanna tour the labs? What for, man, there's nothing down there."

"I'm obviously not prepared to take your word on that," I said.

"Yeah, guess not." He held out his hand. "Look, I'm Ted. Maybe we can work this out, you and me."

I looked at his hand, but didn't take it.

"Nice to meet you, Ted," I said.

"And your name?" he asked.

"Come on."

"Yeah okay. It's just that I'm gonna lose my job."

"I won't tell anyone if you won't."

He laughed.

"There's cameras down there, man. Soon as you pop up on one, I'm out, and I like this job."

"Sorry about that. I can kill you instead, if you want."

"With the sword."

I realized the problem was that he didn't think of the sword as an actual threat.

"Not working for you, huh?" I said.

"I mean, it could be a prop. Maybe you should cut something with it or, I dunno. I mean is it sharp?"

I reached into the bag and pulled out the Beretta M-9. This is an extremely boring handgun that also happens to be very reliable. When you remember that guns used to explode all the time, reliability ends up being something you value pretty highly.

"Is this better?" I asked.

"Yeah, that's better," he said, taking a deep breath.

I slid the sword into the sheath on my back.

"I mean, it's not *better*," Ted said, "but I can respect that. No offense, but if I'm gonna go, I don't wanna be the guy who went down from a sword wound. That guy who took the arrow downtown, remember him? I bet if he dies—"

"What do you say we just go downstairs?"

"Yeah, all right."

He walked over to the door and unlocked it with the card, then led the way through. The stairwell had running lights to guide us on our way, and smelled like a fireplace, even a year later.

Ted stopped at the first landing, at the door which presumably led to the highest of the intact sub-levels.

"How far down does it go?" I asked.

"Two more after this one."

"And you guard it alone?"

"It's abandoned, so yeah. The whole place is empty and burned out. Dunno what you're looking for, but prepare to be disappointed."

"Do you sleep here?"

"What? No, man. What part of abandoned don't you get?"

"I didn't see a car, topside," I said. "You don't look like

someone who walks all the way from the nearest town. No offense."

"I work for a security company. Next shift drives up, leaves the car for me, and I drive it back."

"Odd arrangement."

"Sure, but it's what they want."

"So you're really alone here. There's no bunker of second shift guards or anything."

"Like I said."

"Okay, go ahead."

He swiped his card and pulled open the door.

As with the stairs, there was some lighting. It was just enough to make the place seem kind of creepy.

I saw ten doors.

"Tell me about your routine, Ted. Do you have to clear all the rooms?"

"I go down there, and I turn around, and I come back here. Place is spooky as shit, so you if you're asking whether I check every room every time, I don't. Am I s'posed to? Sure. Don't tell anybody. Besides, sound carries really well, so it's not like an intruder would be a secret. A chair in one of those offices decided to collapse one time when I was on the other side of the floor, and I tell you, I saw God that night. Scared my ass like you don't know. But if you're thinking somebody might hide in here or whatever, I mean I guess, but these are all cleaned-out, so I don't know why. You wanna see one?"

"Yes, humor me."

We walked over to the nearest door. He pushed it open.

"It's not locked?" I asked.

"No, genius, because it's empty, like I been saying."

We stepped in.

I've spent a little time in biology labs. For a good month, I visited one daily, as people with medical backgrounds (I'm assuming; I wasn't in a position to ask for credentials) studied me. I knew what I was looking at, then, when we stepped inside the room.

It was a big space—half the doors on the hallway evidently led into this room. Most of it was taken up by lab counters, and each counter had a hood, i.e., antiseptic spaces where samples could be examined. One wall going all the way down to the other end of the room had a collection of unused devices, and freezer units.

I stuck the barrel of the gun in Ted's back and walked us along the wall with the freezers.

Lab freezers are a little different from regular ones, because they have to maintain a lower temperature, so it was easy enough to see if any were currently in use: they hummed loudly, and they had an LED display indicating the temperature inside. None of these appeared to be running.

I pulled open a couple of the doors just to verify that they were empty. They were. There was a spot on the handle where a lock would fit, if somebody were inclined to seal up something in a powered-down industrial freezer. None of them had locks.

"Are you satisfied?" Ted asked.

"All the floors are like this?"

"Nah, the next two have better lighting."

"Other than that?"

"Look," he said, "maybe this would go faster if you told me what you were looking for."

"I don't know what I'm looking for."

"Super."

"Does anyone else work in this place?" I asked.

"You mean, other guards? We've been through that. There are shifts."

"No, I mean staff."

"You came down the ladder, right? Did that look OSHA certified to you?"

I didn't know what OSHA was, but I got his point.

"Let's try this another way," I said. "Is there any room here that you can't get into? Any door you're not supposed to open?"

"Supposed to?"

"A place they told you not to go, maybe."

He looked like someone having an argument with himself. It didn't last too long.

"Yeah," he said, nodding. "Yeah, there is. It's on the bottom floor."

~

We stopped off on the middle floor first, just to confirm a few things, such as: the improved lighting he spoke of; that the rooms he said were empty really were empty; that they were all unlocked. It looked a little less abandoned than the higher floor, and the lights came from the ceiling halogens rather than the emergency spotlight boxes in the corner. The lab also looked cleaner, and like it was used more recently. But, it was still empty of people and things.

The bottom floor had a layout that was essentially the same as the first two, but when we got to the laboratory door that had been unlocked the other two times, we stopped.

"This is it," he said.

"If the room on the other side of this is the same size as the others, this is a pretty big omission, Ted. You're not allowed to inspect the room?"

"No, it's off-limits. So's the one at the end."

He pointed to a set of double-doors at the far end of the hallway. They were painted white, as were most of the doors we'd come across, so they were probably steel underneath too.

"Any idea why?" I asked.

"They just told us our job was to make sure nobody got into anything on the top two floors, and this hallway. That's the whole gig. I wasn't gonna ask why. I figure they got someone else worrying about what's in there."

"Like, a secret security guard?"

"More like a high-security system. Something pricier than I am."

"Okay, that makes sense," I said. "Does your badge work on the door?"

"You know? I never tried."

He tried. The light turned green.

"Hey, what do you know?" he said.

"You seriously never tried that before?"

"Swear to God."

I was having trouble believing a security guard was that incurious, but this was not the time to review his job performance.

"Well, let's go," I said. "And if there is a high security system in there…well, you first."

"Thanks, buddy."

He re-ran the card and pulled open the door.

There were no lights on, but a bank of switches next to the door took care of that.

"Wow," he said, seeing the room he'd been guarding for who-knows-how-long, for the first time.

The lab setup was the same as the ones on the other floors, but with one key difference: a water tank, right in the middle. It was maybe fifteen-by-fifteen, looked about ten feet deep, and was made of what had to be some pretty thick glass.

The way the overhead lights hit the side of the glass made it impossible to see inside. It was obviously full of a liquid, but the nature and opacity of that liquid was uncertain.

"Look, we found the executive swimming pool," he said. "Is this what you were looking for?"

"I already told you I don't know what I'm looking for," I said. "But this might be it."

I stepped up to a panel next to the side of the tank, and

flipped a few of the switches, until internal lights came up on the other side of the glass.

The water—if it was water—was milky; the lights only enhanced that milkiness, like a headlight in fog. That said, something was clearly moving around in there.

"All right," Ted said, "put down the gun."

In my curiosity—and probably because I didn't think of him as a serious threat—I'd temporarily forgotten I had a hostage. That hostage had pulled his own gun, which I'd never bothered to take from him because again: I didn't see a threat there. So now he was standing near the only exit, pointing a gun at the back of my head, and I still didn't entirely know what I was looking at.

I didn't want to hurt him, but he was making this difficult.

"Don't you want to see what's in the tank?" I asked, turning slowly, so that my back was to the tank.

Whatever was swimming about in there was undeniably coming closer. Also, one of the switches I'd thrown on the panel appeared to be connected to a heart monitor, because I was picking up a beeping noise that was increasing in frequency.

"I'm not even supposed to be here, and neither are you," he said. "Are you gonna drop the gun, or do I gotta shoot you?"

"You might hit the tank," I said.

"You're right, they won't like that. Move over there."

"I don't think so."

"Fine. Fine, stay there, then, but put the gun down, slowly."

I crouched down to the floor and placed the gun near my feet, then stood again. While I was doing that, Ted unhooked his radio.

"Hey, is that a short-range radio?" I asked.

"What?"

"I asked if it was short-range. It looks short-range, but I don't know a lot about radios. We're pretty deep underground, though. Who are you going to talk to?"

"I'm gonna call the office and tell them we got an intruder, and they should send the police," he said. "Does that work for you?"

"Well no, it doesn't. I'm just wondering if you're calling another part of the facility without realizing it. Because you said we're alone."

"Yeah well, maybe I lied about that."

I didn't think he had lied. I thought this was the first time it occurred to him he might be communicating with another part of the same facility. I might have been bluffing too; I'm not exactly an expert in radios, but the last time I used a walkie-talkie, it didn't have the kind of range I'd expect from a cell phone. Maybe that's not true any longer, though.

"Hey, this is Ted, over," he said, into the radio. "I have a…"

He didn't finish the sentence, because something particularly engrossing had just appeared in the tank, over my left shoulder. It was startling enough that he dropped the radio and put both hands on the gun.

"What in the fucking hell is that?"

I turned to look.

The missile-head-shaped body type was the first thing to notice. That came before the face, and the enormous mouth, and the human-like arms. It was staring out at the source of light, its black eyes unfocused, like there was a film on them.

A healthy one would have broken out of this tank long before now. This one was clearly sick.

"That's a merman," I said. "And he's a long way from home."

CHAPTER 15

"A merman, like a guy mermaid? The fuck, you think I'm that dumb?"

Ted did not appear to be interested in taking seriously the evidence being provided by his eyes.

"He's right there," I said. "What do you think you're looking at?"

"I do not know, but I'm rejecting merman out of hand, mister, because they're not real."

There was a Sherlock Holmes aphorism that seemed appropriate in this situation, but Ted didn't look like he was ready to hear it.

"Forget it," he said. "Leave the gun on the floor and step back from…Jesus, whatever that thing is."

"I understand. I would have felt the same way a few months ago, but I've met one since."

Not that this wasn't a shock for me too. Mermen are incredibly strong, can absolutely travel on land, and have a shriek that would probably put a crack in the containment glass. You didn't keep one in a fish tank. The fact that they were, meant…well, I didn't know what it meant.

I chanced another look over my shoulder. The merman's eyes, which had sought out the light a second ago, were already closing. In addition to being sick, I wondered if they were drugging him. If so, that would require regular maintenance.

Actually, everything in the room implied routine visits, or the subject in the tank would have starved to death by now. Either Ted was lying about there being the occasional staffer, or his shift didn't intersect with theirs.

Or, there was another entrance. We were underground, but maybe there was a tunnel somewhere.

If I was the kind of person who thought positively about a large pharmaceutical company like Holitix, I'd conclude that the merman in the tank had the same disease as everyone else, and the employees of this lab were trying to cure him. On the island, I saw a mermaid suffering from the same condition, so it was a plausible explanation.

It was unsustainably improbable, though, because all anyone had to do was head downtown to find plenty of individuals suffering from the same malady, and none of them required special living conditions.

But maybe I wasn't thinking this through. Maybe they needed a live merman in order to come up with a cure.

There was another explanation, though, and since I was *not* the kind of person who thought positively about Holitix, that was the one I gravitated toward.

"Just step away from the gun and have a seat at that desk there," Ted said.

"You don't want to talk about this?"

"No. Look, it's one in the morning, I'm late for my rounds and overdue for a cup of coffee. I'm not gonna stand here in a room I ain't supposed to be standing in, debating an armed invader over the existence of mermaids. And another thing: I recognize you. Adam, right? I saw your face on the TV."

"Then you know I'm armed and dangerous."

"Well yeah, but it didn't say anything about a sword."

"Nobody would have believed them."

"Right. Are you gonna sit, or am I gonna shoot you?"

I sighed.

"Okay," I said. "I'm pretty sure yours isn't even loaded, but we can pretend."

"Don't worry, it's loaded. I was army, my friend, I know my way around a gun. That chair there."

I sat down.

I didn't really want to kill Ted. I didn't even want to hurt him. My plan had been to find a room with a door that locked, and put him in it until I finished looking over the place. The problem had been that none of the rooms we'd come upon so far could be locked in such a manner. I had confidence I could lock one so that someone on the outside couldn't get in, but none of them seemed to be designed so that a person on the inside couldn't get out. I expected this was normal for office buildings, which didn't habitually design places to physically trap employees.

He was definitely pushing his luck, though. I couldn't have him reach whoever picked up the other end of that radio and tell them I was in the building. I can do a lot of things, but evading all the police in the Chicago area in ten acres of woods wasn't one of them. Not long-term. Given I'd killed a cop a day earlier, they would be especially motivated to keep looking, too.

Ted seemed to have some respect for how dangerous I was supposed to be, because after I sat he crouched down to try and find the radio he'd dropped on the floor, while also not taking his eyes off of me. It would have been funnier without the loaded (presumably) gun in his hand, but he was searching the wrong part of the floor by about two feet.

"You want me to help with that?" I asked.

"Shut up."

"I could do hot/cold."

"I said shut up."

The work stations in this lab hadn't been cleaned out; I was sitting at a desk that would have looked at home in just about any medical facility, with a computer monitor and keyboard, various decorative knickknacks, generic motivational sayings printed up and taped to the cubicle wall, and a desk calendar. There was no evidence of a computer, but the wires to the monitor ran behind the desk and onto the floor, so maybe it was elsewhere. There was also a bunch of pens being held in a coffee mug that had the Holitix logo on it, a stack of computer printouts, and…a paperweight holding the printouts in place.

It was a round, polished rock with a flat bottom to keep it from rolling away, about the size of a shot-put.

The gun was five feet away. I could reach it if I threw myself to the ground, but there was a risk Ted could get off a shot in the time it took. He'd probably miss me, but there were plenty of things in this room it would be bad to hit with a bullet. However, if Ted was momentarily distracted, or otherwise incapacitated, even if it was for just a second or two, I could get to the gun.

Then I'd have to shoot him, which again, I didn't want to do, but I was running out of alternatives.

What I needed was for Ted to take his eyes off of me for a second, which I figured he'd have to do eventually if he wanted to get his hands on the radio.

But then he stood again, and the radio was in his hands, and it looked as if I'd missed my moment.

Then the merman made a sound.

It wasn't a huge sound, not compared to what they're capable of. Just sort of a low moan. Since Ted was busy refusing to believe the merman was there, he jumped at the noise.

That was my window. I grabbed the paperweight and threw it.

I was aiming for his chest. A goblin would have been accurate enough to knock the gun out of his hands, but since I wasn't one, it made more sense to target the largest part of his body instead.

Ted recovered from the shock of the merman's vocalization in time to notice the projectile, but not in time to avoid it completely. It hit his right shoulder. He nearly dropped his gun, but didn't. I still had the time to dive to mine, roll a few feet, and come up on one knee with the gun to bear.

The next thing that would have happened, if this were a movie, was that he and I would fire our guns at the same time and see who was the better shot. But Ted was near the door, and evidently didn't watch the same movies I did. He decided to get out of the room altogether before I had a chance to get off a shot.

I actually *did* have a chance, but I didn't take it. I couldn't decide on a kill shot or one to wound, and that hesitation ended up meaning I didn't fire at all.

I couldn't let him get away, though, so I was going to have to figure out which one it was going to be before the next opportunity arose. He couldn't get away, and he couldn't radio anybody, or if he did, I couldn't be on the bottom floor of the lab when one of those things happened, because there was only one exit.

I slipped the Beretta into my pocket and ran to the door. Maybe, I thought, I could tackle him or something. He probably wasn't a fast runner.

I reached the hallway, and very quickly had to come to grips with an entirely different situation.

For starters, Ted didn't have to be tackled, because he was already dead. It was a little gruesome, actually; the first thing I saw in the hallway was Ted's back, with the pointy end of a sword stuck through it, at around the spot where his heart would be.

He crashed to the floor, next to the gun he never got to use and the radio he probably shouldn't have.

There was a goblin on the other side of the body. He and a second goblin were blocking the way to the stairwell. On the left, towards the mystery door at the far end of the room—a door which was now ajar— were three more goblins. All of them had their swords out.

"Hi, guys," I greeted. My hand had already slipped into the bag around my shoulder. "Pretty good security on this floor. Where'd you even come from? The ceiling? Or, wait, a secret tunnel. There's gotta be one, right?"

"You're trespassing," the one who killed Ted said. He spoke quietly, in the same tone of voice you'd use to tell someone their fly was open.

"That's true," I said, "but at least I didn't kill the help."

"That's exactly what you did, with that sword on your back. Where is the other one?"

"Other who?"

"You aren't traveling alone. Your imp is in the hospital; where is your goblin girlfriend?"

"You're suspiciously well-informed for a security team that's happened upon an intruder."

"We'll look for her later," one of the ones to my left said. "He's the important one."

"I'm flattered," I said. "Since I'm so important, I don't suppose you guys feel like attacking one at a time? Just to be sporting."

Without so much as an *en garde*, the nearest one leapt over Ted, his sword in an overhand swing coming down hard. Since the three on my left also charged, I took this to be a *no*.

I drew my sword to parry the overhead attack, but only with one hand, which was frankly not the way to handle this sort of thing. Goblins are too strong and fast, and while this one had completely sold out by leaving his feet, if the sword was all I was equipped with, the correct response was to put both hands on the haft and counter power with power. But, I only used my right, and did my best to force him sideways. Meanwhile, my left hand was seeking out the Mossberg in my shoulder bag.

This was a nifty-looking short-barrel shotgun I fell in love with, despite not knowing such a thing existed prior to my meeting with the gun merchant. (Also, it was likely I remained annoyed at having left behind Rick's gun, and decided to rectify that.)

In my day, you took a shotgun, sawed down the barrel, and voila. Now, gun manufacturers made them that way.

Design-wise, it was almost perfectly contrary to the natural direction of hand-held weaponry, in that it was exceedingly inaccurate, and so became drastically less useful the further away the target stood. I didn't think this one had a chance to hurt anybody at more than thirty feet, basically, which you couldn't say about most other kinds of guns. You might wound them from that far, but you wouldn't stop them altogether.

It reminded me of the old blunderbuss, even though they weren't used in the way I just described, and didn't have as wide a blast range. Actually, it reminded me of every gun before properly-designed rifles came into existence: inaccurate, but loud.

I didn't bother to draw the shotgun from the bag; I just pointed the correct end in the appropriate direction and pulled the trigger. It blew a hole through the vinyl and knocked over everyone charging from the left side of the hallway. Anyone not killed outright by shot lost the use of their ears temporarily, myself included.

The sword blow wasn't easy to parry, meanwhile, because he was strong, and had put his entire body weight behind the attack. (It wasn't, I should add, a smart attack. Goblins are only a little stronger than humans, but they're a *lot* faster. A strength move was the wrong play.) Despite the recoil from the shotgun and the fact that I only had my right arm to blunt his swing, I successfully diverted him into the wall to my right.

Quickly, I assessed the damage from the gunshot.

The blast killed the nearest goblin outright, but it looked like the other two, while down, were only wounded, which was extremely disappointing.

Meanwhile, the second one to my right was completely uninjured, and in my blind spot.

I didn't hear her attack because I couldn't hear anything at all, so I guess it was fair to say I *felt* her attack. It was probably just experienced anticipation. Whatever you want to call it, I ducked from a swing meant to take my head off, turned around and emptied the second barrel into her chest.

Bits of goblin sprayed all over what had been white walls, and the vinyl bag was smoking. As it was still attached to a strap around my neck, I didn't feel like exploring an answer to the question, *can a vinyl bag catch fire*. Also, I didn't have time to reload the gun inside, so I discarded the whole thing.

Then, the one I'd parried into the wall came at me again. I barely blocked the attack, this time pushing him to my left. He was fast, and strong, and not nearly as groggy as I was, evidently, but his full-force attacks were frankly getting annoying; I felt like a matador.

He was also shouting something, but I couldn't hear what.

I figured it out soon enough. He was just keeping me busy, while one of the two wounded ones to my left regained his feet so as to throw sharp things at my head. Thankfully, he was as rattled by the shotgun blasts as I was: the first one missed, albeit not by much.

I needed some distance between me and the dude throwing things, so I started to backpedal from the swordsman. (To my right, where the corridor was clear except for shotgunned goblin parts.) This put the swordsman at the seeming advantage of having to pursue me, but it was really just to make it harder for knife guy to get a clean shot.

After about five steps I stopped, ducked, and turned my shoulder into the swordsman's groin, flipped him over my head, and dropped straight to the ground. A knife flew where neither of us were standing anymore. Meanwhile, I'd drawn the Beretta.

The knife-thrower was tough to pick out at first, in the

assorted goblin bits lining that side of the room, but from his perspective it probably looked like I disappeared too, given I was lying on the ground and partly hidden by Ted's robust corpse.

I spotted him before he spotted me, and fired twice. The first one hit him in the forehead. The second missed but by then it didn't matter.

The swordsman was up again by then. Thankfully, my hearing was coming back so I knew where he was, and rolled away before he buried his sword in my back.

And, this is why you bring a gun to a sword fight. I shot him in the face.

Then the hallway was silent. I really hoped the reason was that everybody other than me was dead, and not that my hearing was still too off to pick up the sound of someone moving.

I got to my feet slowly, and looked down the hall. I had a clean path to the staircase if I wanted it, but something felt off.

By the time I realized that the issue was that I was missing a goblin, the arrow had already been loosed.

He was hiding under the body of the one I'd shot in the forehead, at the far end of the hall. He'd been wounded, but not killed, by the first shotgun blast. The spot I had last seen him lying in was no longer occupied; I should have caught this right away.

I thoroughly deserved getting hit by that arrow, is what I'm saying.

It wasn't lethal, but it sure didn't tickle. I think I must have twisted a bit at the last second, because it struck me in the torso to the left of my heart, took off a layer of skin and skipped off my ribcage. The flak jacket was unquestionably of assistance in preventing more serious damage.

It got stuck in the jacket, though, which was less than ideal. But, it must have looked like it was stuck in me, and not my clothes, because the archer got brazen. He shed his cover and stood to take more careful aim. I was on my knees—I didn't recall falling to them, but that was the position I was in nonetheless—and presenting a decent target.

I raised my gun and got off a shot at the same time he loosed his arrow. Honestly, I don't know if he was aiming for it or not—if he was, it was a hell of a shot—but he hit the gun with the arrow. My shot was already going wide, but I wasn't going to be taking another one because now the Beretta was ten feet behind me.

I took a second to make sure none of my fingers were back there with it. (They weren't.)

"Wow, that was impressive," I said.

He didn't feel like chatting. He fired again as I threw myself to the floor, behind Ted.

I was busy calculating my odds of either, A: finding and reloading the shotgun, or B: throwing the Bowie knife with any kind of accuracy, before one of his arrows found home in a more unfortunate part of my body, when I realized Ted's gun was on the floor next to my face.

I probably had time to see if it was loaded, but with the available options, it didn't much matter. If it was empty, I was dead either way.

"Wait a second," I said, raising a hand above Ted's corpse.

He let me sit up, presumably because he didn't know I had another gun.

"What if I paid you more than the bounty?" I asked. "Would that make a difference?"

"What bounty?" he asked.

"Really? Okay."

I leveled Ted's gun and fired.

He got off an arrow, too. This time, his shot went wide, while my bullets landed true. He sagged against the wall.

I got to my feet again, slowly. I wasn't a hundred percent sure this was really over, so I stood motionless, gripping Ted's gun and listening to my breathing, for about ten seconds. None of the goblin parts tried to jump up and attack, and nobody else came rushing in from the doors on either end of the hallway. It looked like I was in the clear, for at least a few minutes.

I put Ted's gun down next to him—said a quiet thanks to his corpse for being good about keeping his gun loaded—and went about the business of extracting the arrow from my person.

Or rather, I tried to do that. It was stuck in the flak jacket and not me, so I took the jacket off and tried to pull the arrow out, found out that wasn't going to happen without a set of pliers, and gave up.

The cut along the ribs was bleeding, but it was all surface wound. Nothing deep. Annoyingly, it was going to keep on bleeding for a while, though, because I had nothing to tape it shut with, and it wasn't in a great place to tie off.

For good measure, I checked the rest of my body, in case my adrenaline was hiding another wound. I didn't find anything. Then the phone in my pocket started to vibrate, and I jumped a few feet into the air.

I opened the line.

"Uh, yes?" I said.

"This is Han. I am keeping track of the police channels."

"Oh. Okay, good. Good for you. How's that going?"

"There has been a report of a disturbance at your location. You should get out of there if you can. I'll meet you at the edge of the woods."

"Sure, okay. Head there, I'll let you know." I was looking down the hall, and not in the direction of the stairwell.

"Adam, police are on their way."

"I get it, but I'm not finished yet."

There was the nagging problem of that room at the other end. Ted said there were *two* doors he wasn't allowed to open, and we'd only checked one. Sure, the police were coming, but it was an underground lab, they couldn't come in unless they had evidence of a crime, and we were something like six levels beneath the surface. Plus, five goblins had either just manifested out of empty space, or there was another way out of this place. Maybe that other way was on the other side of the door at the end of the hallway. The fact that the door was now open certainly lent credence to that argument.

Secret tunnel meant another way to escape without having to worry about the police. It also could mean more goblins, or something bigger, but I still liked the idea of checking behind that door better than I did fleeing the facility immediately.

I think it's fair to say I wasn't thinking entirely straight at this point in the evening.

First, I collected the shotgun—reloading it on my way to the door—and the Beretta, just in case I was right about both the tunnel and the possibility of more violence.

I pulled the door open. There was no tunnel on the other side; just a room. I stepped in.

It looked like a place that served no real function in either an office building, or a laboratory. There was a wooden table, and a wooden chair. On the wall opposite the door was a glass screen, but there was nothing on the screen. The other walls were metal, as was the back of the door I'd come through. Five armed goblins didn't emerge from this room. I didn't think they'd even *fit* in the room.

All things considered, it was pretty unsatisfying.

Then the glass screen jumped to life.

It acted like one of those old television sets, the vacuum tube ones, that went from unfocused to focused after several seconds. Someone fuzzy was on the other side of the screen.

He spoke before the image clarified, which gave me a little time to prepare for it. Not that preparation helped.

"You can at least give me this much, Jackie," the man said. "I held up my end of the bargain. I stayed out of your way."

I knew the voice, which was both terrifying and completely

impossible. Then the face that belonged to the voice filled up the screen.

It was the man I knew as Herman Mudgett, looking no older than the last time we spoke, over a hundred years ago.

He hadn't aged a day.

CHAPTER 16

"It can't be," I said. "You're dead."

I kept blinking, like that would make it so I wasn't seeing who I was clearly seeing. It didn't help.

He laughed.

"Did you see me die?" he asked.

"No, but—"

"But everybody dies, I know. All except you. Honestly…Adam, now is it? Honestly, Adam, on the subject of immortality, you're the last man on the planet I thought would require convincing."

"But how?"

I was having a lot of trouble with this, if that wasn't obvious. My logical mind was trying to convince itself that this was a grandson, who just bore a striking resemblance, and also appeared to have all of the knowledge of his grandfather. And his laugh. And his eyes. And his gestures. It wasn't working.

"How am I immortal?" he said. "How are you immortal? I never knew the answer, did you? We simply are. Honestly, it's been a great deal of fun, watching you parade about the planet as if you were something unique. The arrogance! Well and the redhead, but we both know she's a little different."

Eve was not, to my understanding, all that different. Just older. She also had a trick that I hadn't learned yet, but that was all. Maybe I knew her better than he did.

"I would have come across you before," I said. "Before this. The world isn't that large."

"You're right! And you did. We've been friends on more than one occasion, separated by many, many centuries. I always enjoyed seeing that flicker of recognition, before you decided I couldn't possibly be the same person you were thinking of."

"I would have figured it out."

"And yet, you did not! Here, I'll tell you the first time we became friends. It was in Susiana, and I was a priest using the name Shif. You were a farmhand who stubbornly refused to learn how to read. You remember?"

"I do. But, no, you looked different."

"As did you."

"Not *this* different."

I thought back to the last time Shif, and Haltamti, were on my mind. It was after I saw the Elamite script written in blood on the wall of the island hotel. I had a dream about Shif right after, and the dream version of him told me I wasn't paying attention. I took it as a portent of doom, which seemed to be borne out by the tsunami that hit the island the next day.

Clearly, that was the wrong interpretation. I hadn't been paying attention all right, but over the course of centuries, not days.

"Susiana was when I realized you and I were the same," he said. "I'd been high priest for fifty years, and took note that two others in the city also did not age: our red-haired priestess; and a lowly farmhand."

"All right," I said. "Let's say I accept what my eyes are telling me, and this isn't some sort of trick."

"What trick could it be?"

"You're not here in person. You could be a simulation."

"Why, I suppose that's true! But someone would need to have digitally captured the entirety of Herman Mudgett, yes? In a time when such a thing was technologically impossible. On top of which, who else could possibly know all I know?"

"I agree. I'm only saying there is a theoretical explanation."

"Very good. I always admired your adherence to the logical. I am unfortunately not going to be joining you in person today, which I expect would be the only evidence you'd find acceptable. Unless you were to then argue the existence of a lifelike robot."

In the back of my mind, I could hear Han screaming that the police were already on their way, and I needed to get out of there. He was right, but I couldn't get my legs to move toward the door. There was just too much I needed to know. The threat of long-term incarceration was about to become very real and I couldn't move.

"You said we've known one another for centuries," I said, "except nobody clued me in on our long-standing friendship. This wasn't *all* about my failing to recognize you. I recognize you now."

"Yes, because I'm allowing it. Do you know what a rakshasa is?"

"Of course I do. You're not going to tell me you're one of those, now, are you?"

Rakshasas are truly awful beings. They combine a taste for human flesh with an uncanny ability to disguise themselves, with the latter bordering on the supernatural. The only reason I don't think it *is* magic is that magic isn't real.

"No, but I studied under one," he said. "This was not long after I parted ways with the temple in Susiana. I wandered…no, that isn't accurate. I fled the city due to a minor religious disagreement concerning human sacrifice. Unimportant. I'd tell you to ask the redhead about it, as I'm certain she remembers, but you won't have a chance. I fled, is the point, and I ended up in what's now Northern India, where I came upon a family of rakshasas.

They taught me everything they knew about deception, and in thanks for their hospitality, I murdered all of them."

"That's an odd way of saying thanks."

"Well, I know, but they were rakshasas." He shivered at the thought. "Can you blame me?"

I was kind of on-board with him on this one. I have learned to find something likable about very nearly every non-human species I've encountered. But not them.

"I thought of it as my final test," he said. "I killed them one by one, each time impersonating another member of their own family. The only thing I didn't do was eat any of them. Although I tried! *Very* gamey. Do you remember that animal…it was like a gigantic rabbit, only with claws?"

"I do. I think it's extinct."

It had been a good forty thousand years since I saw one, so this was a good bet. But what did I know? I couldn't even spot another immortal man.

"Oh, very much so! I don't think archeology has even discovered it yet. Just as well. Do you remember how the meat tasted?"

"We always hunted those as a last resort," I said. "We would go after something twice as deadly first."

"Yes! Take that flavor, only the meat's spoiled. That's what rakshasa tastes like. It's no wonder they never tried cannibalism."

"How old *are* you?"

"No idea! Old enough to remember that rabbit thing. Who can even count that high? But this is nice, is it not? Talking like this, after all our time on Earth? I bet you never expected to meet another man who even remembered that beast."

"I didn't, no. But, why did you wait so long to tell me? You could have done it at any time."

"For the same reason I'm not there in person right now. I'm afraid we're irreconcilable, my old friend. Not that I haven't tried. But your perspective on things is simply impossible."

"I don't know what you mean."

"It was right there, in Susiana. I aspired to a position of power. The redhead fashioned herself a goddess. You were a farmer. And you were content! It continues to boggle the mind. Don't you understand that we are gods to these temporary things? We are forever. They're flickering lights—mayflies, dead by the sundown. That you can bring yourself to care about even one of them is, well, it's disappointing."

"Is that why you're trying to kill all of them?"

He laughed.

"You've figured it out, have you?"

"The merman in the tank down the hall. You're not trying to cure him, right? Even though that's what this company is supposed to be doing. The merman is where you got the strain of the disease."

"I came across my first merman twelve thousand years ago, after a shipwreck that left most of my crew dead. The creatures came ashore to take our deceased. They like meat from the land, when they can get it, but are really quite gentle if you don't bother one of their queens. I befriended them, and while I was stranded on that island, they kept me alive by bringing fish."

"You befriended them how, exactly?"

"Very good! You know me better than you realize. I traded fish meat for human meat, and when I ran out of drowned shipmates, I started murdering them. Anyway, I learned some of their language, and further learned of the wasting disease. When the day came, I sought out a live sample. It took twenty years to capture the one you saw in the tank."

"And then you modified the disease so that it could jump species," I said. "You turned it into a weapon."

"I wouldn't call it a weapon. We manufactured our own plague is all."

"That's really the definition of a weapon."

He waved his hand in the air, as if to say, *never mind that*. It was such an arrestingly familiar gesture, I couldn't possibly deny that this was really him.

"It was released in small doses," he said, "just enough to initiate a panic. In another year, Holitix will provide a cure, and for an exorbitant fee, mass inoculation will begin. The exorbitant fee is what sold the board on it."

"That's horrible."

"It's smart. We own the entire market, why not take advantage? And these species value secrecy above *everything*, including survival, which is frankly their own damn fault. Of course, there *is* no cure. The inoculations will kill all of them. That's the part the board doesn't know about."

"Why would you do that?"

"Why NOT! My lord, you are so infuriating! What does it matter? They're ants! Microbes! Don't you see how weak your irrational concern makes you? I honestly think I would have an easier time explaining this to the other one."

"Eve."

He laughed.

"Is that what you're calling her? How quaintly biblical of you. Yes, her. She was here too, you know. Not in this room; three floors up. She is *far* deadlier, and twice as ruthless. Made such a mess we just burned down the whole building rather than try cleaning it up. Bravo, on all the work you did in the hallway, incidentally. It was good to see the killer come out again. I wish you embraced him more often."

"Come visit in person, and I will," I said. I was a little annoyed that he thought she was more deadly, and yes, I know how dumb that sounds.

"Oh, I know. That's precisely why I'm not there in person."

"There's time. I'll find you, and figure out a way to stop what you're doing."

"Well. That's your other weakness, isn't it? Misplaced bravado. Ill-advised derring-do. An overactive sense of heroism.

I can't imagine you're surprised to find that it has ended up being your undoing."

I would never describe myself as a hero. Maybe once a century, I do something modestly selfless, but that's all. I think the number of times I've headed away from danger far exceeded the number of times I turned towards it. But, if he'd been around me for as long as he claimed, the heroic moments probably stuck out.

"I'm still here," I said. "I don't know where you are, but I'll find out."

He was sitting before an annoyingly pedestrian background, behind a desk, with no windows in view. There was nothing on the wall behind him, and in fact it might have just been a sheet or something, since it was utterly featureless. Also, there was nothing on the desk. The chair was leather, and squeaked when he moved, but that wasn't helpful.

He smiled at the suggestion that I could hunt him down.

"I could go on about how the police are right now surrounding the property," he said, "or how ten minutes ago the door to the stairwell was unlocked remotely for them. Knowing you, you'll murder your way out and come up with some absurd justification for your actions, like always. But none of that is going to matter, because you're not leaving the room. The door locked behind you, and the walls are steel."

I'd left the door to the room open, but he was right; it had since closed up behind me. I hadn't even noticed.

"The screen isn't steel," I said.

"No, it's glass, but the wall behind it is also steel."

"Then I'll knock until someone opens the door from the other side. As you said, someone's already on the way."

"You still don't understand. This is goodbye, Adam. I wouldn't have told you all of that if I expected to ever see you again; this isn't a spy film. You're standing in a kiln right now."

"You're joking," I said, even as I tallied up the facts in support of this: the heavy door; the steel walls; the apparent lack of function. Even the wood furniture made sense in this context.

"I'm really not. Had it built after that mess the redhead left behind, as a better way to dispose of things. It's also just plain fun."

Something in the ceiling began to whirr. There were thin vents at the edge of the walls, and those vents had just opened. Hot air was pouring through.

"I picked this up from Henry, incidentally," Herman said. "He was a flawed man, but also brilliant in his way. Body disposal was his finest feature. He built his own crematorium, and not only disposed of his dead in it, sometimes he actually put them in while still alive. He liked to hear their screams."

"Is that what you're going to be doing? Listening for my screams?"

"And watching. But, this screen is quite expensive, so I am afraid this is the last time you'll be seeing *me*. Or anyone else. Goodbye, Adam."

The screen went dead, and then retracted into the ceiling.

As advertised, the wall behind it was the same metal as the rest of the room.

I tried the exit, as one does. It was locked, which was disappointing, but not surprising. I couldn't even see the locking mechanism in the seal between the doors, and the hinges were unexposed. There was no handle or knob. If I hadn't already known a doorway was there, I might have mistaken it for another wall. Which, I guess, is the point when one wants to create an oven that someone will voluntarily walk into.

I considered trying the shotgun on the door, but steel that thick wouldn't respond well; I'd just blow myself up.

"Herman?" I shouted. "I know you can still hear me. We can work something out. You don't have to do this."

Silence.

The air was already becoming difficult to breathe. I decided for my own safety to relocate the guns to the other side of the room, before the gunpowder ignited. I had no idea what temperature that might happen at, or whether or not it was a higher temperature than that at which I could still survive, but it still seemed like a solid decision anyway.

A minute later, I was adding the knife and sword to the other side of the room. The metal was conducting the heat better than I was; the sword nearly burned a hole in my back.

None of this mattered. If someone didn't open that door soon, the next thing to happen would be the wood of the table catching fire, and then maybe my clothes, and then me.

Maybe if I was lucky, I'd suffocate first.

Another thirty seconds, and I was down on my knees gasping for air. If I thought I could speak, I'd tell him to hurry up with it already. It wouldn't have mattered—probably—because he was clearly interested in my suffering.

Then the table burst into flames.

Strangely, when that happened, it felt like I could breathe a little easier.

The chair went next, and then one of the guns fired off a round. It looked like Herman *had* answered my silent wish that he speed up the process, because the walls were glowing white and the air was wavy with the oppressive heat...and I was fine. The air I was breathing was cooler than it should have been, and I wasn't on fire.

Then I realized why I wasn't currently dead or dying. I wasn't entirely *in* the room anymore. I stood in the middle of it, but I wasn't really there. It was like I was witnessing a particularly impressive interactive movie from the other side of the screen.

There was a hand on my shoulder. When I noticed this I nearly pulled away in surprise, which would have surely been a lethal decision. If memory served, doing that would drop me right out of the veil.

It was Eve. Somehow. I couldn't believe she was not only

there, but actively rescuing me, and I would have asked her why, but then I saw the strain on her face.

She took my hand.

"Don't let go," she said.

I got to my feet, and then she walked us through the doors and into the hallway.

It all felt really strange: passing through the solid door; standing in the hall and feeling like I was taller than I should have been; the continued sensation that I was on the other side of a screen, the same way Herman had been a few minutes earlier.

Then Eve let go of my hand, and we both fell back to Earth.

I ended up on the floor, gasping, as if my lungs had been taking in all of the hot air of Herman's kiln that whole time.

Eve lay on the ground next to me, on her back. I noticed she was wearing a hospital gown, which was the same thing she had on the last time I saw her.

"You came straight from the island," I said.

She nodded.

"How did you know to come here?"

"I know the man," she said. "I knew he would lead you here, as he led me here."

"But you want me dead at least as much as he does. Don't you?"

She smiled that ridiculous smile of hers and sat up, then leaned against the wall when sitting up completely on her own proved too challenging.

"It's possible I have changed my opinion on that point, Urr," she said.

"Well, that's nice."

We were both ignoring the copious amount of blood and guts just out of reach down the hall. Maybe it was just me, but it seemed like the only time we really got to talk was around corpses.

"You may also be the only one capable of stopping him. Perhaps I'm keeping you alive so that I might kill you later."

I laughed, and she joined in.

I'd never heard her laugh before. I liked it.

"Sounds like a deal," I said.

There was a banging on the stairwell door at the other end of the hall.

"That was fast," I said. "He must have sent the police right down to the bottom floor. Can you…"

I was going to ask her about maybe pulling the same trick that got me out of the kiln, to get us good and far from the police, but the question would have been posed to empty space.

Eve had disappeared on me again.

"Hey come on," I said. "That isn't funny. Get me out of here."

Silence. If not for the part where I'd been walked through a solid steel door, I'd have suggested she was never there at all.

At least, I reflected, as the stairwell door flew open, she was being historically consistent.

Three armed men with CPD on their bulletproof vests poured through the doorway with their guns out.

"Don't move, don't fucking move!" the first one barked.

I was unarmed—my guns were undoubtedly slag at this point —and covered in blood that mostly didn't belong to me. So, I didn't move other than to raise my hands.

"Jesus, look at this," the second guy said. It *was* the kind of scene that puts a person off of solid food for a while. "Is that him? Is that him?"

He seemed fully prepared to shoot me right there.

"I'm not armed," I said. I remained on my knees, my hands up, palms empty. Then I waited for one of them to wade through the bodies to get to me.

If any one of these three was actually here to collect on the bounty, this was going to go very badly, very quickly.

"Command, we have him," the first guy said in to his radio.

Guy number three lowered his gun and pulled out a pair of cuffs. Number two still looked like he was going to shoot me.

"Repeat, we have Adam. We're bringing him up."

He nodded at the one with the handcuffs, who started walking.

"You're under arrest," number one said.

Then he began to read me my rights.

~

I didn't do a head-count, but by my conservative estimate, I was being take into custody by every police officer in Illinois. I was marched up from the bottom level by the three officers who found me, and then it took the assembled forces a half an hour to figure out how to get me up out of the hole, since I couldn't climb a ladder while my hands were cuffed behind my back.

Once that was resolved, I was perp-walked past all the television crews in the Midwest—thankfully all were kept at a moderate distance so nobody could Jack Ruby me along the way —and into a squad car.

I was joined in the back seat by the arresting officer—the first guy through the door, whose name was Stanton—a driver who looked like a regular patrolman, and a captain who introduced himself as Dunwitty.

Dunwitty did two things, as soon as I got into the car: he had Stanton change it so my wrists were handcuffed in front instead of behind me (so I could sit comfortably); and he provided me with a bottle of water, which was really nice.

"Were you advised of your rights, Adam?" Dunwitty asked. He was going to try to come off as my very best friend on the ride back downtown. I wondered how strong his case was.

"Yes, I was," I said.

"Good," he said. "Is any of that blood yours?"

"Some of it. I have a wound on my side. Nothing too deep."

Dunwitty glared at Stanton.

"I'm sorry about that, Adam," the captain said. "We should have had a paramedic take a look at that."

"It's okay, I heal fast."

"Which one of those bodies down there did that to you, you reckon?"

Here was where he tried to get me to admit to killing at least the six in the basement. Which was interesting, because I was pretty sure that crime scene wasn't in his jurisdiction; the laboratory was outside the city limits.

"Probably the one next to the bow and arrow," I said. "Hey, how many bodies do you have me down for? Ten, fifteen?"

"Sixteen. Right?"

"Yes sir, sixteen," Stanton said.

"You're going to pin all of those on me?" I asked.

"That's not up to us," Dunwitty said. "But you are the only one still standing. If there's something else going on, now's the time to start talking."

"Why's that?"

"So we can go round up the folks responsible. Just put us on the trail, Adam. We'll do what we can."

I thought back to when I fled England, and why. Now here I was, well over a century later, still getting arrested for murder thanks to Herman. Even though he didn't get to kill me in his oven, he still got what he wanted.

Just like in Whitechapel, and at the World's Fair, he outsmarted me before I could stop him, before I was even aware I was in the middle of a battle of wits.

This time, he was committing mass genocide—for fun—and I might not even make it to the sunrise. There was still a contract on my life, and thanks to the media attention, the entire Western hemisphere was going to know where to find me before we even made it into the police station.

With all that in mind, I started laughing. I couldn't help it.

"What's so funny?" Dunwitty asked. He looked over at Stanton, who shrugged.

"Captain," I said, "I'll tell you whatever you want to know. May as well get it recorded somewhere. But I can guarantee you're not going to believe a word of it."

ABOUT THE AUTHOR

Gene Doucette is a hybrid author, albeit in a somewhat round-about way. From 2010 through 2014, Gene published four full-length novels (*Immortal, Hellenic Immortal, Fixer,* and *Immortal at the Edge of the World*) with a small indie publisher. Then, in 2014, Gene started self-publishing novellas that were set in the same universe as the *Immortal* series, at which point he was a hybrid.

When the novellas proved more lucrative than the novels, Gene tried self-publishing a full novel, *The Spaceship Next Door*, in 2015. This went well. So well, that in 2016, Gene reacquired the rights to the earlier four novels from the publisher, and re-released them, at which point he wasn't a hybrid any longer.

Additional self-published novels followed: *Immortal and the Island of Impossible Things* (2016); *Unfiction* (2017); and *The Frequency of Aliens* (2017).

In 2018, John Joseph Adams Books (an imprint of Houghton Mifflin Harcourt) acquired the rights to *The Spaceship Next Door*. The reprint was published in September of that year, at which point Gene was once again a hybrid author.

Since then, a number of things have happened. Gene published three more novels—*Immortal From Hell* (2018), *Fixer Redux* (2019), and *Immortal: Last Call* (2020)—and wrote a new novel called *The Apocalypse Seven* that he did not self-publish; it was acquired by JJA/HMH in September of 2019. Publication date is May 25, 2021.

Gene lives in Cambridge, MA.

For the latest on Gene Doucette, follow him online

genedoucette.me
genedoucette@me.com

<u>SCI-FI</u>

The Spaceship Next Door

The world changed on a Tuesday.

When a spaceship landed in an open field in the quiet mill town of Sorrow Falls, Massachusetts, everyone realized humankind was not alone in the universe. With that realization, everyone freaked out for a little while.

Or, almost everyone. The residents of Sorrow Falls took the news pretty well. This could have been due to a certain local quality of unflappability, or it could have been that in three years, the ship did exactly nothing other than sit quietly in that field, and nobody understood the full extent of this nothing the ship was doing better than the people who lived right next door.

Sixteen-year old Annie Collins is one of the ship's closest neighbors. Once upon a time she took every last theory about the ship seriously, whether it was advanced by an adult ,or by a peer. Surely one of the theories would be proven true eventually—if not several of them—the very minute the ship decided to do something. Annie is starting to think this will never happen.

One late August morning, a little over three years since the ship landed, Edgar Somerville arrived in town. Ed's a government operative posing as a journalist, which is obvious to Annie—and pretty much everyone else he meets—almost immediately. He has a lot of questions that need answers, because he thinks everyone is wrong: the ship is doing something, and he needs Annie's help to figure out what that is.

Annie is a good choice for tour guide. She already knows everyone in town and when Ed's theory is proven correct—something is apocalyptically wrong in Sorrow Falls—she's a pretty good person to have around.

As a matter of fact, Annie Collins might be the most important person on the planet. She just doesn't know it.

The Frequency of Aliens

Annie Collins is back!

Becoming an overnight celebrity at age sixteen should have been a lot more fun. Yes, there were times when it was extremely cool, but when the newness of it all wore off, Annie Collins was left with a permanent security detail and the kind of constant scrutiny that makes the college experience especially awkward.

Not helping matters: she's the only kid in school with her own pet spaceship.

She would love it if things found some kind of normal, but as long as she has control of the most lethal—and only—interstellar vehicle in existence, that isn't going to happen. Worse, things appear to be going in the other direction. Instead of everyone getting used to the idea of the ship, the complaints are getting louder. Public opinion is turning, and the demands that Annie turn over the ship are becoming more frequent. It doesn't help that everyone seems to think Annie is giving them nightmares.

Nightmares aren't the only weird things going on lately. A government telescope in California has been abandoned, and nobody seems to know why.

The man called on to investigate—Edgar Somerville—has become the go-to guy whenever there's something odd going on, which has been pretty common lately. So far, nothing has panned out: no aliens or zombies or anything else that might be deemed legitimately peculiar… but now may be different, and not just because Ed can't find an easy explanation. This isn't the only telescope where people have gone missing, and the clues left behind lead back to Annie.

It all adds up to a new threat that the world may just need saving from, requiring the help of all the Sorrow Falls survivors. The question is: are they saving the world with Annie Collins, or are they saving it from her?

The Frequency of Aliens is the exciting sequel to *The Spaceship Next Door*.

Unfiction

When Oliver Naughton joins the Tenth Avenue Writers Underground, headed by literary wunderkind Wilson Knight, Oliver figures he'll finally get some of the wild imaginings out of his head and onto paper.

But when Wilson takes an intense interest in Oliver's writing and his genre stories of dragons, aliens, and spies, things get weird. Oliver's stories don't just need to be finished: they insist on it.

With the help of Minerva, Wilson's girlfriend, Oliver has to find the connection between reality, fiction, the mythical Cydonian Kingdom, and the non-mythical nightclub called M Pallas. That is, if he can survive the alien invasion, the ghosts, and the fact that he thinks he might be in love with Minerva.

Unfiction is a wild ride through the collision of science fiction, fantasy, thriller, horror and romance. It's what happens when one writer's fiction interferes with everyone's reality.

Fixer

What would you do if you could see into the future?

As a child, he dreamed of being a superhero. Most people never get to realize their childhood dreams, but Corrigan Bain has come close. He is a fixer. His job is to prevent accidents—to see the future and "fix" things before people get hurt. But the ability to see into the future, however limited, isn't always so simple. Sometimes not everyone can be saved.

"Don't let them know you can see them."

Graduate students from a local university are dying, and former lover and FBI agent Maggie Trent is the only person who believes their deaths aren't as accidental as they appear. But the truth can only be found in something from Corrigan Bain's past, and he's not interested in sharing that past, not even with Maggie.

To stop the deaths, Corrigan will have to face up to some old horrors, confront the possibility that he may be going mad, and find a way to stop a killer no one can see.

Corrigan Bain is going insane ... or is he?

Because there's something in the future that doesn't want to be seen. It isn't human. It's got a taste for mayhem. And it is very, very angry.

Fixer Redux

Someone's altering the future, and it isn't Corrigan Bain

Corrigan Bain was retired.

It wasn't something he ever thought he'd be able to do. The problem was that the *job* he wanted to retire from wasn't actually a job at all: nobody paid him to do it, and nobody else did it. With very few exceptions, nobody even knew he was doing it.

Corrigan called himself a fixer, because he fixed accidents that were about to happen. It was complicated and unrewarding, and even though doing it right meant saving someone, he didn't enjoy it. He couldn't stop —he thought—because there would always be accidents, and he would never find someone to take over as fixer. Anyone trying would have to be capable of seeing the future, like he did, and that kind of person was hard to find.

Still, he did it. He's never been happier.

His girlfriend, Maggie Trent of the FBI, has not retired. Her task force just shut down the most dangerous domestic terrorist cell in the country, and she's up for an award, and a big promotion.

Everything's going their way now, and the future looks even brighter.

Unfortunately, that future is about to blow up in their faces…literally. And somehow, Corrigan Bain, fixer, the man who can see the future, is taken completely by surprise.

Fixer Redux is the long-awaited sequel to ***Fixer***. Catch up with Corrigan, as he tries to understand a future that no longer makes sense.

~

FANTASY

The Immortal Novel Series

~

Immortal

"I don't know how old I am. My earliest memory is something along the lines of fire good, ice bad, so I think I predate written history, but I don't know by how much. I like to brag that I've been there from the beginning, and while this may very well be true, I generally just say it to pick up girls."

Surviving sixty thousand years takes cunning and more than a little luck. But in the twenty-first century, Adam confronts new dangers—someone has found out what he is, a demon is after him, and he has run out of places to hide. Worst of all, he has had entirely too much to drink.

Immortal is a first person confessional penned by a man who is immortal, but not invincible. In an artful blending of sci-fi, adventure, fantasy, and humor, IMMORTAL introduces us to a world with vampires, demons and other "magical" creatures, yet a world without actual magic.

At the center of the book is Adam.

Adam is a sixty thousand year old man. (Approximately.) He doesn't age or get sick, but is otherwise entirely capable of being killed. His survival has hinged on an innate ability to adapt, his wits, and a fairly large dollop of luck. He makes for an excellent guide through history ... when he's sober.

Immortal is a contemporary fantasy for non-fantasy readers and fantasy enthusiasts alike.

~

Hellenic Immortal

"Very occasionally, I will pop up in the historical record. Most of the time I'm not at all easy to spot, because most of the time I'm just a guy who does a thing and then disappears again into the background behind someone-or-other who's busy doing something much more important. But there are a couple of rare occasions when I get a starring role."

An oracle has predicted the sojourner's end, which is a problem for Adam insofar as he has never encountered an oracular prediction that didn't come true ... and he is the sojourner. To survive, he's going to have to figure out what a beautiful ex-government analyst, an eco-terrorist, a rogue FBI agent, and the world's oldest religious cult all want with him, and fast.

And all he wanted when he came to Vegas was to forget about a girl. And maybe have a drink or two.

The second book in the Immortal series, Hellenic Immortal follows the continuing adventures of Adam, a sixty-thousand-year-old man with a wry sense of humor, a flair for storytelling, and a knack for staying alive. Hellenic Immortal is a clever blend of history, mythology, sci-fi, fantasy, adventure, mystery and romance. A little something, in other words, for every reader.

Immortal at the Edge of the World

"What I was currently doing with my time and money ... didn't really deserve anyone else's attention. If I was feeling romantic about it, I'd call it a quest, but all I was really doing was trying to answer a question I'd been ignoring for a thousand years."

In his very long life, Adam had encountered only one person who appeared to share his longevity: the mysterious red-haired woman. She appeared throughout history, usually from a distance, nearly always vanishing before he could speak to her.

In his last encounter, she actually did vanish—into thin air, right in front of him. The question was how did she do it? To answer, Adam will have to complete a quest he gave up on a thousand years earlier, for an object that may no longer exist.

If he can find it, he might be able to do what the red-haired woman did, and if he can do that, maybe he can find her again and ask her who she is ... and why she seems to hate him.

But Adam isn't the only one who wants the red-haired woman. There are other forces at work, and after a warning from one of the few men he trusts, Adam realizes how much danger everyone is in. To save his friends and finish his quest he may be forced to bankrupt himself, call in every favor he can, and ultimately trade the one thing he'd never been able to give up before: his life.

Immortal and the island of Impossible Things

"I thought I'd miss the world."

Adam is on vacation in an island paradise, with nothing to do and plenty of time to do nothing.

It's exactly what he needed: beautiful weather, beautiful girlfriend, plenty of books to read, and alcohol to drink. Most importantly, either nobody on the island knows who he is, or, nobody cares.

"This probably sounds boring, and maybe it is. It's possible I have no compass to help determine boring, or maybe I have a different threshold than most people. From my perspective, though, the vast majority of human history has been boring, by which I mean nothing happened, and sure, that can be dull. On the other hand, nothing happening includes nobody trying to kill anybody, and specifically, nobody trying to kill me. That's the kind of boring a guy can get behind."

Nothing last forever, though, and that includes the opportunity to *do* nothing. One day, unwelcome visitors arrive in secret, with impossible knowledge of impossible events, and then the impossible things arrive: a new species.

It's *all* impossible, especially to the immortal man who thought he'd seen all there was to see in the world. Now, Adam is going to have to figure out what's happening and make things right before he and everyone he loves ends up dead in the hot sun of this island paradise.

Immortal From Hell

Not all of Adam's stories have happy endings

"Paris is romantic and quests are cool. But the threat of a global pandemic kind of sours the whole thing. The good news was, if all life on Earth were felled by a plague, it looked like this one could take me out too. It'd be pretty lonely otherwise."

--Adam the immortal

When Adam decides to leave the safety of the island, it's for a good reason: Eve, the only other immortal on the planet, appears to be dying, and nobody seems to understand why. But when Adam—with his extremely capable girlfriend Mirella—tries to retrace Eve's steps, he discovers a world that's a whole lot deadlier than he remembered.

Adam is supposed to be dead. He went through a lot of trouble to fake that death, but now that he's back it's clear someone remains unconvinced. That wouldn't be so terrible, except that whoever it is, they have a great deal of influence, and an abiding interest in ensuring that his death sticks this time around.

Adam and Mirella will have to figure out how to travel halfway across the world in secret, with almost no resources or friends. The good news is, Adam solved the travel problem a thousand years earlier. The bad news is, one of his oldest assumptions will turn out to be untrue.

Immortal From Hell is the darkest entry in the Immortal series.

Immortal: Last Call

"I'm something like sixty-thousand years old, and I've probably thought more

about my own death than any living being has thought about any subject, ever. I used to be unduly preoccupied with what might constitute a "good death", although interestingly, this has always been an after-the-fact analysis. What I mean is, following a near-death experience, I'll generally perform a quiet review of the circumstances and judge whether that death would have been objectively good, by whatever metric one uses for that kind of thing. I'm not nearly that self-reflective while in the midst of said near-death experience. Facing death, the predominant thought is always not like this."

A disease threatening the lives of everyone—human and non-human—has been loosed upon the world, by an arch-enemy Adam didn't even know he had.

That's just the first of his problems. Adam's also in jail, facing multiple counts of murder, at least a few of which are accurate. He may never see the inside of a courtroom, because there remains a bounty on his head—put there by the aforementioned arch-enemy—that someone is bound to try to collect while he's stuck behind bars.

Meanwhile, Adam's sitting on some tantalizing evidence that there might be a cure, but to find it, he's going to have to get out of jail, get out of the country, and track down the man responsible. He can't do any of that alone, but he also can't rely on any of his non-human friends for help, not when they're all getting sick.

What he needs is a particularly gifted human, who can do things no other human is capable of. He knows one such person. He calls himself a fixer, and he's Adam's—and possibly the world's—last hope. That's provided he believes any of it.

Immortal: Last Call is the sixth book in the *Immortal Novel Series*, and also the end of a long journey for one immortal man.

~

Immortal Stories

~

Eve

"...if your next question is, what could that possibly make me, if I'm not an angel or a god? The answer is the same as what I said before: many have considered me a god, and probably a few have thought of me as an angel. I'm neither, if those positions are defined by any kind of supernormal magical power. True magic of that kind doesn't exist, but I can do things that may appear magic to someone slightly more tethered to their mortality. I'm a woman, and that's all. What may make me different from the next woman is that it's possible I'm the very first one..."

For most of humankind, the woman calling herself Eve has been nothing more than a shock of red hair glimpsed out of the corner of the eye, in a crowd, or from a great distance. She's been worshipped, feared, and hunted, but perhaps never understood. Now, she's trying to reconnect with the world, and finding that more challenging than anticipated.

Can the oldest human on Earth rediscover her own humanity? Or will she decide the world isn't worth it?

~

The Immortal Chronicles

~

Immortal at Sea (volume 1)

Adam's adventures on the high seas have taken him from the Mediterranean to the Barbary Coast, and if there's one thing he learned, it's that maybe the sea is trying to tell him to stay on dry land.

~

Hard-Boiled Immortal (volume 2)

The year was 1942, there was a war on, and Adam was having a lot of trouble avoiding the attention of some important people. The kind of people with guns, and ways to make a fella disappear. He was caught somewhere between the mob and the government, and the only way out involved a red-haired dame he was pretty sure he couldn't trust.

≈

Immortal and the Madman (volume 3)

On a nice quiet trip to the English countryside to cope with the likelihood that he has gone a little insane, Adam meets a man who definitely has. The madman's name is John Corrigan, and he is convinced he's going to die soon.

He could be right. Because there's trouble coming, and unless Adam can get his own head together in time, they may die together.

≈

Yuletide Immortal (volume 4)

When he's in a funk, Adam the immortal man mostly just wants a place to drink and the occasional drinking buddy. When that buddy turns out to be Santa Claus, Adam is forced to face one of the biggest challenges of extremely long life: Christmas cheer. Will Santa break him out of his bad mood? Or will he be responsible for depressing the most positive man on the planet?

≈

Regency Immortal (volume 5)

Adam has accidentally stumbled upon an important period in history: Vienna in 1814. Mostly, he'd just like to continue to enjoy the local pubs, but that becomes impossible when he meets Anna, an intriguing woman with an unreasonable number of secrets and sharp objects.

Anna is hunting down a man who isn't exactly a man, and if Adam doesn't help her, all of Europe will suffer. If Adam *does* help, the cost may be his own life. It's not a fantastic set of options. Also, he's probably fallen in love with her, which just complicates everything.